ON THE SLOPES OF

Tahoe

J.A. FORDE

E-book ISBN: 979-8-9905763-2-2

Kindle ASIN: B0DNWSPQV7

Paperback ISBN: 979-8-9905763-3-9

Cover Design by Sam Palencia at Ink & Laurel

Line editing and proofreading by Britt Tayler

Copy editing by Brooke Crites

Chapter headings and scene breaks designed with Canva Pro

j.a.fordeauthor@gmail.com

This book is dedicated to the families we find along the way and choose to make our own, even in the most unlikely of circumstances.

Author's Note

My writing contains mature themes and explicit language and is therefore intended for audiences 18+. On the Slopes of Tahoe is a fade-to-black romance with implied sexual intimacy, however no explicit scenes are depicted on the page. This story deals with several issues that could be potentially triggering, such as: a cheating ex, unplanned pregnancy (not between the main characters, this is NOT a surprise pregnancy book), childbirth, parental abandonment, the death of a main character's parents (in their youth, not described in detail), and controlling parents. Your mental health is paramount, so please protect your peace and well-being if these are themes you are sensitive to.

I try to keep everything in my books as close to reality as possible... but occasionally the need for some creative freedom comes into play. In researching whether a foreign national is allowed to perform a legal wedding ceremony in the United States, I found that yes they can—in all states but one, Nevada. As Tahoe falls between California and Nevada and the ability for a character to perform such ceremonies in both states is important to the plot, I ignored that little fact for the sake of the story. So, if you happen to be particularly well-versed in Nevada marriage law, just remember that this is fiction and a little creative freedom never killed anyone.

Happy Reading!

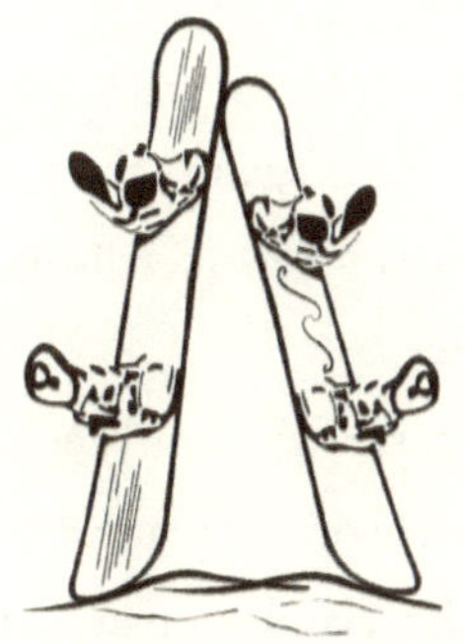

CHAPTER ONE

BRECK

I'm staring at the baggage carousel, going round and round without a single bag in sight—nothing to show for its efforts—and I can't help thinking it's a little bit like a metaphor for my life. I turn on the spot and take in my surroundings. Framed pictures of opalescent casinos and sparkling turquoise waters decorate the walls of the Reno-Tahoe International Airport. The soft Christmas music humming from the speakers and copious amounts of garland mark the cheery season better than the harried travelers I just deboarded with.

The date on the monitor overhead shows December eighth—the same date we left Sydney... nearly twenty-four hours ago. It's as if time stood still while we traveled, not wanting us to miss a minute. Crossing the international dateline is a trip.

My body aches with the weariness that only comes after a travel day like this one, or maybe it's the seven-year-old girl clinging to my back like a koala causing that pain. The tiny arms wrapped around my neck tighten as Willow—my daughter... my reason for breathing—nuzzles in closer against my shoulder. I tilt my chin down to brush a kiss against her hand, relishing the closeness despite my back screaming at me.

Nudging her awake earlier was nearly enough to send her into a meltdown, so once we were off the plane, I propped our backpacks on our carry-ons and let her clamber up my back. I'm sure I was quite the sight. Willow on my back, her long spindly legs wrapped around my waist holding on for dear life, while I wheeled the bags behind me. It's a miracle I made it to baggage claim without dropping anything—most importantly her.

My shoulders sag under her weight as I contemplate the feat of getting all of it, plus two large suitcases and my snowboard bag, to the curb to meet my ride. I'm going to need a cart, but the prospect of tracking one down is daunting. If Willow's mom were here, like I pictured her being when Wes and I originally schemed up this trip, it would be a non-issue. I wouldn't be doing this alone. But she left—me... Willow... She left us.

"Daddy," Willow whispers in my ear, shocking me out of my trance. "Someone is trying to talk to you."

I spin around, eliciting a giggle from my koala baby, who tightens her grip around my neck to the point where I can't breathe.

"Rory?" I croak out, confused and literally breathless. "Willow—" I croak again, then cough to clear my throat. "Can you loosen your grip, baby girl?"

I pull at her hands and she relaxes.

"Daddy, who's that?" Her lilting, sing-song voice is quiet in my ear, but not so quiet that the woman can't hear her.

Rory beams at us, offering a matching smile to the one I see so often on her brother's face back home. Though, his is accented with dimples she doesn't have. Instead, her nose and cheeks are smattered with delicate freckles.

"I'm Rory," she says, addressing Willow, and her American accent brings an involuntary grin to my face. "Are you the famous Willow? Wes has told me all about you."

Willow begins to wriggle and I squat low for her to slide off, my knees protesting with pops and cracks when I stand again. Oh the joys of being in your mid-thirties. Though, I guess it's to be expected after hauling a fifty-pound seven-year-old for the past day, not to mention all our crap.

Willow bounds forward and wraps her arms around Rory's middle. I chuckle under my breath while also noting we might need another "stranger danger" lesson. It's my own fault. As a hugger by nature, she's seen me throw around my affection freely nearly every day of her life.

"I love Uncle Wes. I miss him already. Will you be my friend now, since he's not here?" Willow looks up at Rory, stopping her string of conversation to tilt her head and blurt, "You're pretty."

Rory laughs, and I scrub a hand down my face to suppress my smile—one I'm surprised to find is entirely genuine. *This kid*. She has no verbal filter.

Only now that the travel fog is lifting, I realize I can't chide her for her comment, because she's not wrong. Rory's strawberry-blonde hair is braided over one shoulder, a few strands coming loose to curtain turquoise eyes that defy the harshness of the airport's florescent lights. I squeeze my eyes shut and shake away the thought I'll deny ever having. In my current circumstances, even thinking about another woman so soon after everything with Talia feels... wrong, somehow. Not to mention she's Wes's little sister—one who's eight years younger than me. Yeah, wrong.

She's in a pair of black leggings tucked into fur-lined snow boots. Her cream-colored puffer coat hits her knees and hides everything else about what she's wearing, aside from that smile and those freckles.

"I'd love to be your friend, Bug." Rory looks at Willow, and I hope she knows giving Willow a nickname is guaranteed to earn her hero status for life. She coasts a hand down Willow's dark braid—a far cry from the intricate one Rory is sporting that's giving Elsa from *Frozen* vibes.

Rory's jewel-bright eyes catch mine and I realize I haven't said more than her name in the minutes we've been standing here.

"Sorry," I say with a smile and move to hug her. "I thought we were meeting you outside. I wasn't expecting you to be *here*."

My arms envelop her and I'm surrounded by her floral scent, my nose pressing close against her hair. Apart from Wes, his girlfriend Joss, and Willow, any physical touch I've allowed in the last few weeks has felt perfunctory and forced, but with Rory, it feels natural and comfortable. As if I've known her forever.

In reality, we've only met twice. Once when she and her parents came to Australia for Wes's and my college graduation—she was only fourteen then. The other was last year when we were both in

Hawaii after Wes's crash, but we only overlapped for a couple of days. Now with Wes living in Sydney, and with how much he talks about her, I feel as if I know Rory better than I should.

"It's good to see you," I say, and I mean it. My arms tighten around her, and it's like all the feelings I'm holding in are attempting to physically manifest themselves. I know she's gone above and beyond behind the scenes to help make this trip happen for me and Willow, which means she feels like a safe place to land in this unfamiliar country. This unfamiliar life.

Hold it together, Breck.

"It's good to see you too," she says into my shoulder.

When I pull back, there's a smile stretched across her lips, but I swear there's a hint of surprise there too. At my hug?

I should've asked Wes how much he told Rory about why we're here, about Talia leaving. If she knows it all, she probably expected me to be a mess.

And I'm doing everything in my power not to be.

I can't fall apart. I have to hold it all together because Willow needs me to. I take another step back and squeeze the back of my neck with my hand, attempting to relieve the tension there, my slightly too-long hair curling over my fingertips.

"I thought you could use the extra hands," she says, gesturing to the luggage cart off to her side.

I hold back from hugging her again. "I can't begin to tell you how much I appreciate it. You should've seen the show I made of myself schlepping just our carry-ons from the plane."

"I make a great backpack," Willow says with a grin.

"The best," I say, smiling down at her and ruffling her hair—it already resembles a bird's nest, so it's not like it can get worse.

I follow Rory's gaze over my shoulder to see bags appearing on the carousel.

She steps over to Willow. "You can stand here with me while your dad grabs everything. We can start loading this other stuff on the cart, can't we?"

Willow, despite her exhausted state, rallies with a smile and nods. Her bright blue eyes, a carbon copy of my own, meet mine and she slips her hand into Rory's without hesitation.

"Yeah. Yeah, okay, that would be great. Thanks. I'll be right back, Willow Bear."

I know Willow is safe, that Rory is my best friend's sister, but I still hesitate before turning to grab our bags. I've always been protective, bordering on overbearing, and now—especially after everything—just having Willow out of sight makes me jumpy. Makes me remember I couldn't protect her from her mom leaving.

I join the other tired-looking passengers and let myself recall the look on my daughter's face when I told her Talia wouldn't be coming back. It's branded into my brain, which is why I'm desperate to keep her close and never let her go. But as I spot our first suitcase rounding the belt, I stuff the memory down, because I can't let Willow or Rory see past the façade that says *everything is just fine*.

Within fifteen minutes, I'm pushing an overfilled cart toward the parking garage. The girls walk ahead of me, hand in hand, like it's the most natural thing in the world. Willow's animated voice carries back on the light wind, sweetly contrasting with Rory's American accent. My shoulders relax to hear Willow sounding like herself. I wasn't sure if I was being selfish in leaving Sydney, knowing it was the best decision for *me* but not knowing how she'd fare. Seeing her skipping down the pavement encourages my flailing heart. *I made the right call.*

Rory makes a beeline for a bright red Jeep and a small smile tugs at my lips. I remember when Wes bought it a few years back—how excited he was, sending me pictures and telling me all the off-road capabilities. I don't think he used a single one, but maybe I'll get a chance to test them out while I'm here.

He almost shipped it when he moved to Sydney back in June, but he decided it wasn't worth the hassle for just a year. Lo and behold, it's only been six months, and he has no intention of coming back to the States. But his loss is my gain because it saves me renting a car while we're here for the next seven weeks.

Seven weeks. Willow and I have the entirety of her summer break to enjoy Tahoe, take a breather, and hopefully figure out how to do this "family of two" thing.

We load the bags into the back of the Jeep and as Willow hops into her seat, I'm thankful she no longer needs a booster after her latest growth spurt. One less thing to travel with.

I lean across to buckle her in and she whines in my ear, "Dad, stop. I can do it myself."

Fiercely independent, my daughter. I swear sometimes she reminds me more of a thirteen-year-old than an almost eight-year-old, and I have no idea how to deal with it. And what's worse, I'm going to have to figure it out *alone.*

I raise my hands in surrender but press a light kiss to her mess of dark hair before closing her door and slipping into the passenger seat. Rory already has the heat blasting, and while there's no snow on the ground in Reno at the moment, the bite of the early December air is something to behold. Especially considering we left the height of summer behind us in the Southern Hemisphere. I was lucky to throw together even a skeleton winter wardrobe to bring with us.

"There's seat warmers here," Rory says, reaching across the center console to a button near my knee and turning them on. "I'm sure these temps are a bit of a shock. Wes sent me a picture of him and Joss lounging on the beach this morning after their surf."

I shiver, sinking deeper into my seat. "I'm definitely going to miss those dawn patrol surfs. At least here I can snowboard, though it's been forever since I was last on the slopes back in Australia. I'll be a bit rusty."

"No way. Wes told me how incredible you are on a board. Any board. I'm sure you'll be outpacing anyone on the mountain in no time." She shoots me a cheeky smirk before focusing back to the road. "Except me, of course."

I laugh, and the sound surprises me. Laughter's been rare over the past couple of weeks—longer, if I'm being honest—so I'm left feeling a little more like myself as I relax back on the headrest.

"I guess we'll have to see about that." I offer her a cocky grin and notice her lips twitch with amusement. Wes told me she loves to snowboard, maybe more than he ever did, and that she's competitive about it. A tidbit I don't doubt with the way she just lit up at the mere mention of the sport. Dragging my eyes away, I find Willow fast asleep in the back, cheek pressed against the window like she passed out trying to take in every detail of the world outside.

A light snow starts to fall as we reach the freeway and Rory's hands tighten on the wheel; her eyes fixed on the road ahead. *Responsible.* Another quality Wes used to describe his sister, right up there with loyal. I saw them both in action when she dropped everything to be by his side in Hawaii—also with how she didn't hesitate when he asked her to help us.

I use the quiet moment to take her in as she taps her fingers to the rhythm of the quiet Christmas music emanating from the speakers. She took her coat off when she climbed in, revealing a University of Nevada hoodie underneath. She's a local girl, through and through. I trail my eyes to her face and, even in profile, her freckles stand out on her nose and cheeks, still pink from the cold.

"What?" She shoots a glance across to me, eyebrow raised in question.

Busted.

"Nothing. Sorry, I was just looking at your braid," I say, covering for my gawking. "I have butchered more braids in the past few weeks than I care to admit—as you probably noticed."

Rory's face falls at whatever look she must see on mine when I nod my head toward Sleeping Beauty in the back seat. Hell, thirty minutes in and I'm already failing at keeping my baggage tucked away. Her eyes flit up to spy Willow through the rearview, where she continues to fog up the window with her steady breaths.

"That can't be comfortable." Rory chortles, shaking her head as her shoulders tremble with silent laughter.

I relax, thankful for the change of subject. "I've never met anyone who can fall asleep in any position, and in just about any location, as easily as her. I wish I had those skills. Just looking at her makes my joints hurt though."

Flipping on her blinker to head up the pass that'll take us to Tahoe, Rory says, "You know, you could follow suit and rest up. I don't mind."

"You sure?" I ask, stretching my legs out with a groan. It's tempting, but she already drove the hour to come get us and I don't want to leave her with no one to talk to on the way back.

"One hundred percent. I can turn up the radio or put on an audiobook if I need to. I don't mind the quiet either." She glances sideways, an encouraging smile lifting her pink lips.

"Okay. We'll see, but why don't you tell me more about the condo in the meantime," I say, and slump against my own window.

Rory starts in on the details of the condo I'm renting from her parents, but before I catch anything beyond Willow's room having bunk beds—she'll be thrilled—I'm lulled to sleep by the sound of her voice and the whir of the engine.

When I pry my eyes open next, we're pulling up outside what can only be described as a ski chalet with a dusting of snow coating the ground. It's like a balm to the soul. When was the last time I saw the snow? It's not like we get any in the city, and the closest hills are a three-hour drive from Sydney—at best. So, looking out at the powdery flurries blowing off the roof has a sense of peace washing over me.

"We're here," Rory says with a soft voice. "Home sweet home."

That peace is replaced with a pang in my chest, reminding me that the home we left behind will never be the same.

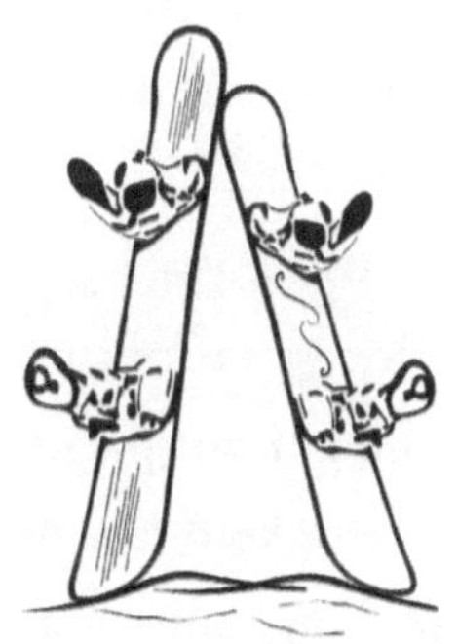

CHAPTER TWO

RORY

The walk to my condo is brisk after leaving Breck and Willow to get settled at their place. I stayed just long enough to watch him—big, sturdy man that he is—extricate his little girl from the back seat and carry her like precious cargo into their new home. She didn't stir, safe in his arms. I think my ovaries nearly exploded at the sight.

I'm glad I'm only a quarter mile away from them in case they need anything. Wes asked me to help them get set up, and I feel somewhat responsible for making their time here as stress-free as I can manage. I know it wasn't Wes's intention to add their happiness to my plate, but I'm determined to try.

Getting home, I have just enough time to swap my fleece-lined leggings and hoodie for dark jeans and a cream-colored sweater before running out to my car. I know Mom will comment on what I'm wearing regardless, but at least I tried, and that might be enough to get through dinner unscathed.

Pulling into Capisce, my favorite little Italian restaurant, I take a deep breath and hype myself up. The fact that my parents pulled the plug on their marriage twelve years ago yet still insist the three of us sit down like this once a week baffles me. Erica James and Dean Anderson are nothing if not pragmatic though, and this is the easiest way for them to keep tabs on what I'm doing and dole out their combined disappointment at my failure to meet their expectations. Maybe Breck and Willow's arrival, or Wes's impending Christmas trip with his girlfriend Joss, will give me a reprieve from the standard questions… but I'm not counting on it.

My fur-trimmed snow boots catch on black ice and I'm glad for their impressive tread. Pulling my braid over my shoulder, I straighten my spine and walk into the lion's den.

In actuality, Capisce is heaven on earth. Their homemade ravioli is out of this world. Add in their family "gravy"—aka red sauce—and I could die happy. I hang my coat by the front door as the savory aroma envelops me, and then follow the hostess to a booth in the corner where my parents sit on opposite sides of the table. *Lovely*. Now I'm tasked with choosing who to sit next to. Dad's back is to me, but Mom stands and walks the last two paces to give me a peck on each cheek, guiding me to her side of the booth.

"Hi, Mom. Hi, Dad," I say, forcing cheer into my voice.

Dad stands before I sit and pulls me into a side hug. I don't think he's given me anything different in… well, years. Maybe at my college graduation four and a half years ago? Did he hug me then? The hug Breck gave me this afternoon was more affectionate than this.

What I wouldn't give for an embrace like that from my parents.

Once I'm adequately trapped on the bench seat, I sense Mom's eyes roving down my body and I know without looking that her eyebrows are pinching together. I tuck my chin, hating the way my cheeks heat under her scrutiny.

"Did you not have time to go home after picking up the Kylies?" she asks, the disdain for my outfit *right there,* but only if you know where to look. And I've had years of practice. "Breck and... what's his daughter's name again? Aspen?"

Breck Kylie. It's the first time I've really put his full name together in my head, and I find that I like the way it sounds.

"Willow. Her name is Willow. And yes, I went home first; I had to get my car," I tell her, not taking the bait. Even though I made the attempt to dress up a bit, considering it's thirty degrees outside and there's ice on the ground, I knew it wouldn't be enough.

She's in an evergreen cashmere sweater dress with black heeled boots that come to her knees, and I can see her full-length wool overcoat hanging on the coat rack next to my puffer jacket. Always immaculately put together. Her long red hair is pinned up in a severe bun that makes my head hurt just looking at it. Her makeup is flawless even at eight o'clock at night, whereas I hastily swiped on mascara and blush *before* I left to pick up Breck—almost four hours ago.

"That's right, you took Wes's Jeep." Dad breaks into the conversation. "Did it run okay? I was worried having it sit idle for six months might've caused some issues."

"It was great. I drive it once a week just to keep the fluids moving and everything." I love driving that car, and I'm going to miss it while Breck and Willow are in town.

"You got them settled in all right, then?" Mom asks, sitting up a little straighter, business-mode activated.

"Yeah, the place looked great when I went in earlier today. I picked up some basics at Safeway so they should be covered for the next few days. I think the bunk beds in the guest suite are going to be a big hit when Willow is a functioning kid again and registers them. She was zonked when we got there."

Mom nods, looking bored, and changes the subject. "How's your condo? Any issues we should know about?"

This is her way of ensuring I never forget *my* condo is really *their* condo. That my home is something they provide, not something that's truly mine. I hold back the immature desire to roll my eyes. Our parents don't just own my and Breck's condos, they own properties all around the lake. Their business is the one partnership that's always worked between them. Even when their marriage fell apart, Stateline Properties never faltered.

"It's fine. Nothing new to report."

"You know, it's been a while since we've come by to inspect it," Mom says, addressing my dad as though I'm not right here. "Dean, maybe we should schedule that for this week?"

"Really, guys, it's all good. If there was anything that needed work, I'd let you know."

"Oh, we know, dear. I just want to ensure we're keeping up with it."

"How's work been? Gone viral or whatever you kids call it these days?" Dad interjects, saving me from having to respond, but my jaw clenches at the condescension in his voice.

Working in content creation for our local ski resort, Empyreal Mountain, isn't exactly what my parents had in mind when they paid my way through a journalism degree from the University of Nevada. They assumed I'd work for some sort of publication—front page dreams and all that. I wanted so badly to make it happen for them, but the reality is there aren't all that many jobs here in traditional journalism. So, when this opportunity presented itself shortly after I graduated, I went for it. I wouldn't say it's what I had in mind for my career either, so I guess nobody's happy.

Not that I don't enjoy my job. It allows me to photograph the most beautiful place on earth, and it gives me unfettered, year-round access to my favorite mountain and all its amenities. Did I mention I get to snowboard as much as I want? So, yeah. It's great. I just wish I could spend all my time on the photography aspect and let someone else do the rest. Unfortunately, the "rest" is the most time-consuming part of the job.

"Work is fine," I say simply.

No matter how many times I explain what I do, they'll never understand how "posting to a bunch of apps" is a real career. They do their best to keep their passive aggression low-key(ish) about it though, unlike when I told them I wanted to go into photography full-time at the beginning of my junior year of college. They were not low-key about that. Not in the slightest. To them, photography will always be something I do as a hobby, not a feasible career path.

"Did you see the article Jamie wrote last week? The one about his parents' work with the whisky distillery down in the valley?" Mom lifts her wine to her lips. "I was really impressed. You know, you could write freelance articles like he does, Rory. You never know where it might lead."

"Yeah, Jamie doesn't write freelance. This was a special case because of his proximity to the subject. And he's between books at the moment, so he had some extra time."

"Well, if he has extra time on his hands, he won't be too busy to have dinner with us next week, will he?"

Shit. I walked right into that.

Jameson Liam Murray has been my best friend since freshman year of high school, when his family moved here from Scotland, and my parents adore him. Of course they do; he's amazing. The problem is, because they adore him, they want nothing more than for us to be a couple. Unfortunately for them, he's never been my type—even if his Scottish and Irish roots blessed him with deep auburn hair, a beard to match, and startling green eyes. We've never felt anything for each other beyond friendship, which is just one more thing in my life for my parents to be disappointed about.

"I don't know what his schedule looks like," I say, trying to walk back what I said, even though I *do* know he doesn't have anything major going on for the next few weeks. He always takes time off after he publishes, and his third book came out last month.

"Maybe if *I* call him, he'll make time in his busy schedule to see us," Mom says, the threat clear. She's persistent, and Jamie's too nice to say no.

"I'll talk to him." I sigh, defeat pressing down on my shoulders.

We've officially covered the two main reasons why they insist we get together on a weekly basis—to needle me about my job and to ask about my love life, or lack thereof—and we haven't even ordered our meals yet. This is going to be a long night.

Walking into my condo what feels like hours later, I'm completely deflated. Sunday nights with my parents are a killjoy, and that's saying a lot when I have very little joy in my life to begin with these days.

I slip my boots off and trudge up the stairs to my bedroom. Flopping onto the bed, I type out a message to Jamie.

Me

> Soooo, don't kill me, but you have to come to family dinner next week.

Jamie

> What have you done?

Me

> I might've implied you're between projects. Mom latched right on to that and threatened to call you herself.

> I'm sorry.

It's not like Jamie doesn't like my parents. It's more that he's indifferent to them. He doesn't like the way they treat me, but the man was raised to be respectful, and he's nothing if not a perfect gentleman. Plus, they're always on their very best behavior when he's around.

Jamie

> I do always like it when you owe me a favor…

I laugh out loud. The last time he was forced into one of these dinners, I got us tickets to see Imagine Dragons at the outdoor arena to make up for it. If I remember correctly, he went home with a girl he met at the bar afterward, so I understand his enthusiasm.

Me

> Fine, I'll owe you one.

Jamie

> Excellent. Now to come up with what said favor will be.

Me

> I can practically see you wringing your hands and cackling maniacally.

Jamie

> You know me too well. What are you up to tomorrow?

Me

I've got work, but I thought I'd make it a half day and take Breck and Willow to lunch if they're up for it. You could join us.

Jamie

Sounds good to me. Night, Rory.

Me

Night.

I hurry through my nighttime routine, ready to put this evening behind me. When I sink into my bed, pillows cradling my head and blankets cocooned around me, my mind wanders down the street. To a man with wavy blond hair and bright blue eyes. Did he get Willow to bed okay? Is he sleeping, or is jet lag keeping him up? Did he eat the pizza I stashed in their freezer? Is he happy to be here, or is he just relieved not to be *there*? The questions swirl around in my head as I slowly drift off to sleep.

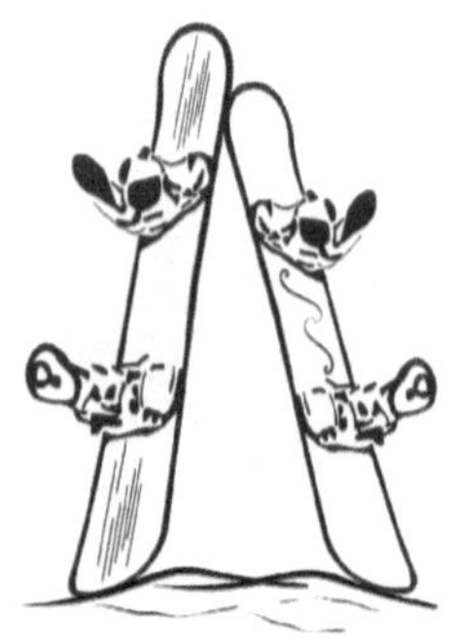

CHAPTER THREE

Breck

I know Willow will eventually love the bunk beds in her room, but she ended up in bed next to me last night. I should've expected it. Her disoriented yells woke me from a dead sleep just after eleven. I might've thought it was comical, me running through the house in my boxers to get to her, but seeing as I don't know the layout very well myself, I ended up running into a wall *and* stubbing my toe on the door jamb.

Needless to say, I'm knackered. Having tiny feet in my face half the night only exacerbated my own restlessness. Though, if being in bed with me is what she needs right now, I'll deal with it.

I yawn and say a silent thank-you to Rory for the stock of coffee grounds next to the coffee maker. If I'd had to go out first thing this morning, I might've cried. In reality, I would've smiled through it and found a way to make it an adventure for Willow, but I definitely would've *thought* about crying.

Pouring grounds into the filter and pushing the *strong brew* option, I take a full breath in through my nose. My shoulders drop away from my ears as I let it out, and the tension I was holding starts to melt away. Moving around the kitchen, I open and close all the cabinets, familiarizing myself with our new space. I find a large mug with an Empyreal Mountain Resort logo and feel the itch to get out there. There's a comfort to the mountains, to the glistening snow covering them, and I intend to make the most of it.

I spent every winter of my early childhood in Perisher Valley—one of the best ski areas in Australia. Those mountains were my first home, the one I shared with my parents before they were taken from me. I haven't been that far south since Willow was born. Even when I coordinated trips there with my tour company, Adventure Chasers, I never went with them.

Not my company anymore.

I sigh, my hands gripping the counter, and let myself wallow until the coffee stops percolating. I stare out the window at the sun illuminating the peaks in the distance, and I think back on my attempts to convince Talia to take a family ski trip. She never had any interest, and I didn't want to leave Willow behind, so the years passed in the name of compromise. I should've prioritized it so I could've shared that connection to my parents with Willow.

What was I so afraid of?

The beep of the coffeemaker draws my attention and I shake away the question. Pulling open the fridge, I find milk nestled between a carton of eggs, some butter, and shredded cheese. It looks like scrambled eggs are on the menu this morning. I pull everything out, spread the ingredients on the counter, and fill my mug with piping hot coffee and a splash of milk.

Ten minutes later, I hear the pitter-patter of little feet on the stairs and turn to see a sleepy Willow shuffling into the kitchen. My mood brightens instantly.

"Morning, love."

If I thought her hair was a mess yesterday, it's much worse now. The braid is in shambles, sticking out in all directions, loosely held together by the elastic at the bottom. She offers me a small smile and climbs onto a stool at the island worktop.

"Morning, Dad," she says with a yawn, so it sounds more like "morig da," which makes me chuckle. "I'm hungry."

"I bet you are, Willow Bear. You slept right through dinnertime last night. Scrambled eggs and toast sound okay?" She nods and swivels on her stool to take in the open floor plan. Behind her is the entryway and the stairs that lead up to our rooms, and the ones that disappear down to the lower level. Both the eat-in kitchen and living room are lined with expansive windows that look out onto the mountains and Empyreal's ski runs. The natural light is nearly blinding, and she squints sleepily.

"I'll give you the tour after breakfast. I think you're going to love your room, *and* there's a game room downstairs"—I wiggle my eyebrows at her, knowing this will be her favorite part—"with a foosball table."

She squeaks with excitement. Her private school back home has one and she fell in love with it. So much so that I bought her one for our house. The house we left behind in Sydney. Damn, it's like a punch to the gut to think of going back there just the two of us. Eventually we'll have to figure that out. I turn away to grab plates so she doesn't see my smile fall.

"Can I go play now? Daddy, please!"

"Breakfast first. Then, you're going down, little ankle-biter." I laugh and she joins in, nothing but glee on her face. The fact that she can still find that kind of joy fills my heart and gives me hope for myself.

Plating our scrambled eggs and toast, I add a sprinkle of shredded cheese and slide Willow's across to her. I carry mine around so we can sit shoulder to shoulder. I moan around my first mouthful of eggs, and it hits me all at once that I slept through dinner last night too. I only took a cursory look around the house before brushing my teeth and falling into bed. The bright side of that was getting a few hours of sleep before I ended up at the stinky end of Willow's feet.

Appreciative sounds interrupt my musings, and I nudge Willow's side. Getting her to eat has never been an issue. The kid can put away some food, but she also has more energy than a kangaroo on crack.

"Done!" She raises her hands in the air and looks at my nearly empty plate. "Come on, Dad, I want to go play!" She tugs on my elbow, and I swallow back the desire to tell her to be patient. She's been cooped up or sleeping for nearly two days and that energy has finally found its way to the surface. She's bouncing on the balls of her feet, standing beside the stool and smiling ear to ear.

"Okay okay. I'm done." I look at the mess on the counter, then at the four-foot form already clearing the first two steps downstairs. I turn my back on the kitchen.

I have a foosball game to win.

I did not win. I don't know how she managed to school me so thoroughly. It was kind of embarrassing actually, and I'm just glad there was no one else around to watch me fail.

Hell, there's yet another metaphor for my life in there somewhere.

After she yelled "In your face, sucker!" at me for the third time, I had to send her to her room so she could take a minute to cool down. *Awesome.* I blame Wes for that little gem of a phrase. However, I'm not sure it's the punishment I intended with how thrilled she is at the bunk-bed situation.

I told her to unpack—maybe a little ambitious on my part—and I'll likely be unable to find a single thing I put in her suitcase when I go in there later. So really, I'm punishing myself.

Ah, the joys of parenting.

I drop back into my pillows and cross my arms over my chest, heaving a sigh. *I'm a single parent.* Officially. I have no partner to fall back on anymore. No one to ask for help. No one to share both the beauty and burden of parenting with. As much as I want to let myself pretend this is a carefree vacation, just me and my favorite girl, it's not. The realization cracks something in me, just like every time I think about the life we had before and the life that awaits us now in the after.

Taylor Swift's voice floats through Willow's door down the hall. I should probably tell her that being in something like a time-out means no music, but right now, if it makes her happy, she can dance around to "Shake it Off" all she wants.

I stare at the unmoving ceiling fan and the raw emotions crest like a wave. I've always had them—big emotions, and lots of them. I learned after my parents died that those things make people uncomfortable though. That negative ones only work to scare people off. So, since I was thirteen, repressing them became as easy as breathing. And after my aunt and uncle—who took me in when I lost my parents—also passed, it became as natural as the skin I wear. At least it was, until my entire life imploded. Now I'm feeling too much and I'm afraid of what that might do to the people around me who have never seen me as anything but positive, happy, and confident.

What will it do to Willow if she sees me like this? I've been trying my best to shelter her. She's struggling in her own way and shouldn't have to see her dad struggling as well. It's my job to protect her. Even from my own feelings—*especially* from my own feelings. She doesn't need another person in her life changing right before her eyes.

Not that Talia changed.

She just left.

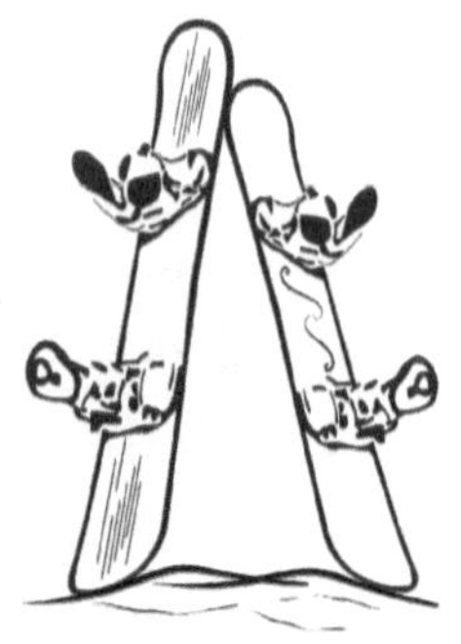

CHAPTER FOUR

RORY

I stare at my phone, at the blank text thread I just opened. Everything I type out feels weird and I delete it before I can hit send. *Hey, just checking in...* delete delete delete. *How did you guys sleep last night...* backspace backspace backspace. Breck's not my friend—not really. I tap my fingers along the side of my phone while worrying my thumbnail between my teeth.

Yesterday was friendly, right? He seemed genuinely glad to see me... but I think that's just Breck's nature. According to Wes, he's never met a stranger, and after years of hearing him talk about his friend, I feel like I *do* know him. When we met for the second time in Hawaii, I was terrified and heartsick over how close I came to losing my brother, my favorite person in the world, so those interactions are blurry.

Otherwise, I'm sure I would've embarrassed myself like I did at their graduation all those years ago. But then, show me a fourteen-year-old girl who wouldn't think their big brother's friend with the blond surfer curls, strong cut jaw, and swoony Australian accent was the hottest guy on the planet.

Did I harbor a secret crush on him? Of course. I was a teenager and it was harmless. He lived half a world away, was eight years older than me, and was never an option. Not that I wanted him to be an option. He was a fantasy... again, a crush. It's always been there though.

Now he's here, and if I'm completely honest with myself, he's even more crush-worthy than ever. The past thirteen years have done nothing but increase his appeal. The rugged, thirty-five-year-old Breck beats out the boyish twenty-two-year-old one by miles...

I shake my head. Even if he wasn't here to escape what sounds like a shitty situation, I'd never, ever date Wes's best friend. I wouldn't chance our relationship, and Lord knows he never liked his Navy buddies sniffing around when I would visit him in Lemoore, where he spent most of his career.

Why am I even thinking about this? I look back at my phone with a sigh and finally type out a message... No more overthinking. This is Wes's friend; I can help him get settled without thinking about his sharp jawline and deep-cut dimples, or the way his lips look when they... *Nope. Rein it in.*

Me

The three dot bubble pops up almost instantly and I watch it dance with anticipation.

Breck

> That would be great actually. We spent the whole morning unpacking. Could probably use a break. What time?

Me

> I can walk over now.

Breck

> Great, see you soon.

See, was that so hard?

I pull on my heavy puffer jacket and a mint green beanie low over my ears. The walk between my condo and theirs is short, but it's in the low thirties outside. My fleece-lined jeans keep my legs toasty as I walk out my door and down the steps to the sidewalk, my breath puffing out in white clouds around me.

I stomp up the stairs to their porch, knocking the snow off my boots as I go. I reach a gloved hand for the doorbell but before I can press it, the door swings open and I falter back a step. Willow's sweet smiling face is a welcome sight, settling the surprise of the moment before.

"Rory!" she squeals and launches herself at me, and I smile ruefully. *Like father, like daughter.*

I'll never forget when I walked into Wes's hospital room and Breck enveloped me in a hug that could only be described as life-changing. If I couldn't have a hug from Wes—who was laid up and unable to move from his bed—Breck's was the next best thing.

It was different from yesterday's, which had an edge to it, something under the surface, almost like he was touch-starved.

You're reading too much into it, Rory. It was just a hug.

I squeeze Willow a little tighter, just in case I'm *not* all that far off the mark and she could use one too. I gently shuffle us into the entryway so I can close the door behind me. It's cold and she's in nothing but little sleep shorts and a T-shirt. This girl needs flannel pjs or she's going to freeze.

"Hey, sweetie. How'd you sleep?" I ask, then let my eyes travel over her head to Breck standing just inside the kitchen. He's leaning against the island, a grin spread across his face like it was carved there. He seems *almost* normal, so close to being the over-the-top golden retriever type guy I remember. Then I remind myself he's likely not that guy right now and that appearances can be deceiving during a crisis.

"Probably would have been better if *someone*," Breck says, shooting a pointed glance at Willow, "hadn't slept with her feet in my face half the night."

Willow's bright giggle escapes her, and she releases me to run over to her dad.

"At least they're not as smelly as yours." She sticks her tongue out at him and bolts.

"I'll get you for that, little ankle-biter." He lurches forward but she's already out of reach, running past me for the stairs to her room. Her laugh cascades through the house as she goes.

"Ankle-biter?" I inquire with a raised brow. He lets loose a laugh, settling against the counter again. He's dressed casually in a pair of jeans and a thermal Henley that hugs his chest and arms. His hair is damp and a little disheveled, like he ran his hands through it just before I walked in the door.

"I guess they don't call kids that here? It's a term of endearment in Australia... at least, it is when they're being little pests." He says *pests* with affection and humor. "Anyway, come on in. She's going to get changed but wanted to wait to see you."

His Australian accent wraps around me, a hug in itself. Damn, I love the way it sounds.

"She's a really sweet kid, Breck."

His face softens at my words, and my heart melts a little with it. I might've only gotten the Cliffs Notes version of what happened from Wes, but I couldn't imagine putting on a brave face and trudging on like he is.

"She really is." He clears his throat and pushes off the counter, walking around it to rinse his coffee mug in the sink. "Thank you. For the groceries. You're a gem."

"You're welcome. That was actually Wes's idea. He told me that you and—" I break off, scrunching my eyes shut, hoping he didn't notice my near-misstep. "He told me you had pizza and beer waiting for him when he got to Sydney. So yeah, just returning the favor!" I wave my fingers in the air, and *oh my god.* I need to calm down.

He runs a hand over his lips, hiding a grin, and the tension that was lingering in his shoulders eases.

"Everything else okay with the house?" I say, moving to a safer topic. "I had dinner with my mom and dad last night and they wanted me to make sure you were comfortable."

"It's great. Better than, actually. Maybe if I'd actually looked at the listing I would've known this place had a foosball table. Willow mopped the floor with me this morning."

"She plays foosball? Isn't she like eight?" I ask, surprised.

"Seven, at least for two more months. But yeah, her school has a table and she's a full-fledged champion now." He chuckles. "We bought our own table earlier this year. You should see her go toe to toe with Wes. The two of them trash talk each other like crazy." He rubs at his chin. "I might've let that get a little out of hand though, so now I'm attempting to reel it back in."

"She's a little competitive, huh?"

"You could say that. She and Wes feed off each other like a couple of feral kids, which of course, she is, but Wes..." Breck laughs and shakes his head. "He's always right there with her."

"He would be. I swear he's just a big kid at heart. So, are you and Willow hungry?"

"Yes!" Willow's enthusiastic voice comes from behind me, and I twirl around to see her standing at the foot of the stairs in a pair of lightweight leggings, a sweatshirt, and tennis shoes.

"Umm, Breck?"

"Hmm?" He steps up behind me, a questioning hum coming from much too close. My body tenses at the unexpected proximity.

"Please tell me she has warmer clothes than that." My voice is quieter, embarrassingly breathy as I catch my bearings. "Otherwise, I think our first stop will need to be Target."

"That's a complicated answer. She has some warmer clothes, but I'll need to supplement her wardrobe now that we're here. Would you mind looking at what we have and helping me come up with a list of what she still needs?"

I turn and come face-to-face with his chest. He steps back but only enough so I can look up at him. He's about six inches taller than me, even with my boots on, and is much more comfortable with this closeness than I am apparently. A sandy blond curl falls across his forehead and he shakes it back. Behind the persistent strands are piercing sky-blue eyes. I'm entranced, a little unsettled, and warmth blooms across my cheeks.

"Sure." My voice squeaks out and I feign a cough in order to continue at a normal decibel. "Do you want to do that now? Or later? We could go get lunch first and then come back, take stock, and go from there?"

"I'm guessing from your reaction that Willow isn't dressed appropriately for lunch, so maybe a quick inventory and then lunch, and you can pick out something warmer while we're at it?"

I turn back to Willow, taking my first full breath since he walked up behind me. "Alright, girly, lead the way."

We walk into pure chaos when we get upstairs. Her luggage is splayed open on the bottom bunk and there are exactly zero items still inside—and it's not a small suitcase. The dresser drawers sit partially open and a few things are hanging haphazardly in the closet. Mostly, there are piles of what used to be neatly folded clothes all over the floor. The only things that look like they were placed with care are her tablet and a small frame holding a picture of Breck, Willow, and Talia.

My eyes catch on it and can't seem to move on. I've seen pictures of Talia before, from Wes's time in Sydney the last six months, but it seems to shine a light on the situation even more. Willow's resemblance to her mom is uncanny—to both her parents really, but there's so much of Talia in her. I'm struck anew by how hard that must be for Breck. Willow, too.

Her dark hair reaches long down her back exactly like Talia's. It's stick-straight and shiny, like inky black curtains. Her coloring is closer to Talia's too, more olive than the sun-kissed bronze of Breck's. They have the same straight nose and matching crinkles at the corners of their eyes.

She's a beautiful little girl, and one day she'll be a stunning woman.

Breck walks in, and his proclamation of "holy shit" draws both my mind and my eyes away from the photo and back to the task at hand.

"Ha! Swear jar for you, Daddy," Willow says, a gleam in her eye. "Wait, you did remember to bring the swear jar, right?"

"Of course. How could I forget the swear jar? I'm pretty sure it's how we're going to pay for this condo," he jokes, and she rolls her eyes. She's got attitude for days.

I stifle a laugh behind my hand. "Oh, you can't be that bad."

He grimaces but quickly follows it up with a smile. "Let's just say Willow has a real chance at Taylor Swift tickets if I don't clean up my act." Willow jumps up and down like that would be the ultimate prize in life.

"I bet Uncle Wes had to contribute to the swear jar quite a bit, didn't he?" I say, looking at Willow, and she bursts out laughing, her nod emphatic.

Breck laughs too. "He started prepaying with a twenty every time he came over because it made more sense than paying as he went. The Navy really did him no favors on that one."

"Yeah, the whole *swears like a sailor* thing rings true, doesn't it?"

Wes was a fighter pilot in the Navy until his near-fatal plane crash. Though he survived, his wingman and friend did not. As much as I miss him, I'm glad all that trauma took him to Sydney to work for Breck's adventure tour company. It brought him to Joss, the love of his life. He deserves that happiness, and I'm glad he's found it. Even if it's half a world away from me.

"It does indeed, but that's beside the point. Willow Bear, what on earth happened here? I thought I told you to unpack, not throw everything around the room like a tornado came through." Breck's hands are on his hips and his lips are pursed. I stifle the laugh that bubbles up. His stern look is so at odds with his usual demeanor.

"Well, I did unpack." She waves her arms around at the wreckage. "Then I got distracted dancing to my music. And then I decided to take a shower and I couldn't find my bathroom stuff. And then you told me Rory was coming so I threw my pjs back on so I could say hi. And then I needed to get dressed and wasn't sure what to wear so..." She looks around her room as if this rambled explanation makes sense of the scene.

"O-kay," I drawl, feeling the need to pipe in and defuse this stand-off. "How about we find you something warmer to wear to lunch and we can go through this when we get back. Organize and take stock at the same time, yeah?"

I offer a kind smile to Willow and quirk a brow at Breck.

"Yeah. Yeah, okay." He huffs a breath. "Do you at least know where the snow boots are, Willow?"

She jumps on the spot, spinning in a circle until her eyes land on the closet. "There!"

She saunters over, not a care in the world that she just kicked over the last remaining pile of mostly folded shirts. Breck groans from the doorway and I bite my lip to hide my smile.

The boots in her hand look sturdy and warm. "Did you order those? I can't imagine you found them in the height of summer in Sydney."

"I absolutely ordered them. She, of course, insisted on the ones with the pink fur."

"Obviously." I chuckle. "Willow, any idea where the pants are?" I ask, scanning the room for jeans or anything heavier than—

"These are my favorite leggings," she says, interrupting my search. They're very cute—black with silver sparkles—but the flimsy fabric is unlikely to cut it when we step outside. Looking at Breck, he just shrugs, so I let it go.

"They are very cute. How about a jacket? Hat? Gloves?" I glance around, seeing none of these things.

"Her jacket is downstairs. As for a hat and gloves, I somehow forgot about those... even though I definitely packed them for myself." His hand tightens at the back of his neck then his eyes follow suit, squeezing shut. If I could see into his mind, I think I'd hear him kicking himself.

"That's okay, I have an extra pair of gloves in my coat. You know, for emergencies." I give Willow a conspiratorial wink. "They'll be a little big, but I bet they'll work just fine. So, lunch?"

"Yes, please!" Willow draws the words out. Her melodic voice and adorable Australian accent make my heart melt.

"My best friend's going to meet us. I think you'll like him," I tell her, and her eyes brighten. She walks out past Breck and I expect him to follow, but his eyes are caught on something behind me. With what I see on his face, I don't have to look to know it's the framed picture of what used to be their family.

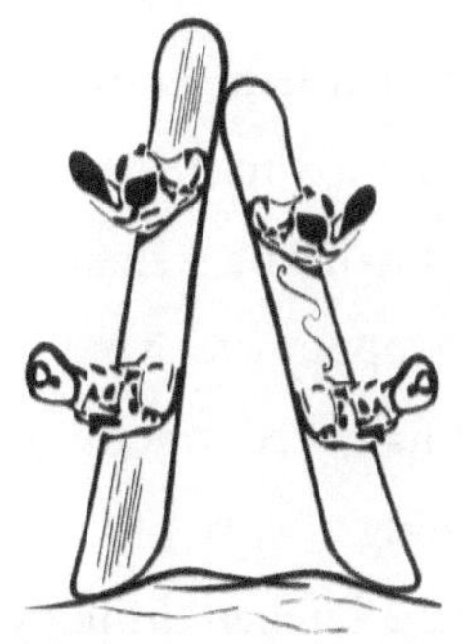

CHAPTER FIVE

BRECK

We piled into the Jeep and hit up a small local burger joint for lunch. It was technically within walking distance, but with Willow's insistence on the flimsy leggings, driving was the prudent choice. Jamie, Rory's friend, had a table waiting for us when we arrived.

I don't know what I was expecting, but a hulking man with red hair and a beard wasn't it. Willow took to him immediately, pointing out the way his slight Scottish accent was different to Rory's but not quite like ours either. Sitting next to each other with her strawberry blonde hair, he and Rory look more like siblings than she and Wes do.

Was I curious to know if there was more between them? Maybe. But with the way she encouraged him to get the waitress's phone number and her pleased expression when he did, I don't think there is. And I don't know why I felt relief with that realization... Not at all.

We didn't linger after lunch, knowing we had a wardrobe explosion to clean up. I tried to help when we got back to the condo, but Rory seemed to have a system going, and I was only in the way. I also couldn't stop my eyes from snagging on the picture on the bedside table. I finally had to walk away, leaving the girls in peace to do their own thing.

So, here I stand, in the kitchen drinking a cup of cold coffee, contemplating my life.

I'm a thirty-five-year-old single dad who ran to a foreign country because the mother of his child left him for a man he called a friend, a business partner. I've been unemployed since we sold the company, but I've promised myself not to dwell too much on that fact given how much the sale brought in. If it was enough to allow Talia to leave with Drew, it's enough for me to enjoy this time with Willow.

Still... Nothing about my life looks the way it did even a month ago, and the future I'd envisioned for myself feels lost in the tumult.

By the time Rory has a comprehensive list of everything Willow needs and they trudge down the stairs, I can tell my little munchkin is waning on energy. Driving thirty minutes to go shopping is a no-go seeing as she's already burrowing into the couch, and I'd like to avoid a meltdown. I scrub at the back of my neck, a sigh escaping my lips.

"I can go," Rory says quietly from beside me. "I can grab you guys something for dinner while I'm out."

"No. It's okay. We can wait until tomorrow to shop and I'll just order something in," I protest. She must have better things to do, but she's not taking no for an answer, and no matter how much it feels like I'm taking advantage of her kindness, I relent. She takes my credit card with a smile and a promise to be back soon.

If my broken, useless heart could feel something for anyone besides Willow right now, I think it would fall for Rory with the way she's taking a bit of the burden off my shoulders.

The door clicks shut behind her and I fall into the couch. Letting Rory help feels like a slippery slope. I can't become reliant on her. I can't let her become a crutch over these next seven weeks, and I know it will be all too easy to do so. She's already been more helpful and accommodating than I possibly deserve. Wes's doing, no doubt. His guilt at not being here has manifested in lobbing the job of caretaking onto his sister. What I do know is that I cannot—*will not*—take advantage.

I tuck my daughter closely into my side and turn on *Bluey*. She got plenty of sleep last night, but jet lag is telling us both that we should've been asleep for the last eight hours. While she lounges against me, her breathing evening out in a way that tells me she's drifted off to sleep against my chest, I pull out my phone to text Wes.

Me

How were the waves this morning? Do they miss me?

It's less than a minute before I feel a vibration in my hand that pulls me from the sight of four animated Queensland heelers dancing on the screen.

I don't know about the waves, but we sure do. I did catch a couple extra ones for you though. Getting settled?

I turn on my camera and flip it to selfie mode, watching a wide smile spread across my cheeks, just enough to cover the exhaustion. I snap the picture at an angle to include a conked-out Willow, then hit send.

I miss her too. She doing okay?

I'm not sure how to answer that. Honestly, Willow has handled this better than I expected. The first few days after I told her, she cried a lot and asked plenty of questions, but aside from being a little moodier, she's her usual bubbly self. I'm not really sure how to feel about that. I know what it was like not to process my grief as a kid—hell, I'm still doing it—and I don't want that for her.

I didn't want any of this for her.

She seems fine, but how can she be?

I'm just going to say it. You seem fine too, but how can you be?

Well, shit. I can't argue with that. I am trying to be fine. I need to be for Willow. Right?

Touché

Wes

Sorry. I just want to be sure you're really okay too.

Me

I will be, mate.

Wes

I'm here, you know, if you need to talk. You didn't push me, and I'm not going to push you.

But I am here.

Me

I know. Thanks.

Rory's been a god-send. She's out shopping for Willow to get her properly outfitted for a Tahoe winter… something I dropped the ball on. There's supposed to be a couple feet of new snow this week.

Wes

She's pretty amazing. I'm glad she's able to help. I wish I could.

I can't wait for the snow. Less than two weeks and I'll be shredding that powder right alongside you.

I chew my lip, wondering if I should tell Wes that his sister is doing too much. That she has a life of her own, and I can do this... but I'm beyond exhausted. Saying no to the help she's offering feels almost irresponsible at this point. *Bluey*'s soft end-credit music drifts through the room and I'm out like a light, my mind blissfully clear in a way it hasn't been in weeks.

A persistent knocking draws me out of sleep, and when I reach for my phone, I discover it's been two hours. I scrub a hand across my face feeling the day's stubble scratch my palm.

The knocking continues.

Shit. *Rory*.

"Coming!" I holler, and Willow startles awake next to me. "Sorry, Willow Bear." I lean down and kiss her head before extricating myself from her lanky limbs.

I swing the door open and Rory stands there, a walking Target ad, loaded down with an absurd amount of bags.

"Bloody hell. Did you buy the whole store?" I ask incredulously, reaching out to grab as much as I can. "You haven't been standing out here long, have you? We passed out on the couch."

"Not too long," she says, but her cheeks are bright pink like she's been standing in the cold for a while. They match her lips perfectly.

I should not be looking at her lips.

I clear my throat and glance away. "Come on inside and warm up. Want a cup of coffee or something?"

"Sure, that sounds great." I swear I see her teeth chatter around the words.

"Rory!" Willow's excitement levitates her off the couch and she tackles her in a big hug. Rory bends to pull her in, rubbing a palm down her back, likely trying to syphon her warmth.

"Hey. Wait until you see all the fun stuff I got you." She glances up from where she's crouched and winks at me. "Your daddy gave me his credit card and I went all-out."

Willow giggles, and a laugh bubbles up in me as well.

"Do you take milk in your coffee?" I ask, moving into the kitchen. "And do you mind if its reheated? Or I can make a fresh pot."

"Reheated is fine and milk's great, thanks. Okay, Willow, let's get to the good stuff."

She grabs a bag and starts pulling out item after item. Fleece-lined pants and jeans, sweaters and thermal tops, hats, gloves, heavy socks. Even flannel pajamas. Then there's the snow gear. A pair of snow bibs and snow gloves that she somehow was able to match to the heavy jacket I bought for Willow. There's flower prints and unicorns, pinks and purples and blues, sparkles and sequins. I couldn't have picked out a more perfect wardrobe for Willow, and Rory's only known her for a day.

"Daddy! Look!" She grins at me from beneath a pink hat with furry poof ball ears. My Willow Bear.

"Well, if that isn't perfect for you, I don't know what is. Did you thank Rory for picking everything out for you?"

"Thank you, Rory!" She jumps into her arms again and Rory laughs, her turquoise eyes landing on me.

Thank you, I mouth, and she nods, everything in her face softening.

I'll never be able to thank her enough for being here. It's only been two days and I feel like I can breathe again—like maybe, just maybe, Willow and I will be okay.

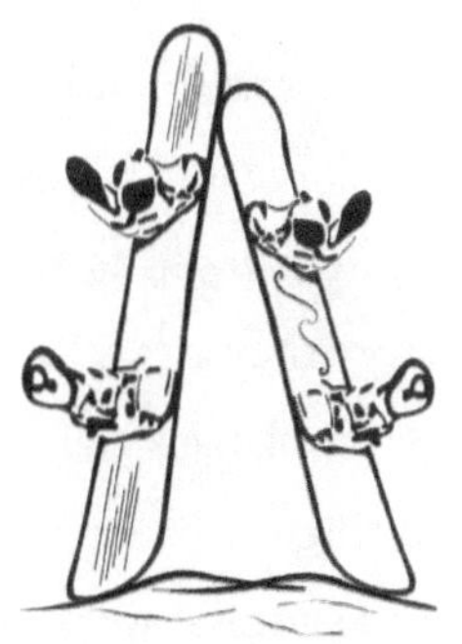

CHAPTER SIX

Rory

A fire crackles in the hearth next to my table in the base lodge of Empyreal, keeping the chill of sitting by a window at bay. My laptop sits open in front of me while skiers and snowboarders meander through on their way to the slopes. I work outside the office as often as I can because where's the inspiration in staring at a blank wall or out a window—no matter how great the view is? I'm constantly on the hunt for a new angle, a new image, a new idea that'll drive traffic from social media to our website and draw more people to this mountain I love so much.

The days I'm on the slopes, camera in hand, are the days I relish this job. I get to partake in some of my favorite activities all in the name of "work," and that never gets old. But then there's all the days in between. The days when I'm knee deep in TikTok trends or

Instagram reels when I'd rather be knee deep in the snow. Those are the days I feel an itch in my palms to reach for my camera and not let go.

I look over the top of my screen and spot a couple snuggled up in the corner in their ski gear. The dwindling snow falling just beyond the window, light filtering through just enough to highlight their smiles before they kiss... I know I could capture it perfectly behind the lens. I look back to my laptop and, ignoring the work I should be doing, click open the Photoshop tab. Pictures of the elopement I shot last weekend fill my screen. We'd gotten a dusting of snow the night before, so the sparkly layer of white that meets me in the images is mesmerizing and ethereal.

A few months ago, Jamie asked me to take photos while he officiated an elopement for his friends John and Bree, and I jumped at the chance. It was just a favor *and* a perfect excuse to be around something I've always loved: weddings. We had such a blast with the first one that we've done a couple more, but always under the guise of it being "for fun." It's not like I'm trying to change jobs or anything... it's just a hobby. I shake my head and smirk. *Imagine?* Mom and Dad would have a field day.

I sigh happily and scroll through the images, remembering every little touch, smile, and kiss as the bride and groom said their vows. Watching two people declare their love for each other helps me feel more connected to it. Especially since the romantic kind of love seems to be on a permanent vacation from my life lately. I guess I thought by the time I was twenty-seven, my life would look a little different. A little less lonely.

Wes is in Australia and my parents are—well, my parents. I have friends, and Jamie's like a second brother, but none of that is the same as having someone to call my own. I want a *person*—my person. I dated a lot in college, searching for that, but no one ever fit the bill.

Then there was Kyle, and the failure of that relationship still hovers around me sometimes. Not because I miss him, but because of what the breakdown between us cost me. Mom and Dad introduced us—he was the son of one of their associates and it made them happy to see me with someone they felt was appropriate. But *I* wasn't happy. I couldn't be myself with him—which shouldn't have come as such a shock, what with our origin tale being what it was.

I didn't need one more person controlling my life, controlling me. The breakup was more than the two of us splitting—it marked the end of a dream for our parents, and it didn't go over well. Mom and Dad lost friends (read: business associates) and it was "all my fault." All those years of constantly trying to please my parents and that was what fractured it in ways I never expected. I'm still trying to fix those broken pieces, and it's been over a year.

I haven't gone on a single date since.

I click into the finished file for a different elopement we did right around Thanksgiving. We hiked up a trail that gave us a perfect view of the lake in the background, and then clambered out onto a huge rock where Jamie stood before the couple and declared them man and wife. Yes, they trekked in full tuxedo and wedding dress, with hiking boots, and they smiled the whole time. So did I.

Some days, the concept of finding a love like that seems so far out of reach, but then I take photos like these and it feels attainable again. Like if these people found it, then maybe I can too.

I want more of that feeling, but I also know Jamie can't take on more elopements. He's busy promoting his new book and once he starts writing the next one, he'll be holed up in his home office. One or two a month is the most he can swing. Not that I have time for more either. I need to focus on my real job. I'm good at it, and I should be content with that. Even if I suspect it'll never make my heart soar the way capturing these couples in the most beautiful location on earth does.

I shake my head and, with a growly sigh, click the tabs closed. This can only ever be a hobby. It's not going to pay my bills. It's not going to keep my parents happy—though that outcome feels more and more out of reach every day anyway.

A ding from my email draws my attention and I open it, an ironic laugh bubbling up. It's an inquiry about shooting an elopement. Of course it is. They're also friends with John and Bree, and their date is in February. This puts us at six word-of-mouth bookings since we did theirs. I pull my phone from my hoodie pocket and text Jamie.

Me

> Whatcha up to February 27th?

Jamie

> I don't know, why? Planning to pay me back for having dinner with your parents this weekend?

I groan, having forgotten about the dinner entirely. Poor Jamie. They're better behaved when he's there, but it won't be pleasant. If they had their way, Jamie and I would be married by now and I'd have a "real" journalism job with a publication somewhere. We'd be a power couple: the published author and the published journalist.

I'm never not disappointing them.

Me

What do you want? I'm pretty sure I owe you my firstborn at this point.

Jamie

Hmmm, still pondering, but I promise it'll be good. So, what's happening on the 27th?

Me

You up for another elopement?

Jamie

Yeah, sure, I guess.

Me

Sound a little more enthusiastic why don't you.

Jamie

Sorry, I just had no idea this would become such a thing. I'm surprised is all.

Me

You and me both. Sounds like they got my email from Bree.

Jamie

I can make the 27th work. I'll put it in my calendar now.

The dots jump and fall on the screen as I wait for him to say something else, but instead my phone rings.

"Hey," I answer, sliding my earbuds into my ears and pulling up my calendar.

"Hey," he says, an air of caution in his tone.

"What's up?" I ask, knowing all too well he wouldn't have called if he didn't have something more on his mind.

"I was just wondering. These elopements. I know you love them, and I love doing them with you, but what's your endgame here?"

"What do you mean?"

"Like, is this your way into the photography world? Are you hoping to take this full-time?" He sounds wary, probably because he knows how much I still secretly covet the opportunity.

"No. Not at all." *Lies.* "It's just a cool way to put my camera to use"—*more lies*—"and I feel like it's a hobby that actually does someone some good, more so than taking pictures of people on chairlifts and sitting around fires in the snow." *Lies, lies, lies.* He knows it too, sitting quiet a minute longer than he would if he believed a word of what I just said.

"Okay. I just—" Jamie breaks off. I know he wants to say "I just want you to be happy" or something like that. In the end, we both know it won't change anything.

"I know." I clear my throat. "So, the twenty-seventh is good, yeah?"

"Yeah, it's good."

"Start your next book yet?"

"Nah, taking a few more weeks off before I start. I'm working on a short story to pass the time."

"Oh yeah? What about?"

"Scotland." He says it like this isn't a bit of a bombshell.

"Really?" I'm seriously shocked. He may have spent his first fourteen years of life in the Scottish Highlands, his now subtle accent only thickening to a true brogue when he drinks, but he rarely talks about his time there, and by rarely, I mean *never*. He did in the early years, when we were in high school. When he'd go back on summer breaks to stay with his grandparents. But he cut his trip short the summer before we started college and shut down every attempt I made to ask him about it. He hasn't been back since.

"Yeah. It felt like a good idea at the time. Not so sure about it now."

"Well, I think that's great, Jamie. You going to let me read it when you're done?" I love getting first dibs—perks of being best friends with the author.

"I don't know. This one might be just for me."

"Yeah? Well, I'm here if you change your mind."

"Thanks, Rory."

I hum and lean back in my chair. "I better go do some real work, especially if I want to get up on the mountain this afternoon. It's a perfect day."

We hang up and I stand to stretch, my legs feeling stiff. I rub my arms and look out into the sunlight that's just breaking through the clouds. I have a perfect view of the learning hill and notice a jacket that looks familiar—it's pink and grey and matches perfectly with the snow bibs I bought at Target. I place my hands on the sill and lean forward, squinting, and eventually confirm that it's little Willow, sitting in the snow. Towering over her is Breck—though I can only really tell from the wispy blond hair sticking out at the base of his helmet. He mentioned last night that he was going to bring her out today for her first time.

I bite my bottom lip between my teeth and smile, watching them talk… Willow throwing snowballs at his feet. I've noticed the loneliness has felt less suffocating over the last few days, and I know it's the newness of having visitors here and getting to show them around my home.

I wish I could grab the gear that's strewn around me and join them, but this is their moment.

Breck pulls Willow to her feet and I sit back in my chair, focusing my attention on the reports in front of me. A few hours of charts and insights and then I can forget the numbers and make my way up the mountain. Then I can fly.

CHAPTER SEVEN

BRECK

This morning has been an absolute disaster and it's only ten a.m. Getting Willow out the door was a struggle from the get-go. She didn't want to wear fleece leggings. She didn't want to layer a thermal top under her sweatshirt. She didn't want to wear snow boots. She didn't want two braids, she wanted one, and she wanted it to be just like Rory's—which I do not know how to do. *Yet*. But I'm bound and determined to master braiding if it's the last thing I do.

Sitting at the base of the magic carpet—a literal carpet conveyor belt built into the snow that will carry us up a tiny hill—Willow is pouting and grumpy. Now it's because I told her she had to wear a helmet for this endeavor. She's "not a baby," apparently. I tried to explain it has nothing to do with how big she is and everything to do with not wanting her to bounce her melon off the snow if she falls.

"Bear, come on, let's just try it. Please." I refrain from tilting my head back and screaming into the blue sky.

"I don't want to." She crosses her arms and juts her lip out even farther.

I pinch the bridge of my nose and take a deep breath. We're both tired. Getting suited up in all our gear, walking to the lodge, and renting Willow's equipment, all to end up here, has been utterly exhausting. Nonetheless, I bought two season passes and I'll be damned if we don't get some use out of them.

"I think you'll have fun if you just try." She rolls her eyes, and I rein in the desire to say "fuck it" and go home. "How about this? Three runs down this little hill and I'll get you a hot chocolate."

Bribery. The ultimate parenting hack.

She perks up at the mention of hot chocolate, finally making eye contact with me long enough to stop lobbing snowballs at my feet.

"Fine." She huffs and reaches a hand up. Mine dwarfs hers as I pull her to stand and try not to laugh when she hops around, one foot still strapped into her board.

I have her watch me get on the magic carpet and she follows suit. *Success*. I think if she had fallen it would've been the end of this deal. We don't get as lucky at the top where she loses her balance, but I'm able to catch her before she bites the dust—or snow.

I clip her other foot into the board and pull her goggles down over her eyes. She's the cutest little snowboarder I've ever seen. Pulling my phone out of my pocket I step back and say, "Smile for Uncle Wes."

She's in the hot pink snow bib Rory got her, layered under her grey and pink jacket, and her pink gloves stand out on her hands. No way I'm losing her in this getup. The helmet is pink and purple tie-dye, tying the whole look together. Maybe I'll send the picture to Rory too.

"Are you ready to do this?" I ask, hoping she'll at least try to listen to my guidance. Wes told me to get her a lesson for her first day, but oh no, I had to be a hero and try to teach her myself. I'm already regretting that decision.

She shrugs and nods. "Sure, Dad."

I set her up perpendicular to the slope and explain how she can push the snow in this position, like a snowplow, and it'll keep her from going too fast. I demonstrate what I mean, then flip around to watch her attempt to do the same. Instead, she turns her board so it's pointed straight downhill. Before she can control it, she catches her heel edge and falls flat on her back.

I cringe and brace for the tears. My girl is nothing if not a little dramatic about things like this. I race over, and her lip quivers when she looks at me. Her glance around tells me she doesn't want to cry in public.

"You okay?"

"You didn't tell me how to stop." She sniffles and reaches her arms toward me so I can pull her up.

"You're right, I didn't. I didn't think you'd take off like a rocket." I tuck her braid over her shoulder. Even through the goggles I can see the sheen of tears in her eyes. "I'm sorry."

She shrugs and sniffles again. I'm surprised the waterworks aren't going in full force, but I'm not going to question it.

"Think we could try again?" I ask, and she nods. "Okay, good. Now, where did I put those brakes?" I look around like I might find a handle or something. She chuckles and the sound lights me up inside.

See, I've got this. It's going to be okay.

A couple of hours later we've done ten *very slow* runs down this hill and Willow's starting to get the snowplow skill down. There's no chance I can attempt the chair lift with her though, so I admit defeat and make a plan to get her into lessons this weekend.

I want snowboarding to be fun for her, and it won't be if I'm grumping the whole time. We didn't have these issues when I taught her to surf back home. Why is this different? Or is it that *we're* different now—more emotional, more tightly wound?

"Okay, that's enough for today, yeah?" I dust some snow off my pants and look at her fresh pile of lopsided snowballs. "Ready for hot chocolate?"

Willow looks up with an evil grin, grabs one, and throws it at me. It's a direct hit to my chest and I dramatically fall to the ground with a groan.

"You got me! You'll pay for that, ankle-biter." I reach for some snow and ball it up, throwing it a good few inches from her feet.

"I think you owe me two hot chocolates. I did more than three runs," she says with a snarky little smile.

"Yeah, I don't think you need that much sugar. Why don't I buy you some lunch instead?"

"Yeah, okay." She sighs. You'd think I've been torturing her for two hours rather than trying to teach her something fun.

We unclip from our boards and I carry them down to a rack, stacking them amongst all the others. Grabbing my girl's glove-encased hand, we trudge upstairs into the lodge. Inside, the warmth surrounds us along with the smell of fried food. I look for an open table, but it's crowded with what I imagine are other keeners trying to make the most of the resort finally having decent snow. Scanning the room, my eyes are drawn to the corner, as if by an invisible tether.

Rory's strawberry-blonde hair is pulled over her shoulder in her signature braid and there's a faint flush across her cheeks, making her freckles stand out. She offers a smile and a little wave, drawing Willow's attention.

"Rory!" She's gone from my side before I can stop her. I offer an apologetic shrug before she's knocked back in her seat. I cross the room, excusing myself as I pass those Willow just blew through. Drawing closer, I see the computer sitting on the table.

Crap. She's working and we've just obliterated her cozy bubble.

"Sorry. We didn't mean to disturb you." I offer her a contrite smile, hoping we aren't too much of an inconvenience. Though she looks perfectly content, as does Willow—who's practically climbed into her lap.

"Not at all. My eyes were going crossed from staring at this screen anyway." Her shiny pink lips lift in a smile when she looks at Willow. "You're the perfect distraction."

I move around to her side of the table and rest my hands on the back of her chair. I see the pictures before she can close her laptop. Rows and rows of wedding photos are splayed across the screen, and an image processor takes up the top corner.

"What're you working on?" I think she does something in marketing for the resort, but it didn't look like the resort in the background.

She tilts her head back, her startling aquamarine eyes locking on mine. There's a deep blush moving across her cheeks and I grip the chair a little tighter, itching to press my cool fingers to them.

Wait... what the hell?

"Nothing. Just editing some photos." She chews her bottom lip and my eyes are drawn to her mouth now. It's even more distracting than the blush. Leaning back into the chair, her shoulders brush across my fingers, and I pull my hands away like I touched something on fire.

"Can I see? Can I see?" Willow asks, and I'm grateful for the interruption. She gives Rory her puppy-dog eyes, a look I know well.

"Yeah. Okay." She gives in and lifts the screen, and I sit down next to her.

Hovering over her felt too close, too intimate. Physical touch isn't something I shy away from, but with her it feels different. Because of my connection to Wes? Or is it because of Talia...

On the screen, there's photo after photo of a couple dressed to the nines and surrounded by nothing but gorgeous views. The blue lake glitters in the background, framed by lush green trees, though the couple stands on a rocky outcropping. It's so different from a typical wedding, more private and intimate. There's no crowds. No fancy decorations.

Jamie—who's an officiant *and* an author, apparently—stands between the bride and groom with nothing but nature's beauty to frame them in. It's positively stunning, but the way Rory's captured it, captured them... I'm struck by her talent.

"These are incredible, Rory. You took these?"

"Yeah." She tucks her chin, like that will stop me from seeing her blush.

"Why didn't Wes tell me you're a photographer?"

She's taken aback by the question, only making me want to press further.

"Can you take my picture?" Willow breaks in, forcing our attention to her instead.

"Sure. You know..." Rory trails off and boops Willow's nose. "I'd love to get some of you snowboarding. How'd it go today?"

Willow shrugs and looks at me.

"She did great. Though your brother was probably right when he said I should get her lessons first. We'll try that this weekend."

"I'm sure you did amazing. I can't wait to see," she says, her full attention on Willow now. "Did you know snowboarding is my favorite?" She leans in and whispers something into Willow's ear.

"Really? You'd go with me?" she exclaims, her face lighting up.

I bark a laugh. *Of course* that's what she said. I think I'd rather like these two giving me a run for my money on the slopes.

"Anytime. You wanna go right now?"

Rory looks at me, eyebrows lifted in question. I raise mine back and shrug—silently telling her Willow won't agree. Not a chance.

"Okay, let's go!" Willow cries, jumping up, and my mouth drops open.

Rory turns a smug smile on me and winks. "Would you mind staying here with my stuff so I don't have to get a locker?"

"Sure." I turn to my daughter. "You okay with that, Willow Bear?"

"Yup! You can get the hot chocolate for when we get back. Get Rory one too," she demands. Little bossy human.

Rory grins wider, eyes glittering. "I never say no to hot chocolate." She grabs her gloves and helmet, then slides on her jacket. I didn't even register she had her gear with her when I sat down. She heads for the door with Willow in tow—wearing a grin she didn't even attempt to offer me when I dragged her up the mountain this morning.

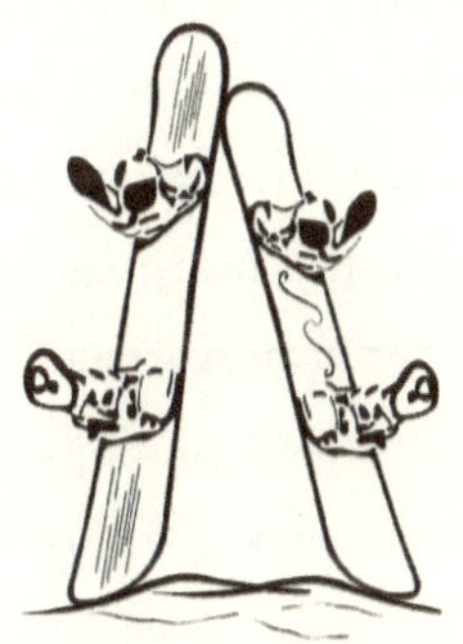

CHAPTER EIGHT

RORY

I flash Breck one last smile before we walk out the door and into the sunshine. I have no idea why I thought I was the best person to do this. I've helped a few friends learn to snowboard over the years, but I've never taught a kid. I have seen enough parents yelling on the slopes to know that they typically learn better from anyone who's not mom or dad, though.

I knew as soon as they walked into the lodge—and from the few peeks I took out the window to watch—that this morning didn't go quite the way Breck planned. Willow's ever-present smile was missing, and he looked weary—even if he was trying to hide it. Willow's going to need some real lessons, like the ones I had growing up, but maybe I can help her end today on a good note.

Willow points to her board on the rack, the standard Burton Grom the ski school rents to all the kids. It's propped against a solid black board with vibrant teal bindings and stickers from a handful of Australian ski resorts. Breck's board. I run my fingers over it and smile. It's practically the reverse of my own, which is sitting right where I left it this morning, a few rows down. Teal and mint swirling together in an abstract design on the top, solid black on the bottom, with black bindings. I tuck one under each arm and head for the magic carpet, Willow's snowpants swishing beside me as we walk.

At the base, I ask, "Do you surf with your dad back home?"

She looks at me, a little confused, and says, "Duh."

She's got spunk, I'll give her that.

"Okay." I hide my smile behind my gloved hand. "So when you surf, which foot do you have forward?"

"This one." She shakes out her left foot in front of her.

"Alright, good to know. I ride with my right foot forward, and we call that goofy foot here. Do they call it that in Australia?" I ask, and she shrugs. "I bet your dad is regular foot like you are."

"I don't know…" Her lips tip up in a half smile and she says, "He's pretty goofy if you ask me."

I snort a laugh. It's not a side of him I've really gotten to see, but I can imagine it based on the stories I've heard.

She shows a certain level of comfort when we clip in and skate over to the carpet, so that's a good sign.

"If you're a surfer chick, you should have no problem with this. We just need to get you as confident on the snow as you are on the water," I say when we reach the top. Willow smiles and straightens her shoulders, a hint of pride in her features. "I'm going to start here." I slide down the slope a few feet and stop right in front of her.

Reaching forward, I grab her pink gloved hands in my teal ones and tell her to lean back into her heels. Then I start inching my way backward down the hill, her following along facing me. "Good job. Keep all your weight on your heels, okay? Better to fall on your butt than on your face."

She giggles. "You said *butt*."

I blanch... Does that count as a bad word? "Uh... well, what should I call it?"

"Daddy says it's my bottom, but I've definitely heard him say I'm a pain in the ass so..." She lifts her shoulders and giggles. I choke back the laugh crawling up my throat—I can just picture him mumbling that under his breath with an eyeroll.

"Let's stick with bottom, I think." It sounds like her swear jar gets enough donations. She gives me a look like *if you say so*.

She inches forward as I inch back and I guide her back and forth across the small slope, like a falling leaf in the wind. We reach the bottom and with a smile she exclaims, "Let's go again!"

"Sure thing, Bug." Her head whips my way and she smiles, her cheeks turning slightly pink. The endearment slipped from my lips just as easily as it did that first day at the airport. I like it, and I'd say she does too.

We've gone up and down the hill three more times and she hasn't fallen. This time I'm not even holding her hands, so I pull out my phone and hit record to capture the last few seconds of her run. She stops in front of me—on her own, thank you very much—and I woop, lifting both hands to give her a double high five. It knocks her off balance, arms flailing by her sides before she falls flat on her "bottom." Luckily she laughs and lies back, swiping her arms through the snow. I snap another picture of her makeshift snow angel.

Once we're both unclipped, we walk back to the lodge where I see Breck watching us from the window, a wide grin lighting his face. He's not smiling for me, but it makes my cold cheeks warm with a blush all the same. We climb the steps hand in hand and Breck abandons his position by the window to run over and pull Willow into his arms as soon as we're inside.

"You did awesome, baby girl! Wow!"

"Thanks, Daddy! It was fun!"

"I'm so glad. You're amazing." He presses his lips into her hair before setting her feet back on the floor. In the next moment, I find myself enveloped in a similar hug, one that pulls me slightly off my feet as well. Strong arms and a firm chest surround me, along with a scent that's all snow and spice. The whispered "thank you" against the shell of my ear has a shiver running down my spine.

"You're welcome," I whisper, and I mean it.

He lets go, taking just one step back, and my breath gets caught in my lungs. I can't seem to let it out. There's so much feeling in his face—gratitude and appreciation, with a hint of something I can't place underneath. The second stretches and I can't look away, don't want to look away.

"Daddy!" Willow pops up between us. "Where's my hot chocolate?"

Breck chuckles and reaches to undo the clasp on her helmet. "I figured I'd get it as soon as you finished so it wouldn't get cold. I'll be right back."

Willow and I strip out of our gear, setting it by the fire to dry. We're just settling in when Breck comes back with two steaming cups of cocoa, a basket of french fries, and chicken tenders.

"I thought you both deserved a snack after all that hard work."

Willow squeals and tucks into the fries with abandon. I shake my head, biting back a smile, and reach over to grab a few myself.

"Thanks for this. I'm glad I decided to work here today instead of in the office."

"Me too," Breck says.

He sits across from me and, when I look up from the food, I blush under his gaze. The attraction that's always been there for me burns anew under it, and I struggle to break its hold. All these years I never thought much of it—he lived in Australia, he was Wes's best friend, he was with Talia, he had Willow. I was just a woman appreciating a man, that's all.

My phone vibrates across the table with a video call from Wes, snapping our connection. I reach for it, swiping without a thought for where we are. I never skip out on a call from my brother. Ever.

"Hey, Wessy," I say with a mischievous smile, and he nearly growls at me. He hates when I call him that, but I don't care even one little bit. I laugh and flip the camera toward Breck.

"Hi. 'Wessy,' was it?" Breck says, his accent wrapping around the word, and I burst out laughing. Wes's groan through the line only makes it worse, making me snort.

"No. You do *not* get to call me that. Take it back," he barks at his friend.

"Ooohhh, can I call you Uncle Wessy? Please!" Willow's signature giggle joins the fray, putting me in stitches. He's going to be so mad at me for this.

"No, you absolutely cannot," he says firmly, but with the way he's smiling, it doesn't sound like he means it. "Only Rory gets to call me that, and I may need to revoke her privileges."

"Impossible. I'd like to see you try." I flip the camera back to myself then stand and move around behind Breck and Willow, leaning my phone against my water bottle.

"You're the worst." He pouts and scrunches his eyebrows. "I'm rethinking my call now. I don't know if you deserve to hear my exciting news."

I stop laughing, my interest piqued. Exciting news? He and Joss are already coming in a couple weeks, what could be more exciting than that?

"Did you get a job offer?" I ask. He was working for Breck in Sydney as a skydive pilot, but when Breck—and Talia and their business partner Drew—sold the business last month, he decided to put in applications for the airlines. He's been hoping for Qantas, the same airline Joss works for as a flight attendant.

"No, the interview is next week." He's toying with me now. Giving me nothing.

"Tell me now, brother, or I'm getting out the baby books to show Breck and Willow."

"You wouldn't dare," he seethes.

"Wouldn't I?" I lift a brow, daring him to contradict me.

"No, don't tell her," Breck interjects. "I want to see Baby Wessy."

Wes glares at his friend and huffs. "Y'all are the worst," he mumbles. "But I'm actually glad you're together right now." He smiles wide, dimples popping behind his soft beard, blue eyes bright with excitement. "I'm going to propose to Joss."

He holds a ring box in front of the screen and pops the lid. My gasp is nothing next to the little scream Willow lets out.

"Uncle Wessy, that's so pretty! I want one!" This draws a laugh out of Breck, and all of us join in.

"I'm so happy for you, Wes." Breck looks almost misty-eyed. Nothing but love for his friends in his expression.

I'm *definitely* misty-eyed. No, I'm a step past that. I have full-on tears rolling down my cheeks. I'm so excited for my big brother. I never thought I'd see him settle down. This didn't seem remotely possible when he was dragging himself from the trenches of his grief last year.

"Rory, for goodness' sake, why're you crying?"

"Because I'm just so happy. Ugh. Why can't you be here right now so I can hug you?"

"You'll be able to hug me real soon. I promise," he says, eyes soft and smile warm.

I nod and wipe the tears from under my eyes.

"Seriously though, this is incredible. What's your plan? Tell me everything," I say, leaning a hand on Breck's and Willow's chairs.

"I can't let you in on all my secrets," he jokes, and I glare at him. "I actually have a question for you though."

"Okay, shoot," I say, back to being seriously intrigued.

"I'm going to ask Joss to elope while we're in Tahoe."

"What?! Are you serious?" I yell, drawing attention from those around us. Luckily the lodge has cleared out quite a bit. I'm so excited I could jump up and down. In fact... I do. I'm jumping around behind Breck and Willow, the two of them staring up at me like I've grown a second head.

Wes's genuine, hearty laugh booms through the phone. Willow joins in, and I can feel Breck's eyes as they watch me.

"Rory," Wes says, but I'm still bouncing around like a kangaroo. "Rory!" he says more loudly, and I stop to look at him. "I haven't even gotten to the best part. I want you to do the photos like—"

He's cut off by my squeak of excitement. "Shut up! You want me to do your elopement? Do you want me to ask Jamie to officiate? Oh my gosh, yes. I can get everything set up here. Just tell me what you want." All my thoughts and questions ramble together.

"Of course I want you to do it. And we could ask Jamie to officiate, unless..." He trails off and looks to Breck. "Would you want to do it?"

Breck's eyes instantly go glassy and he glances away. Wes's face falters, concern written there. "You don't have to. I know right now might not be the best time for this. I'm sor—"

This time it's Breck who cuts him off.

He looks straight at my brother, emotion leashed just under the surface, silver tears pooling in the corners of his blue eyes. "I would be honored, brother." His voice quavers on the word, and I wish more than ever we were all in the same space right now instead of separated by seven thousand miles.

The look that passes between these two men is layered. They may have only spent a few years on the same continent out of the last fifteen they've known each other, but their bond is deep. I can picture it—the way it spans the oceans to reach from where we sit on a snowy mountain in Tahoe, across the world to where Wes sits on his balcony in Sydney.

Wes clears his throat and nods, words failing him.

"Do I get to be the flower girl?" Willow chimes in, and they break eye-contact, looking instead at the darling girl whose eyes are alight at the idea of being part of this wedding.

"Absolutely. Make your daddy buy you a pretty dress, okay?" Wes gives her an over-the-top wink. His dimples are on full display and the crinkles around his eyes are more pronounced. I've never seen him look so happy.

My brother is getting married. My brother is going to elope and he wants me to take the photos, to organize the whole thing. He's one of only two people in my life who knows how much I love this, and it means everything.

That thought crashes over me like a wave, dousing all the elation I was just feeling. Mom and Dad will be part of this. They'll see me in my element, and they'll never approve. My heart sinks, but I keep my smile big and laugh along for the remainder of the conversation. All the while, I can't help wondering how much it will hurt at the end when I don't get to do this anymore.

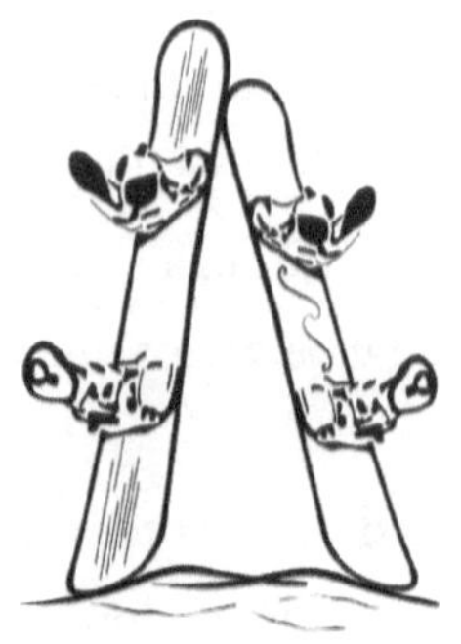

CHAPTER NINE

BRECK

I stand near the windows of our condo, looking out on the mountain beyond, and wonder how I got here. Yesterday was a lot, a roller coaster of emotions. I barely held it together when Wes asked me to officiate his and Joss's wedding. It was a battle for what I felt more of: absolute joy and gratitude that my best friend has found the love of his life and wants me to partake in their union this way, or a deep-seated sense of loss over the future I can no longer see for myself.

I could see his wariness in asking me and I pray I was able to hide the loss behind the joy enough that he didn't notice it. I would never turn him down, but alone in the darkness, I feel the ache everywhere. I'm truly excited for my friends. I miss them. I miss that part of my home, even when most everything else about that place feels wrong and broken right now.

Where being here feels... right. The sun crests the mountains, a new day dawning. I may no longer be a successful business owner, or a partner to Talia, or see the future in the same way, but I do have Willow. I have friends who love and care for me. The freedom to invest in something new. I can find a new path forward for us, can't I? I can find our way, mine and Willow's, and I can do it on my own.

A vision of Willow and Rory high-fiving at the bottom of the slope yesterday pops into my head and I chew my lip. It was incredible and heartbreaking all at once. Why was it so much easier for Rory to get through to her? This is *our* time to bond and forge a new path, and I can't let myself use Rory or anyone else as a crutch. I need to look toward what will work for Willow and me as a team of two. Because in the end, that's what we'll be when we go back to Australia.

I scrub my hand along the back of my neck, my sleep-mussed hair tangling between my fingers. I need to let Rory know I've got this. I'm sure she has better things to do than hang out with a surly mid-thirties guy and his daughter. Rory should be out having fun, not spending the evening watching *Encanto* and eating takeout with us—like she did last night after we got back from the slopes.

The buzz of my phone on the counter draws my attention from the view taking shape beyond the window. Needing another cup of coffee, I walk over and pick it up with a sigh.

"Speak of the devil," I murmur.

Morning! I'm heading up the mountain in a bit for work, but I could drop by with the info Jamie sent me about getting your officiant's license before I go.

I don't want to interrupt your morning with Willow though. I could bring it later. Whatever works best for you.

The texts sit unanswered while I refill my cup and think about how I want to proceed where Rory's concerned. I enjoy her company, obviously, but I'm not sure it'll help anything in the long run.

I do need that information though, and I should probably talk to Jamie at some point. I could use some pointers.

After a swig of coffee, I text her back.

Sure. I'm up and Willow is having a bit of a lie-in, so you aren't interrupting anything.

Okay, see you in a few.

I jog upstairs to pull on a T-shirt. Rocking black joggers without a shirt doesn't feel appropriate around my best friend's little sister.

I keep calling her that in my head, as if it will somehow keep me from recognizing just how beautiful she is. The eight years between us feels like nothing when we're together. She's mature and put together in a way I'd expect of someone older, but that still doesn't change anything.

I take a second to brush my teeth, wishing I had time for a quick shower. My dirty-blond hair stands up like I stuck my finger in a socket. I run my hands under the water and try to calm the worst of the bedhead, then press at the dark circles under my eyes. Despite being used to the time change, I'm still not sleeping well. Too much on my mind. Too much to feel when I'm finally alone in bed and can allow myself to.

The five-o'clock shadow from yesterday has turned into a full-on six a.m. scruff. I'll need to do something about that after Rory leaves. The soft knock from downstairs tells me she's here and it's time to accept that this is as good as it's going to get. Not that I'm trying to impress her, I just don't want to look like a complete vagabond either.

The plush carpet compresses under my bare feet on each stair before I reach the door. Pulling it open, I'm met with a bright smile and rosy cheeks. Rory has a mint green beanie pulled low over her ears, but her braid of rose-gold hair peeks out over one shoulder. My mouth goes dry and I have to clear my throat to speak.

"Hey. Come on in," I say, stepping aside to make space for her. She knocks her boots together, snow falling off in clumps on the mat before she steps inside. She slides off her jacket, revealing a form-fitting thermal top over leggings. *Bloody hell.* I rake my gaze up her body, meeting her questioning eyes, and quickly look away. She definitely saw me check her out.

"Coffee?" I ask, leading the way into the kitchen before I embarrass myself further.

"Oh, uh, yeah. Yes, please." She stumbles over the words, and I want to kick myself for making her uncomfortable.

She sits up at the counter and I focus my wayward brain on fixing her a cup.

"Thanks," she says when I slide it across the counter, her voice clear and bright once again. "Here's everything Jamie had about getting your license. He said it's pretty easy, but he's happy to walk you through it. I put his number on the front for you." She slides me a stack of paper, then lifts the cup to her lips. A soft sigh of enjoyment leaves her as her eyes close, a look of contentment on her face, like that one sip of coffee made her whole day.

I scratch the back of my neck. "Perfect, I'll get the ball rolling today so, assuming Joss says yes, we'll be set."

"Oh, she'll say yes." Her smile is soft, full of love for her brother.

"I know she will. You're going to love her. She's perfect for him, showed up at the exact right time." My own smile lifts my cheeks.

"I've got a lot of work stuff going on today," Rory says, "but if you guys need anything, just shoot me a text. Or if you're up on the mountain, let me know and I can try to meet up with you or something. I'm happy to work with Willow some more too if she—"

"Rory," I cut her off, and she looks at me expectantly. "Thank you for all your help getting us settled. Really, I appreciate it so much. But I've got this. You've got work and a life. I don't want to take advantage of your kindness. I know you're doing this because Wes asked you to, but we're all set now."

I don't look at her, not directly. As much as I'm doing this for her, I still feel like an ass, and I'm scared to see the expression on her face. Even more so when she replies.

"Oh. Yeah, okay. Sure." Her voice is too quiet, almost restrained. "I really should get to work. Have a good day, Breck."

I look up from where I'm scrubbing a towel over the clean surface of the counter and catch the briefest look of hurt across her features. Then she turns and heads for the door. I want to follow her, apologize, but I hold my ground. This will be better, easier.

"You too," I say but the door closing behind her drowns it out. My eyes fall on her full cup of coffee and my shoulders sag.

Fuck, what did I just do?

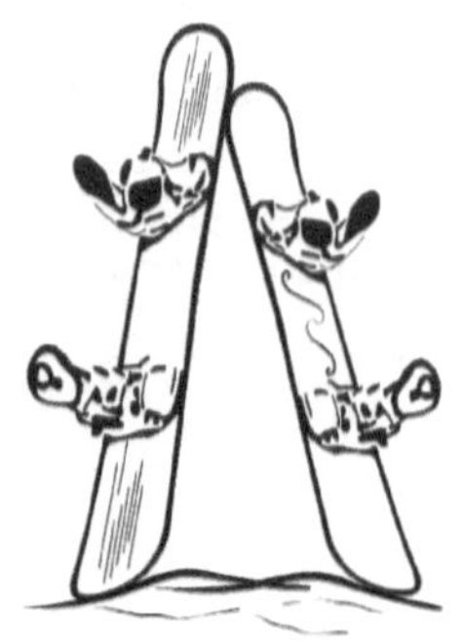

CHAPTER TEN

RORY

I make it down the front steps before the first tear slides down my cheek. There's a sting in the back of my throat as I contain what I'm sure will come out as a noisy cry if I let it. It's a short walk to my condo and the tears I can't control nearly freeze to my face as I go.

So stupid, Rory. It's clear now that what I thought was a budding friendship was really just me being in the way. Overstepping and becoming nothing more than a nuisance to Breck as he tries to heal from the pain of Talia leaving. I thought I was helping; I thought he and Willow enjoyed my company. In reality, I was nothing more than Wes's kid sister hanging around where I wasn't wanted.

I've been here before. My people-pleasing nature often gets me into situations like this. Situations where I try too hard to be what everyone around me wants and I end up falling horribly short at every turn. The only people I've never felt that way with are Jamie and Wes. Here I am though, unable to even help Wes's friend the right way without putting him in a position to tell me to back off.

The really stupid thing is that I could've sworn I saw heat in Breck's eyes when he let me inside. That look had me blushing, but clearly I was seeing something that wasn't really there. I made it up in my head, right along with the idea that we were, maybe, becoming friends.

My head tips back on a sigh and I watch the white wispy clouds churn overhead. At least this overcast sky can match my mood. It's going to be pretty gloomy inside my head today.

Unlocking the door to my condo, I grab my bag from the foyer, slip my board under my arm, and head back out into the cold. I didn't even get to finish my coffee before I was politely asked to leave them alone, but I couldn't let Breck see how it affected me—even if he does make the best coffee. When I get desperate for caffeine later, I'll grab some at the lodge.

Five hours later and I have not had another cup of coffee. I'm over-the-top cranky at this point, and the next person who crosses me is likely to get an earful. After dropping my bag in the office this morning, I headed up the mountain with all my gear in hopes of getting some fresh content. The chairlift was down when I got to it, and that was only the first of many missteps in today's plan.

When I finally made it to the top, the clouds just barely covering the sun and giving off a shiny glow to the fresh snow, I realized my camera's battery was dead. And since I charged it last night, it's likely completely dead and I'll need to replace it. Fine. I strapped in and flew down the hill, determined to enjoy the view of my lake, my town, and my mountain as I went, but nothing was shaking me from the bitter feeling Breck's words brought on.

I made it back to my office and realized my backup battery was in my other camera bag. At home. I didn't have it in me to trudge back for it, so I opted to use my phone for today's footage. Videos for reels instead of static pictures for posts. Also fine.

But by the time I got back up the mountain, those white fluffy clouds had turned mean and were dumping snow in what I can only classify as a complete white-out. I'm rarely nervous being up on the mountain, but no matter how skilled you are on skis or a board, it only takes one novice who isn't to knock you off your feet.

My anxiety was on high alert for the slow ride down, and keeping close to the trees only added to the terror. I decided I'd get a cup of coffee in the lodge and wait out the storm, but the coffee gods decided to double down on my punishment and cut power to the resort. Throwing my proverbial hands in the air, I grabbed my bag from the office and headed home.

I'm so close now, teeth chattering, fingers nearly numb as they cling to my board. I stomp up the stairs of my condo, ready for a hot bath, a cup of coffee, my sweats, and to put this shit day behind me.

I've only just crossed the threshold when a shrill "Rory?" greets me.

Well, damn, I guess today *can* get worse.

"Mom?" My voice holds the obvious question: *What are you doing here?* I lean my board against the rack just inside the door, kick off my snowy boots, and hang my jacket up. I ignore the *drip, drip, drip* of snow melting onto the stone floors and go in search of my mother.

She's sitting at the island in my kitchen, a white mug in her hands. It's the only plain one in the house and was bought specifically with her in mind. I like fun mugs. Mugs in any color and size—well, no, I like ones that hold lots of coffee. I collect them and have a whole cabinet full. My current favorite sits on the counter, next to a steaming pot of coffee. It was a present from Wes and has the Sydney skyline on it.

"Mom. What are you doing here?" I ask, my crankiness just barely leashed.

"I got here about thirty minutes ago. Remember we talked at dinner on Sunday about doing a quick inspection on the place?"

Yes, it was mentioned *in passing*. And she got here *thirty minutes* ago? Why didn't she call or text me? It's a Friday; she knew I'd be working.

"Sorry you had to wait."

She shrugs and picks a piece of imaginary fluff off her sweater. "It's fine. I took a few minutes to poke around, and everything seems to be in order. Then the storm really came up and I thought I'd wait it out a bit. I hope you don't mind I made myself at home."

She knows I *do* mind. I'm aware that this is their house, their investment property, but she knows I hate when they turn up unannounced.

"No problem at all." I plaster on a smile. Everything in my life feels off-kilter today, and I just want to go to sleep and wake up to a better tomorrow.

The gravitational pull of the bean water has me circling the island to the coffee pot. I grab my mug, its comforting size and shape molding to my hand as I fill it. I pull out my favorite maple-pecan creamer and add a large splash. If this doesn't fix my mood, nothing will.

I lean my elbows on the counter across from my mom, where she sits silently watching me—judging me.

"No Dad today?" I ask, wondering if they played rock, paper, scissors for who would get to "inspect" my home.

"No, he had a meeting with Logan about one of his properties." *Logan.*

Though my parents have their opinions about my job, they have no qualms about being friends with my boss. Logan has never allowed their connection to play a part in my work, but my parents absolutely believe they're to thank for any success I might find at Empyreal.

"Ah. That explains why I didn't see him. Though, I was up on the mountain most of the day."

"In this weather? Rory, honestly, is that even safe?" She sounds scandalized.

I don't tell her it likely was *not* safe, instead opting for the positive spin.

"It wasn't too bad while I was up there, but the resort lost power and I figured I'd head home to get some more work done from here." I hope the implication will lead to her leaving, and I almost think I've done it when she stands up in her perfectly pressed slacks and cashmere sweater. Only, she walks around to the coffee pot and refills her cup. I drop my head forward, taking a deep breath before pulling another sip of coffee between my lips.

"So, everything looked good with the house then? I told you there weren't any issues."

"I know, but your father doesn't like to let these inspections go too long," she says, like she wasn't the one who first proposed the idea.

"Yeah, of course."

Silence stretches between us. We've hit on work, and the house, the next topic is sure to be—

"How are Breck and Willow settling in?"

Well, at least it's not my love life. The question smarts a little anyway, because they're great. So great they don't need me bothering them anymore. My chest tightens and the sting that was festering in the back of my throat returns, but I refuse to cry in front of my mom.

Glancing away, I say with as much nonchalance as I can muster, "They're doing great. All settled in."

"Oh good. You'll keep an eye on things over there for us, won't you?"

I swallow. "Sure, of course. Though I think they're just trying to enjoy their time here. I don't want to bother them."

"Well, Wes will be here soon and can help out. I'm sure Breck will be glad to have *him* around."

"Yep." Keeping the hurt at bay is a struggle. But she's right. God, I've never felt more like an unwanted younger sibling in my life. Wes never made me feel that way, no matter our age difference. He was always the best at including me. He never once locked me outside his room when his friends were around or made me feel like I was lame.

Mom pushes away from the island and places her mug in the sink. When she squeezes my shoulder, I lean into the touch, desperate for affection regardless of where it comes from. I look up, our eyes catching, and I wonder if she can see I'm having a hard day. Her eyes soften just a touch but then—

"When Wes and Joss get in next week, we said they could stay here with you since you have the extra room. That's okay, isn't it?"

Of course it's okay, but why couldn't she ask me first? Will I always feel like a visitor in this home? It also irks me the way she says "we," like this was a joint decision between her and Dad, as if they're still a couple.

When their marriage started to fail, they pulled the plug on it, no love lost. It was done with such ease, so few considerations, that I've always suspected they might do the same to me one day.

I nod, unable to find words, and she says, "Great. They'll have more fun here with you than at mine or your father's house. Have a good rest of your afternoon, Rory. See you and Jamie for dinner on Sunday." She plants a perfunctory kiss on my cheek and moves to the door, out into the storm, leaving me to deal with the one raging inside of me.

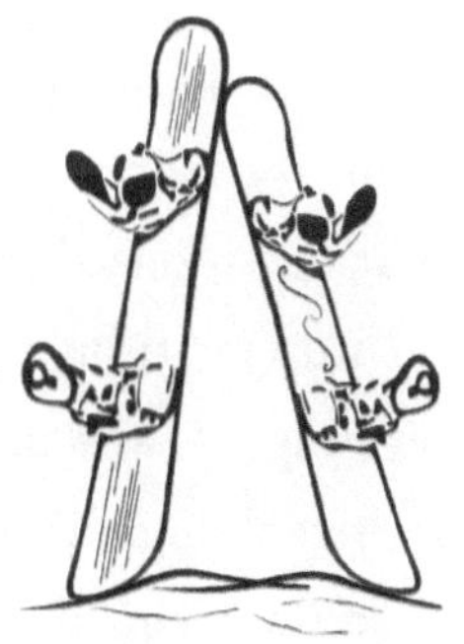

CHAPTER ELEVEN

RORY

Wes is vibrating with energy in the passenger seat of my car, talking animatedly while Joss looks on from the back seat, cracking jokes about how much of a golden retriever he's being. I can't believe they're really here. Wes, of course, gave me a hard time for crying when I picked them up, but I couldn't help it. From the minute I hugged Joss to when I was wrapped up in Wes's arms, I was an emotional mess. I've missed him so much, and having him home makes everything feel right in the world.

The drive was filled with easy conversation, mostly catching them up on the plans for their elopement on New Year's Eve—a mere ten days away. Wes only popped the question a few days ago, so I've been going full tilt to ensure this'll be the most incredible tiny wedding imaginable.

Breck texted me to say he took care of the necessary paperwork to officiate, and that's been the extent of our communication in the last week. Beyond catching the occasional glimpse of him and Willow on the slopes, I haven't seen them either. I don't blame him for wanting space. *I don't.* He's figuring out his life, and he doesn't need anyone else in the mix.

Knowing that doesn't stop me from repeating his words in my head and feeling their sting just as acutely as the day he said them. With Wes and Joss here though, there will be ample time where we're all together, so I'm trying to move past that. Let it go.

Wes must've told Breck that we were close, because when we pull up outside my condo, he and Willow are standing on the front steps. I've barely turned off the engine before Wes jumps out and bounds toward his best friend and his pseudo-niece. Their embrace, Willow sandwiched somewhere in the middle, threatens to make me cry again.

Wes has missed having Breck in Sydney, that much is clear. He has Joss there, but he loves his best friend and would give anything to fix the things that drove him away. But he can't, and I know that kills him.

Joss and I meet at the back of the car, amused looks passing between us at the guys' show of affection.

"Oi, a little help over here," Joss hollers, and they quickly break apart with barks of laughter.

"Sorry, Grey. I'm coming," Wes calls back, using his favorite endearment for his fiancée. Clapping Breck on the back, he saunters over, a look of warmth in his eyes that I've never seen him wear for anyone else. He gives Joss a peck on the cheek and then grabs several of the bags.

I turn from the hatchback to hand another bag to Wes and run into a firm chest.

"I'll take that," Breck says, his voice a raspy caress over my skin. He takes the bag, his hand lingering over mine for a second too long. I feel his eyes on me but don't meet them.

"Aunt Joss!" Willow exclaims, pulling all the attention to herself. She runs forward and wraps her arms around Joss's middle.

She really is like a niece to them. I don't have close friends with kids, and considering I didn't expect Wes to settle down, I figured I'd never be an aunt. Who knows, maybe that'll be in my future after all.

Willow releases Joss and turns to me, offering me nearly the same squeal of excitement. "Rory! I've missed you!"

My heart goes all gooey in my chest. I've missed her too. Who knew that it would take less than a week around this kid to be smitten. Of course, that only made this past week apart that much harder.

"Same here, Bug. How's snowboarding going?"

"Soooo good." She drags out the word, and it makes me smile. "I'm linking turns now!" she says, pride evident in her voice.

"Seriously? I can't wait to see!" I'll get to see her in action while Wes and Joss are here, and I plan to make the most of it.

I look over her head and everyone's watching us. Wes and Breck weighed down with bags, Joss with a small smile on her lips.

"Sorry, you need me to open the door." I slide my hand down Willow's dark braid and note it looks slightly less messy than usual.

She links her hand in mine and I squeeze it tight, walking up the stairs to unlock the door.

"Make yourselves at home," I say over my shoulder, all of us funneling into my foyer. In no time, it's a mess of jackets and shoes. My socks join the pile too, because there's something about being barefoot on these warm hardwood floors that feels homey to me. "Wes, you know where your room is. Breck and Willow, can I get you anything?"

I can play the hostess, no matter how awkward it feels to have him here after everything.

"Do you have hot chocolate?" Willow asks, bouncing on her toes, bubbling with excitement. Breck opens his mouth as if to protest, but I cut him off.

"I sure do. Let's make some." I take her hand again and pull her toward the kitchen. "Do you think Uncle Wes and Aunt Joss want a cup too?"

She nods emphatically. "And Daddy too. Right, Daddy?"

She turns us around and Breck's eyes lock with mine across the space. There's something tentative there, like he's unsure of how to act around me.

"Sure, Willow Bear. Can we keep it to a small cup? I'd like for you to sleep tonight." His gaze never leaves mine while he speaks, and that precocious girl of his notices.

"Daddy, why're you staring at Rory?"

His head snaps her way. "I wasn't staring. I just..." He trails off. He definitely was, but so was I.

I turn back toward the kitchen, leaving a spluttering Breck in my wake.

I get started on the hot chocolate, but it's not enough to distract me from the display of enviable friendship happening in my living room once Joss and Wes join us. I have friends. I do. Well, I have Jamie. There are others in my life I would classify as friends too, but nothing like this. There's a pang in my chest as I watch them interact. They're so natural with each other... Comfortable.

Breck picks Willow up by the ankles. Lifting her high, he blows a raspberry on her stomach, making her cackle and squirm against his hold. Wes and Joss join in with their own laughter from where he's pulled her down against his side on the couch. It's a Hallmark moment. They're like a little family, and here I am, on the outside, wondering how I get an invite in.

The sound of shattering glass rends the air and the moment breaks, right along with the mug I just dropped at my feet—too deep in my head to notice how close it was to the edge of the counter. I look down at the broken shards of what was one of my favorite mugs. Moving without thinking, a large piece of porcelain slices through the delicate skin of my bare foot.

"Ow, shit!" I holler, lifting my foot away from the offending object—blood immediately seeping from the cut.

My body locks up, and the room erupts in chaos.

Breck drops Willow to the couch, his wide eyes finding mine at the same time she yells, "Swear jar!"

Willow attempts to run for the kitchen, also barefoot, and Wes grabs her, tossing her over his shoulder. "Uncle Wes!" she shouts, pounding on his back with her little fists.

"Rory, are you okay?" Wes calls, but I'm still frozen, gaze locked on Breck.

Joss adds, "Breck, you still have shoes—"

"On it," he says, already moving. He rounds the counter, concern flitting across his face when he takes in the mess around me.

"Rory, don't move, okay?" His voice is soft and gentle.

I'm not going anywhere, acutely aware of the fact I'm standing in a minefield of broken glass. Breck's boots crunch over it, the sound scraping through my consciousness and bringing me back to the pain in my foot.

I look down and the room spins. There's more blood now. The edges of my vision blur but snap back into focus when large hands grip my biceps. I look up into brilliant blue eyes. They're the only things that could distract me from the pain radiating in my foot and the tightness in my chest.

"I'm going to put you on the counter, yeah?" His accent wraps itself around the word *yeah* in the most indecent way.

He winds an arm around my waist to hoist me onto the counter, the move obscenely easy for him. I've never been one for being manhandled, but I don't hate it right now. Heat rises to my cheeks, my mind offering up other ways he could—

Rory, what the hell?

"Hey, you okay?" The hand that isn't still wrapped around my waist cups my cheek, forcing me to look at him. Can he see what I was thinking? I make myself focus on Breck, on the pain, on anything but my wayward thoughts.

"Yeah. Yeah, I think so. I don't like blood," I stutter out.

"I guessed as much. Keep your eyes on me. Where's your first aid kit?"

"Upstairs, under my bathroom sink."

"I'll get it," Joss says from across the room.

A minute later, Wes is next to me. "You know, Roars, if you wanted help with the hot chocolate, all you had to do was ask. You didn't have to resort to violence and start breaking stuff." He chuckles, and I try to smile back, but it feels weak.

"If you aren't careful, Wessy," I say through clenched teeth, "I will choose violence and throw the next one at your head."

"Well, there she is. See? You're okay," he says, a genuine smile replacing the look of concern.

"I've got the first aid kit," Joss says, walking into the kitchen. "Bloody hell. That's, well, a bloody mess."

I groan and close my eyes, my head tipping forward as I attempt to pull air into my lungs. My forehead hits something firm and warm with a soft thud. Breck's chest. I can't bring myself to care, forcing a big inhale in through my nose to avoid passing out. He smells good. Really good.

"Helpful, Joss," Breck mutters sarcastically.

It registers through the haze that this is embarrassing. What a wonderful first impression I'm making on my soon-to-be sister-in-law. Passing out would be worse, however, so I really need to pull it together. I hear more crunching of glass and assume everyone has shoes on now to avoid ending up in the exact mess I've found myself in.

Except Willow apparently, because the man holding me to his chest says in his firm dad voice, "Stay there, love. Just wait until we get everything cleaned up."

"Okay." She sniffles, and I hate that I've scared her with my clumsiness. "Is Rory alright?"

"Yeah, sweetheart, she's fine. Just needs a minute." His words puff out across the top of my hair, and my neck prickles at the closeness, the warmth.

The swish of a broom and the tinkle of glass filter in alongside the sound of my breaths mingling with the ones that lift the chest I'm still resting against.

"Joss, can you check her foot?" Breck's voice rumbles out above me and I press my hands into his abdomen in an attempt to push away.

"I'm okay," I say, but I don't make it far. Blinking my eyes open, I catch sight of the bloody massacre that is my floor. "No, I'm not." I squeeze my eyes shut again and feel Breck's hand smooth up my back.

"It's fine. Let Joss look at your foot and Wes can clean up the mess. When we're all done, you'll be good as new, yeah?"

There's that word again. *Yeah.* Why does it only sound that good when he says it?

"Okay." At my acquiescence, his shoulders relax, like he thought I'd fight him on this. I know myself though, and I really might pass out if I look at that blood again. Joss's gentle hands grip my ankle, rolling the hem of my jeans up. I tense, and Breck's hand resumes its gentle strokes. I melt into the touch and don't pay attention to the world around me until I feel Breck's hands slide along my thighs and underneath me to hoist me up.

"Just moving you to the other counter," he whispers against my hair when I inhale sharply.

My instinct is to wrap my legs around him, but I don't need to. He supports my weight fully, and I try not to think about his hands and where they're gripping me. He rotates us, angling me on the opposite counter so Joss can maneuver my foot into the sink.

I hiss when water hits the cut, my other leg tightening around Breck where he stands in front of me. He doesn't pull away but brings those big hands back to my spine.

"Almost done," Joss says quietly. I can hear a smile in her voice when she continues. "And, you made your brother clean your kitchen for you. Well done."

I chuckle weakly at her joke, as does Wes from somewhere nearby.

"Real nice, Roars. Real nice." Wes's voice drips with sarcasm. Then I hear him closer, right next to me. "You doing okay?"

"Yeah, I'm okay," I say on a shaky exhale.

His hand comes to the back of my neck and he plants a soft kiss on the crown of my head—one I wish was from Breck. *Really, Rory?* As if he isn't doing enough, holding me through this whole ordeal. I guess it's good he was sick of having me around, because after this I won't have any trouble wanting to avoid him.

"Alright, all done. Good as new," Joss says. "The cut wasn't that deep, so you don't need stitches or anything."

I lift my head, opening my eyes, and the first thing I see is Breck, his face mere inches from mine. I push away and find my hands fisted in his shirt, over his pecs. I release them, shaking away the feel of cotton and heat.

"Sorry," I say as I look away, glad that my kitchen no longer looks like a crime scene.

Breck loosens his grip too. When he steps back, I realize my leg is still wrapped around his thigh. I untangle myself, his heat leaving me completely.

I look down and see dark crimson spots smudged along his jeans, and it's not my queasiness this time that makes me put my head in my hands.

God, could this get any more embarrassing?

I groan. "I'm sorry. I'll get you new jeans."

His laugh is low and rumbly. I peek between my fingers to watch him take in the state of his pants. "No worries. They'll wash. This isn't the first time I've had a situation like this. Willow's had her fair share of scrapes. Seems to come with the territory of being a dad."

I cringe and squeeze my eyes shut. There I was gripping his shirt and thinking about how easily he manhandled me, while this was all him leaning into *dad mode*. I press back against the counter, ready to hoist myself down onto my good foot and hobble straight to bed, or to find a hole to swallow me up.

I don't make it far before he grabs my elbow. "Hang on, I'll help you."

"You don't have t—" I don't even finish my sentence before his hands are on my waist. Again. He lifts me off the counter and I slide against him until my feet find the ground. Too close. We're too close.

"Thanks." The word is brittle, his presence doing something to me it absolutely shouldn't be, and I sigh. I'm supposed to be mad at him, or at the very least indifferent at this point. Instead, I'm nearly purring at his proximity.

Willow's steps are heavier, like she's put her boots on too, just in case. She pokes her head around her dad's hip and smiles. "Are you okay?"

Breck steps back, leaving me to lean against the counter instead of him, and pulls Willow into his side.

"Yeah, I'm fine. Just a small cut. Nothing to worry about. Sorry if I scared you."

"I wasn't scared." She juts her chin out, defiant and cute as a button.

"No, of course you weren't. I was, though."

"You were?" she asks, looking me over.

"Oh yeah, I don't really like blood very much." I swallow thickly, knowing there was quite a bit of it to clean up. "Sorry I ruined the fun."

"You didn't." It's Breck who speaks this time, and I notice it's just the three of us in the kitchen now.

"Where are Wes and Joss?"

"I think they pulled an Irish goodbye and went to bed. Maybe all the excitement took the last of their energy," he says with a shrug.

"I really did ruin the night then. I'm sorry." My shoulders slump and I look at the floor.

"Hey, you didn't ruin anything. They were bound to go to sleep early regardless. You could probably use an early night too. Do you need help getting upstairs or anything?" The thought of him helping me into bed makes a blush rise in my cheeks.

"No. No, I'm fine. Thank you though. Willow, raincheck on the hot cocoa, yeah?"

"Yeah, okay." She's disappointed, but her dad gives her neck a squeeze.

"Let's let Rory go to bed. We'll see everybody tomorrow." He says it like it's a sure thing, but there's a question on his face when he looks back to me. Honestly, I may just hide out forever.

"Yeah, tomorrow." I don't meet his eyes when I say it, unsure if it's true. He gives Willow another squeeze and they head for the door.

"Night, Rory," Willow calls, the door closing behind them.

My head hangs and I keep leaning against the counter, unmoving, unwilling to consider how I'm going to get up the stairs. Maybe I'll just sleep on the couch.

"Hey, little sister." My head snaps up to find Wes watching me from across the island. "You okay?"

"Oh yeah, just wishing I could erase the last thirty minutes of my existence."

"Ah, come on, it wasn't that bad. It could've happened to anybody." He comes around the bar and leans against the counter next to me, bumping me with his hip.

"Yeah, but it didn't." I drop my head against his strong shoulder, absorbing the comfort that only ever comes from being near him. "I thought you snuck off to bed?"

"Nah. I just wanted to get Joss settled. She's beat."

"I'm sure you are too. I won't be far behind you if you want to head that way."

"I want to hang with my little sister for a minute. You sure you're okay? You've been pretty quiet since we got home—and I mean before the whole mug-throwing debacle." He smirks down at me.

"I didn't throw it." I roll my eyes and bump his shoulder.

"I'm just giving you a hard time. It's my job as your big brother, ya know?"

"Yeah, I know."

"So, uh…" His words drift off as he runs a hand through his hair. "What's up with you and Breck?"

I stiffen. "What do you mean?"

"Come on, Rory. Even before whatever all that was with him helping you with your foot—"

"He was just being nice… His dad mode kicked in. And I'm glad it did because I'd be way more embarrassed if I'd actually passed out."

"Okay, we'll come back to that, but… did something happen?"

"Seriously? No. Goodness, Wes, he's here trying to pick up the pieces after Talia and you're asking if something happened with us?"

"No, I wasn't.…" He looks genuinely surprised. "I just—it felt tense between you two, and I wanted to make sure everything was okay. I know Breck isn't really himself right now so I expected him to be a little off, but you're being weird with him too. What gives?"

"Nothing. I just… I think I overstepped. I was trying too hard to be you for them." I shrug. "It's stupid."

"Did he say that?" Wes sounds defensive. Of me or Breck, I'm not sure.

"I mean, not in so many words, but kind of. I don't blame him. I'm not you, and I shouldn't have tried to be. I haven't really spent much time with them in the past week, not wanting to crowd him. But now that you're here, it's a little awkward being pushed back together. I don't know how to give him space and be around him."

"I'll talk to him. I doubt he was—"

I cut him off. "No, Wes, please don't. It's fine, really. He's going through enough and he needs you to be there for him."

"Yeah, but I need to be here for *you* too." He says it quietly, and I can hear the sadness behind the words. He knows how much I miss him. I know he misses me too. And he misses his friend. It's hard all around.

"He needs you more than I do. He's the one who could use his friend, so I'm glad you're here."

"Rory." His voice is soft and placating, but I don't want his pity.

"Really, it's fine. I'm going to go to bed." I carefully put weight on my foot and am thankful there's only a dull ache as I take my first step toward the stairs. "I'll see you in the morning."

"Okay. You sure you're good?"

"Yep. I always am."

I continue my slow limp away and only just hear him when he says, "Yeah, but you shouldn't have to be."

CHAPTER TWELVE

BRECK

Wes and I head up the chairlift on the backside of Empyreal, a cold wind cutting across our faces. It's just the two of us as Willow is taking one more half-day lesson and Joss is down there with her, taking a lesson of her own. Wes—smart man that he is—told her something along the lines of "I want to get married in nine days, and you might not want to marry me if I try and teach you."

Lessons have been a godsend for Willow over the past week. She gets more confident with each one, more comfortable with the skills they're teaching her. There hasn't been a single tear shed, nor any complaints. Not even when she finishes class and I take her for a couple of runs. She's a natural, just like when she surfs, and I love that. I love that she and I can share this sport, the way my parents shared it with me.

"Man, this feels good," Wes says with a sigh, tipping his helmeted head back to look up at the blue sky.

"Yeah, it does. This mountain is quickly becoming my favorite place. No wonder you love it here so much." I can see now why leaving for good was such a big deal.

"It will always be home in a way. But Sydney feels like it's really mine, you know? I was born to love Tahoe, and it will always have a special place in my heart. But Sydney... It's the home I choose, with Joss."

I sigh, looking over to where the lake sits in the distance, an expanse of blue surrounded by steepled mountains of grey and white. "Sydney's always been home, at least it has been since my aunt and uncle moved me to live with them after my parents died." Wes knows all about my parents, and while Aunt Tracey and Uncle Bill passed before we met in college, he's heard me speak about them plenty over the years. "But I don't miss it as much as I thought I would. Plus, it feels tainted somehow."

I look at my friend and his lips are pulled down at the corners. If not for the goggles, I know I'd see his furrowed brow as well.

At his silence, I say, "We have just over a month left here, and part of me is already dreading the idea of going back."

He gives me a solemn nod, and I know he's taking every one of my words and rooting to the core of them. "Have you heard from her?"

His question lands like a punch and I'm thankful our chair reaches the top of the mountain at the same time—our movement to get off covering my flinch. I don't answer, feigning preoccupation with strapping into my board as my mind reels.

I haven't heard from her. Part of me hates that, hates it for Willow, that Talia really could just write us off and walk away so easily. But I'm also glad for it. It would be harder to have her be one foot out the door. If she wants a clean break, then so do I.

"No, I haven't," I finally reply. Then I take off down the mountain, letting the snow cover the multitude of feelings I have rushing through me.

I don't want to relive the moments of that last phone call, in the wake of her leaving. I didn't expect her to call me back, not after all I said.

I fly down the run, my board cutting through the soft powder like it's butter, and the torrent of memories floods my mind.

I pace the living room, listening to each long ring like it carries me toward a cliff I'll fall over as soon as she answers. But she doesn't. Instead, it's just her voice, melodic and soft. "This is Talia, leave a message," followed by a resounding beeeep. *I breathe against the phone and have to swallow back all the emotion.*

"Talia. Please call me. Please. I don't understand. Willow doesn't understand. Please, don't do this. Don't leave. We can figure it out. We can find a way to make this work. I don't..." My voice breaks and I swipe a tear from my cheek. "I don't understand. Please, Talia. I don't want this for Willow." The emotions surge and anger starts to beat out the rest as I continue to speak into the void. How dare she not answer the phone. She didn't even attempt to have a conversation with me before leaving, and now this. "Talia, you're better than this. We're

a family, and you can't just walk out on your family. Dammit. You can't do this."

I pull each breath through my constricting throat, and it physically hurts. My hands shake, and I want nothing more than to throw the phone across the room, like I did the lamp in my office last night when I found her letter telling me what she'd done. That she'd left—with Drew—and wasn't coming back.

"It's not just about you and me, Talia. What about Willow!? And what about the turnover of the business... You're just going to walk out on our obligations and expect everything to transfer over to the new owners smoothly? You're a coward. You're a bloody coward doing this. I'll never forgive you for this. Willow will never forgive you for this."

I'm saying things I'll never be able to take back if she happens to change her mind, but at this moment, I'm beyond caring. She fucking left us. And it clearly wasn't on a whim; she took the time to have a lawyer draw up the permanent release of her rights to Willow. She gave up her child, for what? A fling? For freedom? Fuck, I wouldn't give up Willow for a single thing in this world, not even for more time with my own parents. She's a part of me. She's a part of Talia too, yet it wasn't enough.

How could Willow not be enough?

"Fuck you, Talia. Fuck you, and fuck Drew. Don't call me. Don't ever come back. We'll be fine. You don't want this? Fine, we don't need you. Goodbye."

I press the red end call button so hard I'm surprised the screen doesn't crack. Then, I do throw my phone—at the couch. I guess I have some semblance of control left.

I hang my head into my hands and cry.

We reach the bottom of the mountain and I'm winded. Planting my hands on my knees, I gulp in air, but it doesn't want to fill my lungs.

"Bloody hell," Wes says, skidding to a stop beside me with a spray of snow over my board. "I don't think I've ever seen you go so fast."

I shake my head and plaster on a smile that I know doesn't reach my eyes, but it's the most I can muster after that. "Just wanted to enjoy the first run of the day on fresh powder before everyone tears it up."

He studies me for a moment, whatever he sees in my face telling him not to press. Not right now. "Right. Well, that was amazing. Again?"

"Yeah, let's go again," I say. So we do, and I take it all out on the mountain.

We reach the lodge at midday to meet with Willow and Joss for lunch, and I'm surprised to find Rory waiting for us with all her gear. I didn't know if she'd feel up to hitting the slopes after last night's excitement. I also don't know if I'm glad she's here or embarrassed because of how I acted.

My brain went into "someone I care for is hurt" mode and I couldn't help myself, but what if I came across more like an overbearing boyfriend? Grabbing her like that, hoisting her around the kitchen like a caveman... Then there was the tension as I held her—her head against my chest, hands gripped in my shirt, leg wrapped like a vise around my thigh. I've never felt anything so electric in my life.

I love Talia—*loved* Talia—and with my affectionate nature, I imagine most would believe we had an intense physical connection. But that wasn't the case. There was attraction, sure, but our chemistry, even when we were first dating, was never... *electric.*

It's confusing to say the least. It doesn't feel right to have any kind of response to a woman when it's only been five weeks since Talia left. The mourning period for a nearly ten-year relationship should be longer than that. But also, if I'm going to feel something for someone... it shouldn't be Rory, *right?*

I shake off my errant thoughts and we all pile in around the table. Willow takes the space between Wes and Joss, looking happy as ever. Part of me feels bad for taking her away from the support system we had in Sydney, but then I watch her wake up every day, positive and ready to take on the world, and I release myself from the guilt. A little.

"How's your foot?" I ask Rory, keeping my tone light as I drop down next to her.

"It's fine, *Dad*, thanks for asking," she says with a sarcastic bite I've never heard from her, and I choke on my own saliva. If I'd been drinking, I would have spit across the table.

Well, hell... that was unexpected. I guess I wasn't giving off the caveman/boyfriend vibes I thought I was last night, but was I giving off *dad* vibes...? I am so out of my depth here.

I'm not the only one spluttering over her comment. Wes is coughing into his hand and Joss snorts a laugh. Rory looks totally nonplussed, shrugging and facing Willow to ask about her lesson. My eyes flash to Wes, and he raises an eyebrow in my direction, just as unsure what to make of that comment as I am.

He joins me when I offer to go grab food for everyone and we walk together through the line.

"Listen," Wes starts, and I stand up straighter at his tone. "I don't know exactly what was said between you and Rory, but I know that y'all are awkward as fuck around each other right now. She didn't give me much to go on, and she asked me to stay out of it, but could you clue me in?"

I stand, staring at my best friend, completely slack-jawed, unsure of what exactly he's trying to ask.

"There's nothing happening between me and Rory."

"I know that. Bloody hell. She said something about you telling her to back off, like she was maybe trying too hard to be me. Ring any bells?"

"What? No, I never said that. I wasn't..." I run a hand through the hair at the back of my neck and give it a tug. "Fuck, that isn't what I meant." I try to remember every word of our conversation in my kitchen. I'm sure I didn't say that, but I guess it doesn't matter if that's how she took it. No wonder she could barely look at me yesterday.

I hurt her, didn't I?

Wes is looking at me and I'm not sure how to respond. "Okay," he says, drawing the word out. "Then what did you say?"

"I just—it was becoming too easy to rely on her help. She was incredible the first week we were here, and I kind of freaked myself out over it." I blow out a breath, relieved to say these thoughts out loud. "We're only here for so long, you know, and when we go home, I have to have my shit together. I have to be able to take care of Willow and handle our lives and do it all. By myself."

When I pull my gaze away from the red tray in my hands, there's hurt in Wes's eyes.

"You will have help there, brother. We're there. Me and Joss. You aren't going to have to do this all alone and you know it." His voice is firm. I know he and Joss will move heaven and earth to help us, but they also have lives... just like Rory.

"I know that, but still. I have to figure out who I am now that both my career and my relationship are gone. Spending so much time with Rory felt like it was muddying the process a little. But mostly, I didn't want her to feel strapped to us either."

Wes's brows pinch together. "What do you mean?"

"Well, man, you practically signed her up for this gig. The one where she got saddled with a broken man and his kid. She'd do anything for you, that much is obvious, and I didn't want her to feel obligated."

We continue to move through the line and Wes says nothing in response. I'm sure I've officially pissed off my best friend, but when we finally reach the end of the line and get our food, he claps me on the back with his free hand and smirks.

"Maybe we all need to work on our communication skills. I never intended for Rory to feel obligated to help you in my place, but I can see how she might've felt that way. I appreciate that you were looking out for her, but nothing you just told me matches up with what she got from your conversation. So, either I misunderstood her or she misunderstood you, but figure it out so you guys can stop tiptoeing around each other, hm?"

I nod. He's probably right, and I feel like a complete ass for it.

"One more thing," he says, his smirk growing into a cheek-splitting grin now. "Why did my sister call you *dad* back there?"

I hang my head and chuckle, shoulders lifting and falling. "I might have said something last night about how I've helped Willow plenty when she's been hurt. I did *not* mean to imply that I was *her* dad... but again, my communication skills leave something to be desired these days."

Wes laughs hard, muttering "daddy" under his breath between his wheezing chuckles. I punch him in the shoulder as we approach the cashier to pay for the mountain of food on our trays.

"Weak sauce, Breck. That was pathetic." He continues to laugh, playfully dabbing at his eyes. "You should know though, as much as I love you, if you hurt my sister for real, not just this miscommunication bullshit, I'll punch you *for real*."

With that, he walks back to the table, leaving me standing stunned in his wake. Well, shit. If that wasn't him drawing a boundary around Rory that screams *do not cross...*

And now, with his brotherly warning bouncing around in my head, I have to smooth over whatever awkwardness is between us.

Easy.

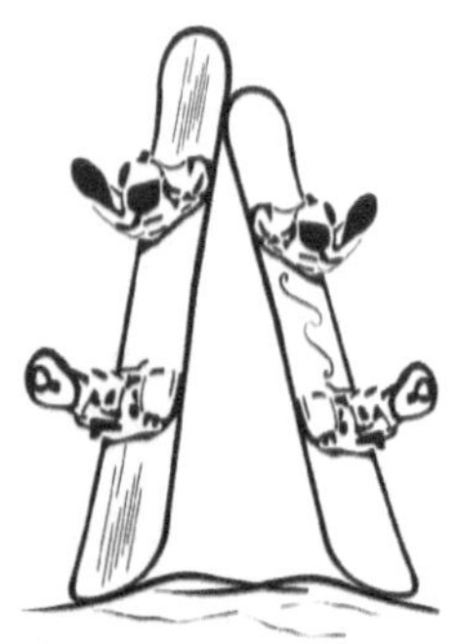

CHAPTER THIRTEEN

RORY

"You look beautiful, Joss." I watch her twirl in front of the floor-to-ceiling windows of the honeymoon suite, the short train of her fitted dress flitting weightlessly. The neckline is high and wide, seemingly modest with only her collarbones and neck exposed, but when she turns, it cuts down low, exposing the soft skin of her back, all the way down to her tailbone. The bodice and long sleeves are fitted, hugging every curve until it reaches her knees where it flares out, pooling on the floor by her feet.

I've been capturing pictures for the last hour while she's gotten ready for her wedding. I'm giddy with nerves at the prospect of watching my big brother marry this amazing woman. She stops mid-twirl and the dress splays behind her as she stares out the window into the light snowfall beyond. I lift my camera and capture the moment in time forever.

"Are you sure you don't want me to get pictures of Wes's first look? I have a feeling his face will be priceless." My voice is pleading. Joss and Wes agreed to share the moment privately before the ceremony and I want to respect that, but dammit, I want to see the look on his face when he sees his bride like this.

Joss laughs, knowing I'm pouting. "Yes, I'm sure. Why don't you send him up and then we'll follow you down in a few minutes."

I give her shoulders a gentle squeeze, not wanting to muss her dress or her immaculate hair and makeup. "I'm so glad he found you. I can't wait to be your sister."

"Oh my god, stop! You're going to make me cry." She pulls me in and hugs me tight, unconcerned with her dress or anything else.

I release her and smooth my hands down her long sleeves. "I'll see you down there."

Outside in the hall, I find my brother pacing. His head snaps up at the sound of the door closing and a wide smile stretches across his face when he sees me.

"Is she ready?" His eyes are wild, dimples cutting deep grooves into his handsome face underneath the perfectly groomed beard. It suits him, like his new life in Australia suits him. I've never seen him so happy, at ease with his life and himself. His deep navy-blue tuxedo suits him too. I don't know that I've ever seen him in a tux. A fancy dress uniform for the Navy, sure, but never a tux.

"She is. You look damn good, Wes. Who knew you could clean up so nice?" He pulls me into a hug and kisses my hair. "I'm so happy for you."

"I'm happy for me too. I can't believe this is really happening."

"Oh, it's happening, I've been planning it for weeks and it's going to be perfect!"

He pulls back, his eyes brimming with unshed tears. "Thank you, Rory, I couldn't have done this without you."

My face softens, knowing he doesn't just mean the wedding.

"I love you, Wes. Now, go get your girl so we can get you married, okay?"

"Okay." He breathes and it's almost a sigh, but in that soft moony way only the hopelessly in love can sound.

He heads for the door and I walk to the elevator, turning to watch him stop dead in the open doorway. I can't see his face, but I can imagine it.

The ride up the Empyreal gondola is filled with chatter. We're all packed into one of the large cars—Mom and Dad stand in one corner with Joss's dad Brian and her half-sister Isla. Jamie and Breck are talking over a few last-minute ceremony details and I'm clinging to Willow's hand while talking animatedly with Jaz, Joss's best friend, and her boyfriend Paul.

The arrival of Joss's closest friends and family was a Christmas surprise from Wes. He organized for them all to arrive a few days after he and Joss did—just before dinner on Christmas Eve—and

Joss looked like she might faint on the spot when they walked into my mom's house.

Dinner that night—Mom had it catered, of course—went surprisingly well considering the eclectic group of people. I was sure my parents would do or say something that would leave me cringing, but they were surprisingly well-behaved. They usually are when Wes is home. Add in a future daughter-in-law, lots of new faces, and people to impress? They were downright pleasant.

In the week since, we've filled every moment to the brim. A Christmas morning in my condo, complete with hot chocolate and presents—mostly for Willow. Days on the mountain where we got all the Aussies strapped to a board at one point or another—even Brian. Mom and Dad worked every day besides Christmas Eve and Christmas, which was fine by me. We ate out, we ate in, we made mulled wine and hot toddies.

Having so many people around also made it easy to ignore the ever-present tension between me and Breck, and I've avoided any circumstance that might leave the two of us alone together. It feels easier that way. Even if I did catch his eyes on me multiple times...

The gondola crests the top of the summit and the reason we're all together is here at last. My eagerness has me bouncing on my toes. We exit into a winter wonderland, where Lake Tahoe is our backdrop and the soft snow falling only adds to the magical feel. All that's left to do is wait for the man and woman of the hour, who are set to arrive in their own gondola.

Jamie pulls me into his side, offering me his warmth. Since he's not officiating today, he's here as moral support for me—and as a buffer. He knows too well how my parents can be, and I think he's extra wary since I'm behind the lens in an official capacity.

Another gondola makes its way toward the top of the mountain, and I bounce on my snow boot–clad feet. I have on a beautiful long-sleeved evergreen dress draped in a faux-fur cape, but the fleece leggings underneath are a necessity, as are the boots.

The entire wedding party is in snow boots, even with all their finery, and it's kind of hilarious.

This is what I've come to love about elopements. It's not about everything being "perfect." It's about the adventure, the experience. So what if we have on boots instead of heels if it means we can do this in fresh powder with the lake in the background?

Everything goes silent as the doors open and Wes steps out. The navy blue of his tuxedo stands stark against all the white. His tousled brown hair blows in the light breeze, tiny snowflakes landing amongst the strands. He reaches a hand back into the car and I lift my camera to catch the moment Joss steps out. Her manicured hand meets his, and then it's a flurry of shutter clicks as I immortalize every movement of her exit.

The long sleeve of her gown. Her hand lifting the hem of her dress to show off a pair of furry boots like mine. Ducking her head, then looking up into my brother's smiling face when she stands. They turn toward us, our little group erupting in cheers and applause, and I capture the moment my brother lifts his soon-to-be wife's hand overhead in celebration. They deserve this happiness; they deserve this moment.

Joss's dress swishes over the snowy ground as they make their way over to us. Her fur wrap covers her back and shoulders but only adds to the simplicity of her dress. Her brown curls hang over one shoulder and her grey eyes are alight as she absorbs the scene around us. She has a simple bouquet of winter greenery in the hand not clasped with Wes's. He's barely taken his eyes off her, and I can't blame him.

The ski lifts haven't closed yet for the day, so there's still a trickle of people milling about, stopping to watch. We don't have an elaborate set-up, and we don't have to walk far through the swirling snow to find the spot I had in mind for the ceremony.

Breck positions himself with his back to the lake, dressed in a dark grey suit and a heavy wool coat—and, of course, his boots. He pushes a lock of hair back from his forehead with a leather-gloved hand and smiles at our couple—Wes to his right, Joss to his left. When Willow sneaks up next to Breck, no one says anything. She's welcome there in her deep purple dress, black fleece tights, and peacoat, holding a small bouquet of flowers and the rings.

There's no music or fanfare, simply the soft snow falling around us.

Breck takes the reins and begins the short ceremony, walking them through the exchange of their vows, giving them space to share their own. Neither has anything written down, but they talk from their hearts and there isn't a dry eye around. I'm trying my best to keep it together so I don't miss a single moment, but it's tough. When Breck asks for the rings, Willow hands a small pouch over to Wes.

The tenderness with which Joss places the ring on his finger breaks me, and I reach for a tissue before my tears can freeze on my face. Lifting my camera again, I happen to glance at Breck and notice the slightest pinch to his features. The click of the camera catches his eye before the look is gone as fast as it appeared, replaced by the proud smile he's been wearing all day. Then the focus is on Wes as he slides Joss's engagement ring, along with the delicate band, onto her slender finger before lifting her hand to his lips to kiss it.

"By the power vested in me, I now pronounce you man and wife. You may kiss the bride," Breck says, stepping aside with Willow so I have an unobstructed view of Wes and Joss flush against each other, wide smiles on their faces as he dips her low. One hand in her curls, the other low on her back. Then he kisses her senseless. They're surrounded by hoots and hollers, and not just from our group. There's a small crowd of onlookers who have stopped to watch, and their enthusiasm only spurs my brother on.

He dips his bride lower, takes the kiss deeper, and I watch her skin flush crimson through my viewfinder. When he finally stands up and they break apart, the laugh that leaves my brother is nothing to the girlish giggle that escapes Joss.

Willow says, "Eww, gross," and the rest of us burst out laughing.

Breck ruffles her hair. The dark strands that I curled for her this afternoon show each and every snowflake that's landed there in the time we've been outside. "I'll give you 'eww, gross,'" he says, and pulls Willow into his arms to plant a wet kiss on her cheek.

"No, Daddy, stop," she protests, giggling through her half-hearted attempts to get away. This kind of affection for his daughter is nothing out of the ordinary for him, but I catch my parents eyeing them. Never once did they show affection like that to Wes or me as kids. I can't even imagine having a relationship built on such overt love. It's the kind of relationship I'd want to have with my own kids...

After the congratulations are out of the way and we're all shivering, Wes and Joss board their private gondola down the mountain, where we'll all head to an early dinner to continue celebrating. Jaz, Paul, Brian, and Isla take the next one, followed by my parents. Another approaches, but before I can board it with Jamie, I feel a hand on my elbow.

"Ride down with me?" Breck asks, a hint of apprehension on his face. I nod, words escaping me, and Jamie jumps in, asking Willow to ride down with him instead. She obliges him with a starry-eyed smile. I think she's fallen a little bit in love with my best friend in the three weeks they've known each other. Breck and I stand in silence while we wait for the next gondola.

It eventually slows for us and my stomach constricts at the realization that we haven't been this close since the night Wes and Joss arrived ten days ago. My cheeks heat remembering how I cut my foot and was wrapped around him like a koala, and the embarrassment steels my spine against whatever might come in the ride down the mountain.

The door opens and Breck's hand falls to my lower back, ushering me inside. I shiver, unsure if it's because his hands are cold from being outside or from the touch itself, and watch in shock as he plops down next to me. When the door closes, the inside of the car charges with energy.

Breck and I have been perfectly *friendly* while Wes and Joss have been here, but he hasn't sought me out and I've given him the space he said he wanted.

But here he is, solidly in *my* space.

"Rory." I don't think I've ever heard my name sound like a caress before. "I owe you an apology."

Oh no. This is Wes's doing. He must've told Breck what I said—big brother coming to the rescue—and now he's been shamed into a pity apology. No thank you, I don't want it.

"Breck, don't." I hold up a hand just as the car lurches and it lands on his chest. Our eyes track to where I touch him, unable to pull away, and I continue. "I'm guessing Wes said something, but it's fine. We're good. Okay?"

"No. It's not okay. I've been looking for a chance to talk to you, but you've been avoiding me."

"I have not," I protest, even though I totally have. "I'm right here, aren't I?"

"*Yes*." He bites the word out. "But you're still not listening."

"I heard you loud and clear the first time." I huff out a breath, then realize I'm still touching him.

"Dammit, Rory, would you just stop? I hurt you with what I said, and I'm trying to apologize. I'm trying to explain what I meant to say." He's not quite yelling, but his frustration is clear in the way his voice has risen. I've yet to see him mad, and it shocks me into silence. His voice softens before he starts again. "Don't be mad at Wes, he was just looking out for you. I know you probably hate that, but it's his wedding day so you can't be angry at him. I *really* wasn't trying to push you away." I lift my eyebrows skeptically and he sighs. "Okay, I was. Sort of. But not for the reason you think."

"Look, I don't need you to do this. I told him not to say anything because I didn't want you feeling sorry for me—Wes's poor little sister who got her feelings hurt. I'm fine. You don't have to smooth anything over because I get it. You don't have to apologize. I'm not mad."

I'm clearly mad. Mostly at myself for getting into this situation in the first place, but also for telling my brother who I knew couldn't keep his mouth shut.

The gondola reaches the bottom of the mountain just as I finish my tirade. The moment the doors open, I'm up and out, leaving Breck behind me. I storm straight past Jamie, who looks adorable holding Willow's hand. I'd smile if I weren't fuming. The surprise on his face is evident, and I only just catch the look of determined protectiveness that replaces it before I'm gone. I hope Breck is ready to be told off by another man in my life.

Right now, I couldn't care less.

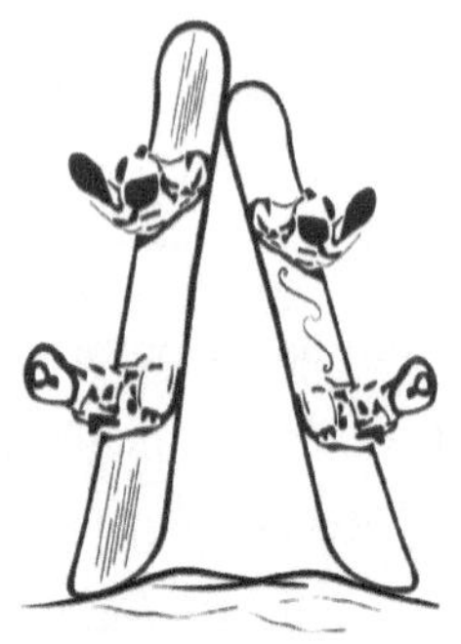

CHAPTER FOURTEEN

BRECK

"That went well," I grumble, my eyes glued to Rory's retreating figure.

I ignore an affronted-looking Jamie, who's just stepped into my path, and look instead to Willow. "Did you have a good ride, Willow Bear?"

"So good. Jamie pointed out all the ski runs and told me about Tahoe Tessie! They have a water monster here too, just like in Scotland." I ruffle her hair with a laugh on my lips, but when I look up at the imposing Scotsman, he doesn't look amused. Best get this over with.

"Willow, I see Jaz over there, why don't you go say hi?" I say, pointing to where the rest of our group is congregated.

"Okay!" She runs off, and once I see her collide with Jaz's legs, I look back to Jamie.

"I—"

"Listen, man," he cuts me off. "I like you. I respect the hell out of Wes, and I know you're his best friend." He pauses and points in the direction Rory stomped off in. "Rory is *my* best friend. She's as much a sister to me as she is to Wes, and if I see that look on her face after being alone with you again, we're going to have a problem. Understood?"

I don't particularly like being taken down a peg by this guy, but I almost don't mind it. Was I trying to do the right thing and apologize to Rory? Yes. But he doesn't know that, and I can appreciate him looking out for her. I swallow my pride and my desire to argue, opting for a nod instead. "Understood."

"Good. I'm going to go find Rory. See you in there for dinner?" Just like that, he's the same casual, easy-going guy I've been slowly getting to know. He's shown up a fair amount over the last week, whenever we went out for dinner or to hang out at the house in the evenings. Wes treats him like a younger brother, and I want to pretend I didn't feel a wash of relief just now when he mentioned Rory being like a sister...

I make my way over to Willow, who's twirling in her dress in front of Jaz and Paul, and the rest of the wedding crew milling about. We all head into the casino where we're booked for dinner. I just hope Rory will give me another chance to explain. I'd love for us to get back to that easy friendship we were finding... before I put my foot in my mouth and it all went to shit.

I watch the setting sun across the lake through the gable windows and I'm awed at what Rory's accomplished. The fact that she was able to get us a private room on New Year's Eve on such short notice seems like a miracle. The space isn't large, but it's perfect for the twelve of us. Plus, there couldn't be a more picturesque backdrop for the evening.

"Rory, bring your camera over here. I want to see some of the pictures you took," Wes calls down the table.

Joss smacks him across the chest and chastises him with a quiet "Bossy." He catches her hand over his heart and holds it there, tugging her closer for a kiss. I've always been affectionate, but I nearly shield Willow's eyes from the show he puts on. Paul catcalls them from the end of the table and Rory mimes gagging. The only ones not laughing are Wes and Rory's parents: Erica's lips are a fine line, though I think that may just be her face, and Dean looks unimpressed.

Rory stands, camera in hand, and meanders over. I try not to notice the way her hips sway in her fitted green dress, or how the reddish-blonde coloring of her hair pops in comparison. She crouches between Wes and Joss, the slit of her dress showcasing a milky white thigh that I'm certain was covered with tights or something earlier.

Yes, I noticed that too.

I stand and swing my chair around between them so she can sit. Her gaze is assessing, like she's questioning my motives.

A curt "Thanks" is all I get.

I peek over her shoulder as she taps through the pictures. I'm again reminded of the talent she has for finding the perfect angle of the perfect moment and capturing it with clarity and creativity. I've garnered more from Wes about what she does for the ski resort, and though some of her work includes taking photos, it's not her primary job. It could be though. Her skill level matches any professional photographer I've ever worked with.

Joss's and Wes's running commentary—accented with laughs and soft smiles—draws more of the group until almost everyone is crowded around us.

"You guys," Rory says, a blush on her cheeks. "I'll get an album up in the next couple days. There's still so much I need to do." She scoffs a laugh. "The real bride and groom are right here, just stare at them."

She's uncomfortable with the attention, and I watch her eyes flick to where her parents are still sitting.

"They're fantastic, Rory, truly," Joss says as she pulls Rory in for a hug. "Thank you for doing all of this. Wes told me you had experience with elopements, but to pull off this whole thing and the pictures—color me impressed, sis."

The color in Rory's cheeks deepens at the compliment. She parts her ruby red lips to speak, but her mother pipes up from the other end of the table. "What does she mean you have experience with elopements?"

It's like the moment in a movie when they dub in the sound of a record scratching to a stop, everyone freezing in place, but it's playing out in real life. Wes's eyes go round as saucers, apology written all over his face. Joss goes a little pale and grips Rory's hand. And Rory... looks nothing like her usual open, warm self. I feel like I'm missing something.

Jamie leans forward, forearms pressed into the table. "Rory helped me out a few months back. A friend asked me to officiate, and I asked Rory to take the photos. She did an incredible job. Much like today." He sends her a wink and her shoulders relax away from her ears.

"Oh, good. Thank you, Jamie." Relief covers Erica's tone. "I thought maybe she was still holding on to those silly notions she had in college about photography being a real career." She dabs the edges of her mouth with her napkin, oblivious to how her words might've landed with her daughter. Then, almost to herself but still loud enough we can all hear, she continues. "Although, playing around on Instagram and TikTok isn't exactly what I'd call a real career either."

I inhale, ready to jump in, but my words are cut short by Rory's chair hitting me in the stomach. It knocks the wind out of me almost as much as the hurt in her eyes as she stalks out of the room without another word.

Erica's muttered "Dramatic" is drowned out by Wes's shout down the table. "Mom!"

Dean stands and scolds Wes for the outburst, and the rest of us—minus Jamie, who left in pursuit of his friend—are stunned silent.

That went downhill fast. Willow looks shocked and confused by the commotion, and I gather her to me, taking it as my cue to get her home for the night.

I lean in close to Joss and explain that the babysitter I hired to stay with Willow tonight should be at the condo soon, but she still has a guilty look on her face. "I was going to take her home any minute anyway," I say in her ear, and she deflates.

"What a mess."

I squeeze her arm. "Don't worry. It'll be fine, and we're going to have an amazing night. See you guys in a bit, yeah?"

"Yeah. Good night, Willow, we'll see you tomorrow." Willow wraps her arms around Joss and I'm thankful she has someone like her she can look up to. Especially now. She's going to need new female role models in her life more than ever with Talia gone.

This is the second time I've allowed thoughts of her into my mind today, my resolve to keep them at bay having held for the most part. Watching Joss slip the ring on Wes's finger during the ceremony was when they first hit. How many times had I wished for that moment with Talia? But she never wanted to get married. She said our relationship was enough, parenting Willow was enough. We didn't need to be married to be a family, but were those all lies? Was that just her way of keeping herself free so she could leave when the opportunity struck?

I shake the thoughts away and slap Wes on the back, the look on his face as he eyes his parents is one I wouldn't want pointed at me.

"Hey," I say, and he finally looks at me. "Don't let it ruin your night. See you back at Rory's in a bit. We're still going out, right?"

"Yeah, see you." He stands and pulls me in for a hug. "Thank you again for today. It meant the world to have you with us." It's probably the fiftieth time he's thanked me for officiating, but it was my pleasure. An honor.

Gripping Willow's hand, we head out of the room and are quickly followed by Jaz, Paul, Brian, and Isla—all trying to escape the tension we're leaving behind.

I got Willow tucked into bed, gave myself a pep talk that she'd be fine with the woman my friends helped me vet to watch her, and headed out on the town. We've been hopping from bar to bar for the last few hours now.

The music in this one thumps inside my skull, and the amount of people jammed into the small space is obscene. It was common to deal with crowds like this in a huge city like Sydney, but it always seemed less oppressive, more spread out. Tahoe is a small town. A small town currently packed to the gills with tourists that flocked in for the snow and the holidays.

Joss's dad and little sister are flying out early in the morning, so they opted to stay in. Also, Isla's only eighteen and wouldn't have been able to get into the bars like she does in Australia—something she complained about *loudly*. Brian probably didn't want to watch Joss suck face with her new husband all night either.

Which is fair, considering that's exactly what the newlyweds are currently doing. They're the only ones who didn't change into something more weather- and location-appropriate. As Wes put it, you only get married once, so they might as well get their money's worth for the dress and tux.

Jaz and Paul could be a cover couple for a fashion magazine with the outfits they changed into. Jaz's russet curls that went a little wild in the wind earlier are pulled back, small tendrils framing her face. She's wearing leather leggings and a slinky red sweater that complements her soft brown skin. The dark green of Paul's sweater makes her eyes pop when he moves in close to plant a soft kiss on her lips. Jaz pulls back with a smile and swipes her thumb across his cheek before pulling him in for one more peck.

Bloody hell. I'm surrounded.

If things were different, Talia would be here right now. We'd be the ones kissing and making the single people around us sick. The reality of having no one to kiss at midnight hurts more than I expected it to.

Rory and Jamie chat animatedly on the other side of our bride and groom and their never-ending kiss.

"For fuck's sake, mate, let the woman breathe," I say in exasperation, and the group around us howls with laughter.

"Got a bit carried away there, didn't I?" Wes says, unapologetic.

"Maybe a little bit," Joss says, cheeks red either from embarrassment or beard burn. It's hard to tell which.

"So, where to next?" I ask, looking around. It's not yet midnight, but I can tell that for the visiting Aussies—Wes now happily included in that group—their energy is waning. If I'm being honest,

I don't want to go home yet. It's been a while since I've had a night out on the town... the closest being the night Wes and I went out for beers in Sydney last month—the night that changed my life.

The night I found the letter. My hand instinctively grazes my pants pocket, where my wallet sits.

Wes looks at Joss, something heated passing between them. Rory must see it too because she wraps both hands around her throat and mimes being sick.

"Get a room," she chides.

"We have a room. I think it's high time we used it."

"Gross," Rory counters, and we all laugh.

"I think we're going to head back too." Jaz smiles up at Paul. "The hotel said we'd be able to see the fireworks from our room, and honestly, I'm beat."

Wes turns to Rory, pulling her into a tight hug. "Thank you. For today. For everything." He presses a kiss to her temple then pulls back. "How're you getting home? There might not be any cabs with this crowd."

"I'll walk. It's not far," she says, and he scrunches his nose.

"I'll walk with her." I move beside Rory, and Wes instantly relaxes.

"Thanks, mate." He pulls me in for a hug too. I swear he's become more of a hugger than even me lately.

Jamie claps Wes on the shoulder, but that's not good enough for Wes. He embraces him too.

They all stumble into the cold night air, laughing as they go.

"One more drink?" I ask Rory, altogether bypassing Jamie, who's still standing at her side.

Please say yes. Let me fix this.

"Yeah, okay," she says, holding my gaze. "One more drink." Then, with a Cheshire cat grin on her face, she says, "Then dancing!"

She spins in her boots, ones that come up above her knees, and I catch her elbow when she loses her balance. We've been out for a while now, but she's barely had two drinks so I know she's not drunk, just excited. She's more carefree than I've ever seen her, and I'm glad she didn't let her parents bulldoze her mood. This isn't her trying to take care of anyone or impress her parents. This is just Rory, out on the town, looking for fun.

"Dancing, huh?" I scrub my other hand at the back of my neck and try to hide my smile. It's been years since I went dancing, definitely before Talia and I had Willow.

"Yup. You coming, Jamie?" She doesn't pull her elbow from my grip and I lazily let my thumb coast up around her bicep. Is it bad that I don't really want him to come? That I kind of want this time with Rory to myself?

There's a wide, mischievous smile on his face. "One drink and dancing. Yeah, let's go."

CHAPTER FIFTEEN

RORY

Jamie dragged us down the street to another bar where he said the dancing would be better. Fine by me. I caught Breck with his eyes on the sky, taking in the bright lights of the town all decked out for the new year. It's chaotic and crammed with people right now, but it's mine, and I love it.

I'm standing at the bar between Breck and Jamie. Their protective stances keep me from getting shuffled around by the crowd. The bass reverberates down to my very bones, perfect for a night where all I want is to let loose. With each drink I forget a little more about my job, my parents, the hurt I was harboring over Breck's words. I want to start the new year not worrying about anything but me for a change.

Breck turns from the bar with a margarita for me and a beer for himself at the same time Jamie turns with his scotch. There's something relaxed in Breck's demeanor now. Maybe he's got ideas for starting the new year fresh too. He hands me the glass, fingers sliding over mine. I blush under his watchful gaze and ignore the flip in my stomach.

Jamie breaks the spell between us. "Dancing?"

I turn to beam at my best friend, grabbing his free hand with my own. "You get the first dance, Jameson."

His exaggerated eye roll makes me laugh out loud. He hates when I use his full first name, but I love it. Just like I love calling my brother *Wessy*. There's some savage pleasure in needling the people you love a little bit.

We wander through the crowd toward the mass of moving bodies. They're playing "Sweet Child of Mine" and I spin on the spot before stopping to jump a little as I sing along. Dancing has a way of making me feel carefree, like the weight I seem to always be carrying is lifted for just a little while.

I gulp down my drink in an effort to not spill it, and the burn of the tequila mixed with the chill of the ice makes me shiver. Breck leans against the bar top watching us—watching me—his dimpled smile disappearing behind his frothy glass.

Another song later and Jamie excuses himself to the bar. He was making eyes with a girl at the other end and I'm not going to hold him back from enjoying his evening. One of us should have someone to kiss at midnight.

I continue to sway despite the heat pressing in from the crowd around me. I'll be glad later for the heavy tights I have on under my black flippy skirt and my heavy sweater when I have to walk home, but damn, it's hot in here. I pull my hair up with my hands, letting the slightly cooler air caress the back of my neck.

With the alcohol running through my veins, I lean into the freedom I feel on the dance floor, smiling. I feel loose and uninhibited. That is until I slip on someone's spilled drink and lose my balance.

A pair of strong hands grip my waist from behind. I'm instantly taken aback by the possessiveness of the gesture, but my brain quickly catches up and I'm grateful not to be sprawled on the dirty floor right now. Spinning, I come face-to-face with Breck, my arms instinctively wrapping around his neck. His eyes are wide and there's a glint of something there, like he might be pleased at this turn of events.

The heat of his hands at my waist intensifies. My sweater rode up when I flung my arms around him, so his hands are grazing bare skin. His gaze roams my face, landing on my mouth, and I feel a pull low in my belly. His stare burns into me and I lick my lips. He lets out a wicked chuckle, shaking his head and breaking himself out of a trance. *Same here, buddy.*

"Thanks." I tell myself the breathy quality to my voice is from the exertion of dancing, but it's a lie. I'm flustered by his proximity. "For not letting me fall."

"You're welcome," he husks in a low voice. It's growly, a little undone, and I like it.

I begin to move my hips in time with the music. Hips that Breck's strong hands are splayed over.

His eyes widen a little more, as if surprised I'd choose to dance with him after my outburst earlier. That's the last thing on my mind right now, and it's my turn to flick my eyes to his mouth. The buzz around my brain wonders how his lips would feel on my skin. The top one is the perfect bow shape and the bottom is slightly fuller than the top, perfect for...

I snap my eyes back to his, finding them smoldering in the low light. He moves closer, pulling our bodies flush, and heat rushes through me. He's warm, and the muscles of his torso press into mine as we move. I have no idea what I'm doing, what I'm thinking, but this feels good. It doesn't feel lonely, and it doesn't feel like I'm doing it for anyone but me.

I haven't done anything in a long while that was for me and me alone. I don't care that he's Wes's best friend. I don't even care that he's a dad or that he's from Australia or that he's leaving soon. I just don't care, and it feels damn good.

His hands tighten on my waist, thumbs firmly gripping me under my sweater, and I feel that touch like a brand. With my arms around his neck this way, I could have my fingers tangled in his hair with only the slightest movement. It's not the first time I've had that crush-fueled fantasy. I spent years as a teenager wondering what his hair would feel like.

The music changes, giving us an ideal opportunity to separate, get some space. For me to stop fantasizing about running my fingers through his silky strands. I glance to the bar and see Jamie happily ensconced with a blonde, head dipped toward her ear. He catches my eye over her shoulder and winks. I likely won't be seeing much of him for the rest of the night.

Every time my eyes meet Breck's, I wish I could read his mind. I can't reconcile the Breck of the last few weeks with this man who's warm and inviting and wearing a smile that is one hundred percent in the "panty dropper" category. I wonder if this is the Breck that Wes knows, the one who was fun-loving and full of life. The one Talia broke.

Was he this way with her?

Why do I care?

It's an excellent question, because I shouldn't. I like this carefree version of him and want to let myself believe it's a version that's just for me. Tonight, I don't want to be Wes's little sister. Or Jamie's best friend or my parents' biggest disappointment. I want to be a woman with a man looking at her like he doesn't want to look anywhere else.

And Breck doesn't. His eyes never waver. They're just for me. I don't know how long we dance like that, smiling, laughing, touching, watching, but we've slowly migrated to the far end of the bar. Without the crush of people, I can hear my breathing, fast and labored from the exertion.

I press onto my tip toes and it drags my body along his. "Another drink?" I ask against the shell of his ear, and I swear he leans in, like he wants me that close... closer. I slide away and his hands slip from under my sweater, making me miss the roughness of his palms. I grab his hand, pulling him up beside me at the bar, and order two tequila shots. Looking up from under my lashes, I take my bottom lip between my teeth and his grip on my hand tightens.

I'm going all in tonight. I can't remember the last time I took a shot. College?

The smirk on Breck's face says he's onto my game, or at least that he's willing to play. The bartender sets down my order, and I slip him some cash before he walks away. Before I lose my nerve, I grab a glass, lick my hand and salt it, and lift it in a salute toward Breck, expecting him to do the same.

He moves his hand, but not to grab the second shot. Instead, he takes my hand and brings his mouth down to lick the salt from it before his lips find the shot glass and he shoots it back.

I'm sure the look on my face is priceless, my mouth gaping open. My brain attempts to turn itself back on after being thoroughly short-circuited, but to no avail. Especially when he reaches for the lime wedge and pops it between his lips to suck the juice through his teeth. The visual pulls at something deep inside me and a shiver rolls down my spine. He hasn't broken eye contact since he first touched my hand and is staring at me now with a look of triumph... and heat.

Oh. My. *Lord.*

Breck's lips tick up on one side and just the one dimple appears. "Your turn." His low voice caresses my skin even from a foot away.

This night has veered off in a completely different direction than I anticipated. Breck reaches for the other shot while my mind whirs out of control. His tongue darts out to wet his hand before he salts it, and I nearly expire on the spot. Damn, that was hot.

Am I doing this?

I'm *so* doing this.

I set my shoulders, smirk at his handsome face, and opt for reckless bravery. Sliding my hand up his wrist, I feel every inch of the sinewy muscle of his forearm where his shirtsleeve is pushed up at his elbow. When I lower my head, I don't just lick the salt. I suck at his skin, eliciting a groan from deep in his throat. I smile and release him, having gotten exactly the reaction I was hoping for, and lift the shot to my lips.

I don't even taste it, too focused on his eyes, which are like molten lava. I bite down on the lime he holds up between us, the tartness dancing across my tongue. A drop of the juice slips from between my lips and Breck catches it with the knuckle of his forefinger. The touch makes me lose my mind entirely as I close my lips over it, sucking the last of the juice off.

"Bloody hell."

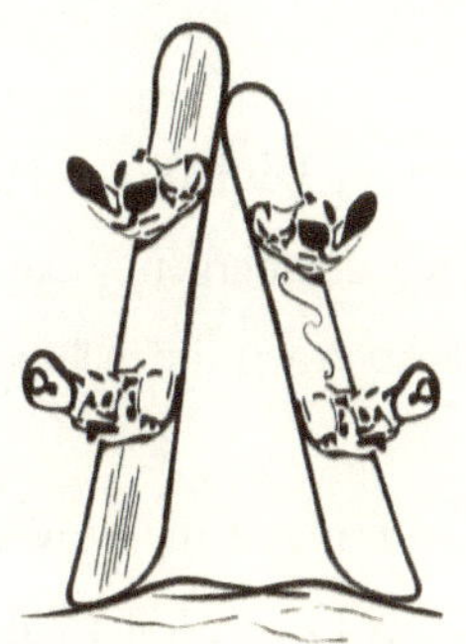

CHAPTER SIXTEEN

BRECK

The tug of Rory's lips on my knuckle sends a shock wave through my entire body. She looks up, dark lashes fluttering, soft strawberry-blonde hair framing her face and floating around her shoulders. The coy smile that lifts her brightly painted lips says she knows exactly what she just did to me.

I hold her eye contact and watch the color rise in her cheeks, the red there is a near match for the lipstick she's wearing. Lipstick that stains my hand where she sucked off both the salt and juice, and I swear I can still feel the gentle pull. She bites her bottom lip and my jeans feel uncomfortably tight all of a sudden.

For fuck's sake, Breck, I chastise myself, but it doesn't do anything to change the rising desire in my body. Something I haven't felt in a while.

The noise level in the bar increases around us, but I only see her. *Rory*. I wish it was only us, but the bar is exploding with people counting down the seconds to the new year.

45... 44... 43... 42...

I act on impulse, grabbing her hand and pulling her toward the back of the bar where I see an emergency exit. She squeals a little in surprise, and I have to tamp down the feeling of pride.

30... 29... 28... 27...

I've taken a complete leave of my senses, pulling her out the exit. The door spits us out just inside an alley off the main drag through South Lake Tahoe. The alley is empty, though there are people scattered around the street, shouting the countdown.

8... 7... 6... 5...

I look into Rory's too-bright eyes, a question in my own, and she reaches up to grab the front of my button-down. Taking that as my answer, I press her up against the brick wall of the building.

The first firework explodes above us, and I claim her mouth with mine.

The taste of her lips is euphoric. Her fingers find the nape of my neck, tangling in my hair. I grip her hip with one hand and twine the fingers of my other into her waves, tugging. Her mouth pops open in a gasp and I take advantage, allowing my tongue to slide against the seam of her lips. She tastes like tequila and lime, and the reminder of that moment makes me more insatiable.

The intensity of her answering kiss nearly knocks me backward. I graze my teeth along her bottom lip before sucking it into my mouth, wanting to leave it a little bit swollen, marked by me. A reminder for tomorrow. She moans and pulls me closer. I pin her more fully into the brick wall, and I can't find it in myself to be embarrassed by how obviously turned on I am. If she notices, she doesn't appear to care. If anything, she pulls me closer.

I grab her hand that's tangled in my hair, pressing it above her head, and kiss my way down her neck. When I nuzzle over her collarbone, she moans again, her head falling to the side, giving me more space to work and permission to keep going. I feel the heat radiating off her body, and I want to be closer. I want more. I shift, pulling back from her neck, and press a knee between her thighs. Her half-lidded eyes snap to mine, illuminated by the fireworks popping off above us.

I hardly hear them, their loud cracks and booms. I can't focus on anything but Rory. The gasping breaths, her heady moans. She shudders when I adjust my leg, and her eyes catch fire. I hold her gaze, fingers sliding down her side, skimming her ribcage. I stop to grip her hip, letting my thumb graze underneath the fabric of her sweater just like I did when we were dancing. When I thought this was only a bit of harmless flirtation.

We're beyond that now, and I'm fucked. Because this is *Rory*. Only... I can't bring myself to care. My mouth moves back to claim hers and my hand wanders lower, sliding along the edge of the little skirt she's wearing. I slip my fingers just under the hem, along her thigh, and she whimpers against my lips. I can only imagine how soft her skin is underneath these tights. I need to find out.

Another firework explodes overhead, lighting up our secret space, and someone from the street yells, "Get a room!"

The moment breaks and I pull back suddenly, releasing Rory's hand from over her head. My breathing is ragged and my heart beats a frantic rhythm in my chest. Rory looks wrecked too, her chest heaving where she leans against the wall. The finale of the fireworks show is a cacophony of noise and light that feels like too much right now.

My brain can't settle on anything with the chaos ensuing around us. The only thing coming through in perfect clarity is that I just made out with my best friend's sister. His only sister. His little sister. Dammit, what was I thinking? I run a hand through my hair and look at the ground.

Fuck. Wes is going to flip his shit when he finds out. Or... maybe we can keep this between us. Maybe there'll never be a reason for Wes to know. This wasn't supposed to happen—not just with Rory, but with anyone. Not now at least, and not in Tahoe.

My hand slides to the back of my neck and it awakens the memory of Rory's hand there, tugging at the too-long strands. I lift my head to find Rory's eyes are downcast. Is she wondering how in the hell we got here, pressed together in a dirty alleyway?

How the hell *did* we get here? This afternoon she was pissed at me and I wasn't sure I'd ever get her forgiveness. Now I'm at a complete loss for how we move forward. We have to see Wes and Joss in the morning for brunch before they leave for their honeymoon. Can I even attempt to hide this from him? Will Rory want to, or will she tell him and let him eviscerate me?

"We should probably walk home. It's late." Rory draws me from my spiraling thoughts. She's no longer looking at her boots and she's sucked her lip between her teeth again. Heat licks at my chest, and I force myself to look away.

"Yeah." My voice is hoarse. "Need to relieve the sitter."

If nothing else will sober me, the thought of my daughter asleep back in our condo while I stand here panting after mauling Rory sure will.

"Breck?" Rory's voice is quiet and timid, and her eyes have flicked back to the ground. Can she see the regret on my face? No, because I don't regret it, not exactly. I'm honestly not sure what I'm feeling right now.

"Yeah?"

"Nothing," she says, but I know it's not nothing. "Let's go." She turns away, taking a step toward the street.

I reach for her hand, grabbing it tightly and making her face me. I push a stray tendril of hair behind her ear, then I run my fingers along her jaw until they rest at her chin and tip it up.

"It's not nothing, Rory." I hold her gaze, wanting to run my thumb over her bottom lip. It's swollen, and *damn* does that do something to me.

"Are you going to tell Wes?" She straightens her shoulders, a hint of defiance snaking through the uncertainty.

"Do you want me to tell him?"

"No. I don't. Is that going to be a problem for you?" Her voice is steady, the fire she hit me with in the gondola coming back.

"If it's not a problem for you, then it's not a problem for me. He doesn't need to know our personal business." A hint of a smile lifts the corner of her lips and I relax my grip on her chin. She nods and steps back, my hand falling away completely. She grabs it and tugs me along toward the street and through the crowds of people.

Leaning down close to her ear, I whisper, "Happy New Year, Rory."

The lights from the casino cast a bluish tint to her cheeks, but it's not enough to hide her flush or her freckles that stand out a little more prominently. Damn, I really like those freckles. I like the way she smiles too when she says, "Happy New Year, Breck."

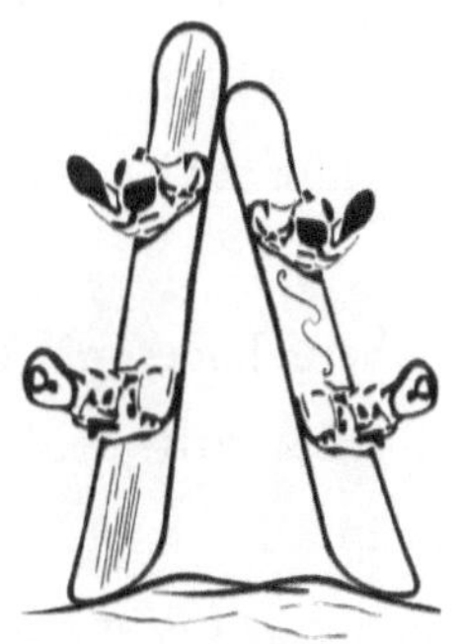

CHAPTER SEVENTEEN

RORY

There's a loud pounding in my head. That tequila shot was maybe not my best idea... or maybe it was. I run my tongue over my bottom lip. It's not as kiss-swollen as it was last night, but considering it's only—

I glance at my clock and see it's eight a.m. Ugh. I've been in bed for less than 7 hours... why am I awake? The pounding resumes and I realize it's not inside my head but at my door. For the love of all that is holy, isn't there a rule against knocking on someone's door at eight o'clock the morning after New Year's?

I roll over, hiding my face in the pillow to drown out the pounding. For goodness' sake. I sit up, smacking my hands down beside me on the heavy down comforter. It better be a freaking emergency. I push my feet into my white fuzzy slippers, then I stomp down every single step to the main landing.

Swinging open the door with a huff, I almost stumble into Jamie. There's a wicked grin on his face and two paper cups held in his gloved hands. I give him my best glare and stand aside to let him in.

"What are you doing here, Jameson?" I lace my words with venom, but the smell of coffee wafts behind him and my brain gives up on the missed sleep.

"Oooh, feeling a little snippy this morning, are you, Roars?" he teases.

I growl at him—like, literally growl. He knows I hate that nickname. Jamie might be as good as family, but that's crossing the line.

"I thought you might be in a better mood this morning..." His eyes trail down my pajamas and back up to my messy hair. "Considering the night you had."

I narrow my eyes and reach for the cup in his hand, but he pulls it away—hovering it above his head. Stupid tall man. "What's that supposed to mean?"

"Oh, it just seemed like you and a particular Aussie were having a rather enjoyable time."

I blanch, stumbling mid-jump for the cup. "What?" I let out a sound that sits somewhere between a croak and a squeak.

"Rory, Rory, Rory," he chides, dipping his eyebrows and smirking. "Did you think I wouldn't keep an eye on you? We both know the kind of creatures this town sees during the holidays."

Shifting my gaze away, I chew the edge of my thumb. Busted.

"You saw the shots?" I flick my eyes up, and his grin is knowing. Smug bastard. I slap his chest. "Jamie! Just tell me what you saw. And give me my coffee."

He laughs, deep and throaty, and lowers the cup to me. "So bossy this morning. To answer your question, I saw you dancing and, yes, I saw the shots." He wags his eyebrows at me suggestively. "Then I watched him haul you off toward the back of the bar like a man on a mission."

"And you just let him run off with me? What if I didn't want to go?" I volley back, knowing I never would've forgiven him if he'd interrupted us.

"Oh please, you're a grown woman and you went willingly—very willingly, from the look of it. Am I wrong?"

I hide my face by taking a very large gulp of very hot coffee and end up spluttering it down my pajama top. Jamie just laughs again.

"Fine. No. You're not wrong." I stick my tongue out at him, not feeling overly mature this morning.

"Care to spill? I brought your jacket, by the way," he adds, lifting his arm that does, in fact, have a jacket draped over it. Oh shit. I completely forgot about it. It was definitely cold on the walk home last night, but between the tequila and the heat from our kiss, I hardly even noticed.

"His too." He raises his eyebrows and hangs them both on the hook by the door. His smirk is like a permanent fixture on his face at this point, the auburn whiskers of his beard twitching each time it grows.

"Thank you for grabbing them. How was your night? You and that blonde looked pretty cozy." I change the subject, preferring when he's in the hot seat, which is standard.

He blushes under his scruffy beard.

"Oh-ho, good night then. Sorry you were left hauling our jackets when you likely had other, *better* things to do with your hands." I sip my coffee to hide my smile. "Thank you for this, by the way."

"Welcome. And yes, it was a good night."

I pause to look him up and down. "Oh my god, you didn't go home? Did you sneak out of that poor woman's hotel room to get me coffee?" I'm not actually that surprised, ladies' man that he is.

He shrugs. "Sort of. I mean, I was leaving regardless. I wasn't exactly sneaking out. She knew the deal when she took me home with her."

"Uh-huh, and you thought you'd just come here and wake me up too?"

"I'm honestly shocked you were still asleep. Don't you have breakfast with your family in half an hour?"

The color drains from my face. Crap.

"No, no, no. I totally forgot. Thank god for you." I press up on my toes and kiss his cheek. "I have to get ready. Are you coming? You might want to change..."

"Do you want me to come?" He gives me a loaded look.

I know his ask is genuine, but after last night, after finally doing something for myself, I feel a tiny bit steadier at the prospect of seeing my parents. Plus, Wes and Joss will be there, and Willow and Breck too.

I blush at the thought of Breck. Jamie must notice because his knowing grin is back.

"No, I'll be okay. Thank you though. Go home and take a shower. You're a mess," I tease, shaking my head. His hair is tousled and there's a smudge of lipstick on his collar.

"If you need me, just call, okay?" He lifts his coffee my way before heading back out into the cold.

I have to get ready, and I have less than thirty minutes to do it.

I'm jogging down the stairs to pull my boots on when there's more knocking at my door. *Who is it now?*

"Coming," I call as I skid to a stop and yank it open.

"Morning." Breck's smile tilts up on one side, allowing just one of those perfect dimples to pop, making me weak in the knees. He has his hands pushed deep in his jeans pockets, and he looks like he's *freezing*.

"M-morning," I stutter, feeling a warmth spread across my cheeks. "What're you doing here?"

I force my eyes away from the face of the man who kissed me senseless against a wall last night and focus on the smiling little girl beside him. She's bouncing on her toes and is wearing the bear-eared hat I bought for her.

"Thought we could all drive together to breakfast. You know, for the environment." His smile quirks up a little higher, like there's definitely more to this invite than saving the sea turtles.

"I'd love that."

"Can you sit in the back with me, Rory?" Willow asks, and I smile brighter. She's really good for my ego.

"Sure thing, Bug," I say, giving Breck a shrug that says *There's no saying no to her, is there?*

I slip my boots over my dark jeans and pull my heavy puffer jacket on over the bright purple sweater I chose for today. It's cut low in the front and hugs my body in a way that makes me feel flirty and sexy. It would appear Breck likes it too, from the way his eyes follow my zipper with rapt attention.

He clears his throat. "Ready to go?"

I grab his jacket from the hook and gently push it into his chest. "Yup." I smirk at the look of surprise on his face. "Jamie grabbed them for us last night. Since we left, um, rather hastily."

He looks down at my hands and his lips twitch. "Oh. Well, great. Thank you."

There's a thick tension in the air when we all pile into the Jeep. My attention is focused on Willow's retelling of yesterday's festivities, but Breck and I sharing the same space comes with desire and want that shouldn't be here in the light of day.

The restaurant we're meeting at for breakfast is nestled between the semi-frozen lake and a forest of deep-green pines. I'm desperate to capture the mountains in the distance, the blue of the lake, the clouds gliding low across the horizon. I wish I brought my camera, even though I know it would've led to more commentary from my parents.

We follow a hostess to a table in the far corner, away from other diners. Everyone else is already here and seated, and they turn our way as we approach. Breck takes a chair next to Wes, and Willow immediately takes the one next to Joss. So much for the idea of putting some space between us today. I slip my coat off and drop into my seat, carefully avoiding brushing my arm against Breck's.

"No Jamie this morning, Rory?" Mom inquires from the other end of the table. At least I'm not sitting next to her or Dad.

I busy myself with my menu when I answer. "Nope. He swung by the condo early this morning to drop off my jacket"—I shoot a sidelong glance at Breck—"and he was still in last night's clothes. I think he was headed home for a nap."

"Well done, Jamie," Wes jokes, eliciting laughs from everyone. Well, almost everyone. Mom's huff of displeasure doesn't fit in. When will she finally get it through her head that Jamie and I are never going to be a thing?

"What did you guys get up to after we left?" Jaz asks from across the table, and I school my features. *Don't blush, do not blush.* Breck's thigh presses against mine under the table, and I know I've lost the battle.

"Jamie dragged us to a bar to go dancing." I play it off like it wasn't really my idea. Breck's thigh shifts. Does he know what he's doing to me right now?

"Did you stay out until midnight for the fireworks? We caught some of the show from our room." Wes yawns.

"Uh…" I look at Breck, feeling Joss watching me intently.

"Yeah," Breck says. "There were definitely fireworks."

He doesn't look at me, but I hear the implication behind his words and hope no one else does.

"We passed out before they happened." Jaz pouts, and Paul wraps an arm around her shoulders, pressing a kiss to the side of her head.

"Luckily we don't have to wait long for the Australia Day fireworks over the bridge. I'll make sure you have the best seat in the house," he says, and Jaz smiles, sinking closer into his side.

"Will you guys be home by then?" Jaz asks Breck and Willow, and I hate the way my stomach drops. I don't want to think about them leaving. It's been hard enough with Wes on the other side of the world.

"I need to check our return flights, but they're somewhere in that time frame." Breck's voice is tight. Maybe he isn't ready to think about leaving just yet either.

"Rory, when do you start back to work?" Dad asks, and my shoulders sag. Even with everything else going on and a dozen more interesting topics at his disposal, this is what he chooses?

"Monday. I took this whole week off." I was off last week too, not wanting to miss a minute with Wes and Joss.

"Do you really need the whole week? Wes and Joss leave this afternoon," Dad says, eyebrows pulling down into his typical disappointed scowl.

"Dad, she deserves a break. She never takes vacation," Wes interjects.

"Is it really a vacation when she's just sitting at home? Why not go to work if she's going to be here anyway," Mom adds, teaming up with Dad—just like I knew she would.

"Just because you guys never take a day off doesn't mean that's how everyone wants to live their lives," Wes shoots back, and Mom stiffens. It's rare anyone talks back to her, but he is not having it this morning. I don't know what words they exchanged yesterday after I left dinner, but Wes is unusually prickly toward our parents today.

"As long as she isn't filling her time with silly elopements and photography dreams." Mom's voice drips with disdain. "She knows better than that. She's smarter than that."

It's like a slap to the face. It's nothing new, and I shouldn't be shocked, but...

"That's enough. Please stop. You're ruining our breakfast." Wes glances at Joss, whose eyes are on me, full of concern.

She mouths, *I'm sorry*, as if this is somehow her fault.

Mom sits back in her chair, shoulders squared and lips tight. "My apologies," my dad starts. "I didn't realize the question would cause such a stir." Condescending, infuriating man. "Are you two ready for your honeymoon? I'm sure New Zealand will be wonderful this time of year."

The conversation falls back to a normal rhythm, though a bit more formal and awkward than before. I just sit quietly, ruminating over Mom's words.

She's smarter than that.

Smarter than what? Smarter than to do what I want with my own life? I guess so, since I never have. I stare blankly at my plate, not listening to the words flowing around me. It's like I'm sitting in a little sound-proof bubble, invisible and unnecessary to anything happening right now.

The bubble bursts when a hand finds mine—balled into a fist, fingernails nearly puncturing my palm—under the table. This one is strong, masculine. I glance to my right and find Breck staring down at me. There's concern etched into his features as he tilts his head, a silent question.

Are you okay?

An infinitesimal shake of my head is all I can muster, but I know he sees it because he squeezes my hand. I can't sit here anymore. As casually as I can, I place my napkin on the table and excuse myself. I go to the bathroom, but even after washing my hands with hot water for a full two minutes, I still don't want to go back out there. I settle for pacing up and down the corridor instead. At least I can get my steps in.

Breck doesn't say anything when he finds me, just lets me walk it off.

"They're always like that, yeah?" he asks, and there's no judgment. He's giving me an opening.

"Yeah. Pretty much. With me at least. Wes can do no wrong in their eyes." I look up and backpedal. "Well, it's more like Wes was always going to do what he wanted, and they were always too busy to get involved. Wes wants to go to college in San Diego? Sure. He wants to spend his last two years of college in Sydney? Sure. He wants to join the Navy and fly fighter jets? Of course."

I bite my cheek and shrug. "I never got that lax attitude. Never got to apply to that out-of-state school. Big no to majoring in photojournalism and becoming a travel photographer." I smile, but it's tired. "So what did I do? I got a job—one that uses my degree, pays me well, and has one of their friends as my boss. And it's *still* not good enough. I should be writing for a publication, using my degree 'for real.' It never mattered what Wes did, so long as he was doing something. But what I've done has never been enough."

I slump against the wall, defeated. Breck's footfalls bring him to the space next to me, and I'm grateful not to be alone, even though I'm already reeling at how much I just shared. Of all people, he doesn't need my crap laid at his feet. My problems must seem so trivial to him.

"Sorry. I shouldn't be complaining about this to you. I'm fine, really, let's go back." I push off the wall, but his hands grasp my waist and pull me back to him. "Breck... What... What're you doing?"

"Taking your mind off your shitty parents." He threads one hand in my hair and pulls me closer, feathering his lips against mine. It's not a kiss. It's a tease—like they aren't *right there.*

"Someone could see us," I say, keeping my lips a hair's breadth from his.

"So I only have a minute then." He runs his nose along my jaw until it's right under my ear. "Is the distraction working?"

"Yea—yes." I stumble over the words, unable to believe this is happening. Last night felt like a fluke, a stupid mistake after too much tequila—but this? This feels intentional and so, *so* good.

"If we only get a minute, will you kiss me?" My voice shakes and Breck inhales against my neck.

"You smell so good. How do you smell so good?"

I laugh under my breath, my chest moving against his. I'll be damned if I admit to putting on this perfume because I thought he might like it.

"A laugh. Good, my plan is working." He watches me, eyes intent on my face, the ghost of a smile on his lips.

I'm still wondering if he's going to kiss me. *Really* kiss me. Kiss me like he did last night. Like a man starved, searching for something he's been without for far too long. Instead, he just draws a thumb over my lips.

"Still want that kiss?" he asks, holding my gaze.

I nod once, and in the second between that nod and his movement to close the distance, voices carry to us from just beyond the hallway. I jump back like there's a snake at my feet and nearly collide with the wall behind me.

"Hey, guys," Joss says.

"Hey," Breck and I say in unison. *Smooth.*

"Everything okay?" Wes looks from Breck to me.

"Yup. Was just coming back," I say, walking down the hall toward them, away from Breck who's leaning oh-so-casually against the wall. I squeeze Wes's shoulder as I pass, but before I turn the corner, I flick my eyes to Breck only to find him watching me as well, a small smile on his lips.

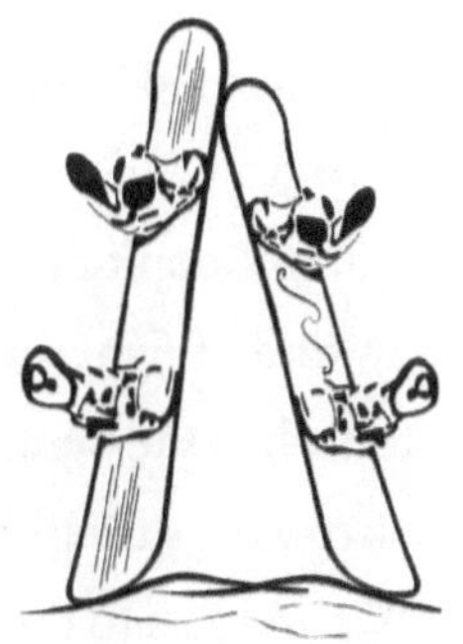

CHAPTER EIGHTEEN

BRECK

Dropping Wes and Joss at the airport was harder than I expected it to be. It was nice to have them here, separate them from the feelings I have about the place we all call home for a bit. In the three weeks after Talia left, Willow and I spent nearly every free minute with Wes and Joss. Those three weeks were brutal. Me wrapping up the sale of a business that felt like an extension of who I was. Willow trying to finish school when the stability in her life was crumbling. Both of us unsure of what our future looked like.

We even stayed in Wes's vacant apartment since he'd already moved in with Joss. His lease wasn't up until after we left for Tahoe, so it was perfect timing, and I didn't want to spend more time than necessary in our house.

My house.

Thank goodness for that. I bought it with the money I inherited from my parents. It was the first time I touched those funds. The day I found out Talia was pregnant was the day I contacted a real estate agent. I didn't want to raise a kid in an apartment in the city. I wanted my kid to have space to grow and roam. We never got around to putting Talia on the deed, so I don't expect her to fight me for it. Not that she put up any kind of fight for us. She walked away, brushing the dust off her feet when she went.

I shake my head and look to Rory sitting shotgun, staring out her window. I offered to take Wes and Joss to the airport by myself, but neither Willow nor Rory wanted to stay behind. It was a crowded and loud drive there, but it's been anything but since we got back on the road. It's late for Willow, especially after last night. Her sitter let her stay up to watch the fireworks from the east coast on TV, but she was happily asleep by the time I got in.

Rory was the only quiet one on the drive to the airport, allowing the more boisterous voices (Wes and Willow) to overtake the conversation. She's still quiet. Because of earlier? Because she's tired? Or is it because of last night? I stifle a yawn and run my hand up over my hair and down to my neck. When I glance into the back seat, Willow is out like a light.

Rory looks back at her too. "Someone was tired," she says quietly.

"Yeah. I can relate. I imagine you can too." I smirk at her. The light of a streetlamp illuminates her face and the soft blush across her cheeks.

"Yeah. I'm tired." Her tone implies more than a "I could pass out right here" exhaustion.

I don't say anything, giving her space to talk it out if she wants.

"Emotionally, mentally, relationally... all of it." She leans her head against the headrest but doesn't close her eyes, keeping them solidly on the dark road in front of us. I'm reminded of our ride from the airport to Tahoe last month and how natural it felt to be around her then. It still feels that way.

"Yeah, I thought so. I'm sorry about your parents."

She blows out a breath, lips vibrating over the exhalation. "All I've ever wanted was for them to be proud of me." Her shoulders slump. "But I don't think they've been impressed with me a day of my life."

"Not for a lack of trying on your part I'd bet," I say under my breath.

She stiffens. "What's that supposed to mean?"

"I just meant that—" I stop at a red light and get a good look at her face. Her lips are in a firm line. "I can imagine you working your ass off to please them because that's who you are. With the way you jumped in when Wes called and asked you to help us get settled... I can imagine."

Her eyes don't hold mine, instead looking back out the window next to her. I glance to where Willow rests in her seat, glad she's still asleep. This is as good a time as any to have this conversation and I'd rather not have it with her listening in.

"You were amazing when we got here. You made it easy for us to find our footing. You were great with Willow. Hell, you were great with me." I clear my throat because it's hard to admit that out loud. "Can I explain everything?"

"Okay," she says, not sounding like herself.

The light turns green and I nod, forced to focus on the road. I take a deep breath and start. "I felt pretty normal that first week here, and something about that didn't sit right. I didn't think I should feel normal, not after everything. I was afraid I was growing to rely on your help, on your companionship for both Willow and myself. I'm supposed to be figuring out this single dad thing while I'm here, and I didn't feel like I was much of one when you were around."

I chance a glance at her and—shit. She looks stunned, so I rush to cover my blunder. "Not that I thought... I didn't think of you as like—" I clear my throat. "I just mean that I always had your help if I needed it. You shopped for Willow. You brought us dinner. You helped her learn to snowboard and not hate it, unlike when she went with me.

"Then Wes called to tell us his news and I was reminded that you were there, helping me, because *he* asked you to. I couldn't be sure if you were spending your free time with me and Willow because you wanted to, or because he asked. Then I started to think of all the things you'd likely skipped out on to make time for us. You have this whole life here. You're young, you have a job, you have friends. I felt guilty for taking you away from all of that.

"So, when I told you I had it all under control and you stopped calling, I assumed it was true. That I had done the right thing."

"Breck," she says quietly, but I need to say everything, get it all out so it doesn't weigh me—or her—down.

"I know now that I was being stupid and was thinking too hard. Do you ever do that? Overthink every little thing? It feels like that's all I do these days."

She chuckles. "I overthink *everything*, so you're in good company."

"I think I made a real mess of things."

Her laughter dies on her lips and she looks down at her lap. I pull into the parking spot in front of her house and put the Jeep in park. I want to force her to look at me, but just this once I'll let her hide.

"I'm sorry, Rory. It wasn't about you. I know that sounds cliché, but it really wasn't. If it helps, Willow and I both really missed having you around."

It's a cop-out to include Willow. It's not untrue, but *I* really missed her. It bothered me on one level, but I also wished I could have that friendship back as soon as she walked out the door.

"I didn't do it for Wes, you know?" she says, finally looking at me. "I did it for you. For Willow. For me too. Like, yeah, I work too hard to please the people around me, but I've never had to do that with Wes. He's the only person in the world who's ever been proud of me for just being me. I never have to work for his love. I would do anything for him because I love him. But with you and Willow..." She bites her lip between her teeth and shrugs.

"With me and Willow what?"

"I guess I thought we were friends. It felt like we were, or that we could be, and I wanted that. Wes can't be here and it kills him. I'd guess it's killing you too. But with what you said—I thought maybe I tried too hard to be him for you and ended up being the little sister who was too much. A burden, a nuisance."

Rory's eyes moved to her lap halfway through her monologue and I could kick myself for making her feel like she was less than.

"Rory, you're none of those things. You feeling that way was never my intention. We are friends, okay?"

"We are," she says, her head lifting. Then she clears her throat and smiles. "Do you, um, have a habit of making out with your friends in alleyways? If so, I might've just learned something I didn't need to know about my brother." She laughs, and I appreciate her breaking the tension.

"No, that isn't something I make a habit of. No need to put images of that in my brain either, thank you very much. I've had to see him make out with Joss enough to last me a lifetime, yet that's how long I'll have to live with them."

"So last night then? Just a lapse of judgment, we blame it on the tequila?" she asks, leaning just slightly closer.

"I can't blame my actions in the hallway this morning on tequila..."

"No, I guess you can't. Not unless your orange juice was different to mine. So, what then? Why'd you kiss me?"

"Because I wanted to. Because for once my mind was clear, and that felt good. Because it felt like you wanted me to—"

She interrupts me with "I did... want you to." She blushes but holds my gaze.

"Because it felt good to be wanted," I continue, and that admission hurts. Over these past few weeks, it's become painfully obvious that Talia hadn't wanted me, wanted us, for quite some time. It's left me questioning everything.

Her eyes widen slightly, and just when I think she's going to swing the door open and disappear up her porch steps, she sinks into her seat.

"Why did you let me kiss you?" I ask, emboldened. "I'll feel like a real asshole if it actually was just the tequila."

"It wasn't that. Though it helped." She bites her bottom lip again and I force myself to keep my hand on the steering wheel so I don't pull it free. "I told you I'm tired. Tired of never measuring up. Tired of doing everything for everyone else and still not being enough. With you last night, I was doing something just for me, because I wanted to, and it felt *really* good."

"Really good, aye?" I quip, and she pushes my shoulder.

"You know what I mean," she says, and instead of letting her pull her hand away, I grab it and wrap it between mine on the center console.

"I do. You weren't trying to impress anyone. You were just being you."

"Yeah." She breathes out through her nose, resting her head against the headrest again. Her shoulders are relaxed, and she's drawing a small circle with her thumb that's making me crazy.

"I wasn't lying when I said what we do in our personal lives isn't Wes's business. It's not anyone's business. But I don't want for us to end up in a place where Wes is stuck in the middle of something that would hurt our friendship. I'm—" I break off, unsure of how to continue.

"You're not interested in anything serious," she says, succinct and to the point.

"No, I'm not. God, right now I feel miles away from being able to handle something serious. Plus, we're only here for a few more weeks."

"What if I said I just want to feel like I did last night? Enjoy choosing something for myself for once. I know you're only here until the end of January. I'm not expecting anything from you, but I'm not going to lie—I'd really like for you to kiss me again."

"Yeah?" I lift an eyebrow.

"Yeah. So, what do you say? You can choose to be a little irresponsible, to not overthink it. And I can choose to want you while you're here just because I can."

I lean an inch closer. "Okay."

Her face is lit only by the glow of the lamplight as snow cascades around the car.

One more inch.

In the space of that inch, Willow stirs behind us and I startle back, hitting my head on the window.

"Ow, shit," I mutter.

From the back seat, I hear a quiet voice. "Swear jar for you, Daddy."

Then she's back to sleep and I'm feeling completely and totally untethered. Rory's in the seat next to me, her shoulders heaving with silent laughter, and I wonder if what we just agreed to is a terrible mistake or the perfect escape.

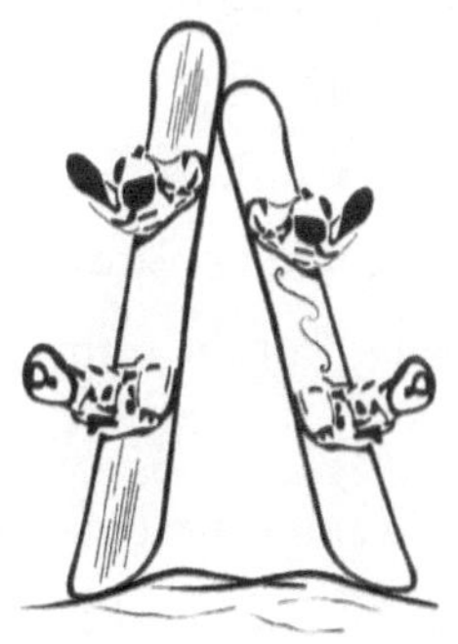

CHAPTER NINETEEN

RORY

I t's been four days since our almost-kiss in the Jeep and despite me asking Breck point-blank to kiss me again, he hasn't. It's understandable; Willow's been around every minute we've spent together, but there's a constant frisson of anticipation under my skin that I can't shake. I go back to work tomorrow, and after two weeks off I'm struggling with the prospect of jumping back into the grind.

Anytime I haven't been with Breck and Willow over the last few days has been spent on my laptop, knee-deep in edits. I love the pictures from Wes and Joss's elopement so much. They're personal, which makes holding these memories in my hands even sweeter.

Wes sent me a couple pictures of him and Joss in New Zealand, along with some videos of them bungee jumping and luge-ing down a mountainside, twin smiles on their faces. That's what I want someday: a partner to go on adventures with, to share my life with.

My eyes bounce across the screen, over Breck's face. In this one, Joss is slipping Wes's ring on his finger. There's so much tenderness in her eyes, but it also captured the look in Breck's from where he stands just beyond them. I couldn't place that look at the ceremony, but I can now—it's longing. For the future he lost? For a love like Wes and Joss's?

In the following picture, his handsome dimpled smile is back in place. It must be exhausting for him… trying to be "fine" all the time.

My phone vibrates on the coffee table and I reach for it, setting my computer aside. I have a perfectly nice desk in my guest room-slash-office, but I rarely use it—preferring the cozy couch with my legs under a soft blanket and a fire in the hearth.

Breck

Still coming over for dinner and a movie?

I glance at the clock and shoot off the couch. I was supposed to be there fifteen minutes ago.

Me

Yes, sorry, on my way. Got sucked into editing.

Breck

Bring your computer with you. I want to see.

Oh. An odd mix of emotions fills my chest—a little bit of pride but also wariness. The fear that I won't measure up rearing its ugly head. I ignore that and slide my laptop into its sleeve before grabbing my backpack.

Five minutes later, I'm trudging through heavy snowfall toward Breck's condo. The soft, picturesque flakes from earlier today have morphed into wet masses of white that coat everything I see. I clearly missed the turn of the storm while in my editing cocoon.

I knock on Breck's door, tucking my gloved hands deep into my pockets. My head is down when the door pulls open and a hand reaches out, grabbing my upper arm and pulling me into the house. My down-covered body collides with a large, solid one. My cheeks instantly flame, Breck's warmth permeating through all my layers. This is the closest we've been in four days.

He squeezes my bicep. "I'm sorry you had to walk here in that. I didn't realize it was so bad until after I texted you. We could've rescheduled." He cups my very cold cheek—I know it's cold because his hand feels like fire against it. I lean into the touch and melt inside when he grazes his thumb across my cheekbone.

"I really like these freckles," he says. Then he leans forward to dust the lightest kiss over them.

"Breck," I breathe, my gaze scanning the space around us, on the lookout for little eyes.

"She's in the bath." He glances up the stairs toward the sound of running water. He pushes the hood off my head, sending melting snow falling around my feet. My hair cascades around my face and his fingers slip against a strand, pushing it behind my ear. "Let's get you warmed up."

"Okay," I croak out, and a chuckle vibrates through him. He moves behind me to help me with my coat and my brain short-circuits with his proximity.

Once I'm bootless, coatless, and gloveless, I settle onto a barstool across from where he moves around the kitchen.

"So you cook too?"

"I do."

"More than just *shrimp on the barbie*?" I attempt to mimic his accent but butcher it horribly.

He barks a carefree laugh and bends at the waist, planting his hands on the counter and shaking his head slightly.

"You know? I think I've maybe cooked shrimp once, and never *on the barbie*."

"Well, that's disappointing. Here I've spent all these years imagining you working over the grill and it's all a lie."

Eyes alight, he says, "You've been imagining me for years, huh?" His smirk morphs into a grin that presses his dimples deep into his cheeks.

Oh shit. My cheeks flame and I duck my head. "I—Well, I, uh…"

I'm saved from the stuttering mess I've turned into by a squeal behind me. I turn to find tiny legs, in a pair of flannel pink pajamas and fuzzy slippers, running toward me.

"Rory!"

"Hey, Bug. I was trying to get your dad to tell me what we're having for dinner. Maybe you can convince him."

"Dad let me help make homemade pizzas. Mine's shaped like a heart, and yours is too." She looks so proud of herself, as she should be. I love pizza but can never get the dough right.

"What about your dad's, is his a heart too?"

"No, he made himself a snowboard," Willow says with an eyeroll.

Breck reaches across the counter and boops her nose. "Aka an oval. A little heart wasn't going to cut it. I'm hungry."

"Same." I didn't eat lunch, jumping straight onto my computer when we got back from our morning on the slopes. The snow started around eleven and we left shortly after for Willow's sake. Breck and I could've gone all day, but she's not there yet. She's comfortable on several of the intermediate runs now and she doesn't fall much anymore unless she's trying to do something she probably shouldn't. Like attempting a bunny hop over a bump in the snow or going faster than she's ready for.

"What movie did you pick, Willow Bear?" Breck asks, opening the oven door and sliding a pizza onto an oversized spatula. It manages to get the whole thing out in one go, and I make a mental note to ask my parents where they got it. Once we're on speaking terms again, that is. Thank goodness for this storm pushing them to cancel family dinner tonight. Not that I was planning to go regardless.

"*Frozen*," she says matter-of-factly, and I chuckle.

"Because it's snowing, right?" I ask, and she nods. The smile on her face is beautiful, just like her dad's.

"But we've watched that one a hundred times... since we've been here," Breck says, exasperated.

"It's my favorite though." She pouts, and I know he won't win this argument.

His shoulders sag in defeat and he just nods. "Okay, go get it set up and I'll bring in dinner." He looks at me. "Would you like a glass of wine?"

"Whatever you're having is good."

He slides a bottle of red wine and a bottle opener across the island to me and then collects a couple of stemless glasses. He opens the oven again, pulling another pizza out, and slides it onto the counter.

"Those look fantastic. Thanks for cooking," I say, pulling the cork free of the bottle. I relish the sound of the cabernet sloshing into the glass. The benefit of living less than a quarter mile away is I can enjoy it and have no issue walking home... assuming the snow isn't up to my knees by the time we finish the movie.

Breck pulls out the final pizza and fishes a cutter from a drawer, ready to massacre their hard work.

"Wait." I stop him and pull out my phone to take a picture. The hearts have expanded so they look more blobby than anything, but it's the thought that counts. I also notice my pizza doesn't match theirs. His is covered in red sauce, cheese, and every kind of meat imaginable. Willow's is just cheese and pepperoni. But mine—mine has pesto and feta and sundried tomatoes and chicken... It's almost identical to the Mediterranean one I ordered when we went out with everyone last week.

I look from the pizza to Breck and note a nervous smile playing around his eyes.

"Does it look okay?"

"It looks perfect," I breathe. "I can't believe you bought all the stuff to make this..."

It should be mortifying that I'm getting choked up. But... when was the last time someone remembered what I like well enough to make it from scratch at home? My ex couldn't even remember how I took my coffee.

Breck remembered. Even though we were hardly talking then. Even though I was practically avoiding him.

I hand him his glass of wine and we toast over the pizza while I attempt to get my thoughts and feelings about this small kindness under control.

Willow fell asleep about thirty minutes ago, leaning heavily against Breck's side. After muting the movie, he asked me to grab my computer while he took her up to bed. We've been sitting close on the couch ever since, slowly scrolling through them. With each new image, his interest grows. He asks me questions and smiles as he remembers certain moments. I love hearing pieces of the experience from his perspective.

"These are incredible," he says, and I squirm under his startling blue gaze. I've never met a compliment I haven't tried to bat away. "Why aren't you doing this for real, Rory?"

The question startles me, but I answer the way I always do. "Because it's not a real career."

"Is that you talking or your parents?"

I bristle. "That's not fair. They just... they want me to have a steady job. One with a salary and benefits. They don't want to see me fail."

"Why do they think you'll fail? You have all the skills to start a business and be successful. So why don't you?" Breck holds my gaze. His words pelt me like hail, leaving stinging discomfort in their wake.

"I don't. I mean, yes, I can take beautiful photos. But the rest? I don't know how to do any of that. I can't run a business. I wouldn't know the first thing about starting something like that." *You're getting defensive, Rory.* I take a deep breath through my nose. "I'm good at my job at the resort. I'm capable. I can live with that."

"Stability is great, but not if you're unhappy."

"I'm not *unhappy*," I say, and he lifts an eyebrow at me. "I'm not. I like my job." The protest sounds feeble even to my own ears.

"Yeah, but it doesn't light you up like this does." Breck's voice softens with a nod toward my computer. I can feel his eyes searching my face, but I refuse to look at him.

"Yeah well, getting *lit up* doesn't equal success. I have responsibilities. I have bills and people who rely on me, and—"

"And your parents," Breck interrupts.

"Yes, them too. They want what's best for me. Deep down, I believe that's true." I *need* to believe it's true. Otherwise, what the hell is all this heartache for?

"Rory. If they wanted what's best for you, all they'd want is for you to be happy. Have you ever thought about how *they* built their own business? They started from the ground up, right? That's what Wes told me. They didn't have salaries and benefits when they got started in property management and investment, but they got there." His fingers tilt my chin so I have to meet his gaze. "I know how much work it is—I spent years of my life pouring my heart and soul into Adventure Chasers. But it's worth it. Your parents keeping you from doing the same is just, well, selfish."

"Just stop, okay?" I pull back and move farther away on the couch. "I don't have time to do this as more than a hobby anyway. I have a full-time job that keeps me plenty busy."

"Maybe it's time for a change."

"Like what? I should just quit my job and start taking pictures? Hope people hire me? Yeah, that's a great idea." I scoff, a little frustrated sound that feels childish.

"No, I'm not saying that." He scratches the back of his neck. "You could start considering what it might look like if you wanted to though. I could help you."

That catches my attention and I whip my head to look at him instead of intently staring at the fire. "What do you mean?"

"You need help with the business side of things, which is something I happen to excel at." He smirks. It's a little bit cocky and a whole lot sexy. I'm stunned by his words, by his proximity. When did he move so close? "I know a good idea when I see one, Rory. You could take this 'hobby' and make it into something really cool. It's a niche that's underserved, especially in this area."

"Wait. Did you research this?" My eyes go wide. He cups my jaw and his thumb traces over the warmth of my cheek, over the freckles he said he liked.

He nods. "I did. Like I said, I know a good idea when I see one, and this is a great idea. Let me help you choose yourself for once. Please."

His words, his desire to help me—not for his own gain, not for his own purposes, but because he sees me and sees what I really want—makes me feel something I haven't felt in a long time.

Worthy.

I press forward, my lips finding his. They're soft and warm, the taste of red wine still lingering. I melt into him, wanting more... wanting him.

Then the lights flicker, and everything goes black.

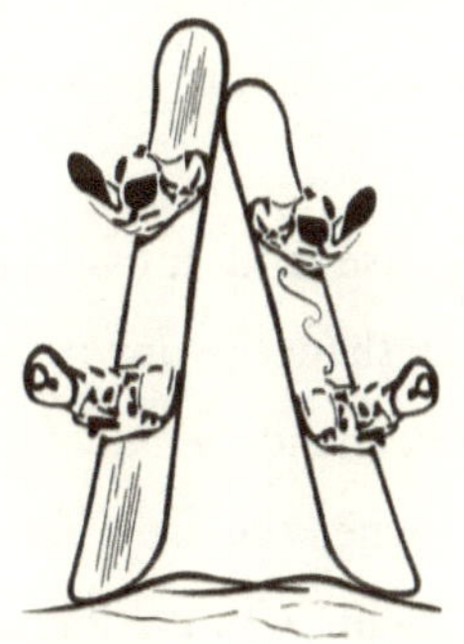

CHAPTER TWENTY

BRECK

The current between Rory and me is so intense it's like it sapped the rest of the world of its electricity. We pull apart, the glow of the gas fireplace emitting a dull light in the otherwise dark room.

She giggles, pressing her forehead against my chest. We were so ensconced in our little bubble that I didn't notice the storm raging. The windows whistle with the wind, causing a howling as it moves through the trees. I turn to look outside and the view is nearly black. Nothing but a bright blurry orb doing its best to shine through the heavy clouds.

I turn back to face Rory and she's watching the view out the window as well, her lip caught between her teeth. I'm reminded of how good it felt to have mine pressed there.

"You're staying here tonight." Hell will freeze over before I let this woman walk a quarter mile in the blizzard outside.

She swallows and glances down at the couch, then back to me. "I'd argue, but I really don't want to go out there. You're sure you don't mind?"

"I definitely"—I pause and move closer, right into her space—"don't mind." I crash my lips down on hers and she responds with equal fervor, lacing her hands behind my neck to tug at the ends of my hair. God, I love it when she does that.

There's a war in my brain with every movement. The one side telling me this is a terrible idea. I'm not ready for this after everything with Talia. This is Wes's sister. My daughter's right upstairs.

The second side is telling its counterpart to fuck off and enjoy this moment. Enjoy this uncomplicated and beautiful woman who, for whatever reason, wants me. It really does feel good to be wanted. The first side of my brain finally shuts up when a little moan escapes from Rory. My hand slides down her neck, over her collarbone, and she arches forward into the touch. I smile against her mouth, glad I'm not the only one who wants more.

There's no tequila to blame now, no conversation about her parents' idiocy driving me to distract her. It's just me wanting her and her wanting me. In the end, that's all we need. I stand from the couch, using all my strength to lift her with me. She wraps her legs around my waist, hooking her feet behind my back. I walk with purpose through the dark. Up the stairs. Down the hall. To my room. I lower her onto the bed, pulling away only long enough to close the door, blocking the last of the light from the fire downstairs, and then I flip the lock.

There's a soft giggle from the head of the bed as I make my way over. Then I crawl toward her with nothing but feel to guide me. My fingers linger on an ankle bone and rasp against denim stretched over toned legs. There's a soft strip of skin where her shirt has ridden up—a strip of skin that grows as I push it up a little farther, and then a little farther still. Her breathing hitches and I shift forward, putting my weight on my arms on either side of her head. I'm nestled between her thighs, our bodies lined up and humming with arousal. Her breath caresses my skin through the thick black around us.

As my eyes begin to adjust I can only just see her lips an inch from mine. I lower my head as she lifts hers from the pillow. Our lips meet, and I'm lost.

There's a yell from down the hall and I jerk awake.

Shit, Willow.

Movement in the bed beside me startles me almost as much as the yell did. The bedside lamp in my room is on now, and it may as well be the sun. Maybe that's what woke Willow, the lights coming back on... The reason doesn't matter, I need to go to her before she comes to me and finds the door locked, or worse, finds Rory in my bed.

I jump up, scanning the room for sweats, when fabric hits me in the back of the head and Rory stifles a laugh. It's my boxers.

"Very funny," I say in a hushed voice, trying to ignore the fact that I'm very naked right now and completely exposed to her—so unlike our rush of hands in the dark last night.

She laughs again and whispers, "Go."

I shuffle into my boxers and slip out the door, closing it quickly behind me.

"Willow?" I ask, walking into her room. "You okay?"

She sniffles from her place on the top bunk. I wish she was on the bottom. I can't climb in beside her and comfort her from down here.

She nods and wipes a tear away from her face.

"What's wrong, love?"

"I heard a noise and then the light in the hallway came on. I was scared someone was in the house."

"There's no one in the house, baby. The power went out last night after you went to bed. It just came back on." I swipe a tear from my girl's cheek, hating that she's upset. "Sorry it woke you up."

"Oh, okay." She nuzzles her head into my hand and I feel my heart squeeze tightly in my chest. I love her so much. I wish I could protect her from anything that might scare her, hurt her, but I've learned in epic ways recently that I can't.

"You want to come down to the bottom bunk and snuggle?" I ask.

She shakes her head and nestles down into the blankets again. "I'm okay now. Thanks, Daddy."

"I love you." I lean forward and press a kiss to her temple.

Back in the hall, I need a minute to get myself together.

I had sex last night.

With Rory.

That was definitely not on my Lake Tahoe bingo card, but here we are. I wanted to kill Wes when I unpacked and found the box of condoms in my suitcase with a note that said *just in case*. If he ever finds out I made use of them with his sister, I imagine he'll want to kill *me* instead. My lip quirks up in a smile and I shake my head, unwilling to feel any sort of regret over what happened.

With the inky darkness beyond the windows downstairs, you wouldn't know it's already five a.m. The kitchen light is on ahead of me, but I take a detour for the lamp in the living room, squinting to make out the shadow of someone sitting on the couch.

"Rory?"

There she sits, legs stretched long in front of her, leaning back against the arm rest with a blanket over her fully clothed body. "Hi. I didn't want to be in the way if Willow needed you."

I crouch down in front of her and interlace our fingers. "Thank you for thinking of her. Her finding you in my bed would not have been good."

She glances down at our hands, one of hers still held in mine while her other fiddles with the blanket.

"I'm not saying last night wasn't good. It was great. I just don't think I want Willow to know about it. Is that okay?" I internally plead with her to say yes. It's the only answer that'll allow this to work.

She looks up and nods, the worry over my words lifting from her features. The side of her mouth tips up in a smile before she bites the bottom one between her teeth. "It *was* great, wasn't it."

"Oh, it definitely was." I lift up higher on the balls of my feet so I can press my lips to hers. I want to lay her out on the couch, but it's too risky.

"Do you want some sweats or something to wear if you're going to go back to sleep?" I ask, running my hand up her jean-clad leg under the blanket.

She shakes her head. "Nah, I think I'm up now. I go back to work today, so I can't stay too long before I need to go home and get ready."

I stand up and stretch, realization dawning that I should probably put some sweats on over my boxers. Ignoring that thought for a minute, I walk to the window. It's a winter wonderland outside, lit only by the streetlights which all have white snowy Santa hats on top. There has to be at least eighteen inches of snow on most every surface. The cars are buried. The sidewalks are non-existent. I can see a snowplow down the road working its way through the streets, but it's going to be hours before anything gets cleared.

"I don't know that you're going anywhere for a bit," I say, turning back around. Rory's eyes jump to mine and I'm sure I just caught her checking out my ass. I grin and add, "You have your laptop, right? Could you work from here today?"

"I don't know." She shrugs. "Maybe. I wanted to work in the office today since I've been off for two weeks."

"Do you really think anyone will be in the office with all this snow?"

"Oh, Breck, you sweet little Aussie. You know nothing of this wintery world we live in. We don't let a little bit of snow hold us back."

"A little bit of snow? A *little* bit of snow? There's at least a foot and a half out there. Six inches might be doable, but eighteen..."

She stands, wrapping the blanket around her shoulders, and joins me by the windowsill.

"You know... you're actually a pretty good judge of measurements. Most men don't know what six inches looks like, let alone eighteen." She says it with the most deadpan expression, and I tilt my head down to look at her. There's a beat of silence, then another, and we both burst out laughing.

It feels good to laugh. With her, everything feels good.

I wrap my arm around her and kiss the top of her rosy hair. "How about some coffee while I convince you?"

She pulls back a few inches and smiles. The freckles across her nose and cheeks stand out bright against her pale skin, her turquoise eyes sparkling. "If you insist." Then she brushes her mouth over mine before sauntering into the kitchen. Her lithe hips sway with every step, and I follow her without another thought.

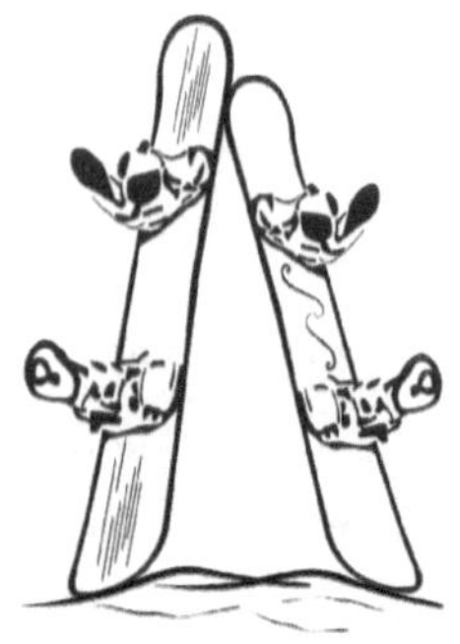

CHAPTER TWENTY-ONE

Rory

I texted my boss over my first cup of coffee and got the go ahead to work from home. The rest of the marketing department would be doing the same, including our intern Hannah, who I had handling most of our social media the last two weeks.

"Looks like I'm working from here. You're sure you don't mind?"

Breck's head pops up from the stovetop. *Please let that be bacon.* "So long as you don't mind us being underfoot while you're working, you're welcome to work here for as long as you'd like."

I nod, walking over to sit across the counter from where he's cooking, and take another long sip of my coffee. I smile when he slides over a steamy plate of eggs and crispy bacon. *Yes!*

"Thank you." I sigh.

Breck stands with his hands braced on the counter, T-shirt pulled taut across his muscled shoulders and chest. I blush, thinking about how I traced those muscles in the dark last night, how I finally got to see them under the light of the lamp early this morning.

Breck clears his throat and our gazes collide, a cheeky grin pulling up his lips. Smug and clearly satisfied to have caught me gawking.

"What?" I say, a little defensive.

"Nothing. I'm not going to complain about you undressing me with your eyes." The grin transforms into a full-blown smile. He shoots a quick glance behind me. "I'm guessing that means we're good. After last night?"

He's confident and assured in his question, but it *is* a question.

"Yeah." I smile. "We're good. *Very* good actually." I don't mean for it to sound sultry, but he lifts an eyebrow as if to ask *Very good, huh?*

I give him a one-shoulder shrug and he chuckles, turning to gather his own breakfast. Yeah, last night was very good. One of the best nights I've had in a long time, and it was *definitely* the best sex I've ever had. The intimacy was like a living, breathing thing between us as we moved together in the dark.

He carries his plate around to sit next to me at the counter. "Should we talk about how this will work? I've got Willow to think about, and I don't want for us to end up somewhere neither of us is looking to be when it's time for me to leave." His words pour out fast and, with his accent, I almost don't catch half of them.

"We both know this isn't serious. We're friends," I say, using my thigh to press against his, wanting to catch his eye. "We hang out, and when we want to do more and it works, we do. I don't want

Willow to get confused either. It doesn't have to be complicated. When you go back to Australia, we're still friends and that's the end of it."

"I'm not supposed to overthink this, right?"

"Right. This is for fun. Just for us. Now, I need to eat so I can get to work. So, could you be quiet? Your overthinking is killing my appetite." I knock his shoulder with my own, drawing a rumble of laughter from his chest.

By the time lunch rolls around, I'm mostly caught up on emails and have touched base with Hannah. I had the majority of our social media set to run on auto-pilot, but it's nice to know she was there to back me up. Maybe with her around I could finally make that trip to see Wes and Joss this year?

And Breck... Nope, not thinking about that.

I shuffle into the condo from his back deck where I was taking pictures of the mountains and kick my boots off by the door. With the holidays behind us and winter in full swing, I'll need new content to pull skiers and boarders to the slopes each week.

A shiver rolls across my shoulders, the warmth of the space a stark contrast to the chill outside. Willow is at the table with a book in front of her. Breck's clicking away on his laptop on the couch, ankles crossed on the coffee table, wearing dark grey joggers and that damn T-shirt. Combined with his tousled hair, he's mouthwatering.

I join Willow and peek over her shoulder. "What're you reading?"

She looks up from under her dark lashes. "A book about a mermaid. Dad says I have to keep up with my reading while I'm on summer vacation." She glances outside and giggles. "Doesn't feel like a normal summer." Then her face falls and she goes back to her book, saying under her breath, "Nothing feels normal these days."

My eyes shoot to Breck and I see the blow land. The happy-go-lucky smile that was on his face dims to a scowl and his eyes freeze over. She didn't mean for him to hear her—she probably didn't intend for me to either—but now I'm at a complete loss for what to say. She's so confident and silly all the time that it's easy for me to forget she lost her mom less than two months ago. What must that be like for her? Having never lost a parent, I can't relate. Especially considering Talia could still be here, could still be in her life, but has chosen not to be.

Everything about Breck has tensed, and the way he stands from the couch is stiff. He looks more unsure than I've ever seen him. I can almost see the place he's kept all his grief locked up tight starting to crack open. "I'll be back in a minute," he says quietly before heading upstairs.

"Can I get you anything to eat, Bug?" I ask, trying to soften the crackling energy in the room.

"Daddy said he'd make me a sandwich when I finish this chapter. I'm almost done, wanna see?"

"Sure." I smile and sit next to her, hoping that if nothing else, she'll know she has people who are here for her.

Breck rejoins us fifteen minutes later with wet hair from a shower and a smile firmly in place. I wonder how he got so good at hiding it all.

"Lunch, Willow Bear? Rory?"

"Sure," we say together and then fall into a fit of matching giggles.

We eat our sandwiches with chips and Tim Tams—Australian cookies Wes and Joss brought over from Sydney.

I swallow a bite of crispy chocolate and grab for my phone that's vibrating on the table.

My phone rings in my hand. This must be bad if he needs to call me to talk about it. As soon as I answer, he's talking.

"I can't do the shoot this weekend. I'm sorry, but I have to go to San Francisco and meet with my agent and publisher. I'm leaving tomorrow and will likely be there for the week."

"Oh—oh-kay. There's no way you can be back in time?"

"I wish I could. They've got me scheduled for meetings all week and a last-minute signing this weekend. I'm sorry, Rory, I can email the couple and take the heat for having to cancel."

"I guess that's our only option. I can't exactly take pictures of a wedding if there's no one to officiate it." I scrub a hand across my face, using my thumb and middle finger to press into my temples. I can feel a headache coming on. Letting a couple down this way is going to send my people-pleasing heart into a death spiral. Plus, I was really looking forward to this shoot.

Attuned to his energy and warmth, I feel Breck beside me before his fingers make contact with my wrist, drawing my attention to him. He's pointing at his chest, a questioning look on his face.

Can I do it? he mouths.

I scrunch my eyebrows as my brain hums with the possibility. Yes, he can do it. He got ordained to do Wes and Joss's wedding. But does he really want to?

"Rory?" Jamie says through the phone. I almost forgot about him for a second.

"Uh, hang on a sec," I say, and move the phone away from my mouth. "Are you sure you want to?" I ask Breck, and he nods.

"I told you I would."

"Yeah, but that was when you were talking about the business side of things, not about officiating the ceremonies."

"I'm happy to help however I can."

Gratitude wells inside me, and it's about to spill over and force me to hug this beautiful man.

"Rory?" Jamie says again.

"Sorry. I'm here. Okay, new plan. We don't have to cancel. Breck's going to officiate."

"Seriously? That's generous of him. Tell him thanks. I hate the thought of leaving you high and dry."

"I will, and I get it, Jamie. This isn't your real job. It was supposed to be a one-time thing, yet here we are."

"Here we are. I really do love doing it with you, but I can't miss these meetings."

"I know. It's fine. I promise. We have it covered." I glance up and bite back a smile. That *we* sounded way too good and came out way too easily. *Reel it in, Rory, reel it in.*

Jamie continues, oblivious to the fact that I'm only half paying attention to him. "Well, I better get packed. I also need to figure out how to get my Defender out of the two feet of snow it's buried in. You okay after the storm?"

"Yeah, I'm good. I was at Breck's when the power went out so I hunkered down here." Those tingles erupt again at the memories.

"Oh yeah...?" Jamie drawls. I can almost hear him waggling his eyebrows through the phone.

"Yeah," I snip. "Talk to you later, okay?"

"You better. If you're finally getting out of your slump I—"

I cut him off. "Bye, Jamie." I hang up and press the phone to the table, willing my face to cool. God, that man. I blow my breath out in a huff only to find Breck silently shaking with laughter. I smack him with the back of my hand.

"What's so funny, Daddy?" Willow says, glancing between us.

"Nothing, sweetheart. Want to go play in the snow?"

"Yes!" Jumping up, she knocks the table and sends my coffee sloshing over the lip of my mug. Luckily it misses my laptop... and Breck's.

"Oops." She covers her eyes with both hands.

"Grab a towel and help me clean this up." He's gentle but firm. "And apologize to Rory, please."

"Sorry, Rory," she says, quiet and timid.

"It's okay, Bug. Accidents happen."

She slips in next to me to mop up the coffee and asks, "Will you come play outside with us?"

"I've got a few more things I need to finish up for work, but if you're still out there when I'm done, I'm all in."

"Okay!" She runs off in the direction of the laundry room with the damp towel, and then up to her room to get ready.

"I didn't mean to insert myself into your time. I can go home after I finish up here. The sidewalks are mostly cleared now I think."

"We need to work out the details for this weekend, right?"

"Yeah, I guess we do. I don't want to impose though."

"You're not imposing. You're invited." He leans down close, breath coasting against my ear. "Wanted."

My breath catches in my chest, awakening something deep inside me.

What have I gotten myself into?

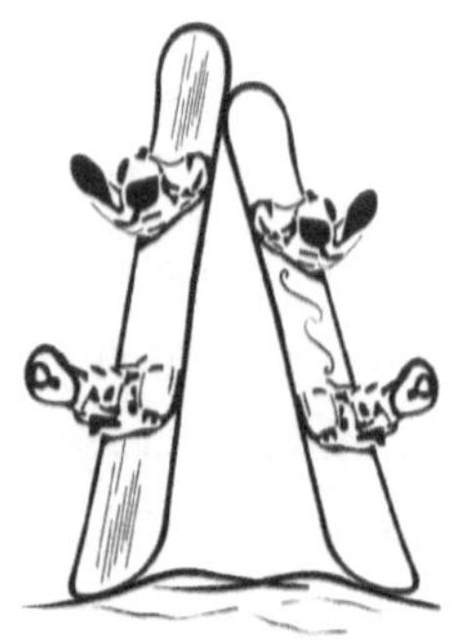

CHAPTER TWENTY-TWO

BRECK

T he week flew by and I'm almost surprised to find myself driving down a windy road in the Jeep, headed for the valley on the Nevada side of Lake Tahoe and the elopement that awaits us. The view as we crested the ridge took my breath away, and I couldn't believe this hidden gem of a town was nestled on the other side of the mountains we've been snowboarding down for a month.

We bump along toward a small ranch surrounded by fields, but it's the mountain backdrop that leaves me speechless. They loom over the valley, tall and proud. Majestic.

"Have you been here before?" I ask Rory, my head spinning as I try to take it all in.

"Yeah, the owners are friends of the family. I used to come here as a kid," she tells me before turning in her seat to look at Willow. "They have chickens. And peacocks. And ostriches!"

"Really?" Willow's voice jumps an octave. She's never been to a real ranch before and was already excited.

"Yup." Rory pops the P, wearing a wide grin, eyes alight. I cut the engine outside a building that's half-barn half-home. "You ready for this?"

I nod and reach for the door handle. We've gone over the plan countless times since Monday. The ceremony isn't that different from what I did for Wes and Joss.

Cold air hits my face and I pull my jacket tighter around me. I round the hood to open Rory's door, then Willow's. The sound of boots crunching on frozen snow is interrupted by Rory's curse when she slips on a patch of ice. Her feet go out from under her and I catch her around the waist, pulling her tightly into my chest. I'm grateful for the superhuman reflexes they issue when you become a dad—though there is nothing dad-like about the way my scorching eyes trail over Rory.

"Thanks," she breathes, gaze dropping to my lips before looking sideways at Willow. It's all the reminder I need to loosen my arms.

"Welcome," I husk, giving my attention to Willow, who's eyeing us. I pull her into my side and ruffle her hair with one hand. "You ready to be Rory's special assistant, Willow Bear?"

Her nod is emphatic, excitement taking over her sweet face. I love when she smiles, showcasing how much of me there is in her. Talia's unmistakably there too, with her straight dark hair and olive skin tone, though the sparkle in Willow's baby blues is all me.

"Alright, let's go scout our location," Rory says, hefting her mint green camera bag out of the car and leading us past the house. We cross an arched bridge over a dry creek, where two large trees jut up to frame the view of the mountains standing in sharp relief above the valley floor.

Rory rotates on the spot, glee and anticipation illuminating her face, and I know she's happy with this location.

"Let's run through it one more time."

With the ceremony concluded and nothing but pictures left to take, I stand to the side and watch. It's clear this is where Rory's heart lies. There's an energy beneath her skin when she has her camera in hand. She's focused and determined, constantly moving to find the best light, the best angle, the best shot. She doesn't falter, doesn't waver, and her confidence is something to behold.

She whispers quiet instructions to Willow, who moves beside her, a second camera around her neck. Willow follows without question and in complete silence, a rarity for her. Willow moves as Rory does and exudes a similar confidence. I've never seen her like this, and I hide a smile behind my gloved hand as I watch. She's finding her footing with something new, something untainted by the heartache of the last couple of months.

I wish I could say the same for myself. Without Talia, without Adventure Chasers, I'm not sure what our lives will look like when we leave Tahoe behind.

Questions are my constant companion. What am I supposed to do with my life? Start from scratch with some new venture? Go work for someone else? I've been my own boss for so long that the thought rattles me.

And what about Willow? She was already struggling with some of the kids, the schoolyard rumors poking at where her mom went... Maybe they'll have moved on to other things by the time we get back, but what if they haven't?

I pull out my phone and snap a photo of Rory and Willow moving in tandem. There they are, all smiles, thoughts fully fixed on what's in front of them, and here I am, with nothing but a jumbled mess inside my mind.

Rory leans in to hug the bride, so I shake myself out of it. Uncrossing my arms, I push off the tree I was leaning against and walk over to the group. The thank-yous and congratulations are quick, and before long, we're waving goodbye to the newlyweds as they head off to the Sierra Nevada mountains. As soon as they're out of sight, I'm engulfed in a hug from Rory.

"Thank you so much for doing this. I couldn't have done it without you." Her lips find my cheek and even though they're cold, warmth spreads through me like a wildfire. It was only a friendly peck, something appropriate even for Willow to see, but it felt like more.

"You're welcome. I was happy to help. It felt good to do something useful."

"What about me? Did I do good?" Willow pipes up and I pull her in, smushing her between us. Then I lean down to plant a kiss on her bear-hat covered head.

"You did amazing." My look of adoration for Willow is mirrored on Rory's face. She's beaming with pride.

"You were incredible. I couldn't have done it without you either."

"Maybe I'll have to always be your assistant," Willow states, and I melt for how sweet she is. I also internally flinch knowing that can't happen. We won't be here. I want to say something, set her straight, but I can't bring myself to dampen the mood.

"I wish you could, Bug. If I have another photoshoot while you're here, you can be!"

"Okay." Willow accepts her answer, and I sigh with relief. Seven-year-olds know how to push a subject, and I never know which one she's going to choose as her hill to die on.

I'm quiet on the ride home, letting the girls fill the car with their chatter, which is why I don't immediately notice when the silence descends. I glance in the rearview mirror to find Willow leaning against the window asleep, again. Then I flick my eyes to Rory. She's watching me, thought lines carved around her mouth and across her forehead.

"You okay?" Rory asks, tentative and quiet.

"Yeah. It's just been a long day. Thank you for including us—Willow especially. I've never seen her so excited over something. She really took to being your assistant."

"She was a huge help. I'm excited to see what kind of shots she got. I pretty much gave her free rein to do whatever she wanted with that camera. She's a natural."

Pride for my daughter blooms. She's incredible, I know that, but having others see that in her too…

"Do you want to grab your computer and come hang out for the evening? I'm making spaghetti, and I think it's time I taught you how to do a Tim Tam Slam." I beam, and her brow furrows.

"A what?"

"You'll see." I smirk.

"Yeah. I just need to cancel dinner with my parents…" She trails off and looks down at her lap before she starts worrying her thumb between her teeth. Her nervous tell. As far as I know, she hasn't seen them since breakfast on New Year's, which was almost two weeks ago.

"Hey," I say, waiting for her to look at me. Wide eyes meet mine after a minute and I continue. "You don't have to. If you want to have dinner with them, we can do it another night."

Her quiet *hmm* is all that fills the space between us. I reach across the console and lace my fingers with hers. They're still cold from the time we spent outside—her fingerless gloves clearly didn't do enough to keep her hands warm—so I press a kiss to her palm before placing it over a heater vent.

"I'd rather have dinner with you," she whispers, and my heart expands. Partially because she's choosing me and that feels damn good, but mostly because she's choosing herself.

Tim Tam Slams were a hit. Willow has perfected the technique of biting off diagonal corners of the rectangular cookie before submerging it in her hot chocolate and sucking the warm liquid through like a straw. Rory couldn't believe we'd held out so long on showing her this piece of Aussie culture, and our supply is quickly dwindling now with three of us vying for them.

Despite her nap in the car and the sugar from the Tim Tams, Willow crashed hard not long after dinner and I had to carry her limp body up the stairs to her room—not bothering with pajamas or teeth brushing.

Rory's in the kitchen washing dishes when I return, so I slide in behind her and press a kiss beneath her ear. She jumps, but I tighten my arms around her and chuckle into her hair.

"You know," I whisper against her neck, "we have this magical invention called a dishwasher that's designed to do exactly what you're doing."

"You don't say?" She continues to wash the dishes, pretending she's unaffected by me, but I know better. Her breathing is shallow and there's color rising up her neck.

Work kept her busy this week, so we haven't had any real alone time since the storm. To say I've been eagerly awaiting an opportunity to have her to myself would be an understatement. It was only one night, but the memories of her body fitted with mine make me ache for more. She sways her hips against me and it's all I can do to hold in a moan. Giving up on any semblance of self-control, I slide my arms down hers into the sudsy water and grip her hands. She inhales sharply and releases the cup she's holding with a plop.

Not caring that our hands and forearms are covered in bubbles, I spin her around and press her back against the counter. I weave a hand, bubbly fingers and all, into her hair and pull her lips to mine. Her arms weave around my neck, wet droplets sliding beneath the neckline of my shirt, and I shiver.

I can't get enough of her. I can't get close enough. I can't breathe. I can't think. My other hand slides down to cup her ass and pull her tighter. She moans, and I slip my tongue along her lips, then inside. She tastes like chocolate, and I want to devour her.

I release her hair, gripping her ass with both hands instead, and lift, spinning us. With a squeak of surprise and a soft giggle, I settle her on the counter across from the sink. It feels so good with her. So easy. How long has it been since intimacy with someone was like this? With Talia... no, I'm not going there right now. Not with Rory's legs around my hips, her hand snaking between our bodies to where my belt is buckled.

"I can take you here or..." I mutter against her lips, feeling them twitch into a smile against mine.

"Bedroom... please," she says between breaths.

She doesn't have to ask me twice.

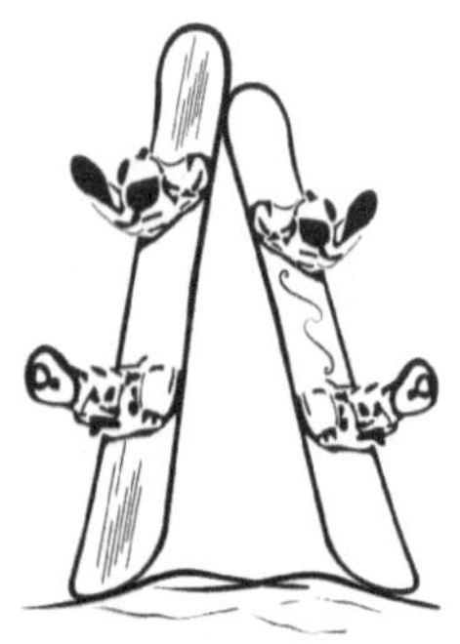

CHAPTER TWENTY-THREE

Breck

One more week. We have just one more week before we board a plane back to Sydney, and I'm dreading it with every passing minute. The positive attitude I wear like a second skin is waning, and unfortunately Willow's picking up on it.

What other option do we have though? We've been living in ignorant bliss, ignoring every bit of the chaos and heartbreak we left behind, but we have to pay the piper eventually.

"Let's go snowboarding today, just you and me," I say to Willow across the breakfast bar. She's been scarfing down the pancakes I made with a scowl in place of her usual smile.

She shrugs and pushes her food around the plate.

"Come on, Bear, it'll be fun."

"Fine. Can we invite Rory?"

I button down the hurt, reminding myself she's a young girl who, maybe, would rather hang out with another girl. Not that I don't love hanging with Rory, but we need to talk about going home, and I don't think that should happen with an audience or while we're trapped in the house.

"She's working today, but I bet we can see her later."

"Fine." She huffs again, her stomping footsteps reverberating all the way up the stairs.

"Dress warm!" I shout after her.

I hang my head and run my hands into my hair. I really need to get it cut. It's nearly long enough I could pull it up, and that's never been my vibe.

My phone vibrates against my leg and I'm greeted by a text from Wes.

Wes

Rory just sent me a couple of pictures from Sunday. They're incredible. Thanks for giving her a hand.

I groan at the unbidden thought about how I gave her more than a hand that night. I want to punch myself. Keeping my relationship—well, friendship with benefits—with Rory separate from the one I have with Wes hasn't been difficult with the seven thousand miles between us. When thrown together in this way though, I'm very much aware of what I'm doing. Sleeping with my best friend's sister. *Fuck.* I hit my head against the counter a couple times before typing out a reply.

Me

> It was my pleasure.

> Willow has been talking about it nonstop for five days. She wants to be Rory's permanent assistant.

Wes

> Well, I appreciate it. I know she did too.

> Are you guys all set to come back next week? Joss is home and will pick you up. I'll be in training.

Me

> Yeah. Everything is set with the tickets. I just wish we felt ready to go back.

My phone rings in my hand. Expecting this, I swipe my finger across the screen and hit the speakerphone button.

"Hey." I keep my voice even, steady.

"Hey." There's concern in his voice. "What's going on?"

I sigh. "I thought I'd feel ready to deal with everything back home by now, but I just... don't."

"You don't have to do it alone."

"I know, I just feel lost." I squeeze my eyes shut, vulnerability oppressing my senses. It's the first time I've said that aloud. "It feels like all we have left there is you and Joss. It's just hard to imagine walking back into our lives like nothing's changed."

"I understand that. You know I do," he says, and he's right. I watched him rebuild his entire life after the crash. "Do what you need to do, brother. Even if it means staying longer."

I shake my head, though he can't see it. "We can't. Willow starts school the first week of February. That's only two weeks away and I want us to have a week to get settled before that."

But, god, I wish we could.

"You're a smart man," he says. "I bet you could workshop a solution."

I scoff. "Like what? Her school's in Australia. I can't exactly put her in school here. They're mid-year."

"I know. What about remote school? After Covid, you can't tell me there isn't some way she could do school from afar for a bit."

That's an idea, but... "I don't know. I'd need to talk to the school and her teacher. And Willow. I don't know if she'd even want to stay."

"Well, like I said, do what you guys need to do. We'll support you."

I wish I could hug him. I had no idea the friend he would become when we first met as two stupid kids in college, but I'm so grateful for him now.

"Yeah. I'll think about it. Thanks, mate," I say, and I can hear Willow coming downstairs. "We're about to head up the mountain. Talk to you later, yeah?"

"Yeah. Enjoy the snow, and say hi to my sister for me if you see her."

"I will. Later, Wes."

I'll definitely be seeing Rory—if not on the slopes, then ideally in my bed. I'm so screwed. The more we hook up, the less I want to stop, and it's going to end up as another thing I have to let go of when we leave.

The slopes are pristine, covered with fresh snow that sparkles like diamonds in the morning light. Willow has moved on from the beginner runs and is pretty comfortable on the intermediate slopes now. She rarely takes me out when we get off the chair anymore either, which is a bonus. I breathe a sigh of relief when today's first exit from the chair is perfect.

Willow straps into her bindings like an expert—she's got a knack for this sport and it makes my heart soar every time I watch her. There's also a pang of longing that goes with it. Longing for my parents to see her like this, for them to help me figure out what on earth to do—with her, with us, with our new, smaller family... With my life. I miss them all the time, but I've lived without them for so long now, and I manage that grief by putting on a brave face and suffering mostly in silence. Just like I did when I was thirteen. And again at twenty when I lost my aunt and uncle.

My parents would know what to do to help me navigate this whole situation. The only other time I felt their loss so acutely was when I found out Talia was pregnant. I wanted to share that news with them more than anything—tell them they were going to be grandparents, ask for their advice. I didn't get that opportunity, and it left a little hole in my heart for what *they* lost when they died too.

"Daddy, let's go!" Willow bellows from where she stands at the top of the run. I'm not even clipped into my second binding yet.

"Sorry, Willow Bear, I'm coming." I make quick work of it and slide in her direction. Instead of stopping, I pass her and flip one-hundred-and-eighty degrees so we're facing each other. "Wanna race?"

I can't see her eyebrow raise under her goggles and helmet, but I can picture it. Her smile dazzles me and she nods before flying past me. This was probably a bad idea. I take off after her, the wind tickling my neck beneath my helmet.

A flat section is coming up in the terrain ahead, so I holler at Willow to keep up her speed. If she doesn't, she won't make it up the small hill at the end. My focus is on her, gauging whether she's going to have enough *oomph* to crest the hill, so I don't see the person standing just at the top until it's too late. I slide my board perpendicular to the slope to slow my speed and attempt to maneuver around them, but I clip the edge of their board with mine.

Using every bit of skill in my arsenal, I flip around, hoping I can catch them before they fall. I register only one thing before we tumble together into the snow—turquoise eyes.

I take the brunt of it, falling onto my back and losing my breath as she lands on top of me. We slide a few feet down the slope and her eyes go wide—which I can only see because she's not wearing her goggles.

"Hi," I croak, unable to take a full breath. My hands work fine though, and I push her strawberry-blonde braid back over her shoulder.

"Oh my god, are you okay?" Rory attempts to clamber off me, but I hold tight, enjoying the unexpected press of her body against mine. She pushes some of her weight into her hands though, and air rushes into my lungs.

"I'm fine. Are you?" I let go of her braid and swipe my thumb across her freckled cheek.

"Yeah." She puffs out a breath then inhales another big one. "You just surprised me is all."

"You and me both. I'm sorry, I was focused on Willow." The reminder has me moving again, trying to dislodge myself while Rory moves with equal urgency, or as much as we can while still strapped to our boards and tangled in the snow.

Once I'm up, I take several large bunny hops up the slope until I can see Willow. She has one foot unstrapped and is skating her way toward us slowly. She clearly didn't carry her speed enough and got stuck. I'm just glad she didn't come flying up to add to the dogpile I created. I offer a wave and she waves back, her face a little grumpier than it was a few minutes ago. No one likes getting stuck in the flats.

Rory hops up next to me, a grin playing around her lips. "I can't believe you crashed into me."

"I can't believe you were just standing at the top of the hill," I retort, incredulous.

"You have me there, but I couldn't pass up the chance to take in the view of home for a minute." She turns to face the lake below, where the sun glitters on the blue water that, despite the low temperatures, never freezes over. The shoreline turns icy, but the center of the lake is always like this.

"I'm going to miss this place," I admit, mostly to myself, but she turns to look at me.

"It's going to miss you too," she says, and I hear what she doesn't say. *I'm going to miss you too.*

"Rory!" Willow calls, finally making it up the little hill to us. "You're here! Daddy told me you were working today." She glares at me like I lied to her.

Rory, picking up on the tone too, comes to my aid. "I was... well, I am. I needed some fresh shots of the mountain, so I came up for a couple runs. I can finish this one with you if you want, but then I have to go back to the office."

Willow's face falls but she rallies a small smile and nods. "Okay."

"Maybe you can tell your dad not to crash into me this time."

The race to the bottom is much less exciting than the first half, at least in terms of collisions, and we're all a mess of smiles and laughs, standing off to the side of the growing lift line.

"Time for me to get back to work. Thanks for letting me ride with you, Willow. See you guys for dinner later?" she asks, eyebrow raised. That look holds more promise than the possibility of a meal.

"Absolutely." I wink, though I'm not sure she can see it behind my goggles.

She pats Willow on the top of her helmet. "Give your dad a run for his money, okay?"

"I will," she responds in her sing-song voice.

Rory slides away with a wave and a backward glance, and we join the lift line to make our way back up the mountain.

"Willow?" I ask, and she turns to face me on the chair.

"How're you feeling about going home next week?" It's time to stop dancing around the subject.

She shrugs, but when her shoulders drop, they slump in a little. "I don't know. Mom won't be there, will she?" I hate the tiny bit of hope in the question. It cuts like a knife. We haven't talked much about Talia, and something about Willow calling her "mom" right now breaks my heart. I've lost a mom, now she has too, and I understand just how painful that is.

"No, sweetheart, she won't be there."

She sniffles and grabs my gloved hand in hers, tilting her helmet-encased head up. I wish I could see her face more fully.

"I thought I'd miss being home for the summer, miss my friends. But I'm glad we came here. I like it here."

"I like it here too." I squeeze her hand.

"I keep thinking... will everyone still be talking about Mom leaving? Like, when I go back to school?"

"I don't know. I wish I could say they won't be, but I just don't know."

"Why did she leave?"

The question crushes me like a ton of bricks and I choke on the silence that ensues. I don't know how to answer. She hasn't asked the question that directly before. After Talia left, we talked about how she was gone, that she wasn't going to come back, but I think the shock overtook a lot of the deeper, more painful questions. Then we came here and we've kind of lived in la-la land ever since.

"I think—" I swallow thickly. My heart is in my throat. "She decided she wanted a life that looked different than ours. She couldn't see how incredible the life we had was and chose to go after something else. It was selfish, and I'm sorry. I wish I could've made her stay—for you, for us." I wrap my arm around her, her snowsuit sliding across the leather seat as I pull her close. "I will *always* stay. I will always be here. I'm not going anywhere," I promise, praying I can be enough for her.

She nods but doesn't speak. The chair nears the top of the hill, signaling it's our turn to get off. We don't fall, so that's something. We're standing at the precipice of the mountain once again, looking down at the place we've called home for six weeks.

"I wish we could stay," she says, breaking the silence, and then she takes off down the hill.

"Me too," I mutter. "Me too." Then I take off after her, my mind moving faster than we are, trying to figure out how I can make that wish come true for both of us.

CHAPTER TWENTY-FOUR

RORY

I tap on my steering wheel as I stare down the red light. Driving to have dinner with my parents is the last thing I want to be doing tonight. But it's Sunday night, and seeing as I skipped out on dinner last week—and forgot to call and cancel—there's no escaping it this week.

I've been summoned—to Dad's house, no less—which feels ominous somehow. We usually meet at a restaurant because they can never agree on whose house to eat at if we try for a home-cooked meal. Not that I'm expecting anything. Mom barely cooked when we were kids, and I've never seen Dad lift a finger in the kitchen.

As I pull up to Dad's A-frame house, the gravel crunches under my Subaru's tires even through the layer of snow. I don't want to leave the comfort of my car, but I'm here now, so I might as well get this over with. I watch each step I take over the slick ground, ignoring the anxiety building in my veins.

I want to be holed up in a little condo drinking hot chocolate through a cookie straw, watching kid movies on the couch with Willow and getting lost in Breck's arms when the lights go out. They leave on Friday, and this dinner is taking me away from one of my last nights with them.

My gloved finger barely brushes the doorbell before the door swings open. Mom stands on the other side, looking me over with irritation in her eyes. *Oh good, it's going to be one of those nights.* At least I won't have to wait out their small talk before we get to the disappointment part of the evening.

"Come in," she says and turns on her heeled foot. Did it just drop fifteen degrees in here?

"Good evening to you too," I mutter under my breath, sliding off my boots.

The smell as I move through the lavish house alleviates a little bit of tension in my shoulders. Scents of curry, spices, and coconut milk make my mouth water. The aromatic dishes sit on the long oak table and, just as I open my mouth to compliment the food choice, my dad's voice cracks through the room like a whip.

"Sit, Rory." Deep blue eyes, identical to Wes's but with none of the warmth, bore into me. They're cold as ice and my body freezes under their stare. I don't even know what I'm in trouble for, but it's clear that I am, and I feel ten years old again.

I duck my chin and move to my seat, awaiting the hammer that's poised to fall as soon as Mom takes hers across from me.

"Anything we should know, Rory?" he questions, eyes narrowing. He sits stick-straight; shoulders tense around his ears.

Shit. Do they know about me and Breck? No, that can't be right. I shake my head, the confusion clear on my face. Dad's features harden and Mom's face holds nothing but disappointment.

"What's going on?" I ask, worrying my thumb between my teeth.

"What's going on?" Dad condescends. "I'd love for you to answer that question. I'd love for you to own up to what you were doing last week when you didn't show up for dinner."

"I... I told you I wasn't feeling well," I stammer. I've never been good at lying.

Mom scoffs and Dad slams his hand on the table beside his plate, rattling the silverware and glasses.

"You're really going to pretend you weren't too busy with another elopement to show up for your obligations? Too busy dragging Wes's friend into your nonsense?"

My mouth pops open. Their knowing shouldn't surprise me, but somehow it does. And their referring to Breck as "Wes's friend" stings too. He's my friend—maybe a little more than a friend—and yeah, spending time with him felt more important than dinner last week.

My mom sees the realization as it dawns and purses her lips with a nod. "You really thought we wouldn't find out you've been taking on more of these photography projects? It wasn't just the one for Jamie's friend and then your brother's. We know about all the others. You think we don't know what you do? Like we'd let our daughter run amok and tarnish our family name in this community."

"But I—how?" I can't form words. I don't understand.

I avoid Mom's eyes, glancing at Dad instead, and the look in his gaze crushes me. I've strived not to disappoint my parents for years and here I am, a bigger disappointment than ever. I can almost feel it radiating off them.

"Does it really matter how we found out?" he says, and his voice is tired, strained. "But if you must know, I met Logan for lunch this week and he mentioned how impressed he was with the photos from your elopement last Sunday. That your photography just gets better and better with *each one*. He told me how proud he was to have you working at the resort with talent like yours."

Normal parents might've beamed with pride... but to them, to learn from my boss that I'm doing something they expressly disapprove of... It's more like a betrayal.

"I was just—"

"You were just what? Trying to embarrass us? Trying to do more than you're capable of? Do you have any idea how likely you are to fail?" Each of Dad's words cut me to the quick. "What's your plan? Abandon your real job for this stupid whim and then come crying to us to bail you out when it falls apart?"

Stupid. That's what this whole thing has been. Stupid for even entertaining the idea that I could do this somehow. Stupid for letting Breck make me dream of something bigger and letting myself get so caught up in him, in them, in a man who won't be here in a week and my life will implode around me the moment he leaves.

"No, I—"

"Don't forget we already support you. We've allowed you to live rent-free because you held down a steady job—maybe not the one we wanted for you, but still, a steady job." Mom's voice drips with disdain. "You were a good investment for that property. If you become a risky investment, we might have to reconsider."

"What? Are you threatening to kick me out?" My lip quivers and I bite down on it. I can't cry. If I cry, it'll be one more weakness for them to look down on. I close my eyes and will the tears to absorb back into my tear ducts. That condo has been my home for over four years. I can't imagine living anywhere else.

"I—where would I go?"

"The correct response should be 'I'm sorry, it won't be a problem again,' because like you said, where would you go?" my mom says with as much fierce resolve as I've ever heard in her voice.

My tears finally get the better of me, one slipping free as I look at my dad. There's nothing but stoic dissatisfaction there. I can't stay here, no matter the heavenly smells wafting around us. I have to leave before they see me weaken any further. I slide my chair out and walk away. They don't follow. I yank the door open, not even bothering to zip my boots up when I slip them on.

As I walk out, I hear my mother's voice behind me. "We expect an apology and your word that this business is over by the end of the day tomorrow, or we move forward with the eviction."

I close the door behind me and the tears fall in earnest my whole drive home.

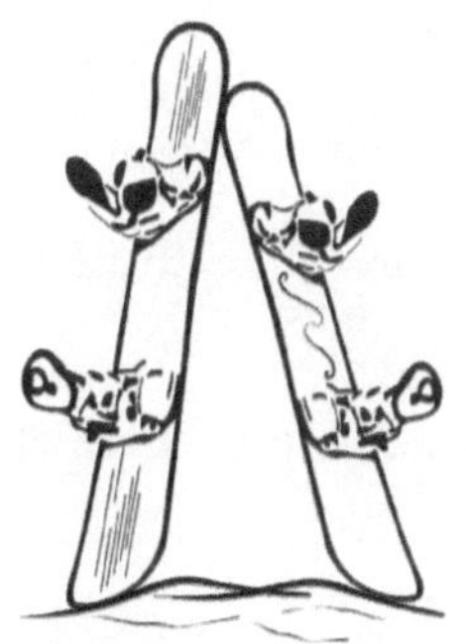

CHAPTER TWENTY-FIVE

BRECK

A knock on the front door startles me out of my TV stupor. I'm not even sure what's on at this point. I was zoned out, in my head about the plans I want to put into motion starting tomorrow. I jump up from the couch and glance toward the clock on the microwave in the kitchen. Eight thirty. Who...?

The river rock floor is cold under my feet when I pull the door open. The sight of Rory chewing her thumbnail, looking up at me with red-rimmed eyes from under her long lashes, is a shock.

"Rory? Bloody hell, what's going on?" I reach out and pull her into the warmth of the house, encasing her in my arms, my hand finding her face to wipe a stray tear that tracks down her cheek.

She sniffles and presses her forehead into my chest. She says something, but it's muffled and watery through her tears. "What was that?"

"My parents—" she whimpers. "They're threatening to... kick me out."

I push her back to an arm's length away. I need to see her face, need to see her.

"You've got to be kidding me," I growl out, but then rein in my anger. "Why?"

"They know about the elopements." She hiccups. "They said they only let me have the condo because I'm a good investment, but if that isn't the case anymore, they won't let me stay there."

I close my eyes and will the red filling my vision to subside. They called her a fucking *investment*?

"Baby..." The endearment slips from my lips, but it doesn't feel wrong. If anything it feels right. I let it sit between us while I reach again for her face to wipe yet another tear. "Come on, let's sit and you can tell me what happened."

I lead her to the couch, pull her down next to me, and wrap my arm around her shoulders.

"Okay, start at the beginning."

"I forgot to call them last week when we got back from the elopement, so when I texted them the next day, I told them I wasn't feeling well."

"I'm sorry, I shouldn't have pressured you to have dinner with us. I—" I press my forehead against hers, hating that I played a part in this mess.

"No, I wanted to be here. That's what's so frustrating. I did exactly what I wanted to do, and I got burned for it." She sounds defeated. "And then my dad had lunch with my boss this week and he brought up the elopements."

"Asshole," I mutter.

"No, it's not Logan's fault. He doesn't know my parents are—well, the way they are. I'm sure he assumed my parents knew and supported me." She slumps against me, like the weight of that hurt on her shoulders is crushing her.

"I'm sorry, Rory. I'm so sorry. How can I help, what do you need?"

"I don't know. The condo's been my home for years and I don't know where I'd go without it." I nod, hearing the pain in her voice. "So I need to cancel the elopements I have booked over the next few months and—"

"What? Why?"

She pulls away, breaking our connection as she slides back on the couch. "Didn't you hear me? They know, and me staying in the condo is dependent on not doing them anymore."

"But Rory—"

"No. It was stupid. I don't know what I was thinking. It was a pipe dream, Breck." She wraps her arms around her knees, hugging them to her chest.

"You don't believe that."

"I don't think it really matters what I believe. I won't have a place to live if I don't quit. Do you know what it would cost for me to find somewhere else to live this close to the mountain? My parents aren't playing around. If they say they'll kick me out, they will."

"What if you did?" I ask tentatively. "Have someplace else to live, I mean." I was going to tell her about my plan tomorrow anyway. I don't have all the details worked out yet, but I'm not going to change my mind.

She raises both brows. "Like where?"

"Okay, hear me out. I've been looking for a new rental the last two days. I'm not ready to go home yet, and neither is Willow. Your parents said this place is rented after we leave, and also... they're assholes." She almost smiles. "What if you come with us? I can find a place with three bedrooms. You could leave their condo on your terms, make your own decision about what you want to do about the business and your current job."

"But that's a short-term solution, Breck. You'll go home eventually. It's not like I can bounce from rental to rental with you forever."

"You're right, it is short term, but it would buy you until the end of February. A little over a month to figure out a plan, find a place of your own. I can help you. I need something to focus on if I'm going to put Adventure Chasers behind me for good, and helping you set up Adventure Elopements could be that thing. If you want it to be. I won't pressure you, but I don't want to see you give up."

She chews her lip, thinking, eyes flitting around the room. "Adventure Elopements?" She smiles, just the smallest lift to her lips. "Sounds a lot like Adventure Chasers."

"I was just trying it out. You're going to need a name one way or another, and it can be whatever you want." I shift to close the distance between us and ask, "Do you really believe they'll kick you out?" She nods. "Do you want to quit? Do you want to let Rory's Elopements go?"

She shakes her head but also chuckles. My little "name the business" game is helping.

"Then we figure it out. We have an opportunity to help each other here, Rory." Our eyes clash and I see the wheels turning, her brain working to see every angle of this option. It's not ideal, I know that, but if quitting isn't what she wants, then I'll be damned if she does it because her parents told her to.

"What if they hate me?" she whispers, the words barely audible as her head lolls back on the arm of the couch.

"They won't hate you, Rory. They might not like your decision, but they'll eventually see that they're wrong. You can do this. Then it'll be up to you if you want to forgive them for not believing in you."

She lifts her head and looks me straight in the eye. "Do you believe in me?"

The question hits like a tornado, creating a swirl of emotions in the center of my being. "I believe in you, one hundred percent."

Her eyes water and her lip trembles.

"Why does that make you sad?"

"Because it's rare that anyone does."

"You know that's not true. Wes believes in you. He'd be ripping your parents a new one if he was here right now."

"But he isn't," she says, and though she tries to hide it, there's hurt in her voice. "I know he can't be. I wouldn't want anything different for him, but I feel his absence like it's a physical thing."

"I know, and I get that. But you have Jamie too. He's doing what he can to help you here. He's agreed to officiate the elopements you already have booked, right?"

"I know. I guess I'm just so used to their support. They feel like anchors that are always there, but someone else believing in me... I haven't had that in a long time."

"Well, I can't imagine why; you're easy to believe in. You're not just 'trying' to do this, you *are* doing it. You've already got, what? Four more elopements scheduled for February and March? These are all word-of-mouth recommendations. You aren't even advertising Elope to Tahoe yet." She smiles again and I smile back, reaching to grab her hand. "This isn't a pipe dream. It's your passion. I can see it every time you pick up your camera. Your clients see that too, and they're bringing their dreams of getting married here to you. You can't walk away from this."

"What if I fail? What if I throw away the life I have now and I fail?"

"You won't."

"But what if I do?"

"Then you'll figure it out. Do you think I haven't spent some part of every day for the last two months wondering how I failed so epically that I no longer have either my business or the family I always envisioned?"

"Breck, I—no, you didn't..."

"Believe me, those things *feel* like failures. I might've sold the company and made a profit... but to be without it, to have nothing left of the legacy I thought I was building..." I scratch at my jaw. "To have poured everything I had into a nine-year relationship with a woman I thought I'd be with forever, only to have her walk away without a second glance? Yeah, that feels like failing."

She's so quiet. I wonder if I've said too much, but I can't seem to stop. "You know what, though? I'm learning that *I* am not that business, and I wasn't just a partner to Talia. Those two things didn't define me then, and they don't define me now. Adventure Chasers lives on, maybe not with my name attached to it, but I built it, and that sale has given me the means to build something else, maybe something better.

"Even if you fail at Runaway Elopements—which you won't, I won't let you—it will not make you a failure. It'll be something that you build on, create around, grow from. So long as you're fighting to move forward, you'll never be a failure. Never."

Her turquoise eyes haven't left my face for a second, and I've watched every word hit their mark. They're hitting their mark for me too. Even though I'm saying these things about myself, it's the first time I'm fully and completely understanding just how far I've come in the last couple of months.

"Please, Rory. Let me help you."

She smiles. "We can build Willow Tree Elopements together?"

"Willow Tree Elopements?" Tears prick my eyes, each word said with awe.

She nods. "I've been thinking about names since we talked about expanding this into a real business. Did you know that willows represent strength and resilience, vitality and new life? It seems fitting, doesn't it?"

It's my turn to nod. I can't speak, too choked up that Rory would consider naming her business after the most important person in my life.

"She's going to be okay, Breck." She wipes a tear from my cheek and I lean into the touch. She's right. Willow will be okay, and Rory will be too.

CHAPTER TWENTY-SIX

BRECK

I stand in the middle of a condo, its panoramic windows lining the back wall and showcasing the imposing Sierra Nevada mountains beyond. Our last condo was comfortably spacious, but this one, this one is something else. I might be splurging a little, especially considering I'm no longer getting the friends and family discount from Rory and Wes's parents, but screw them. I'll happily pay a bit more to distance myself and Rory from their control.

Then there's the—

"Daddy, can I go in the hot tub?" Willow asks as she slides up next to me, *Risky Business*-style, with socks on her feet and a swimsuit on. I give her a once-over and laughter bubbles out of me, my shoulders shaking with it.

"That is quite the look, Bear."

She huffs likes she's seventeen, jutting her chin up, and ignores my comment. The hot tub she's pointing to is roomy enough for at least six people, and we are only three.

Three.

My brain's been gnawing on the idea of Rory moving in with us since I began my search in earnest on Monday morning. By some twist of fate, this brand-new listing popped up and I immediately booked it for the next five weeks.

"Let me help you get the cover off." I slide my bare feet into my boots, not bothering to tie them or to grab a jacket. The frigid air hits my lungs when we step out, and I make quick work of the cover, checking the temperature isn't too hot for Willow, and leave her to it. She seems content to sit with her arms crossed on the ledge, chin resting there, watching the skiers and snowboarders make their descent down the snowy slopes.

I'd happily watch her stare up at the mountain all day, but the doorbell rings. "Holler if you need me, okay?" I shout over my shoulder as I close the door, leaving a slight crack so I'll be able to hear her.

I swing open the light blue door to find Rory with two suitcases behind her.

"We have to stop meeting this way," I quip.

"What way would that be? At doors?" The pink of her cheeks matches the pink of her lips—lips that part in a smile when she looks at me.

There's extra tension in this particular doorway. We've been crossing boundaries with each other for a while now, but this one feels different.

"Come on in." I step aside, grabbing her larger suitcase, and lead her down the hall toward her room. "Is this all you have? Do you need help getting anything else from your car?"

"This is it. Well, and a few boxes, but Jamie took those to his place for now. It's kind of sad to think I lived in that house for four years and this is all I'm walking away with, you know?"

"The furniture?" I ask.

She shakes her head. "It's all theirs. The condo was furnished as a vacation rental when I moved in."

"And Jamie's okay storing your stuff? There's space here."

"It's fine. It's only a month. He even offered me a room if I can't find something of my own before you leave..." She trails off.

"We'll find you something." I'm glad she has a backup option, but she deserves to finally have somewhere she can call her own.

"Where's Willow?" she asks.

"In the hot tub. There was no stopping her from changing into her suit the minute we got here."

"I can't say I blame her."

A vivid picture of Rory in a bikini pops into my mind unbidden, and I have to physically shake the thought away. That's not going to make this living situation easier. This is what's been constantly on my mind for the last few days. How do we maneuver around our physical relationship while also living in the same house? It shouldn't be all that different from the sneaking around we were doing before, when Willow was asleep, but we cannot let those lines blur in front of her.

"Mm-hmm," I hum under my breath, trying and failing to come up with the best possible way to bring this up.

"Breck?" Rory says from the doorway of her room. It's the only one downstairs. Mine and Willow's are both upstairs.

"Yeah?" I ask.

Her head is tilted to the side, like she's studying me. "You're overthinking again, aren't you?" She gives me a knowing smile, and I snort a laugh.

"Yup."

"I know this changes things. Me living here with you and Willow complicates the..." She hesitates. "The friends with benefits situation we had going. It's probably not a good idea for that to continue now, right?"

"Right." I nod, wishing it wasn't true, but this new situation is tenuous as it is. I've already spent almost a month hooking up with my best friend's sister. Now I'm living with her, and something in combining those two things feels like it's too much, too far. "Have you told Wes? About this?" I swipe one hand out to encompass the condo and squeeze the back of my neck with the other.

Her gaze drops to her feet and she shakes her head.

"Me neither. Why don't we call him in a bit?" Her shoulders sag. "How did it go with your parents, by the way?"

I tense, waiting for her answer.

"I still haven't talked to them. I called their office Monday and left a voicemail saying I'd be out of the condo by this afternoon. I never got a response. I figured they'd make contact today, but nope." She drags her toes across the carpet and watches the way the color changes as she does.

"It's their loss, Rory. They'll realize that eventually." I leave her suitcase by the bed, listening for any sound in the house to indicate that Willow's coming back inside. I brush my hand up her arm, past her shoulder, until it reaches her neck. "I'm proud of you. Wes would be too if he could see you."

I brush my thumb over her lips and feel her body shiver against mine. "What do you say? One more kiss?"

When she presses onto her toes, our lips meet. It's soft and languid, unhurried—even though Willow could walk into the house at any second. As seconds fuse into a minute, then two, the way our lips move together becomes more insistent.

My tongue glides against hers, one hand fisting in her hair while the other slides to her ass and pulls her hard against me. If this is our last kiss, I'm going to make it count. She meets me stroke for stroke with her tongue, her teeth, her body as it moves against mine. There's something in the way we are together. It's like the sun, burning so bright, but also dangerous if you look too long. Kissing Rory leaves me with sunspots in my vision, in my mind, for hours... and every time it only lasts longer.

I break the kiss, my breathing ragged and my heart slamming like a drum against my ribs. Rory is just as affected. I love it and I hate it. I feel like a million bucks knowing I can make her lose control like this, but I also know I have no control with her either.

"Dad!" The shout echoes down the hall and I startle back. Rory does as well, tripping over the suitcase behind her and falling flat on her ass in the hallway.

"Shit," I say, lunging for her.

"I heard that," Willow bellows.

"Yeah, yeah," I grumble. "We'll be right there."

"Rory's here?" Willow's voice brightens and Rory's face does the same.

"I'm here, but I fell and need a second to get back up." Rory hollers back to her.

"Okay, I'm going to go take a shower," Willow yells, followed by the wet slap of her feet on the floor as she heads for the stairs.

I hold back from hauling Rory into my arms again when I pull her up, but her hand lingers in mine a second longer than necessary. Then she smiles and leaves me standing there in a daze. I take a minute to move her suitcases to the far side of the room, then I take a deep breath and resolve to figure out this whole roommate situation.

Rule number one is no more kissing.

When I hear Wes's voice coming from Rory's phone a few moments later, my determination to stop sleeping with his sister only solidifies.

"Where are you, baby sister?" he says as I walk into the living room.

She glances over her shoulder toward me. I'm not in the frame yet, so I shoot her a wink and a blush stains her cheeks—I did not kiss her just now like she was *anyone's* baby sister.

"Well, uh..." She flounders.

Not one to beat around the bush, I move so he can see me too and jump straight to it. "This is our new place. You know how Willow and I extended our trip...?" Wes nods, still looking confused. "Well, Rory's going to be staying with us."

Wes's eyes bulge, and he opens and closes his mouth a couple times.

"But why?" Joss's voice comes from the background before she moves into the frame.

"I—" Rory tries again. "I needed to move out of the condo. Until I can find somewhere on my own, Breck offered for me to stay with him and Willow."

I'm leaning over her slightly, my elbows on the back of the couch, just out of reach of her shoulders. If I lean forward any farther my chin will be resting on her head. That position would feel natural *if* we weren't on the phone with her brother, or if we weren't trying to keep our physical relationship in check.

Wes's eyes lift from Rory to me and then flit back to her. "What happened with the condo?"

Rory tilts her head back and I give her an affirming nod when our eyes meet. She needs to tell him.

"Rory, seriously, what's going on?"

"Mom and Dad were going to kick me out, so I left." She lifts a shoulder, letting the sentence slide off her with feigned nonchalance.

"They *what*? You—but what happened?" Wes's face grows red and his brows pull down in the middle like confusion and anger and uncertainty are manifesting all at once. Joss squeezes in next to him, a similar look of concern etched across her brow.

"Breck and I—"

A coolness I've rarely heard in Wes's voice fills the space. "You and Breck what?" His eyes are moving between the two of us at a rapid rate. Can he read in our body language what's been happening here?

I see her roll her eyes through the screen and she continues with more confidence. "Oh, stop it, Wes. For god's sake. Breck and I did that elopement, the one I sent the pictures from. He wants to help me get going with a business of my own. Mom and Dad don't want me doing anything of the sort. They gave me an ultimatum and I called their bluff."

"Wait, what? Why didn't you tell me about any of this? How long has this been going on?"

Again, the question seems to address things Wes doesn't even realize. A hint of guilt niggles my gut.

"What would you have done? You're not here to handle them. You don't understand what they're like with me. How they've *always* been with me. You never have."

"Rory." His voice softens and there's sadness in his eyes.

"No, it's fine." She waves a hand, dismissing whatever he wanted to say. "But working toward this with Breck is the most fulfilled I've felt in a long time. Maybe ever. I don't—I don't want to give that up."

She's come so far in the last few days. I smile broadly, hoping she can sense the pride I have for her in this moment.

"Okay, but what about your job with the resort? What are you going to do when Breck comes back here?"

"Oh, for fuck's sake, Wes," I say, and he startles back from the phone at my tone. "Sorry, mate. It's just that she's not a kid. She's not quitting her job... at least not as far as she's said, and obviously she knows this is temporary, but it's better than the alternative. You know how talented she is. Are you really telling me she should've given up on her dream because your parents were trying to bully her?"

"No—I—that isn't what I'm saying. I'm just trying to process." He runs a hand through his hair and heaves a sigh. "I'm sorry. I didn't mean to imply you don't know what you're doing. I just want what's best for you, and this is a lot of change at once."

"I'm okay, really. Or I will be. I'll be using this time to find a place of my own for when Breck and Willow leave, but for the next month, I'm going to take advantage of his"—she shoots me a wink over her shoulder—"business brain to get this thing up and running. I'll figure out the rest as I go."

"Okay." He still sounds a little skeptical, but he doesn't push any more. "If you need anything, you'll tell me, right? I don't like that I've been in the dark." His eyes fall and he sounds a little wounded. "You're supposed to tell me this stuff."

"I know," she says, her voice low. "But you just—you haven't been here. I know that's not fair. But it's hard to explain it all when you're not here to see it." She glances at me again. So does her brother, and I think he sees it. There's something sad in his features when he looks away from me and back to his sister. The sister who's been coming to me instead of him for the last month.

CHAPTER TWENTY-SEVEN

Rory

I pull my laces tight, tying them around the tops of my ice skates, then slip the lens cap off my camera and snap some pictures of the rink that sits in the middle of the Empyreal Resort village. Strings of Edison bulbs crisscross above me, casting an amber glow on the shiny ice. Fire pits and Adirondack chairs surround the entirety of the rink for merry-watchers and parents to relax while the skaters move and glide along the ice... or slip and fall.

Breck sidles up close to me at the railing, his solid shoulder pressing against mine. My body responds by leaning into him, even though it shouldn't. It can't... not with Willow standing just on his other side. His features are illuminated under the lights, the golden hues in his hair sparking brighter. When a long strand falls in front of his face, I push my hands deep into my pockets to keep from brushing it back.

"Ready?" he asks. Willow stands next to him in a pair of white figure skates that match mine and stand out in contrast to his black hockey skates.

"Yup, let's go."

He reaches for Willow's hand and they walk stiffly on their skates to the opening of the rink. A few skaters have started cutting large ovals around the ice while others cling to the boards, their feet splaying about like baby deer learning to walk. Willow balances precariously on her blades, squeezing the life out of her dad's hand, but you'd never know from the easy smile on his face.

We made it through our first weekend in the new place as roommates, so tonight we're celebrating with this little excursion to the skating rink. We're also celebrating Breck's new job title—as homeschool dad. He spent much of the past week on the phone with Willow's school back in Sydney, working out the best way for her to study remotely for the next month. He'll be working off the same curriculum, keeping pace with her class, to ensure she's where she needs to be when they get home.

I maneuver around them and turn to skate backward. "So, Bug, are you excited to start school next week?"

"I can't wait. I get to do school in my pjs every day!"

I chuckle, understanding her glee.

"What about you?" I ask Breck, whose posture is relaxed as he glides along.

"Being a teacher will be a new challenge for me. At least it'll keep me busy though, and we can take snowboarding breaks, right,

Willow Bear?" She nods up at him, a big dimpled grin on her face. Her eyes shine with love for her dad.

"It's like PE, but *better*," I chime in and Willow giggles, melodic and sweet.

"Just like ice skating," he says, taking in the rink that is growing busier by the minute.

I lift my camera and the snick of the shutter draws their attention, allowing me to capture their matching smiles. I also capture their crash. Willow leans back too far, pulling them both onto their butts. I let my camera fall into its strap around my neck and surge forward. There's nothing but the sound of laughter—boisterous and joyful—coming from where they're sprawled.

"You know? I was just thinking you're a natural at everything, but maybe I was wrong," I joke, needling Breck, who grins back at me. He rights himself quickly, then we each grab a hand to get Willow standing again, and neither of us lets go as we resume a slow pace around the rink.

"It's not my first time on skates," Breck says, "but it has been a while."

"When did you go ice-skating Daddy?" Willow asks—always full of questions.

"I used to go every winter when I was your age."

"With Grandma and Grandpa?" Breck's face softens at her question. He's mentioned them a few times, usually in reference to learning to snowboard. I know they passed in a car accident when he was young, but not much else. I like that even though Willow never got to meet them, she still knows who they are.

"Yeah, Willow Bear, with Grandma and Grandpa. Then I went with my aunt and uncle when they took me to the mountains, but it was much less frequent. I think the last time I was on the ice was in college. I went on a date to a local skating rink."

"With Mommy?" Willow asks. It's a casual comment, but her face falls a fraction. The moment stands still, and I wonder how best to disappear into the background. It's a question she likely would've asked with ease a couple months ago, but there's a quiet wetness gathering in her eyes now.

Breck shakes his head and clears his throat. "No, uh—no, it wasn't."

"Sorry, Daddy." Willow's voice quavers. I want to give them a minute, but I'm afraid she'll fall if I let go of her hand.

"It's okay, sweetheart. You didn't do anything wrong."

"I don't like talking about her anymore."

Ugh. This kid is breaking my heart.

"That's fine, but you can if you want to. Or need to."

"But you don't like to talk about her either." He recoils as if she physically hit him with those words. It's true. I've heard him mention Talia less than a handful of times since he's been here.

"I don't, you're right, but that doesn't mean we can't. I'm sorry I haven't given you a way to do that. I'll do better, okay?"

She nods and pulls her hand free from mine, swiping it under her eyes.

"You know," I say, grabbing Willow's hand again and squeezing it to bring her attention to me. "I have another elopement booked for this weekend, and I need you to be my assistant again... if your dad's alright with it?"

Her sadness morphs into something brighter, and a quick glance at Breck shows relief in his features at the change in subject. He mouths a silent *thank you* and I offer him a brief nod in return.

"Do you need me to officiate this one?" he asks.

"Jamie was on board when we booked it, but since you're here, I'm sure he'd be fine with you doing it."

Breck nods. "I'm happy to help." There's more meaning behind the words than his offer to officiate another wedding. He wants to help me make this—Willow Tree Elopements—a reality, but I'm scared. It still feels like a dream, one I've wanted for so long but never dared to believe would come true.

We tug Willow around the rink while I tell her where we'll be going for the next shoot, what I know about the bride and groom, and what kinds of pictures we might take. She fires back questions and throws out suggestions like she's a pro.

We finish off the night with dinner at Base Camp Pizza Co., followed by a brisk walk home. Breck carries Willow on his back—her little legs too tired after a solid hour of skating. Her head rests on his far shoulder, her eyes heavy and her breathing slowly evening out. I admire her ability to fall asleep like this, and I admire his ability to carry her for this long.

We walk in companionable silence, but somewhere along the way, Breck's fingers brush mine. First, it's just our pinkies, then slowly his gloved fingers twine through mine. His firm hold sends an electric current up my arm, and despite the chill, my whole body feels warm. I want to melt into him, let him wrap an arm around me and hold me close, but we can't do that. So we finish our walk, hand in hand, and even though I probably should, I don't pull away.

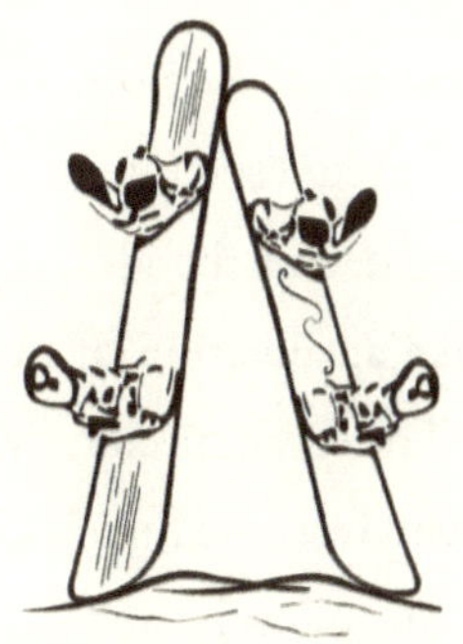

CHAPTER TWENTY-EIGHT

BRECK

I'm staring out the wall of windows, across the deck, up to the darkened mountains beyond. Snowflakes fall, coating everything in a soft blanket of white. I'm the only one awake, and the silence around me is barely a match for the volume of my thoughts. After hours of restlessness, I finally gave up on sleep and have been sitting here ever since. Staring at nothing and contemplating everything.

For the past two months in Tahoe, it's felt like Willow and I have been on vacation from our real lives. This week has been a bit of a wake-up call, but even the dose of reality that comes with Willow starting school tomorrow has nothing on the email sitting in my inbox. The one that arrived just before I went to bed last night.

It's the proverbial pin that has obliterated the cocoon of perceived normalcy we've been basking in.

The new owners of Adventure Chasers are asking for a video call with me, Talia, and Drew to go over some logistical issues they're having. On the surface, the request is innocuous: new owners asking previous owners for insight. But the idea of getting on a call with Talia and Drew feels like an invasion of the safe space I've been building since they left. The email specifically asks for all three of us to be available, and I have to assume there's a reason for that.

It's hard enough to think of my business in the hands of someone else, but to have to deal with Talia and Drew seems insurmountable. Adventure Chasers was *my* baby. I wanted to work with people, offer them the best experiences Sydney had to offer, and participate in those adventures with them every day. I never wanted to sell. In fact, when the offer came in, I said no on the spot. I wasn't interested in the slightest. It was Talia and Drew who pushed me to consider it.

I didn't understand why they'd want to sell and start over, have to find new jobs when the one we had was perfect. Apparently, it was only perfect for me. Apparently, they'd been waiting for just such an opportunity to get out, leave, and never look back.

The sun illuminates the slopes outside in slow increments as my cup of tea grows colder in my hand. A new day dawning. One I've been looking forward to for weeks.

Of course this email would come on the eve of Willow's birthday, and bring with it the rain cloud of the past that I've been avoiding. A reminder that the future I saw for myself is forever changed. A future I saw in vivid clarity on a Tuesday in June almost nine years ago.

My knuckles have barely lifted from the door when it flies open and, before I even have a moment to process, a white stick is thrust into my hands. I take it and Talia turns her back on me, walking away, while I study it. The stick shows two pink lines.

Pregnant.

Talia is pregnant.

I drag my eyes to the woman sitting on her living room floor, head in her hands. A sheet of dark hair falls across her face, shoulders shaking, and her muffled cries pull me toward her.

This was not what I expected when she called me over here today. If I'm honest, I thought she was ending things. Instead, this feels like a cementing of things. I look back to the stick, and even though I'm absolutely fucking terrified, there's a jolt in my system too. I'm going to be a dad.

There's a lot happening in my head, in my heart, in my gut right now. The emotions are threatening to overwhelm me, like they're doing to Talia, but I need to be the one to hold her up now. I can be that guy for her. Maybe I can even be as good at this as my father was. That's the goal. From this moment on, that's the goal.

"Talia?" I gentle my voice.

She looks up from her hands, her eyes puffy and swollen. I lower myself next to her, draping an arm around her shoulders.

"It's going to be okay. I promise. We've got this, yeah?" I kiss her head, but she jerks away.

"How will this be okay, Breck? I'm—" She breaks off on a sob. "Pregnant." She forces the word from her lips.

"I know, Tal, I know. This wasn't the plan, but I'm here. We will figure it out together."

"You're... you're not mad?" Her lip quivers.

"Mad? No, Talia, I'm not mad. Honestly..." I let a smile grow on my face, pushing my dimples up my cheeks. "It might not be the timing I would've chosen, but I've always wanted to be a dad."

What crosses her face looks more like anguish than anything else. This is a much bigger shock for her than it is for me. I understand that. Everything she knows about her body is about to change unexpectedly, but I can be here in every way possible to make this easier for her.

"I don't... I didn't think I would ever be a mom." She looks away, and her admission feels like a punch.

Does she not want this? I mean, beyond the shock, beyond just being freaked out. Does she truly not want this at all? Not with me, not with anyone? My heart constricts in my chest.

"Talia... I know it's only been a few months, but I'm all in with you, with this baby, if you want me to be." I give her an imploring look and hope she sees that I'll support her. She won't ever have to do this alone. I know she didn't have a positive experience growing up with a single mom. She doesn't want that for her own life.

I hold her eyes, bring my lips to hers in a gentle kiss, and silently beg her to let me be there for her, for them. I beg her to let me in, to let me try.

When she pulls back, her eyes are tipped down, but there's a small smile on her lips. She nods, and that tiny movement lights me up from the inside out. My smile grows wider and I hug her to me. I whisper that I'll always be there for her, that she'll never have to do this life alone.

Eight months and thirty-six hours of active labor later, I think Talia just might want to kill me for this. We both know her getting pregnant wasn't completely my fault—turns out condoms really do break and birth control isn't as effective when you're on prescription antibiotics—but for the moment, she gets to blame me all she wants because she's the one pushing a tiny human out of her body.

She squeezes my hand so hard I wince, but I suffer in silence, rubbing her back as she pushes through another contraction. The doctors and nurses, the beeping and noise… it's overwhelming in this small space, but my sole focus is the woman in front of me who just made me a father.

The doctor lifts the crying, wiggling mess up so we can see her.

Her.

"It's a girl," he says, and I go weak at the knees.

Talia didn't want to find out the sex ahead of time and the suspense has been killing me. A girl. My cheeks hurt from the way my smile overtakes my face. I turn to Talia, who's slumped back against the bed in exhaustion, and I beam with pride.

"Want to do the honors, Dad?" The doctor holds out the scissors for me to cut the umbilical cord and I am the proudest dad there ever was. Dad. Tears form in my eyes as I wish mine could be here right now. I wish he could meet his granddaughter. The tears slip over with the snick of the scissors. The doctor quickly finishes what I started and hands our daughter to Talia. Her sleepy eyes take in the tiny creature in her arms and there's a small smile on her lips when she looks at me.

Rearranging the baby on her chest, she reaches for me and skims her thumb across my cheek, wiping a tear away. I can't stop them as I take her in. Sweat-slicked hair in a messy bun, no make-up, IV in her hand… but with our daughter in her arms, I've never loved her more or thought she was more beautiful. She's going to be an amazing mom.

"I love you." I lean in and kiss her forehead, lingering there for a moment. My fingers come to the tiny body in her arms, lightly tracking to wrap around an itty bitty foot. "I'm in awe of you, Talia. Look what you brought into the world." She glances down at the same moment I do and stares like she can't believe it either.

"Thank you for making me a father." I kiss her. This is it. This is my family. This is all I ever wanted. "Marry me."

She gasps against my lips and pulls back. It's not the first time I've asked, and I'm sure it won't be the last. I asked her the night she told me she was pregnant and she said no—said she wasn't ready. I've been persistent, asking her every month since, but she keeps telling me no. It's become a bit of a running joke.

"Thought it was worth a try."

She laughs and kisses me again. "It was a nice try, but the answer is still no." I know it's not her rejecting me. It's her rejecting the need to get married in order to be a family. Marriage just isn't important to her, and though it is to me, it isn't something that's worth fighting over. We're a family regardless, and a piece of paper or a ceremony isn't going to change that.

"Your turn." She adjusts the baby, and I quickly pull my T-shirt over my head so I can be skin to skin with her. The books all said it's important, and I'm nothing if not a perfect student. I take my baby girl in my arms and feel everything inside me melt. My heart no longer beats only in my chest but in her tiny one as well. A nurse hands me a swaddle to wrap around us, and I take it without once looking away from the bow of her lips or the button size of her little nose.

Sitting down in the rocking chair next to the bed, I tuck her more closely into my chest and place the blanket over us both. A hand fights *its way out and I reach for it. Her fingers wrap around one of mine and I know, without a doubt, that I'll never be the same.*

"You look pretty content over there." Talia's quiet voice pulls me out of the haze of baby love.

"Yeah. This is—" I clear my throat, the knot of emotion threatening to overwhelm me again.

"You ready to name her?" she asks.

We talked about names and settled on one for a boy and one for a girl so we'd be prepared at the birth. I won't lie and say that I wasn't hoping for a girl, and part of that was for the name we chose.

I track my eyes over my daughter's face. "Ten minutes in this world, Willow, and it's so much brighter because you're in it."

The scrambling of feet on hardwood floors brings me out of the memories just in time to brace myself before Willow crashes into me.

"Dad! I'm eight!" she exclaims.

"You sure are. And you know what?" I smile down at my beautiful girl.

"What, Daddy?" Anticipation shines in her eyes.

"Eight years in this world, Willow, and it's so much brighter because you're in it." She hugs me hard, and I hug her back. Words can't fix all the hurt of the last few months, but maybe these ones—that I say every year on her birthday—will remind her that she's my whole world and I'll always be here.

Rory helped me plan a little birthday celebration for Willow—just the three of us plus Jamie. He was invited at Willow's request, because she's absolutely harboring a girlhood crush on the redhaired Scotsman. Not sure how I feel about that, but I do like Jamie.

The doorbell rings and Rory runs to open it, finding the man himself standing there, arms filled with presents.

"He makes a good pack mule, don't you think?" She laughs lightly and it chimes with mirth.

"Ha-ha." He grunts. "Can I come inside now so I can set all this shi—stuff down."

"Good catch," I say. "Willow doesn't need any more funds in her swear jar."

"Swear jar?" Jamie grins.

"Yeah, man. How do you think I'm paying for this condo?" I help him with the bags and boxes, revealing his face to the room. As soon as Willow sees him, she starts running and I have to set down my stack of gifts and grab the rest from him so they won't topple to the floor when she collides with him.

My phone rings in my pocket and I take the moment when everyone's distracted to pull it free.

Talia's name flashes on the screen.

I didn't block her number because even with everything she did, she'll always be Willow's mom. There's a tearing and a swelling in my heart all at once. I hate her for calling right now, but I'm also glad in a way. Willow deserves a phone call today at the very least. Maybe Talia still has some love left in her for this little family she obliterated.

I swipe across the screen before I can think better of it. "Tal—" I say, lifting the phone to my ear. Every head in the room snaps to mine and there's barely masked hope behind watery blue eyes.

"Breck." Her voice feels like a physical blow, but I attempt a smile and remind myself I'd do anything for one more phone call from my own mom. "We got the email and thought we should coordinate the meeting."

Every bit of air in my lungs leaves me in a rush and I physically feel my face fall, along with my shoulders. I can't look at Willow. Turning my back on the prying eyes, I hurry up the stairs without a word.

"Breck?" she says again, but I'm not saying another word until I'm behind a closed door.

The moment I'm shut in my room, I whisper-hiss into the phone. "You're calling about the fucking meeting Talia. Today?" I should've never answered. I'm going to be the one picking up the pieces of this shitstorm yet again.

"Yes, what's wrong?" She's so fucking oblivious it makes me seethe.

"Over two months, Talia. Months without a word, and you pick today, of all fucking days, to call about a goddamn meeting. Do you care so little that you've already forgotten today is Willow's eighth birthday? She heard me answer the phone..." I scrub a hand across my eyes, trying to keep myself in check. "She thinks you called to talk to her. God*dammit.*"

"Her birthday was yesterday," Talia says matter-of-factly. I can almost picture her looking at her nails as if this bores her. "Or... where are you?"

Fuck. She's right. She doesn't know we're in Tahoe. Damn time change. The anger boils higher now though, because she didn't forget. She knew it was yesterday, and she still didn't call.

"How dare you, Talia. How fucking dare you. You know what? You and Drew"—I spit his name with as much venom as I can muster—"take the call with the new owners and tell them if they have specific questions for me then they can call me personally. Do not call me again. Do not reach out to me again. You didn't want us. You didn't want me. You didn't want her. Fine. But you don't get to call and disrupt the lives we're trying to rebuild in the wake of your departure. Fuck you, Talia."

I hang up the phone.

My breathing is labored, barely sucking air into my lungs. They feel tight and uncomfortable. I sit on the bed and put my head between my knees, trying to get the shaking in my hands to subside. What the fuck just happened? Wet tears track down my face, everything I said running a loop in my mind. I hope I made the right decision, but I can't have her calling whenever it's convenient for her and destroying the progress we make in between.

My head is heavy in my hands, the weight of the whole world on my shoulders. How do I go back downstairs and face Willow?

"Fuck." I push off the bed as the door swings open. Rory stands there, calm just covering the concern shining in her eyes.

My body moves without my brain weighing in. I pull her to me, closing the door and pinning her against it, and crash my lips over hers. It's a distraction that *I* need this time, and I take it without asking. We're not supposed to be doing this anymore, but she's not protesting. Pulling at my hair, she flips us around so I'm pressed against the door. She lifts on her toes, raking her body up along mine as she goes. I grip her hips and pull her closer.

The kiss slows and she pulls back, wiping a stray tear tracking down my cheek. "Are you okay?" I shrug and she continues. "That was Talia?"

I nod.

"She wasn't calling to talk to Willow I take it?"

I shake my head. "New owners of Adventure Chasers want a meeting. She was calling to set it up. Not a care in the world for it being Willow's birthday... which she thought was yesterday." The pain of that lances through me again and I hang my head on Rory's shoulder. "I told her not to contact us again. I can't even be sure whether that was the right thing to do. Why isn't there an instruction manual for how to navigate this situation? That's what I need. I need someone to tell me how to deal with this and come out on the other side unscathed. Can you do that?"

I look down at her, a plea in my eyes.

"I wish I could. I don't know if there is a way to escape this. Life never leaves us unscathed; it changes and molds us. But, I promise, you will get through this," she says and presses a light kiss to my lips.

"I'm sorry for just now. I got lost in the moment. I know we're not supposed—"

"I know. It's okay. We don't overthink what we do together, remember?" She gives me a sweet smile. "But right now, we need to figure out how to pull it together for Willow. Yeah?"

"Yeah..." I blow out my breath. "Did she... Did she say anything after I came upstairs?"

"She told Jamie she thought it was her mom on the phone."

I shake my head. *Her mom*. Talia doesn't deserve that title. Not anymore.

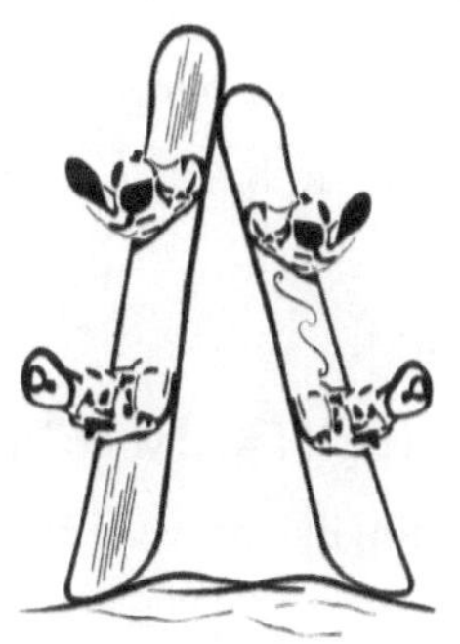

CHAPTER TWENTY-NINE

RORY

With one more quick kiss to his salty lips, I leave Breck so he can gather himself. Walking down the stairs, I prepare myself to distract Willow as best I can from the heartache that's sure to come.

"Who wants an early present?" I say, mustering my enthusiasm and catching Jamie's eye.

"How about the one I bought you?" he suggests, and Willow squeals, jumping up and down. His pile of presents included the ones from me and a couple that Wes and Joss mailed to him so Willow would be none the wiser.

She stops mid-jump to ask, "Shouldn't we wait for Dad?" A look of hope is barely disguised in her eyes.

"He won't mind if we open one little present without him," I say like I'm conspiring with her and Jamie in some evil plot.

"It's not a little present," Jamie says with a scoff. He walks over and pulls the largest one from the pile.

Willow's nearly salivating at the sight, weight bouncing from one foot to another.

"What is it? What is it?"

"Wouldn't it ruin the fun if I told you?" he asks, pulling her into his side. She looks up at him like he hung the moon.

"Can I open it?"

"You sure can," Breck says as he walks into the room. His megawatt smile is on full display. If I hadn't just wiped tear tracks from his face, I'd have no idea anything bad happened.

There's a slight pinch to Willow's brows when she sees he's no longer on the phone, but the desire for presents overpowers it. "Okay!" She grabs the package from Jamie and flops down on the floor, ripping in.

Paper discarded, she's met with a plain brown box, which she spins and examines before pulling out a large nylon bag. "It's purple! My favorite color," she says, looking at it with interest and a hint of confusion. First, her eyes travel to Jamie, then to me, and finally to my camera bag that sits by my feet.

"It looks like yours," she says, half questioning.

"Mm-hmm, and it goes with this." I pull a square package from the pile and hand it to her. She tears off the paper, scraps flying everywhere, and opens the cardboard flaps to reveal—

"A camera?" Her lips stretch into a wide smile, and I think it's the happiest I've ever seen her look.

"A very special camera," I say, my eyes feeling misty. "Wes gave me that camera when I started high school, and it was my constant companion for years after that. I got a new one several years ago, and this one looked just right in your hands at our photoshoots. I thought you should have it."

Breck is staring at me, his mouth slightly gaping despite his lips tilting up into a grin.

"Really? Like, for real?"

"Yeah, for real. It's all yours."

She shoots to her feet and almost chokes me out with a hug. "Thank you, thank you, thank you!"

"You're welcome, Bug. I know you'll take great care of it. I can't wait to see the pictures you take." I squeeze her tighter, my gaze tracking over her shoulder to Breck. I can't place the emotion in his features. The sadness from earlier is gone, replaced by something more tender, more powerful, almost overwhelming. It projects across the space between us, and if I released Willow, I think I could hold it in my hand. Maybe even bring it to my own heart and keep it there.

Willow pulls out of my embrace and looks at the camera in her hands. "Will you teach me how to use it? Like, really use it? All the buttons?"

"It'd be my pleasure."

"Daddy! Rory gave me her camera!"

"I see that. You'll have to take really good care of it."

"That's what the camera bag is for," Jamie pipes in, bringing everyone back together, and the attention back to his present. When

Willow invited him, he wasn't sure what to get the prodigious eight-year-old, so we coordinated.

"Thank you, Jamie!" Her hug for him is almost as big as mine was and he beams. "What's next?" she says, taking in the pile of presents with a sparkle in her eye. You've got to love the one-track mind of an eight-year-old. Especially when it fixates on anything other than the near-miss phone call with her mother that's sure to come to a head eventually.

To Breck's credit, he didn't let Talia's call taint a single second of the day. Not during dinner, not during cake, not during the FaceTime call with Wes. Not for even a breath was he anywhere but in the moment with Willow.

Now she's in bed, wrapped in her comforter and surrounded by all her gifts, when Breck falls into the couch cushions with an exhausted sigh. All the emotion he's been holding in escapes with that breath, tendrils of the strain permeating the space.

He sits reclined against the back of the couch, head tilted up, eyes closed, and I park myself on the coffee table in front of him, my knees just inside of where his sit splayed. What is it they call this? Manspreading? I won't lie, I kind of like it, especially with the black joggers he's sporting.

"Hey," I say, knocking his knee with my own. He lifts his head like it weighs a million pounds.

"Can't thank you enough for the camera," he says, and his eyes go soft. "It's too much, but I know you won't let me argue with you."

"I want her to have it. It was time for it to go to a new photographer. Maybe she'll fall in love with it like I did." I keep my knees pressed against his, liking the warmth where they connect. Wanting more of that warmth, I run my hands up his thighs. I'm pushing the roommate boundaries between us, but he blurred them first with that kiss today.

"I think she already has." He brightens and continues. "Hey, you just referred to yourself, at least sort of, as a photographer, so that's pretty awesome."

"I did, didn't I? Your influence must be rubbing off on me."

"You deserve that title."

I duck my head and blush at the praise. "Well, I don't know that I'd be making much progress without you."

"You would've, I just gave you a nudge." To drive the point home, he squeezes his knees around mine, trapping me in.

"Maybe so." I bite my bottom lip. "How're you doing?"

"I'm just so tired," he confesses, craning his head toward the ceiling once more.

"I know."

"I don't know how to do this, Rory. I don't know how to be both parents, to protect her from the hurt. I don't know how to make it alright while also giving her the space so she knows she doesn't have to be alright. I buried my grief for a really long time because it was uncomfortable for other people. I don't want that for her. I don't want any of this for her."

"I know. She knows that too." He lifts his head and his eyes bore into mine for a minute, absorbing the words. "She may only be eight, but she knows how much you love her and that you're working to make everything okay. She knows."

A subtle nod is all I get. I wish I knew how to comfort him, but I feel underqualified. A crinkling sound draws my attention to his hand, which is clutching a worn piece of paper.

"Whatcha got there?" I ask, and his grip tightens around it.

"Did Wes tell you about the day she left?" The firelight from behind me dances in his eyes.

"No." I shake my head. "He didn't think it was his story to share, so he just told me she left and wasn't coming back. That you guys needed to get away for a while. I—I never wanted to pry."

Another small nod and the crease between his eyebrows deepens. "I've been carrying this around since that day." He slides a finger up the creased side of the paper. It looks like it's been folded and unfolded, crumpled and smoothed out more times than I can imagine. "I don't really even know why. I think I did it at first because letting it go meant letting go of the future I'd envisioned for us. Then I think it became about holding on to the anger. I needed to feel something toward her that wasn't sadness. But I don't want to hold on to that now either."

Breck extends the paper to me. I'm afraid to touch it, but with one more squeeze to his leg, I finally reach for it. He offers me an encouraging smile and nods. He wants me to take it. He wants me to know. I offer him a small grin in return and bring my full attention to the paper, unfolding it with trembling fingers.

It's a letter. Loopy script flows over the whole page. Before even reading a word, I know who it's from.

Dear Breck,

I'm sorry. I know this will be a shock to you, but I'm leaving Sydney. With Drew. By the time you read this, we'll already be gone. I never wanted to be a mother. This wasn't the life I envisioned for myself, and I can't pretend any longer that it is. I couldn't be the partner you needed. The mother Willow needed. I'm not those things, and deep down I've always known it. With Drew, I can be who I've always wanted to be.

I know the only thing you're thinking about right now is Willow. That's why you're her dad, why you're so amazing in that role. You've always thought of her first. Always. It was never me you wanted, not truly. It was her. I know if anyone can get through this, it's you, and you'll help her get through it too.

In the manila envelope you'll find the legal release of my rights to Willow. I wanted a clean break so you could move on with your lives as easily as possible, just like I'm moving on with mine. There's a part of me that will always love you, and her, for the years we had together. But I'm going to put myself first now. I need this. I want a life with Drew.

I'd say I hope you'll understand, but I know you won't. I never should've carried on like this for so long. I wanted to be what you wanted so badly, but I never was and I'm tired of trying. I'm tired of hiding what Drew and I have. I hope someday you'll find someone to love, who loves you, in this way.

I know you'll never forgive me for this, but know I wish you nothing but the best in your future.

Talia

My exhale when I reach the end of the page is like a release valve on a pressure cooker. I lift my eyes from the paper in my lap, seeking Breck's, and I don't understand what I'm seeing. My shoulders have tensed over the last couple of minutes—but his have lowered, relaxed, like a weight's been lifted.

"This is—this is how she left?" My voice is calm, lethally so.

"Yeah. She left it on my desk at work while I was out with Wes one night. Willow was at a sleepover. I called her once, the day after, but she didn't answer. Today's the first time I've heard her voice since."

"I'm so sorry." I understand why this letter looks so worn. I want to crumple it up myself... throw it... stomp on it with muddy boots.

"It's okay."

"Breck—" *This is not okay.* He stops me with a hand over mine, steadying the shaking paper.

"What she did is *not* okay. I know that. But I am." I raise my eyebrows, and he smirks. God, that smirk. "Or at least I'm getting there."

"You are," I say, letting the letter drop to the floor so I can hold his hand between mine. "The future might look different for you and Willow, but you have so much to look forward to. There's something better waiting for you. A better job, a better relationship..."

I trail off, not wanting to sound like I'm implying anything. I'm not. That was never what this was meant to be. We were meant to be the easy, don't-overthink-it situationship. Nothing more. Eventually though, when he goes back to Australia, there will be someone for him and Willow who will fill the gaps in his future. I ignore the pang in my chest at the thought—at the picture of him finding someone out there while I'm here in the exact same place I am now. Because no matter how hard I try to see that future for myself, I can't. It feels out of reach, far away and blurry.

"What do you need?" I ask, breaking the tension.

"I don't want to keep holding on to something that isn't there, and being angry at her isn't serving me or Willow. I need to let this"—his long fingers reach to pick up the letter from the floor between us—"go."

He balls it between his fists and stands. I slide back, giving him room to get around me, and spin to face the fire. He looks at it, flames dancing high in the grate, shoulders square and strong. Then he turns and extends his right hand to me. I jump up and place mine in his before I can blink. The light makes his eyes look brighter and the stubble of his five-o'clock shadow more prominent. He doesn't look away from me as he tosses the paper into the blaze and finally lets go of the past.

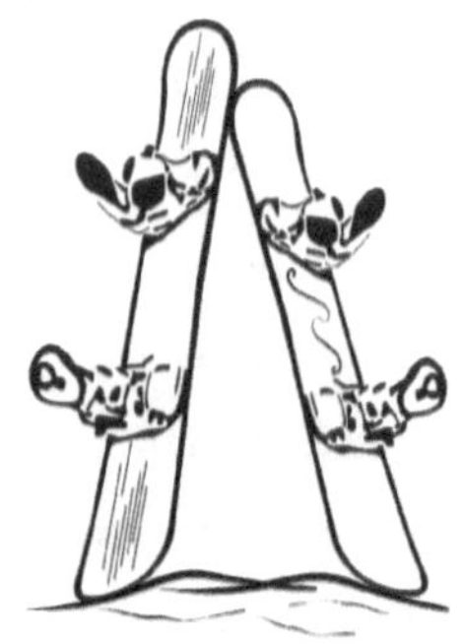

CHAPTER THIRTY

Rory

I read the message and my stomach sinks. There's been zero contact between us since the blow-up at dinner almost three weeks ago, or in the two weeks since I moved out. Now this. Does she really think I'll drop everything when summoned?

"Ugh," I groan, sliding my phone across the marble counter and reaching for my cup of coffee. I don't know how Breck makes better coffee than anyone else, but he does. I may never go to a coffee shop ever again, or at least not until he leaves... in less than a month.

"What's up, Roars?" Breck's smooth, sexy accent comes from behind me, and I throw a little glare over my shoulder at him. He throws his hands up. "Whoa. Was it the nickname or are we just that cranky before coffee?"

"Both. I hate that nickname."

"Ah, come on, you're telling me you hate it when Wes calls you Roars?" I roll my eyes like a petulant teenager and Breck laughs. "Maybe I'll keep calling you that, especially if it gets this reaction."

"Don't you freaking dare. That one is reserved for annoying older brothers, and you're not mine."

"No, I certainly am not," he says, voice lowering to a husk I can all but feel against my skin. There's warmth spreading behind his eyes too, a dark desire flooding his blue irises, making everything within me tighten with anticipation. There should be no anticipation as there's nothing to anticipate. Not anymore. Since Willow's birthday, we haven't so much as touched each other. But that doesn't mean the attraction, the pull between us, is somehow less.

"Morning," comes Willow's sleepy voice.

"Morning, Bug. Coffee?" I ask, like it's totally normal to offer coffee to an eight-year-old.

"Eww, gross. Dad says it'll stunt my growth," she grumbles.

"I was kidding." I laugh and ruffle her hair, and then look back to her dad, all heat and longing gone from his features. "Really, Breck? You told her it would stunt her growth? She's already taller than most kids her age. I think she's just fine."

"That's because I don't let her have caffeine," he jokes. Then, looking at Willow, he says, "Ready to round out your first week of school?"

She shrugs and mumbles something that sounds like "whatever" while she scrounges around in the fridge for the milk.

Breck and I exchange an exasperated look. This week has been a challenge.

On top of them starting school on Monday—which has given him a new appreciation for educators everywhere—he also had to address the call from Talia. That conversation was fraught with tears and anger, a likely months-long buildup finally surfacing. Understandably, Willow's been moodier than normal this week, and we've been doing our best to take it in stride.

But she's not the only one dealing with extra stress. In addition to school with Willow, Breck's week has been filled with communication from the new owners of Adventure Chasers—who reached out to him after their unproductive meeting with Talia and Drew. Turns out Breck's the only person who could actually answer their questions. He doesn't want to see the company struggle, but it's pulling him into the stress of a business he thought he was done with.

I'm doing what I can to help around the house and with Willow, but it was a busy week at work for me too. We're all on edge and I'm glad it's Friday. We could all use a break.

Over his coffee, Breck asks, "What about you, Rory, what do you have on the docket today?"

"I've got to work in the office this morning for a while, but..." I grin mischievously and turn to Willow. "I thought we could do something fun this afternoon to celebrate your first week of homeschool." I waggle my eyebrows at her. "Want to go sledding?"

I probably should've clued Breck into my plan, but it's too late now. Willow's sullen demeanor instantly morphs into one of excitement.

"Can we, Daddy? Please!"

"Absolutely. That sounds like a perfect plan. What time will you finish up at work?" Breck smiles at me, relieved.

"Probably around one."

"That's perfect. Think we can get all your schoolwork done by lunchtime today, Willow Bear?" he asks her, raising an eyebrow.

"Yes! Can we start now?" she exclaims, running over to the kitchen table that's laden with all her school stuff.

I lift my coffee cup in a salute as he walks backward toward the table. This is exactly the incentive he needed to get them through another day. Hopefully it'll get us all out of the funk of the week.

I've fallen into a scene from *National Lampoon's Christmas Vacation*, and I realize I might've made a grave mistake in letting Breck give me a running shove down the sledding hill. I'm screaming, the wind whipping my hair around my face despite my pigtail braids and beanie. The braids were at Willow's insistence. I'm usually a single braid kind of gal, but she wanted to match, and I couldn't say no to her. Just like I can't say no to her father, who I can hear, *laughing*, over my terror-filled yells.

My sled finally slows to a stop—much farther along the flats than anyone else has gone—and I roll myself off the thing and into the snow, breathing hard. I stare up at the trees that surround the clearing and inhale the smell of fresh snow and pine.

There's a delighted shriek and a whoop from up the hill, and I decide to wait here until Breck and Willow come to a stop. My arms and legs move, swiping up and down, in and out, creating a perfect snow angel where I lie in wait. The shriek is now a giggle and there's a boisterous laugh that complements it. Both are drawing closer, and with the sound of boots on snow, I look up into the most beautiful pair of blue eyes, surrounded by a halo of dampened, messy blond waves.

Breck stands over me, the corners of his eyes crinkling. His smile is pushing his dimples into sharp relief, and even from my upside-down angle, nothing about it could be misconstrued as a frown. We have only a second, lost in each other this way, before a tinier version of his face stares down at me as well.

"You went so fast, Rory!" Willow exclaims, her expression gleeful.

"I know," I grumble, trying and failing to keep the grin off my face. "It sounded like you had a much more…" I pause, looking for the right word. "… *enjoyable* ride down the hill with your dad." I try to glare at him, but it's impossible to even pretend I'm mad when that was such a rush.

"I wanna make a snow angel like you." Willow plops down next to me, swishing her arms and legs in earnest. "You make one too, Dad." She lifts her head off the snow, her bear ears standing up on her hat, and I stifle a giggle at the crease that splits his brow.

"I've never understood the point of snow angels," Breck murmurs, groaning as he lowers himself to the ground on my other side. "Why does anyone want to lie in the snow and purposely make themselves wet and cold?"

"Because it's magical." The words slip out at the same time my fingers brush against his. The current of electricity between us heightens with each touch.

On the next pass, Breck's fingers catch mine. Holding my gloved hand in his, our eyes lock on each other while Willow continues to swish her arms and legs beside me.

"I guess it is," he whispers.

I swallow, or try to, but my breath catches in my lungs—in my throat. The urge to say something is impossibly heavy in my chest. This moment *is* magical, with him, with Willow. I've never felt this connected to another person.

"I'm ready to go again." Willow pops up and Breck releases his grip on my hand—and on my heart. "Daddy, you drag the sleds up the hill, okay? This time I'm going by myself. You can go with Rory."

There's a renewed mischief in his eyes when he stands, and I wonder what on earth I've gotten myself into with this man.

I lose count of the number of times we fly down the sledding hill. Sometimes it's me by myself on the saucer—though I never let Breck push me again—while the two of them take the sled. Other times, it's me and Willow in the sled while Breck takes a running start to launch himself down the mountain. My favorites, though, are when Willow is dead-set on going down solo and I find myself nestled between Breck's firm thighs, back pressed against his chest, his raspy voice whispering in my ear as we soar down the hill.

By the time we're done, the sun is setting, the temperature's dropping, and our energy's fading, but we're all smiles on the walk back to the car. The sullenness of this morning is long gone, replaced by Willow's typical bubbly demeanor, and I can tell we all feel less burdened.

Breck grabs my hand after we've finished loading the sleds into the back of my car. "Thank you. We needed this."

I brush my thumb over the top of his. "Today was the most fun I've had in a long time."

"Yeah, me too." His face softens and there's something I can't read behind his expression.

Breck has never asked for anything from me, and I haven't asked for anything from him, but it's getting harder and harder not to want to give him more of myself than I've ever offered anyone else.

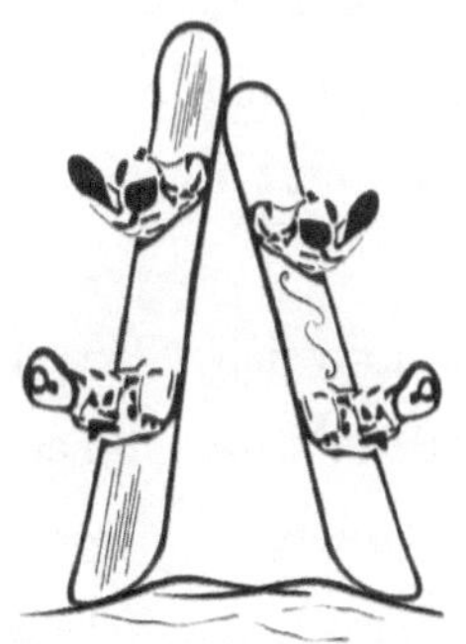

CHAPTER THIRTY-ONE

RORY

"Breck?" I ask from across the living room, anticipation and trepidation in my voice.

He's hunched over, helping Willow with something on her screen at the kitchen table. "Yeah?" He raises his eyebrows in question.

"I know setting up the website was an important step in making Willow Tree Elopements a thing... but, um, I keep getting inquiry emails and don't know how I'm going to have time for all these?" I chew the corner of my thumbnail, my mind racing. I'm totally freaking out.

He presses a kiss to Willow's head. "You keep working on this one and I'll be back in a minute, sweetheart."

There's a purpose in his movements, almost a swagger, that I can't ignore. He inclines his head toward the hallway leading to the stairs and I shift my computer off my lap to follow him. I round the wall that separates the living room from the foyer only to be pulled into strong arms, braced against a firm chest. My anxiety cools in an instant.

"Rory," he says against my hair. "This is a good thing. I know it's a lot right now, but that's what I'm here for. This is what you wanted, yeah?"

I search his face for the truth, that this really is a good thing and not a mistake.

"More inquiries *is* good. That means the website is working and people are looking for what you offer."

"But some of these requests are for mid-week weddings. I have a job, what am I supposed to do?"

"In the beginning you'll have to limit the number of those mid-week shoots to the ones you really want to do, since you'll have to request days off from the resort. Have you considered what you want to do about Empyreal long-term?" He pushes a strand of hair behind my ear and his fingers linger on the skin of my neck. I want to melt on the spot.

"Ideally this becomes a full-time thing, but right now, I can't imagine letting go of my real job."

His eyes go soft, full of understanding. I'm scared and he knows it. "You need to remember that photography is a real job too. You're a professional. You're incredibly skilled. You have two 'real jobs,' and that's a lot. You can do it though, and eventually you'll know what the best road forward is." He rests his forehead against mine. It's the closest we've been since our kiss on Willow's birthday ten days ago. "I'm incredibly proud of you."

The praise lights me up inside, and I smile. I can't stop it, and I don't want to.

"Thank you," I breathe, and it mingles with his in the inches between us. We can't move any farther, but I'm content to share this tiny sliver of space with him.

"Let's look at the calendar tonight after Willow goes to bed and we'll figure out what elopements you can take on, especially if they're while I'm here and can help. We can coordinate with Jamie for the rest, yeah?"

"Yeah, okay." Some of the strain lifts on my inhale as I push away. If we continue to stand like this, I won't be able to resist brushing my lips against his.

Willow's asleep upstairs, my laptop sits on the table, and Jamie's just arrived with his calendar so we can coordinate. Yeah, I called in reinforcements. Muffled voices carry from the foyer while I continue to focus on the screen in front of me.

"Hey, Roars," Jamie says when he rounds the kitchen, a smirk hiding under his beard.

"Ugh, not you too."

Breck joins us and chuckles. "Who needs a drink?"

"Wine?" I ask.

Jamie shakes his head, pulling a bottle of champagne from behind his back. The bright yellow-orange label tells me it's my favorite. One I never get to drink—because who's going to spend that much on one bottle? "Jamie!"

"What? I figured we were celebrating. You're finally doing this thing, and you deserve to be celebrated. Right, Breck?"

"Absolutely, I approve of this message." He beams and goes to the cabinet to retrieve three champagne flutes. The pop of the cork and fizz of bubbles echoes the way my stomach feels.

Glasses in hand, Breck speaks first. "To Rory, making her dreams come true."

"To Rory, I'm so proud of you," Jamie says, lifting his.

I avert my eyes. That's twice today I've heard those words and, damn, it feels good. A tear slips down my cheek with the clink of our glasses. "Thank you both. I wouldn't be here without either of you." The crisp liquid hits my tongue and I shimmy, its effervescence making me giddy.

"Alright," Jamie says, a determined look in his moss-green eyes. "Let's make our girl the most sought-after Tahoe elopement photographer."

More tears. I set my glass down to pull him into a hug.

"I love you, Jamie. Thank you."

"You don't have to thank me for this. You know I'd do anything for you," he says against my hair.

We work our way through the inquiries, the schedules, the logistics. If I take on every client that's requesting services, I'll have an elopement almost every week through the rest of ski season, plus a couple in the summer. It's a heavy mix of excitement and terror—it's so much. How is this possible?

Jamie succinctly summarizes the plans for us. "Breck will take the two elopements between now and the end of February, which works well for me because I'm in the writing cave the rest of this month. Once he leaves," he says, and I flinch internally at the thought, "I'll take on the officiant role again. We will need to figure out a secondary officiant for a few of these, but if we start looking now, I'm sure we'll have someone by the time they come around."

"Rory, are you comfortable taking off two days a month for mid-week sessions through the rest of the season?" Breck asks, pulling my hand away from my face.

I nod. "Yes, I'll request these dates when I go in tomorrow and hope Logan doesn't mind."

"Other than Christmas, I don't remember when you last took time off. Maybe when Wes was in the hospital? If your boss has an issue with it, that's his problem." Jamie's green eyes burn into mine, daring me to argue.

"You're right. I'll talk to him tomorrow."

"Good." He pauses, removing the glasses he typically reserves for evenings in front of his computer, and rubs the bridge of his nose. "Have you talked to your parents at all?"

"Nope. Unless you count Mom demanding I join them at dinner this past weekend. I didn't respond though." Jamie darts his eyes away from me. "What?"

"They called me." Jamie's auburn beard twitches with the clench of his jaw.

"They *what*?" I shout, and Breck shushes me on reflex. "Shit, sorry," I whisper, glancing up toward where I hope Willow is still sleeping.

"Yeah. Your dad called me yesterday."

"My dad?" Interesting. I'd expect something like this from Mom.

"He thought I might be the only person who could get through to you." He offers an apologetic shrug. "Everything else he said was unimportant, and I had some choice words for him in return. I don't imagine he, or your mom, will call me again. They know now that I'm not their ally in this fight."

I kind of do want to know what he had to say, but it won't do me any good to hear those words, so I shrug it off. "I'm sorry, Jamie."

"Why are you apologizing? You didn't do anything wrong. I should've said something to your parents a long time ago. I only held my tongue because I didn't want to create extra drama for you. Now though... It felt good to finally give him a piece of my mind."

I chuckle, then let out a long-suffering groan. I'm going to have to address the issue at some point, but I want to bask in my freedom from their control, their judgment, for a while longer.

"I don't know what I'd do without you both." My gaze trails away from my best friend and lands on Breck. He winks, and the soft, ever-burning flame in my chest grows a little brighter. Jamie's watching us closely, so I break the connection and look at my hands.

"I'm going to turn in. Gotta be up early with Willow tomorrow. I swear her teachers need a raise." Breck yawns and pushes away from the table. Before he leaves, he leans in and whispers in my ear, hands braced on my shoulders. "You're going to be great. I'm excited to see you fly."

The touch of his fingertips sears my skin, and I duck my chin to hide my flushed cheeks. "Thank you."

His footsteps fade away up the stairs and I lift my head to look at Jamie. His right eyebrow is arched and a smirk plays on his lips.

"So, I take it that's still happening?" He jerks his chin toward where Breck just disappeared.

"Don't know what you're talking about."

"Don't play coy. I know you hooked up on New Year's, and I can only assume it continued." He gives me a look like *don't even try to deny it.*

"We only made out on New Year's," I say defensively.

"Semantics. You've more than made out since then."

"That's none of your business."

He laughs. "Oh please. You know *all* my business. You know I won't judge. I just want to make sure you're being careful."

I flush. "Oh, for god's sake!"

His laugh grows more boisterous. "That's not what I meant." The words are barely there between his laughs. "I mean, yes, that's important too. But I was talking about you being careful with your heart."

Said organ feels like it's in my throat. I can't speak.

"I don't want you to get hurt. So long as you're on the same page about what it means when he leaves…" He trails off with a slight lift of his shoulders. "Because he will go home. He's not like Wes, he can't stay. He has Willow to think about, and their whole life is in Sydney."

The apologetic note in his voice only makes this harder—he's more on the money than I care to admit.

"We already stopped… whatever it was. It's too complicated now that we're living together. Thank you for worrying about me, but I'm fine. I'll miss them when they leave, of course, but I'm not harboring any ideas that they'll stay. That was never an expectation."

"Sometimes our expectations grow without our permission."

"It was just something fun, something for us, and now it's over." I'm not sure who I'm saying all this for… him or me.

"And you're really okay with that?"

"Yes," I say but don't meet his eyes.

"Okay. Just be careful. I like Breck. I'd hate to have to kick his ass for hurting you." Jamie chuckles, then he gentles his voice. "I don't want to be picking up the pieces of you after he leaves."

"You won't. I promise."

"Don't make promises you can't keep."

"I'll keep this one."

"Okay. I trust you." He presses a kiss to the top of my head and leaves the way he came.

I'm left with his words spinning on an endless wheel in my mind.

I don't have expectations.

I don't.

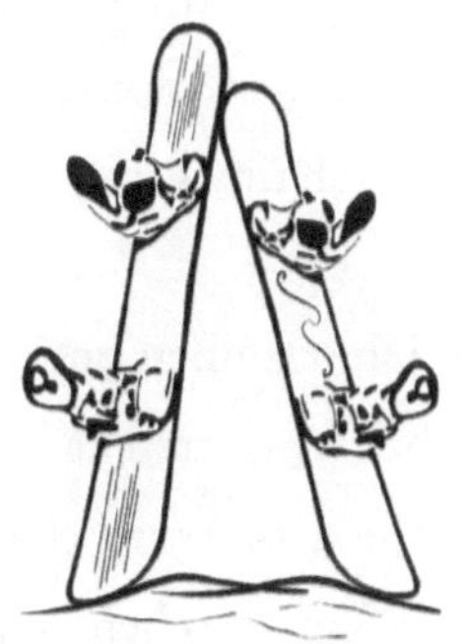

CHAPTER THIRTY-TWO

BRECK

Willow and I walk down Stateline Blvd with the late afternoon sunlight bouncing off the sleek pavement as we head toward the condo. We wrapped up school early and went to the ice rink for a quick skate. By the time we get back, Chinese food containers in tow, Rory should be home from work, and we can all enjoy a casual dinner together.

Her boss was out sick at the end of last week, so today she was supposed to ask him about taking time off. There's only one mid-week elopement this month, but there are two scheduled for March and two for April, so I'm hoping it won't be a problem. I could tell this morning that she was nervous. This is a lot for her. I remember how stressful it was in the early days of starting a business... Hell, I feel it now with how intrinsically invested I am in her success. It feels good though, to be doing something, to be helping.

"Daddy, can you take my picture sitting in the giant chair?" Willow gestures to the wooden monstrosity as we pass. The Adirondack chair is at least ten times the normal size and is painted in a myriad of colors.

"Sure, Bear," I say, and she clambers onto it. She's unable to even reach the armrests with her arms stretched out to both sides. Her smile is broad and warm, the setting sun behind me lighting her face with a golden glow. I wish Rory was here to take the picture, but I pull my phone from my pocket and do my best with what I've got. "Got it."

"Perfect! Can you send it to Uncle Wes?" she asks, hopping down.

"Absolutely. Are you excited that we get to see him and Joss again soon?" I've started mixing in comments about our return home in two weeks whenever I can. One month of homeschooling was as much as Willow's school would allow without forfeiting her spot, and we can't avoid reality forever.

"Can't they come see us again here?" She deflects the question, like she's done every time I've brought it up. She talks a good bit about Wes and Joss, but the mentions of her friends have become few and far between. I don't know what to make of it. I'm nervous she'll be on the outside with them after three months away.

"Aren't you missing your friends?" I want to kick myself for pushing this. It's not like I'm desperate to go back either.

"Yeah, I guess. But I really like it here."

"But you don't have any other kids to play with."

"I don't mind just hanging out with you and Rory." She shrugs her shoulders, her braids moving with them. "She's more fun anyway."

"More fun than me?" I ask with feigned offense, clapping my hand across my chest.

"Never, Dad, you're the funnest. Thanks for taking me ice skating today. I'm finally getting the hang of it."

I don't correct her use of the word "funnest," because what kind of fun dad would I be if I did?

"Yeah, you only fell about twenty times," I say, needling her.

"Dad! I wasn't that bad. And you fell too."

I chuckle under my breath. She has a point. I did fall, but only after I saw a flash of strawberry-blonde hair. My eyes followed the woman, wondering if it was Rory, and the distraction cost me. I slipped and fell, landing hard on my ass. I'm going to have to take advantage of the hot tub later.

A mouth-watering aroma fills the space when we walk into the condo. "Mmm, smells like Rory might be baking."

Willow takes off toward the kitchen, her wet boots sliding on the floors. "Hey, ankle-biter, boots off first. Then go change into your pajamas, please."

She turns back and rolls her eyes. "Fine."

I hold back the reprimand sitting on the tip of my tongue. I don't want to ruin the fun day we've had by getting into it. Not today. I'm still learning which battles to pick, which hills to die on as a parent. Normally, attitude is one of them, but I don't have it in me right now.

The scents of cinnamon, sugar, and butter meld into something heavenly, but it doesn't compare to the sight of Rory bent over and pulling a tray from the oven. She has on tight black leggings that stretch over her ass in the most sinful way. I adjust myself in my jeans, itching to reach for her. The full view of her when she stands up—loose sweater draping low off one shoulder, the lace of her bra peeking out—has me stepping behind the counter to conceal the way she affects me.

Her eyes blaze a trail up my torso as she slides the tray onto the counter. There's a dusting of flour on her nose, making the freckles on her cheeks stand out. Her hair is a wild mess of rose gold curls, and the turquoise of her eyes is bright, sparkling like the Caribbean Sea. She's at ease, comfortable. I like this look on her.

"Hi," she says, breathless, pushing a stray curl back from her face. Her flour-dusted fingers brush against her cheekbone, leaving more on her face, and my lips tilt up in a grin. Does she have any idea what she does to me?

Do I?

"Hey. We picked up dinner." I lift the bag onto the counter next to the cookies. "Looks like you got started on dessert already."

She licks her lip, clearing the flour with her tongue. It makes me want to spread some across mine so she can give them the same treatment. *Damn*. Ending our friends-with-benefits arrangement made sense at the time, but I'm struggling to remember why right now.

"I'll share," she says, pulling my gaze up her face to meet her eyes. There's something heady in her tone, a tease, a promise.

I groan and let my head fall back. She just laughs, bright and melodic. She definitely knows what she's doing to me.

She reaches for the bag of Chinese food and starts unpacking it. "What were you two up to today?" she asks.

"We went ice skating!" Willow says, joining us and hopping onto a stool.

"Nice! How'd you do?" Rory's words are full of enthusiasm, like she truly cares.

"So good. I didn't fall much. Dad did though."

"Hey! I thought we were going to keep my *one* fall between us," I say, indignant. "Little traitor."

I ruffle her hair and she giggles. "Dad, stop, you're messing it up."

"Am I? Well, we can have Rory fix it." Having Rory around all the time means she's pretty well taken over doing Willow's hair every day. There are far less tears and hardly any eye-rolling when she's in charge.

"Or I could teach *you* how to do it properly. That way you can do it yourself," Rory pipes up, her grin lifting her sweet, freckled cheeks.

"Am I teachable? I don't know. I've tried. Plenty."

"I have faith in you," she says, and my heart swells at her words.

I know she only means them in reference to my hair-styling abilities, but there's something that makes me believe she could mean them for so much more.

A couple of hours later, with a belly full of Chinese food and dessert, I'm ready for a quick soak in the hot tub and then bed. Willow is finally asleep. The sugary cookies right before bed weren't my best idea, but I couldn't deny her when they were so good. Not quite like a Tim Tam, but Rory's snickerdoodles are a pretty close second.

I pull out a pair of boardshorts from my dresser. Rory and I have been taking turns with the jacuzzi at night. We never explicitly discussed it, but it's been necessary for obvious reasons. I tie the drawstring and head downstairs. There are no lights on in Rory's room so I expect to see her in the kitchen or the living room, but I don't. Maybe she's...

My brain trails off. Looking out the sliding glass door, the soft lights of the hot tub just barely illuminate her. Her arms are spread wide on the lip of the tub, head tipped back toward the sky, looking peaceful. I swallow. I guess our dancing around this moment is about to end because I *am* going out there.

I pull the door open and her head snaps up. "Mind if I join you? My tailbone is protesting after that fall earlier."

I reach back and pull my T-shirt over my head with one hand. It's her turn to swallow thickly, eyes trailing down my chest and abdomen then back up to my face. Her cheeks were already flushed, but the color's deeper now.

"Y-yep, sure," she stutters, and I step into the tub, my leg brushing hers under the water. Her eyes never leave my body as I slide in amongst the bubbles. "The tattoo? It's for Willow?" she asks, her hands trailing over the surface of the water.

"It is." She's seen it before, touched it, kissed it, but we've never talked about it. The black ink that permanently lines my ribcage.

The roots that reach down to my hip bone. The trunk that grows up my entire side. The branches that sway down around it. My very own willow to carry with me always. "I got it the week after she was born. I needed something that showed how wrapped up I was in her."

"I like it. It suits you." She sneaks a glance at it beneath the water.

"You think so?" I ask, and she nods. I stand and lift my arm, all but asking her to inspect it further.

She moves to the edge of her seat and the water sloshes around us. Her fingers dance over the dainty branches etched into my side. A shiver dances down my spine despite the hundred-and-four-degree water I'm standing in. Her touch holds reverence, her eyes hold desire.

This is why we've been playing trades with the hot tub. It's too intense. The pull we have, my eyes burning into hers, is too much. I want so badly to touch her. I've missed the comfort of that touch, of her mouth, of her body. I've missed when it's just her and me, no one else, nothing else. When we can just *be*.

Be what, I don't know, but I miss it.

Her fingers trail lower down my side and I suck in a breath, the muscles tightening. When her fingers reach the waistband of my shorts, she looks up. The blazing heat in her irises matches the burn of her fingers where they skate across my lower abdomen to the tie on my shorts. I catch her hand, a tremble in my own, unsure of what I intend to do now that I've caught it.

She licks across her bottom lip before drawing it into her mouth, and I lose any semblance of restraint.

"Fuck it."

I bend over her, pressing her back into the side of the tub, forcing water to slosh out onto the ground. I lace my hand into her hair and pull her head back until it rests against the top of the tub. I slant my lips over hers and don't bother taking my time. My tongue seeks hers, sliding between her lips and tasting the sweet cinnamon and sugar of the cookies. I press forward, towering over her, one knee bent on the seat between her spread thighs. Her chest lifts on each inhale and brushes against my bare skin.

"Breck," she pleads.

She doesn't need to beg; I'll give her anything she wants.

"Rory," I murmur against her mouth, sliding my other arm behind her back. I shift us so she's straddling me. She squeaks with surprise but quickly finds her way back to my mouth, letting her hands delve into my hair and pull me closer. She rocks against me and I groan against her lips. Her hand trails down and over my tattoo. Up and down, again and again, until I can't take the soft touch any longer.

"*Rory*." She knows I'm unraveling. Every part of me is giving up the attempt to stay away, to keep my distance, to keep this platonic. I lift my hips, seeking friction—seeking her. She moans, teeth grazing my tongue, as she arches into me. "Yes. Fuck. Rory."

"I'd like that." She trails kisses down my neck before nipping at my collarbone and positioning herself so she's closer, showing me exactly what she wants. I chuckle, but it's dark and heavy, full of promise.

"Okay, baby." I wrap my arms around her back and stand up. She squeezes her legs tighter around my waist like putting any space between us would be a tragedy.

I settle her on the edge of the tub, letting the cold air heighten the sensitivity of her skin, and trail my fingers up her arms. When my hands reach her neck, I look into her eyes and see the anticipation. She's waiting for me to bury them in her hair again and take her mouth, but I don't.

Instead, I trail my fingers lightly away along her shoulders then back again before I grip the strings of her bikini and pull. I slide my hands lower and repeat the motion at the tie on her back. We're still pressed together, my body holding her top in place. I quickly glance around to ensure none of the neighbors are out and then I put an inch of space between us, feeling the fabric slip.

With a nip at her collarbone, I say, "You're going to have to let me go so I can get us out of here without falling."

Desire flames bright in her eyes and she slides her legs from around my waist. She whimpers in protest when I step back. I get it, I miss her body against mine too. The wet fabric slips the rest of the way off her and I catch it in one hand. My eyes rove over her, sitting like a goddess on the ledge of the tub. Need overtakes every other thought, and I guide her out. Our feet land on chilled wood boards, but the heat between us makes that unimportant.

Her hands slide across my slick torso, over each ridge of my abdomen and up to my pecs, the light brush of her thumb over my nipple making me jump. Our mouths fuse again, and with one lift, her legs are back around my waist. I stalk toward the house, the skin of her naked torso slipping against mine with every step. It's glorious torture.

"Still want this?" I ask against her neck, kissing down the column and stopping just at the hollow of her throat.

"More than I should."

"Same, baby. Same."

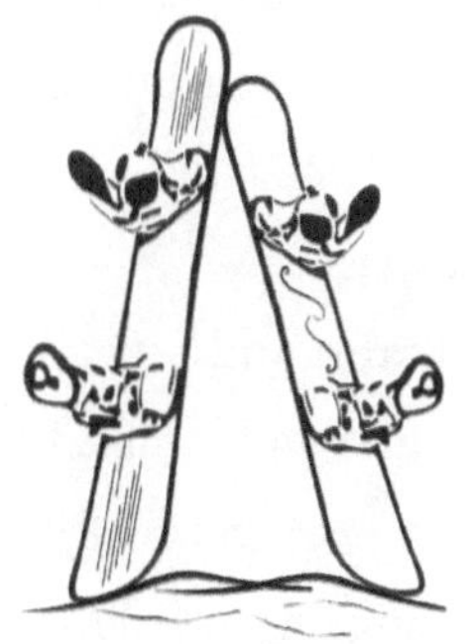

CHAPTER THIRTY-THREE

ROR4

I sit up and pull the sheets tight around my bare torso. The place beside me is empty and cold, and I flop back into my pillows with a groan. Last night was a mistake. Breck and Willow have less than two weeks left in Tahoe, then they'll be back on the other side of the world. Yet here I am, falling into bed with him—maybe falling in other ways too.

Jamie's words come back to me. Last night wasn't careful. It was reckless—it was also *so* good. My bed smells like Breck, fresh and clean with a hint of something spicier, something manly. I bury my face in the pillow he fell asleep on and breathe him in. At least I think he fell asleep with me. I remember falling into a sated heap of tangled limbs, our breathing evening out into soft inhales and exhales. After that, I don't remember a thing.

Maybe he didn't stay at all, just rolled out from beneath my tired body and scampered off to his own room. That would've been the smart choice. Willow finding us tangled up in each other would have been disastrous. That girl has too many questions on a good day. I don't even want to imagine the rapid-fire explosion of words that would escape her in that scenario.

We said we couldn't do this, and it wasn't only for Willow's sake. Now I have to walk out there and act like I can't vividly remember how his skin felt against mine when we fell into this bed—swimsuits discarded, towels and drying off not even a consideration. Pretend I can't remember every sweet word he whispered in the dark as our bodies moved together.

I squeeze my eyes shut and roll my lips over my teeth. I'm an adult. I can go out there and act like one, keep up the pretense that there's nothing between us.

But... what if I didn't? What if—

A light knock at the door derails my train of thought and I pull the covers tighter against me. "Come in," I say, my voice high and squeaky.

Breck peeks his head around the door. The sexy smirk on his face when he sees me sunken down into the bed makes my toes curl.

"Coffee?" he rasps.

Between that sound and the smell wafting in, I could melt into these sheets right here and now.

"Always." I pull one arm away from my chest and reach for it. He slips the door closed and walks with purpose to the bed. He doesn't put the coffee into my hand, instead sliding it onto the nightstand. My outstretched hand fists into his T-shirt. He rakes a hand into my messy waves and our lips move in tandem like they were made to fuse together.

"I hoped I'd get back in here with your coffee before you woke up," he murmurs against my mouth.

Back in here? So he *was* here with me last night—at least physically. I shouldn't want him to be here with me in the mess my emotions are quickly becoming, but part of me wonders if he is.

He moves his lips across my jaw to my ear. "I wanted to be the one to wake you up."

The sound I make as my head falls back has his lips trembling with a laugh against my skin. My body is definitely awake. I tighten my hand in his shirt and pull him back to my mouth.

"Best wake-up call ever," I say against him, and his dazzling blue eyes sparkle. "I'm talking about the coffee, of course," I deadpan, and his head tips back in a hearty laugh before he covers it with a hand over his mouth and glances toward the door.

"I left Willow at the breakfast bar. I should probably get back out there before she comes looking. I just didn't want you to wake up alone."

My heart.

"I wake up alone all the time."

"Yeah, I know. But you didn't have to today." He traces his thumb over my lip and then walks backward, watching me until the very last second when he slips out of my room. I bury my face in the pillow covered in his scent and quietly squeal into it.

I am never washing this pillow.

Ever.

I let myself imagine not having to walk out there and pretend we're only friends. If I could have him how I'm realizing I want to. I could walk into the kitchen and wrap my arms around his middle, resting my cheek against his warm back. He would turn in my arms and kiss me, spatula in hand, eggs popping in the oil on the stove.

I slap both hands to the sheets on either side of me and hop out of bed, pulling on the closest pair of joggers and a hoodie, then spot my swimsuit hung neatly on the hamper. I'll never be able to wear that bikini again without the memory of Breck's hands on me, pulling the strings and taking it off me, playing in my mind. Then I wonder with a smile if Breck had to run upstairs naked this morning to get clothes.

There's soft music emanating from the space when I start down the hall, Willow's unmistakable giggle chiming as the kitchen comes into view.

Breck has a whisk in his hand and is lip-syncing to the music, dancing around the kitchen—hips swaying, head bobbing, shoulders shimmying. It's a sight to behold and it makes my heart stop. He looks so... happy. I want what he's having, so I take the last few strides at a run and slide on sock-covered feet into the kitchen. I collide with Breck who doesn't see me coming because his head is tipped back, whisk-microphone held high.

He drops the whisk, eyes popping open and landing on me. Then he smiles, dimples cutting deep into his cheeks, and his eyes soften. I can't catch my breath. I'm mesmerized, entranced, stuck in his orbit and unable to move away. Willow's laugh breaks through and my heart stutters back to life when he grabs my hand and spins me around.

We're dancing.

In the kitchen.

It's even better than my daydream, and I let myself melt into the moment. My head tips back on a laugh, eyes closed when he pulls, spinning me into him. My free hand connects with his chest and my eyes find his. I can't read what I see there, but it's something new, something I've never seen in the eyes of any man before; at least not directed at me.

A tug on my sweatshirt draws my attention down to where Willow stands, smiling, hair a mess. "My turn to dance with Rory. Dad, you're supposed to be making pancakes."

Breck lets me go, hands sliding reluctantly away while he keeps me pinned with that look. He leans down and presses a kiss to her hair. There's a moment, just a split second, where he moves closer, like he might do the same to me, but then he thinks better of it.

We groove to the music, Willow dancing with me and then by herself while Breck cooks, the smells of pancakes and bacon surrounding us. We dance our way through setting the table. I dance my way across to the coffee pot for a refill and brush my fingers along the small of Breck's back when I pass. He gives me a wink that makes my cheeks heat.

I duck my head and sit down. This is the best morning I've had in a long time. Breck sits next to me, bringing with him a plate piled high with pancakes. Willow sits on the opposite side of the table and digs in, not even bothering to use a fork.

"How'd it go asking for time off with your boss yesterday?" Breck asks around a mouthful of pancakes.

"Manners, Dad," Willow chides him, and I cover my laugh with a hand when his eyes bug out at her.

"Really? Really, Willow?" he says after he's swallowed. "You're one to talk."

"Now now, children," I say in my sweetest, motherly voice and they both gawk at me before we all fall into fits of giggles. I pull myself together, hiccupping over one last chortle. "As to your question. It was fine. I think Logan was surprised, but with how much vacation time I've accrued, he can't really complain."

"I would think not. So we're good for next Thursday then?"

"We are. I wasn't sure if I should tell him why I was asking for the days off or not. It feels a little like I'm cheating on my job there." I shrug, feeling silly. "He's been very supportive of my photography, but it's never interfered with my work at the resort before. I don't want him to think I'm not happy there."

"Are you?" Breck asks, and when I just stare at him dumbfounded, he continues. "Happy there?"

"I-I don't know. Yes. No. Sometimes," I ramble on. I used to think I was, but when I compare it to the way I feel about photography, I'm not so sure. When I compare it to the way I've felt this morning...

"Well, that might be something to think about going forward. You won't be able to do both forever. You deserve to choose the things that make you happy, yeah?"

My mind is screaming at me that he deserves to be happy too. That we both deserve mornings like this all the time. But I can't go down that road, so I change the subject.

"Yeah. So, Willow, you good to be my assistant again?"

She beams and nods, opening her full mouth to speak, but with an arched eyebrow from her dad, she swallows first, then gives him the biggest, cockiest little grin. "I can't wait."

"Me neither." I love having her by my side. She's a natural, and I hope she won't forget how much she loves photography when she goes home. By the time they leave, we'll have done four elopements together. It feels like this whole idea blossomed overnight, but now I can't imagine ever going back.

We finish breakfast and move in our own directions to get ready for the day.

Dressed and ready for work, I walk into the kitchen again to find Willow set up for school at the table, her dark hair flowing down her back while Breck braids it. I finally made him sit and watch me do it after dinner last night, and he studied every movement with rapt attention. I don't know how it was any different than the multitude of YouTube videos I know he's watched, but he's nailing it—fingers moving deftly so when he wraps the elastic around the bottom it looks exactly like it should.

He reaches for the coffee on the table and turns to see me staring. He glances at Willow's hair, then back to me, and his proud smile is all I need to carry me through my day. Though, a goodbye kiss would be even better, but I can't have one of those. I offer him a smile in return, grab the travel mug of coffee he left sitting on the counter for me, and head for the door.

"Bye, see you guys this evening," I call out, but before I fully close the door behind me, a hand shoots out to stop it. Breck steps outside, hissing when his bare feet hit the freezing concrete, and lifts a palm to my face. Then he pushes back the stubborn strand of hair that's peeking out from under my beanie.

He brushes his lips against mine, smiles, and says, "Have a good day."

My gloved fingers fumble over the keypad, the wind whipping my hair up like Medusa. The walk home was cold and miserable, and I just want to kick off my boots and sit by the fire with something warm. Mulled wine maybe? I hum at the idea.

"You're home!" shouts Willow when the door swings open. She flings herself at me, wrapping me in a hug... in her sopping-wet swimsuit.

"I am."

From the kitchen, Breck shouts, "Willow. Shower. Now." It's lighthearted but also firm, like he's probably told her multiple times already.

"Better go, Bug." I lean down and kiss her wet hair. She must be freezing.

"Okay, okay, I'm going," she says loudly enough for Breck to hear her and then sprints up the stairs.

I peel off my layers and walk into the kitchen to find Breck opening a bottle of wine.

"Red?" he asks, one side of his mouth quirking up. "Or do you want something warmer?"

"I was thinking of making mulled wine... but if you have another idea for how to warm me up, I'm open to that too."

Breck steps into me, his tilted smile morphing into something sinful. "I'm sure I can think of something." His hands slide down my arms, to my ass, and he hoists me up.

"This feels familiar," I mutter against his lips, and he chuckles.

"I believe this is the third time I've had you on a counter."

My brows draw down. Third?

"The first," he says, kissing my nose, "was on your counter when you cut your foot."

I groan and attempt to bury my face in his shirt, the embarrassment of that moment flooding me. He continues with a kiss under my ear. "The second was on my kitchen counter, and you had bubbles in your hair."

"That was your fault, you could've let me finish the dishes."

"Ah, but I didn't want to wait." He finds my collarbone, shifting my sweater to the side so he can suck on the sensitive spot there. The one he knows makes me whimper.

"I wish we didn't have to wait now either, but Willow will come down soon for dinner and..." He trails off. No matter the closeness we feel, bringing Willow into it—whatever *it* is—won't help anything. He slides my sweater back into place and presses a light kiss to my lips before stepping back. "Cook with me?"

"I'd love to." I take his extended hand and jump down from the counter.

We move around the kitchen seamlessly. He boils the water for pasta while I brown the meat. The smell of the rich, spiced tomato sauce melts away the strain of the workday. The small touches Breck seems unable to hold back with each pass in the kitchen are helping too.

The first few leave me with goosebumps and a hitch in my breath, so I start giving back as good as I'm getting. I slide my body against his when I pass, even though there's plenty of room in the kitchen. My fingers trail down his forearm to his hand where he's cutting fresh tomatoes before plucking a piece to put in my mouth. It only escalates from there. Each small touch filling the space with more and more tension, and with Willow still up in her room, we're getting bolder.

When I slide my hand across his ass, perfectly sculpted in jeans that look like they were made for him, his restraint snaps. He presses me against the door of the pantry with a low growl, leaving me panting and mewling, wanting more.

Footsteps approach, and I press my fingertips to my lips, smiling as I slide them up to finger-comb my hair.

"Hey, Bug," I say when she comes around the corner. "Hungry?"

She nods and then engulfs me in a hug. I relish each and every one she gives me.

"Good. We made pasta, and you know what? I was thinking we could pick out a board game from the closet. What do you think?"

The smile I love so much grows on her face, dimples showing.

"Can I pick?"

"Sure," Breck says, walking over.

Instead of pulling her from me for a hug of his own, he just joins ours, squishing Willow between us. She doesn't protest but nestles closer. I can't move my eyes from Breck's. They're filled with that same look from this morning. It's tender. It feels like *more*.

More is dangerous, it's risky, but I let myself want it.

Willow finally wiggles to get free and runs to choose a game. She settles on Attack UNO, a personal favorite.

The evening progresses with a fire burning in the hearth, warm food in our bellies, and laughs surrounding us each time the machine spits cards across the table. It feels natural. Right.

It feels like home.

"One more game," Willow begs, but the sun set a while ago and the clock's already reading an hour past her normal bedtime.

"Sorry, sweetheart, it's time for bed," Breck states, then adds, "for Rory too it would seem," when he catches my yawn.

I'm exhausted, but there's a buzz under my skin that makes me think I won't be following Willow straight to sleep... To bed, maybe, but definitely not to sleep. I raise an eyebrow at Breck and his eyes smolder, lips tipped up in a smirk.

"Fine." Willow pushes back from the table.

She starts to walk away but comes back to wrap her arms around me. "Good night, Rory."

"Good night," I say, kissing the top of her head.

She makes her way upstairs, leaving her dad and me at the table. His foot slides across the space and presses against my calf, then his hand snakes across the top of my thigh to grab mine.

"You'll wait up for me while I get her to bed." It's not a question, and I bite my lip, nodding. Then he follows her upstairs.

I sigh and walk over to the couch. Settling in, I lean back against the arm, resting my head against the cushion. I let my eyes slide closed—just for a minute—and then jolt awake at the feel of being lifted from the couch.

"Shh. I've got you." Breck's smooth accent caresses my ear and I melt against him.

He doesn't have to take me far, but I curl in closer to him with each step. When he leans over to set me down, I don't release his neck, pulling him down with me. His *oof* in my ear makes me chuckle.

He folds his body around me, pressing his chest against my back.

"Sleep, Rory. I'm not going anywhere."

I do just that, and I let myself believe him.

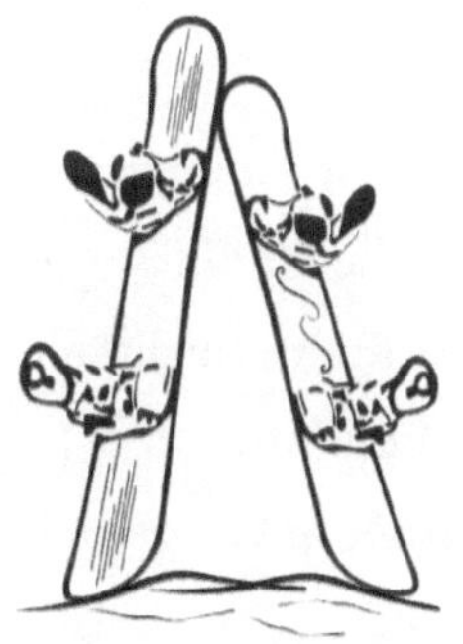

CHAPTER THIRTY-FOUR

RORY

B reck and Willow are carving their way down the mountain through the snow we got last night, but they haven't seen me yet. He texted that they were headed up for an afternoon session and I've been waiting for our paths to cross. I've been up here since midday, having wrapped up in the office so I could take advantage of the spring-like conditions to get some new content. The sun is shining, glinting off the snow like diamonds, and the lake is bright blue under an equally dazzling clear sky.

My camera hangs around my neck, and I stop every couple of minutes to get as many pictures as I can of the adorable daddy/daughter duo laughing their way down the run. Breck stops, facing uphill toward me, attention on Willow working her way down the mountain, a wide smile on his face. He's in a long sleeve

T-shirt and his snow pants, the full sun making it feel warmer than it is. His hair peeks out from under his helmet, and though I can't see his eyes with his goggles on, I know they'd make even the lake look dull in comparison.

I lift my camera just in time to capture a picture of him. In the next second, I capture another of Willow sliding to a stop just above him, spraying fresh snow up his thighs. She sits down on the hill, her tinkling giggle and Breck's bark of a laugh carrying up to me. He falls to his knees in front of her, grabs her board, and pulls her toward him, her butt sliding against the snow.

Watching them together is a dopamine hit. Since that very first day in the airport months ago, their love has been plain to see. He never holds back even a little bit of his devotion or makes her feel like she has to earn it. And what she returns is a love that's tender and carefree. Given without thought.

This thing with my parents, this "fight" we're having… it runs deeper, cuts deeper. It's made me understand that our love has always been transactional—at least from their end. And I worry that there's no coming back from this awareness now that I've seen the real thing.

I huff out a breath and cut my way down to Breck and Willow, drawing their attention with a whistle, and their heads snap to look at me, smiles crossing both their faces. I end up twenty feet below them and take another picture. These are for them. For them to remember their time here. For them to have memories they can look back on. For them to decorate their house with.

They're also for me, to remember how I got to help Willow learn to snowboard. That I got to be the lucky woman who had a part of

Breck, even if for only a short time. That I got to be part of helping them heal.

"Wait there," Breck bellows down to me, pushing himself up and extending a hand to Willow. "Can you take a picture of the three of us?" he asks, sliding down next to me.

"I mean, this isn't the ideal camera for selfies, but I'll do my best," I joke, flipping the screen out so I can manage to see what I'm doing.

They crowd in and our boards bump into each other, nearly knocking me off-balance. Breck's arm bands around my waist to hold me steady. His fingers splay against my hip and I feel it like a brand, warming me even through all the layers of fabric. The casual touches have lingered more and more the last several days, since our morning dancing in the kitchen. I revel in every single one like the gift they are.

I lift the camera up at an awkward angle to attempt to capture the three of us and the lake. The shutter clicks and my board shifts on the sun-softened snow. There's no catching us now. The three of us fall in what feels like slow-motion, Breck and I mostly side by side, Willow landing square on top of us both. I hit the button again on a whim, capturing us in a heap of laughter.

Our breathing evens out, people zipping by giving us odd looks, and we start the process of untangling.

Willow gets upright first and asks, "Can I take a picture of you two?" She raises an eyebrow, holding her hand out for my camera.

I hand it over, knowing she'll be just as careful with it as she is with the one I gave her. She slings it around her neck while Breck and I push to our feet and shimmy closer together. He wraps his arms around my shoulders and mine loop around his middle, both of us smiling at the camera. Willow smiles too, looking at us with her head slightly cocked, the camera pressed to her small face.

After the first click, I pull back and glance up at Breck. He looks down at me, the moment frozen in time, committed to memory. This is where the couple in a rom-com would kiss. Where the guy would say he can't leave. That he can't live without her, that they'll find a way to be together. This is where the girl reaches up to kiss the guy and tells him she loves him. It is *that* moment, and I want it to be ours. It's right here, so close, yet neither of us reaches for it. The shutter clicks again and it's gone, like a snowflake in the wind.

"Race you to the bottom?" Breck asks, head tilted to the side, grin illuminating his face.

Flicking my braid over my shoulder, I give him a playful shove. He topples back onto his ass and I wave to Willow. "Let's go. Last one to the bottom has to buy dinner."

My stomach is rumbling when we walk up to Azul Latin Kitchen for dinner. They seat us at an outdoor table near a firepit and a heat lamp, making it balmy despite the dropping temperature as the sun begins to set. The waiter takes our drink order and walks away just as Jamie walks up. His first kiss lands on Willow's cheek and her whole face flushes under his attention. The second kiss is for my cheek before he slides into his seat across from me.

"What, no kiss for me?" Breck jokes.

Jamie laughs and claps him on the back. "Nope." He turns to me. "Thanks for the invite. I needed to get out of the writing cave and this was the perfect excuse."

The waiter comes back with menus, a basket of chips, and the promise of our margaritas being out shortly. I reach for the chips at the same time as Breck and when our fingers graze, sparks fly between us. I grab one and break our eye contact, looking instead at Jamie—who's staring at me with a raised eyebrow and a smirk.

"How was the elopement yesterday?" Jamie asks.

Willow pipes up first, wanting Jamie's attention. "It was amazing! You should see the pictures I took. It was so fun!"

He peppers her with questions, and while his attention is on her, Breck's hand finds its way under the table to my knee, then slides higher until it's resting possessively on my leg, his fingers wrapped around and pressing into my inner thigh. My breath hitches, and a pleased grin appears on his face even though his eyes stay fixed on Jamie and Willow.

I slip my hand over his, enjoying every moment when we can touch like this.

The margaritas arrive, our food coming shortly after, and we relax into easy conversation and laughter.

Willow talks Jamie's ear off about the last week of school and he listens with rapt attention. She tells him about our fall on the mountain today and insists I get out my camera to show him the pictures. She's squealing with excitement over each candid one I took of them, and the look of gratitude on Breck's face softens me like butter.

The waiter drops off our check and Jamie reaches for it.

"I've got this," he says. "You two should stay and have another drink. I'll take Willow home for you."

"Wh-what? Why?" I stutter. Is he wing-manning me?

"I thought you two could celebrate. It's just one more drink. Willow and I will be alright for an hour, won't we?" He turns to her, leaving me confused.

Celebrate?

"What are we celebrating?" Breck asks, just as confused as I am.

"I found Rory an apartment," Jamie says with a boyish grin and a wink.

"Wait, what? Seriously?"

"Yeah. It's down in the valley. You'll have to commute, but it's yours if you want it. The rent is cheap, they're family friends so I know they're good people, and I think you'll love it." He stands up and extends a hand to Willow—who eagerly takes it. "Stay and have a drink. We can talk more details tomorrow, yeah?"

"Okay. Yeah." I stand and throw my arms around him. "Thank you, Jamie."

"You're welcome." He hugs me a little tighter, then whispers, "Have fun, but not too much." When he pulls back, there's a hint of warning behind his eyes, but it's gone with another wink my way. "We'll see you both in a bit."

"Bye," Willow says, not even bothering with hugs for her dad or me.

Our eyes collide once they're out of view and I duck my head, my cheeks flaming under his perusal.

"Want to go somewhere else?" He inclines his head, reaching for my hand like it's the most natural thing in the world. It feels like it is.

"Sure. Maybe no tequila shots this time," I joke, leading us away from the patio and down the sidewalk in the opposite direction of Jamie and Willow.

Breck's rumbling laugh wraps around me. He releases my hand and pulls me into his side—arm slung over my shoulder. It's the kiss he plants on the side of my head that makes me weak in the knees. We've never been like this with each other. Not in public. It feels like a treat, a gift, a dream.

The bar I lead us to is quieter, more subdued. The darker lighting and cozy seating give off a comfortable, romantic vibe. Breck slides onto a velvet loveseat in the corner, crossing his ankle over his knee, and pulls me down into his side. I look up at him from under my lashes and lean closer, ready to brush a kiss to the underside of his jaw, but Breck stiffens.

A throat clears and I turn, expecting a waitress but finding my parents instead. Mom's eyes dart between me and Breck. Dad is shaking hands with another man and nods his farewell before turning his attention me, hitting like a ton of bricks.

I inch away from Breck, trying to be subtle, like maybe I totally snuggle up to all my friends in bars. No biggie.

"Rory," Mom says flatly.

"Hi." I swallow hard and chance a glance at my dad. His expression is hard to read.

"Dean. Erica. It's nice to see you," Breck says, snapping the tension with just a smile.

"You as well. What's going on?" Dad asks, and the question feels like an accusation. My stomach sinks. I wish Breck could hold my hand, but he's keeping his distance.

"Celebrating," he says with utter confidence. "Rory found a new apartment." This news surprises both my parents, their eyes widening.

"That's wonderful, Rory. Is it here at the lake?" Dad asks. I would expect the question to be hostile, judgmental almost, but it's not.

"Oh, um, no. It's down in the valley. I'll have to drive a bit, but it's a great location." A lie, since I haven't seen it yet, but I trust Jamie and know he wouldn't let me live in a dump.

"Good. Good. Maybe we can come see it sometime," Mom says.

I think my jaw might be on the floor. I'm speechless. Was that an olive branch? Breck's thigh presses against mine under the table and I try to relax.

"Yeah. Maybe." I don't know what else to say.

"And Breck, how much longer do you have before you go back to Australia?" Mom asks, focusing on him. "Or are you extending your trip further?"

"No. We really can't extend any longer at this point. We leave on Saturday," Breck states easily, readily. My gut clenches.

Less than a week.

"Ah. Well, safe travels," Mom says, and she sounds like she actually might mean it.

"Thank you."

"We don't want to keep you. Enjoy your evening," Dad says. "Erica, I'll walk you to your car."

She nods, walking one step behind him to the door, but then she glances back at us and I think she almost smiles.

What the hell was that?

"I have no idea," Breck muses, and I realize I spoke the question aloud.

He reaches his arm around my shoulder and pulls me back into his side before burying his nose in my hair.

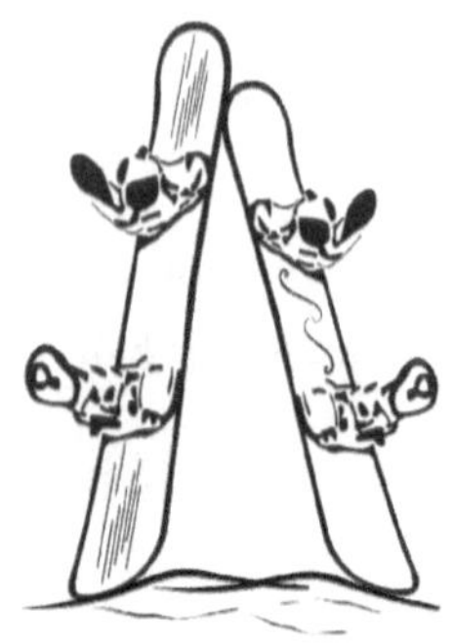

CHAPTER THIRTY-FIVE

Breck

I stand, eyes closed and face tilted up to welcome the sun, as the water laps around the dock at Valhalla. Today's ceremony was simple and perfect, and I find myself walking through every moment, proud of what we accomplished.

Each elopement I've officiated over the last few months feels like an insight into the true value of love and companionship. These are couples who aren't looking for the fanfare of a big wedding: the trappings, gifts, and praise of those around them. They long for something pure, to cherish the union as something that belongs only to them.

My heart constricts like it's physically grasping for a love like that. Like my parents had. Not for show, but because you want to be tied to your partner unconditionally. In hindsight, I should've known when Talia refused to get married over and over again that something wasn't right.

In the weeks since I burned her letter, I've been ruminating on Rory's words.

The future might look different for you and Willow, but you have so much to look forward to. There's something better waiting for you. A better job, a better relationship.

And I'm finally beginning to believe her. That's what I want—for me and for Willow. Where I'm struggling is with picturing it. All I can see right now is Tahoe—and Rory. I refuse to think of her as a rebound or as anything less than the gift she is. She's been my rock in this storm. But even with the squall finally settling around me, trying to imagine being back in Sydney in a few days is like looking through murky water. It's all blurry and indistinct.

My professional future is hazy at best, a complete blind-spot at worst. Helping Rory get Willow Tree Elopements up and running has been a distraction from that. The way she's embraced this new business, even if a little cautiously, is inspiring. It makes me hopeful I can reimagine what I thought my life would look like. I can't see it though. Not yet, at least.

I turn on the dock to face the buildings of Valhalla. The rustic, shingle-style siding and green trim are unique and meld perfectly with the imposing pine trees that surround them. The girls stare down at the camera around Willow's neck, checking the images she took and comparing them to the ones on Rory's camera. Rory's head kicks back at whatever Willow says. I owe her so much for the progress Willow's made too. For Willow to be so far away from home for so long was a gamble, but Rory's been her friend, inspired her with photography, and I'm glad she can take that with her when we go home.

We only have two days left, and we can't extend our time any longer no matter how badly I may want to. Willow's teachers are excited to have her back in the classroom, and I know she needs to be with her peers, her friends. I can't expect Wes and Joss to keep up with my house and everything else I left behind in Sydney forever either.

I'd love to live out my days with zero responsibilities and be on constant vacation, but I need to find a way for myself, a new goal, a new passion to filter my skills into. Working with Rory has been incredible, but it's time for her to fly on her own. She's set to move into her new apartment a few days after we leave, and I wish I could help her get settled, like she did for us. She needs to do this on her own though, to prove to herself she can. And I need to find a way forward for me and Willow. To prove to myself that *I* can.

I shuffle my boots over the slick boards, turning to take in the view of the lake. I've loved Sydney for as long as I can remember, but Tahoe is going to keep a piece of my heart. When I make the full circle, Rory's there, a few feet from me on the dock, and I know it's her I'll be leaving that piece with.

"Ready to go?" she asks, her smile not reaching her eyes.

"Yeah. I was just taking it all in one last time." My throat feels thick and my eyes burn.

I need to keep it together.

"It will still be here if you ever come back." There's a tremor in her voice and she looks past me to the lake.

"Yeah. I hope it will." I inhale the fresh mountain air and wrap an arm around her shoulder, nudging her playfully.

I look for Willow, finding her by a tree, and my brow furrows. What's she up to? She's bent down, hands moving over the snow. I'm squinting so hard under the sun's bright rays that I miss the snowball that comes sailing at me. THWACK. It's a direct hit square to the chest.

"Bloody hell!" I shout, but it's drowned out by Rory's laughter. She's bent double next to me, hands on her knees. Then it's her turn as a ball of ice and snow hits her in the shoulder and she squeals. Jerking up, her eyes go wide then narrow into a playful death glare.

"You're going down, ankle-biter," I yell in Willow's direction, but she just snickers and picks up more snowballs.

Rory and I fan out, moving in opposite directions. I hide behind a tree, making as many as I can. The crunch of fallen pine needles and leaves alerts me to someone's presence. I sling my arm out around the tree and throw the snowball, only to have it collide with Rory's stomach with an *oof*.

"Shit, sorry," I say at the same time she says, "I thought we were on the same side." Her hands find her hips, brows quirked up, cheeks flushed with exertion and cold. We move closer, turning in circles, eyes darting around the trees, on the lookout for our target. I use our new proximity to my advantage and push a tendril of Rory's hair from her face. "Where is she?" I whisper.

"I don't know," she whispers back.

"HA!" I hear from behind me just before a snowball collides with the back of my head.

"Hey! No head shots." I spin and hit Willow in the back. Catching up to her as she runs away, I throw her over my shoulder, tickling her ribs.

"Dad! Stop!" she screeches through her giggles. I let up and slide her to the ground, in direct view of Rory, who tosses one final snowball, splattering Willow's chest. "Ah, man! No fair!"

"Well, you had time on your side with your little stash of snowballs," Rory says, her breathing a little ragged from chasing after us. "You're fast," she tells me.

"For an old man," I quip.

"You're not that old, Daddy. Melissa's dad is forty." Willow makes a face as if that's unimaginable, even though it's only five years away for me. But I guess to an eight-year-old, five years seems like a lifetime.

"Are you excited to see Melissa when you go home?" Rory asks.

Willow looks down at her shoes and shrugs, all the playfulness from a moment ago vanishing in an instant. She's been avoiding any mention of Sydney. I get it, since I don't really want to think about it either, but we can't ignore it. Tomorrow, we pack. The next day, we get on a plane.

Rory looks at me, eyes wide and mouth set in a grimace. She mouths *sorry*, but I shake my head. It's not her fault. She inclines her head toward the car and walks that way, giving us a minute.

"Willow?" I feel like I'm approaching a wounded animal.

She kicks at a pile of snow with her boot and hits a rock. "Ow!" Her shoulders slump before she jumps up and down a couple times and then hobbles over to me.

"Hey." Small cries escape her as I rub my hand through her hair. I doubt hitting her toe was enough to bring on this level of distress. "Wanna tell me what's bothering you?"

"I don't want to go back. Can't we stay longer?"

"We can't, love. It's time for us to go home."

"But why? I'm doing fine with school. And Rory is here. I like Rory, and I get to help her with her work," she rushes out.

"I know. But aren't you ready to see your friends again? You haven't had many kids around the last three months."

"So," she huffs. "I have you guys, and Jamie. We could stay, couldn't we? You don't have a job at home now. Mom is—Mom isn't there. I like it here."

"I know you do, and so do I, but we can't—"

"Why not?" she shouts, tears glistening in her eyes.

"Because, sweetheart. It's not our home. I may not have a job right now, but I will have to get one eventually. Your school wants you to come back and be in the classroom too. They've given us a lot of freedom for the past month, but this wasn't supposed to be a long-term arrangement."

I swipe the tears from under her eyes and hold her close.

"Let's make the most of the time we have left, okay? I promise we'll come back and visit. You know Uncle Wes will want to come back again soon. We can come with him."

She sniffles and pushes away from me, storming off toward the car. I blow a breath out through my lips.

That could have gone better.

CHAPTER THIRTY-SIX

RORY

I'm pulling off my damp socks when the sound of a slamming door echoes through the house. *There goes Willow*, I think with a sigh.

In the kitchen, Breck is hunched over, forearms propped on the counter, head in his hands. He looks exhausted, dejected. I saw the sadness in his eyes on the dock, the same as my own.

Turns out I lied to Jamie when I promised I would protect my heart, because standing here, I wish I could ask Breck to stay. But I know I can't. I want to go to him, hold him, but his expression is unreadable. I don't know if the comfort of my touch, my body even, is what he wants or needs right now.

I know it's what I want.

"Come here." His voice is rough, and I take up the spot next to him, letting our shoulders brush.

Why is it so right being near him?

"Rory, look at me," he insists, shifting his body so he leans on one arm to face me. He pushes my hair, which I was using as a shield, behind my ear. His fingers find my chin and force my eyes to his. I don't know what he sees there, but I imagine they broadcast my swirling emotions.

He opens his mouth, but afraid of what he might say, I lean forward and press my lips to his. Avoiding this conversation doesn't help anything. It will happen eventually, but I don't want it to be right now. I don't think he does either.

I break the kiss first, my breathing ragged. There's a sound from upstairs that draws both our attention.

"Is she okay? I could go talk to her," I offer, wondering if talking to someone besides her dad could help, but I don't want to overstep. I've grown to love her over these past few months, but I know I'm not her mother. It's going to hurt to be separated from her just as much as from Breck.

"She'll come down when she's ready. I think she just needs a little time." He shrugs. "Why don't you go and get changed out of your wet clothes. I'll get started on dinner."

Thirty minutes and a hot shower later, I walk out of my room to music and the smell of sauce and dough and cheese. Willow grabs my hand the second I round the corner from the hall.

"We made homemade pizzas, and I made yours in the shape of a heart again." She's less solemn than earlier, her voice back to her normal octave. "You know, because I love you."

It should feel amazing to hear those words from someone who I know means them, but my stomach hollows out.

"I love you too, Willow," I say, pulling her hand until she's in my arms and I can hug her tight. I will my eyes to hold back the tears threatening to spill out for how unfair it is that Sydney stole my brother and now it gets to have Breck and Willow too.

I'll be left here. Alone. Again.

"What's going on here?" Breck's joy-filled voice comes from behind us. I let Willow go and she saunters over to the fridge.

"Nothing. Just talking about dinner," I say, attempting to control the quiver in my voice. "I hear it's pizza night."

"It is, indeed." Breck comes up next to me, hair wet and smelling of fresh snow and spice, making me wonder what soap he uses. "You want a glass of wine?"

"Sure."

"Okay. Go take a load off and I'll bring you one, yeah?"

"Yeah, sounds good."

Willow snuggles into my side on the sofa and I rest my head on hers. For a minute, I let myself imagine I could have a life that looks like this. A life where I have a man in the kitchen making me dinner and a daughter who's excited to cuddle up and tell me about her day.

"Hey." Breck's voice is quiet, and when I open my eyes, he's standing over me. He holds out a glass and I take it, our fingertips brushing.

"Thanks."

"Dinner's ready too."

Willow jumps up and pulls me toward the table. There's a heart-shaped pizza with *RORY* written in pepperonis. It may not be my preferred Mediterranean one, but this one is even better.

Willow is back to her normal, happy-go-lucky self as we eat dinner. I don't know if Breck talked to her since she shut herself in her room earlier, but I'm glad to see her smiling again.

"Willow Bear, go brush your teeth. Call down when you're in bed and I'll come say good night," Breck says once the counters are back to sparkling and the leftovers are put away.

"Thanks for dinner," I say through a yawn.

Breck smiles. "Willow wanted to do something special for you and it's the only thing she knows how to make."

Everything inside me warms and I stand in silence, watching him, soaking in the moment and all the things it's making me feel.

"Daddy!" Willow's voice carries down the stairs, cutting him off as he was about to open his mouth to speak again. "I'm in bed."

"Okay, I'm coming."

He jogs off, bounding up the stairs two at a time, and I quietly follow. I never participate in bedtime, but part of me wants to, just this once, even if only as a silent observer.

When I approach the doorway, Breck is reading her a story, then she starts to read it to him instead. I close my eyes and imagine sitting with them, listening to her read. When the story's over, I hear them shifting around and peek my head around the door. Breck leans over her, tucking the blankets around her small body. Leaning close, he whispers something in her ear, and she whispers something back. Words that are just for them.

An hour later, Willow is fast asleep and Breck and I are hunkered down in the living room, an empty wine bottle and our two glasses on the coffee table.

We've been going over every possible detail for Willow Tree Elopements. Which dates I have booked, who's officiating... As of last week, Patrick is now part of the team. He's a friend of mine and Jamie's from college who recently moved back to the area. With his confident, outgoing personality, I have no concerns about his ability to be an amazing officiant. And he's available for all of the dates Jamie isn't.

Breck has the website fully up and running and has walked me through all the necessary steps of the scheduling and CRM software. It's a lot, and even though he's been showing me everything as he's set it up, touching on all of it at once is overwhelming.

"Do you really think I can do this on my own?" I ask, chewing my lip. It's a question I've been terrified to voice for weeks.

"You absolutely can." He walks his fingers up my arm. "You can and you will. And you won't ever truly be on your own. I'm only a phone call or an email away. Or hell, a flight even. I know I can't just jump on a plane whenever I want, but if you really needed it, I could be here."

Never in a million years would I ask that of him, but it fills my heart with something warm that he would even offer.

"You aren't alone." His thumb coasts over my jawline. "You have me. You have Wes and Jamie and Joss. You have support, you just have to lean into it. But at the end of the day, all you really need is you. I believe in you."

My eyes swim with tears. As much as I was dreading that question, I'm glad I asked. I needed those words in a way I never knew. I needed them from *him*.

"Okay."

"Okay," he says back. "No more doubting yourself. You've got this. Your new place is good to go next week?"

"Yeah, on Monday. It'll be weird living down in the valley and not right on the mountain. Maybe that change will be good for me too. Some space."

"I wish we could help you get settled in. You did so much for us when we got here."

"Don't worry about it."

"I promise I'll bring you a fancy candle or something when we visit." He grins, but it falls a little flat.

"Don't—" I cut myself off by biting my lip again, this time so much that it hurts.

"Don't... what?"

"Please don't make promises you can't keep."

"I won't. I'm not. We will come back. Wes and Joss are going to want to come visit and I already told Willow we'd come with them when they do. I don't know when it'll be, but we *will* come back, okay?"

I nod, but something in me says it's not true. He and Willow will go back to their lives in Sydney and figure out how to move forward after everything. Even if they do come visit, it'll never be the same. It'll never be like this. He'll find someone to love him, and she'll be the one to pick my housewarming gift. Or maybe it'll be me who finds someone, and the thought of that should make me happy, but it doesn't. Either way, we won't be *us* like we are right now. It'll change, and I wish it didn't have to.

"We'll still be friends, right? I know you'll go back to having Wes when you get home, but..." I can't finish the sentence.

Breck pulls me into him and hugs me tight. "Is that what you're worried about? That I'm going to go home and forget about you?"

"Well, when you put it like that, it sounds childish... I'm only making it more obvious that I'm just Wes's little sister, aren't I?" I try to escape his hold, feeling exposed and raw all of a sudden.

"Stop," he says, keeping me close. "You're not *just* Wes's little sister. God, don't you know that? Rory, you're like sunshine. You bring light to everything around you. You're warm and bright. And you know what else makes you like the sun?"

I shake my head, too nervous to speak.

"There's no alternative to the sun. It may get eclipsed sometimes, but it's always there, shining anyway. That's you. Your parents have tried to control you, you've felt overshadowed by Wes, but in the end, none of that matters because you will come through brighter than ever."

"How do you know?"

"Because I used to be a sun too. I thought all my light, the positivity that I lived by, the brightness of my future was gone when I got here. I couldn't see through the darkness Talia left me in. *You* lit up those shadows. *You* showed me your light. *You* let me pull from it so I could find mine again, and for that I'll always be eternally grateful to you. And you know what I love?"

My breath hitches on the word even though I know he's not going to say it's me. He can't say it's me. He won't.

"I love that the sun in Sydney is the same as the sun in Tahoe. We'll never be that far apart. Does that answer your question about if we'll still be friends when I go home? Does that soothe your worries that I'm going to walk away and forget you? How could I forget the sun?" he says, letting the words sink in as he holds my gaze.

I press forward and seal my lips over his. I have only two more nights with this man and I want to enjoy every last minute of them. He may think I'm the sun, that his light was dimmed and it was me who brought it back, but I've never burned as bright as I have with him.

He encouraged me to fly while also being the soft and stable landing place I could rely on. With him leaving, it's like I'm standing at the precipice and have to decide if I can fly on my own. I know that's what I need. I know that I can. But it's terrifying to look down and know he won't be there to catch me if I fall.

I need to believe in myself to take that final leap, and I never will if he's constantly there as my safety net.

I lean into him farther, afraid to lose the way *he* lights *me* up. He's going to take that with him too. I realize I don't mind if he does, so long as it means he can be the sun to Willow. If it means he'll have a light to see his future—because it's going to be great, and I don't want him to miss it.

I wish I understood why we were only meant for this. For this short space of time. Maybe we were destined to help each other so we could go on to the futures we deserve, even if they aren't the same.

"Rory." He groans against my lips, moving me so I sit astride him on the couch. "Be here. Be with me, right now. Let me distract you from all those thoughts in your head, and you can distract me from all the ones in mine. Just be here, yeah?" His voice is ragged with emotion and desire, and I give in.

We choose each other one more time, before we have to choose ourselves.

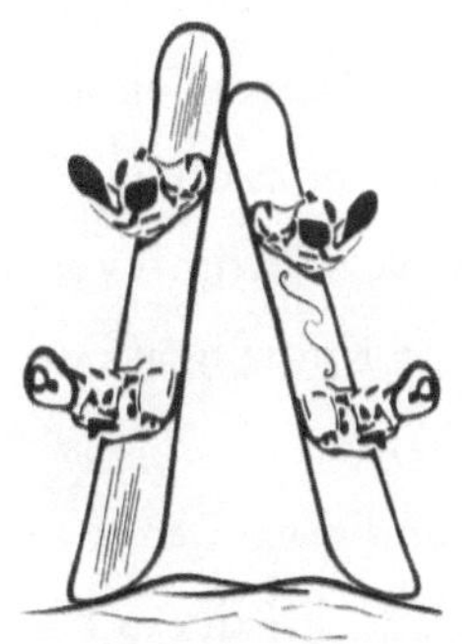

CHAPTER THIRTY-SEVEN

BRECK

"Willow, why don't you go to the bathroom before we go through security, yeah?" I say, wanting a minute alone with Rory.

"But I don't need to go." Willow stomps her foot. Literally stomps her foot. I know I shouldn't encourage her, but I can't hold back a laugh.

"Doesn't matter. Go try anyway." I nod toward the bathroom behind where we're standing.

One aggressive eye-roll later, she takes her stomping feet with her to the bathroom. As soon as she rounds the corner, I pull Rory into my arms. I slide a hand up her back and into her hair, not caring that we're in public, not caring who's watching. We have only minutes.

I tilt her face up and slant my lips over hers, insistent and wanting, using this kiss to convey all the things I can't say.

I want her to know how much I appreciate her for being the support I didn't know we needed. For being a friend. For being a woman I'm proud Willow looks up to. More than all of that, for helping me see I'm capable of intimacy again. For things I won't let myself put into words. Knowing if I do, even in my head, this will become infinitely harder.

I want more and I don't want to stop, but it won't be long before Willow is back, and she doesn't need to find us tangled up in each other. I slow the kiss and pull back enough to press my forehead to hers.

I take a steadying breath and whisper, "Thank you," into the space between us.

She sighs against me and her shoulders relax. She hugs me, resting her head on my shoulder, and breathes the same two words into my ear. I squeeze her a little tighter and she shudders in my grasp.

Another set of arms wrap around us both and I pull Willow into our embrace. Her smaller shoulders shake. She's upset and I know, for her, this is only making it harder.

I close my eyes and inhale, then pull away. We've put off the inevitable long enough. I gather our things and give Willow a minute with Rory, who drops down to her haunches. My throat feels thick watching her hug my daughter. Willow whispers something in Rory's ear and they tighten their embrace as Rory whispers something back.

I brush my hand down Willow's back and she looks up at me, eyes red and puffy. I give her a little nod and her shoulders sag. She stands up and Rory follows, averting her wet gaze.

"Keep me posted on your travels so I know you make it home, okay?" Her voice quavers and I look at the ceiling, wishing gravity could pull the tears back.

"I will," I manage to get out but have to clear my throat to keep going. "We'll talk soon. I want to hear how the elopement tomorrow goes with Patrick."

"Right, yeah, of course." Rory looks up and our eyes catch. Seeing both my girls so sad is eviscerating my heart. But Rory's not my girl, not really.

I wish more than anything this wasn't so damn hard.

"Bye, Rory."

"Bye." Her voice cracks and she turns at the same time Willow and I head for security.

I won't look back. *I won't look back.*

I look back.

She doesn't.

But I can tell she's crying as she walks away, and my throat stings with unshed tears. I will not cry. I can't. If I lose it, Willow will fall apart, and I can already feel her trembling under my arm. I pull her closer and try to send all my love into that touch.

It takes an hour and a half to get through security and to board our plane, but we're finally seated comfortably on our first flight to Los Angeles. Willow leans against my side, legs pulled up under her, head on my chest. I wonder if she'll always let me snuggle her like this. I hope so.

"Daddy."

"Yeah, Willow?" I say against her hair.

She sits up and I look down into her blue eyes.

"Did you tell Rory you love her?"

My heart stutters, along with my brain. "Wh-what?"

"Before we left, did you tell her you love her?" Her eyes are wide, innocent and questioning.

I don't know what to say. I'm blinking too fast and my breaths are shallow.

"You told me once when I saw you kissing Mom and thought it was gross that it was because you loved each other."

I blink again. "Oh-kay…"

"I saw you kissing Rory while I was supposed to be in the bathroom," she says, unapologetic. I purse my lips and tilt my head down in annoyance at her sneaking around. "What? I told you I didn't need to go. Anyway, it's okay if you forgot to tell her. I told her. So at least she knows."

My heart cracks under the strain. Of course that's what she said to Rory. I want to ask what Rory said in return, but those words were for Willow.

"I—thanks, sweetheart." I pull her toward me and kiss her head so I don't have to look in her eyes. Eyes that are like mine but belong to a girl who's so much braver than me. Her willingness to put her heart out there after what she's been through both inspires and terrifies me. I hate that I brought someone new into her life that she started to love and is now losing all over again. I hate it for me too.

"Daddy?" she whispers, and I tense with anticipation. "Why didn't Rory come with us?"

I close my eyes against the swell of emotion, swallowing thickly. "Because her life is here." A life I hope will flourish now that she's doing what she really wants. A life I'll only get to see through images, maybe phone calls, and the occasional visit.

"Why couldn't we stay here then?"

"Because our life is in Sydney." Even if it's a life that feels entirely unfamiliar to me now.

"But Mom said she loved us and she left. It feels like we're doing the same thing to Rory. I don't want her to think we don't love her."

I sniff, staring at the ceiling again. This kid is killing me. She's too smart, too observant, and it's breaking my heart.

"I know you're sad to leave, and so am I, but it's not the same as when Mom left. Rory is our friend, and we have different lives. She knows we aren't leaving because we don't—" I can't get the word out, so I stumble on without it. "We don't always get to live near our friends, sweetheart. Like when Wes lived far away. I knew it was because that's where his life took him, not because he didn't care about me anymore."

"Do you kiss all your friends?" she asks, a hint of sass to the question.

"No, I don't. But you also weren't supposed to see that."

"Why not?"

So many questions.

"I-I don't know. You've only ever seen me kiss your mom. I didn't know what you'd think and I didn't want to upset you. Kissing aside, Rory and I are just friends." *Lie.* But then... that's all we were ever supposed to be. Short-lived, an itch scratched, less overthinking. It was never meant to be more.

Then it was. And now it's not.

"Okay." Willow sighs, her body slumping in defeat. "I'm just really going to miss her."

"Me too, Bear, me too."

As hard it was getting on the plane to leave, getting off the plane in Sydney is a relief. Joss worked some airline magic and got us upgrades to lie-flat seats from LA to Sydney, but I'm still knackered.

Our luggage expanded with the snow gear we accumulated during our trip, so Wes offered to meet us at baggage claim. There's a sense of déjà vu as I approach the carousels with Willow on my back, heavier than she was three months ago, pulling two carry-ons.

I'm so focused on getting past the secure area doors and into the main terminal that I'm only alerted to his presence by Willow's scream in my ear.

"Uncle Wes!"

My head snaps up.

There he is, Joss behind him, walking toward us with big smiles in place. Willow releases my neck and hops to the ground, sprinting for Wes, and it's not just her weight that drops from my shoulders. He scoops her into his arms, squeezing until she starts to protest. Willow's words are flying at a million miles a minute, and Joss makes her way over to wrap me in a bear hug.

"Thank you for the upgrade," I say. "That was a very nice surprise. I doubt either of us would be standing right now if not for you."

Joss stands much shorter, wearing only a pair of flip flops, yet she looks me straight in the eye. "You're welcome. We're glad to have you home."

"Ain't that the truth," Wes says, nearly shoving past Joss to get to me and scooping me into his arms. "We've missed you."

"Us too," I say, my throat feeling thick again, clogged with exhaustion and emotion. It's on the tip of my tongue to say it's good to be back, but I'd be lying. I'm not sure how to feel about being here again.

"How many bags are we looking for?" Joss asks.

"Too many," I say with a groan. They laugh, but I'm not kidding. "Three large ones, plus my snowboard bag. I had to buy an extra suitcase for all the winterwear. Then of course there were the birthday presents, and all the random souvenirs, and just *stuff*. Do you know how much you can collect in just three months?"

"A lot... But I think I snagged the best thing of all in my first few months here," Wes says, looking down at Joss.

"Goodness, can you be any cheesier, Wes?" Joss smacks his chest with a soft thump.

"I'm sure I could try, Grey." He waggles his eyebrows at her.

Their banter has always been my favorite part of their relationship. Even when they were "just friends," they could rib each other and make the other laugh so easily.

"Daddy, there's my bag!" Willow shouts, pulling our attention toward the bright purple suitcase on the conveyor belt. Rory helped

Willow pick it out, and there was no changing either of their minds when I suggested a more neutral color.

"Ah, very pretty," Joss says, pulling it off with an *oof*. "What do you have packed in here? Bricks?"

"Daddy put all our shoes in that one… and my books."

"Well, that would explain it."

The other bags arrive shortly after Willow's and we make the slow trek to the parking lot where Wes has my Hilux parked. There are two things I definitely missed about Sydney: the friends standing around me, and my ute. I drag my hand over the back bumper before releasing the tailgate so we can slide all the bags into the bed.

"Think you'll remember how to drive on the left side of the road? Or are you fully Americanized now?"

"I think I'll manage." I give his shoulder a shove and open the door for Willow to hop in the back, preparing myself for this drive.

We're going home for the first time in three months. For the first time since it stopped feeling like our home at all.

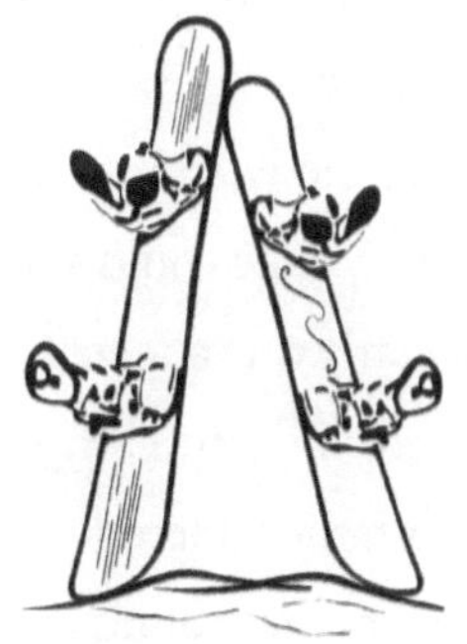

CHAPTER THIRTY-EIGHT

RORY

I quit my job.

I *quit* my job.

I. Quit. My. Job.

Well, sort of. I guess you could say I half quit.

No, I fully quit, but Logan convinced me to stay on part-time for the rest of the season so I can train Hannah, the intern.

Did I really just do that?

Bloody hell.

God, I'm even thinking like Breck, Aussie accent and all.

My feet carry me down the hallway toward my office and away from Logan's. I went in there ready to turn in my two weeks' notice. I want to take my photography full-time and with the trajectory of what Breck and I started, my schedule is already filling up. In the end, I'm glad Logan offered the option of staying on temporarily. This way I won't have to dip into my savings to stay afloat.

I think I was more worried to see the disappointment on his face when I told him I was leaving. Though, when he asked for the reason behind my decision, he was more than excited for me. He even offered to help in any way he could and said he'd be happy to reach out to some of his marketing contacts.

Four years of working for him and he's been a more supportive male figure than my own father. Here I am, a girl whose parents built their own business from the ground up but refused to help me chase my dream. Not that I asked. Why would I with their blatant disapproval for the whole idea?

I sit in my office chair and spin, pulling my legs up and letting my head fall back. I haven't seen them since the bar a week ago, but the tension *has* shifted—slightly. Mom texted me yesterday to *ask* me to join them for Sunday night dinner. I declined, offering the honest reason of having an elopement shoot and needing to pack. Really, it's more that I'm not ready to open myself up to them.

I stop my spinning, bring my hands to my desk, and look around my office.

Noting the time, I stand. Jamie will be at the condo soon. *Our condo.* I've been there alone for the last two days and nothing about it feels right anymore. I'm ready to get out of there.

Without Willow's giggles, Breck's boisterous laugh, the sounds of *Bluey*, the smell of Breck's freshly brewed coffee... It feels like there's no life there. It's like the three of us were playing house for the last month and the bubble of imaginative bliss popped the second he walked away in the airport.

I haven't stopped missing him.

A little piece of my heart went with him that day, and I don't think I'll ever get it back. I'll never regret it though. I gained so much of myself just by knowing him. By having him here. I'm not a different person. I'm just a better version of the woman I was. One who stands up for herself, goes after her dreams and what she wants.

And I can understand that chasing a man to Australia wouldn't have been what was best for *her*.

And it was never even a question for Breck. He had to choose the life that was best for him and Willow, and uprooting them for a fling from Tahoe wasn't it.

Fling.

No, we weren't that. As much as we said it was only physical, friends with benefits, *whatever*, there was more to it. There *is* more. Unfortunately, sometimes life gives you something incredible, but it's only meant for a season. Meant for a space in time.

That was us. A perfect alignment of the stars so we could be friends, lovers, partners... more. For a time.

I can accept that.

Or, I will. Eventually. Right now, it hurts more than I'll ever admit out loud. I miss him. I miss Willow. I miss all of it.

He's putting on a pretty good front, but I think he misses me too. We've only FaceTimed once since he left, mostly to let me know they'd made it home. Willow was adamant she wanted to get on another plane and come back, and Breck looked so tired I could see the tension in him that had all but disappeared these last few months. With Willow there, I didn't ask how he's really doing. I can only imagine it's not great being back in the house he shared with Talia.

We've texted some, but it's mostly been about business stuff: the shoot I had yesterday, the condo, and my move to the new place. It's very surface-level from both sides, and I don't know if that makes it better or worse.

I think he's keeping it friendly, focusing on safe topics so we can move beyond whatever those last moments in the terminal were. I can still hear Willow's whispered "we love you," still feel the ache in my heart. What I told her in return was true: I love them too.

That's the hard thing about loving someone. You want the best for them even if it means letting them go.

I walk up the steps of the building that will no longer be my home in mere minutes.

The sight of my suitcases at the door sparks a reckless feeling in me. How *easy* it would be to take these bags straight to the airport and be in Sydney tomorrow.

But I have a life I'm building here. I owe it to myself to give myself this chance to do what I've always wanted.

My phone vibrates in my pocket and I find Breck's name on the screen. A sad smile lifts my lips. It's like he knows I'm about to leave this space that was ours.

Breck

Big day!

He doesn't know how big, as I didn't tell him about my plan to quit at the resort. That was a decision I wanted to make a hundred percent on my own.

Breck

> I hope the move goes smoothly.

> Wish we could be there.

The dots pop up and disappear, pop up and disappear.

Breck

> Wish I could be there.

My eyes prick with tears.

Me

> Me too.

I write and delete "I miss you" at least five times, then chicken out, going for the less vulnerable option.

Me

> Tell Willow I miss her.

Breck

> She misses you too.

The first tears spill over and I press a hand over my mouth to stifle the sob that wants so badly to escape. The door behind me opens and Jamie envelops me in a hug, holding me as I cry into his shoulder.

"Shhh, m'eudail, shhh." His slight Scottish accent wraps around the Gaelic endearment and I melt into him farther.

I cling to his sweater with my fists and let myself—finally—experience all the feelings.

"I miss them."

"I know you do. So do I."

"But—" I start, but Jamie interrupts me.

"I know it's not the same." He pulls back and his thumbs swipe the tears from my cheeks. He looks right into my eyes. "You promised me I wasn't going to be picking up broken pieces of you. Am I going to have to fly to Australia and kick some ass?"

"I'm not broken." I hiccup. "I'm more whole than I've been in a long time." I choke out a sob. "It's just... a piece of me went to Sydney with him, and I'll never get it back. That hole feels really empty, but everything else feels so full, so I don't know what to do with that."

"You take it one day at a time." His arms come around me again and he kisses the top of my head. "For what it's worth, I'm so proud of you, Rory. Now, let's get you out of here and into your own place, shall we?"

We load my stuff into my car and head down the mountain. I was so busy with Breck and Willow last week, and then with the elopement and packing this weekend, to make it down to see the apartment. My new landlords sent me pictures, but I'm anxious to actually experience it in person.

When we pull up to my new home, I take a deep breath and step out, looking up to the mountains I used to live on. This change will be good.

We're parked in front of a large garage, attached to an even larger home. One of the bays will be mine—a first for me—and I let myself feel hopeful. Our shoes crunch on gravel until we reach a staircase that leads to a separate unit.

The wooden stairs creak on our ascent, laden down with large suitcases. I enter the code into the keypad and the door swings open with a squeak. I nearly melt as I take in the cutest space I've ever seen. It came furnished, though they said I could decorate however I want. For now, this is perfect. It's even better than the pictures.

My parents' condo was clean and modern, but I prefer something warmer, comfier.

There's a plaid blanket hanging over the back of a buttery-soft brown leather couch sitting in front of a gas fireplace with a TV mounted above it. The worn oak coffee table looks like it's been the setting for many a card game or movie night, with water rings stained into the wood right next to the coasters that never got used. The small dining table sits opposite a quaint kitchen, and it's more than enough space for me to set up my laptop. The kitchen is rustic with an assortment of mismatched mugs sitting by a coffee maker, and I can't wait to add my own eclectic collection to them.

The coffee maker isn't as fancy as the one in the last condo, but I've resigned myself to the fact that Breck had a magic touch with which he ruined me.

That magic touch definitely extended to more than the...

Nope, not going there right now. My cheeks heat as I follow after Jamie, finding him in the bedroom.

Jamie plants himself on the bed. It's draped with a dark green comforter and is nestled between rustic side tables that complement the cream walls and dark wood bed frame.

"Nice bounce to this mattress." He smirks and raises an eyebrow.

"Oh my god, stop. Get off my bed." I laugh, pushing at his shoulder. "Of course that's what you'd check first."

"What?" He scoffs with mock offense. "A good mattress is important—for a lot of reasons. Get your mind out of the gutter."

I bend over laughing even harder now. I love this man. I wonder if there will ever be a woman who will tangle herself deep enough into his heart to keep him. One can only hope. He deserves that.

"Let's check out the bathroom," I say.

He whistles when he walks in behind me, bracing his hands on the doorframe, and it's clear why. The large glassed-in shower has not one, not two, but *three* shower heads. One on each side of a rainfall shower head in the middle. The rest of the bathroom is pretty standard, but I think I want to live in that shower.

"Yup, it's settled, I'm moving in too," Jamie jokes before he heads back out to the living room.

"I don't think this place is big enough for the both of us."

He laughs. "Okay, now say that while standing with your hands on your hips like you're challenging me to a shootout."

He assumes the position and playacts pulling two imaginary revolvers from his holsters.

"You're a loon. You know that?"

"I do. Now let's grab your boxes out of my car so we can go get some dinner. We need to celebrate!"

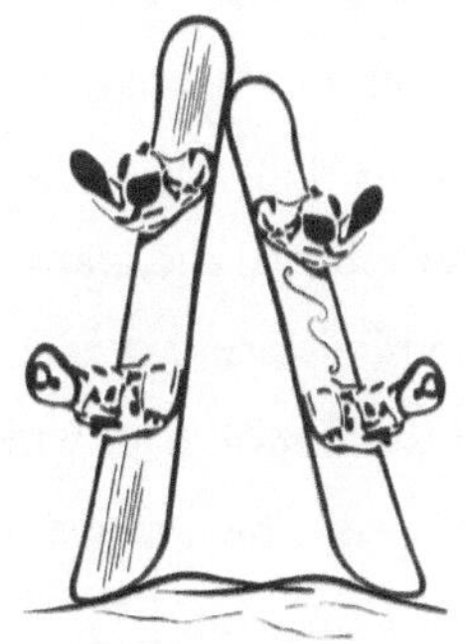

CHAPTER THIRTY-NINE

BRECK

I walk along the harbour, a coffee in each hand—pondering if I should've ordered them iced. The transition from Tahoe's winter to Sydney's summer has been an adjustment. It's a constant reminder that we're nowhere near the place we found solace the last three months. It's not just the sweltering temperatures that have been an adjustment. Everything here feels both old and new.

The house is the same yet different. It's still the house we brought Willow home from the hospital to, that we lived nearly nine years of our lives in.

Willow and I are the ones who've changed, moved into a new phase of our lives.

It took me less than a minute of standing in the master bedroom to know I'd need a new bed. Not just a new mattress, but a whole new bedroom set—and soon. Five nights in the guest room is plenty, thanks.

"Hey." Wes's voice pulls me out of my head as I see him sitting on the concrete sea wall that lines the harbour.

He stands, stretching his right leg, the scar from the crash just visible under the hem of his shorts, and grabs his cup from my hand. It's the first time I've seen him since they picked us up at the airport on Sunday. Both he and Joss left on trips with Qantas the next day. Willow and I have been on our own to get settled which has been both a good thing and the worst thing.

He claps me on the back, studying me as he steps back. "How're you doing, brother?"

I wince internally at his use of the word. We've always been that close, our relationship that easy. But it's hard for me to reconcile our relationship with the one I had with Rory—his *sister*—that he knows nothing about.

"I've been better," I say honestly, and he purses his lips. I don't have the energy to pretend all is fine and good when it's not.

"That was a stupid question. I'm sorry. I wish we could've been here this week."

"No worries, mate, it's fine. We're going to have to figure out this whole *get back to real life* thing sooner or later." I shrug, looking out at the water. I sit down and dangle my legs over the side of the concrete wall, picking up my coffee just for something to do with my hands.

"Yeah, but still. How's Willow handling being back?" he asks, taking a seat next to me. We stare out at the city that's been my home for so long, a view that's brought me peace and comfort for years.

The Harbour Bridge is to our left and the Opera House sits to our right. There are yachts bobbing in the water directly in front of us, and I wonder for a second what it would be like to get on one and just set sail for the horizon.

"She's trying. School's been weird. She missed a month of time with her class, so even though she's not behind, she feels like she's on the outside." I squeeze my neck, feeling the sharp prickle of hair there. I cut it the day after we got back, feeling like I needed to change something I could control. "I worried this would happen when we extended our vacation, but neither of us was ready to come back at the end of January. We're paying the price for that now."

He just nods and drinks his coffee, giving me space to continue.

"I think the kids are saying stuff to her about Talia too, but she's being vague about it. The moms at pickup this week have all been pleasant. You know, in the *we're going to start talking about you as soon as you turn your back* way."

"That's shit, man, I'm sorry. I can pick her up next week if you want."

I shake my head. "I can handle it. It just makes me wonder what they're saying, what their kids are hearing, and what they might say to Willow. She's doing her best, putting on a brave face, but I don't want her to have to do that."

"If I can help somehow, just let me know. I don't have another trip until Thursday." He looks away and continues. "I talked to Rory this morning."

"Yeah?" I keep my eyes locked on the water too, afraid they'll give away how my heart lurched at the sound of her name.

"Yeah, she showed me around her new place. It's pretty nice. Did she tell you she went down to part-time at the resort?"

"What? No." I swing my gaze to his and find him studying me.

"Yeah, a couple days after you left. I guess she was planning to quit outright, but they offered her the option." He shrugs. "I always liked her boss. Anyway, I haven't properly thanked you for helping her. I know I was unsure about the whole situation when you guys first told me, but I'm man enough to eat crow when I need to, and you both proved me wrong."

"It was all her, man. I helped with some of the finer points of the business side of things, but she's got all the talent to back it up. If anything," I say, working to keep my voice even, "she helped me more. I don't think I'll ever be able to repay her for all she did for us."

Wes raises an eyebrow, and I keep going. "It felt good to be back in the saddle, building a business from scratch. I remember those days with Adventure Chasers, and they were the best. Exhausting but exhilarating. Helping her revived that drive in me, and though I'm unsure what that might turn into here, I don't feel as stuck as I did when I left."

I don't go into how she helped me to feel less stuck in other areas of my life too. Or how I can't go a night without dreaming of her in my bed, my arms.

"That's incredible, mate," he says, and I could almost take his words as a response to my unspoken ones.

But they're not. He doesn't know about us, and he doesn't need to. There's seven thousand miles of space that dictated the end to that relationship. I was supposed to leave all those feelings behind, but it's so much more than her body I'm missing when I'm alone in bed at night. It's just *her. I miss her.*

"I wonder why she didn't tell me she was going to quit?" I say, breaking through my wayward thoughts.

"I don't know. Have you guys talked much?"

I shrug again. "Not really. We FaceTimed Sunday night after we arrived and texted some earlier in the week, but it was mostly about business." It's not like I don't want to talk to her. Talking to her just makes it harder to be here right now though, and this is where I need to be. But, *I miss her.*

"I know the time difference can be a bitch, but I think she'd love to talk to you." He lifts his coffee again, letting his words land.

"Did she say something?" Nonchalance is not my forte, and I'm pretty sure I fail at it here. I feel like a schoolgirl talking about her crush. God, I'm pathetic. *I miss her.*

Wes smirks. "No, but I can tell she's missing you guys. It's just an observation. Do with it what you will."

I lean back on my hands, letting my legs kick along the wall. "That's not—it's not weird for you if I call her?"

"Not at all." He grabs my shoulder, pushing it until I turn to face him. "Look, I wish I could've been there for you in Tahoe, but it is what it is. Y'all lived together, I imagine you formed a bond in that time." His gaze pierces mine, sincere and knowing. "I'm never going to stand in the way of you getting the support you need, wherever you need it from. I think you did a lot of good for her too."

I could tell him now. Tell him about how much deeper that bond went. I could ask him what the hell I'm supposed to do.

"I'll talk to her," I say instead. We go back to staring out over the water and I let the conversation drop. Internally though, I'm screaming that I. MISS. HER.

And I'm kicking myself for walking away.

Willow slams the door to the house and my head snaps up from where I'm sitting on the couch, staring at Rory's name on my phone. My fingers hover just above it, as if I could reach through and touch her by just tapping on her name.

"Bloody hell. Willow, what's going on?" Her tear-stained cheeks have me jumping up and over the back of the couch. I had another mom drive her home today, thinking maybe the extra time with one of her friends would be good for her. Looks like I fucked that up.

"I hate it here!" she yells, storming into her room and slamming that door behind her too. Well, shit.

My bare feet slap against the tile and I lean my head against her door with a light knock. "Willow Bear?"

"Go away." I flinch and my heart cracks in my chest. Do I force her to talk to me? Give her space?

"Can I come in?" I try again, but all I hear is a muffled cry from the other side of the door. "Come on, baby girl, please?"

Shuffling footsteps sound on the other side of the door before it opens a few inches. Her head is down so I can't see her face.

She immediately turns back to her bed and climbs on, pulling her favorite stuffy, a kangaroo that was the same size she was when she was born, into her lap. She's picking at the fabric that's pilled and worn.

Not wanting to crowd her, I sit at the end of the bed.

"Can you tell me what happened?"

She shakes her head.

"You can tell me anything."

"I don't want to make you mad." Her lip wobbles.

My eyebrows pull down. Make me mad? Did she get into trouble?

"You won't, sweetheart. Promise."

She looks up from under her onyx lashes, long dark hair framing her face. "The kids at school—" She puffs out a breath and starts again. "The kids at school said you cheated on Mom and that's why she left you. Left me. It's not true!" She shouts the last words, and if my mouth wasn't already hanging open, it would've been after that exclamation. I want to know how she even knows what "cheating" is in reference to a relationship, but that's a conversation for another day.

"No, it's not true, sweetheart."

I promised Willow I wouldn't get mad, but I want to rage. The kids at school didn't get to that conclusion on their own. I won't take it out on her though.

"I told them it wasn't true, but they didn't believe me. Then Andrea asked why Mom didn't want to take me with her and I started crying." The tears begin anew and she buries her face in her pillow. "Then I had to ride home with her."

I crawl up the bed so I can lie down next to her and pull her into my body. She turns over and hides her face in my chest. I hold her, my own tears threatening to spill over. I lose the battle when she whispers the question I've dreaded for months.

"Was it my fault she left?"

I drop my head back and breathe, eyes squeezing so tight I feel it pull everywhere on my face. I hold in a sob for my girl who's been through too much.

"No, baby. It wasn't your fault."

"You're sure?"

"Yes." For that one word, I pull it together, because I'll be damned if she hears even a quaver in my voice.

"But why didn't she want me anymore?" Her voice cracks.

Fuck. It's like my heart is in a blender.

"Because she was selfish, sweet girl. I know that's hard to hear and hard to understand, but it's the truth. She chose not to keep either of us in her life because she wanted something different. Her making that choice had nothing to do with us and everything to do with her. I'm so sorry, baby girl. I'm so sorry."

I hold her tighter and she cries until she runs out of tears. With a little hiccup, she looks up at me. "I miss her, but I don't want to."

"Both of those things are okay. To miss her and also to wish that you didn't."

"Do you miss her?"

"I miss her for you and for what you lost. You deserved a mom who'd always be there. I didn't have that growing up, and I wanted it so badly for you."

"I have you though," she says as she nestles closer. "I think that might be all I need anyway."

I roll onto my back and bring her with me. She may not know it, but her words were exactly what I needed to hear.

"You'll always have me, and I think you're all I need too, Willow Bear."

We lie there quietly for a couple of minutes, and just when I think she's fallen asleep, she speaks.

"I miss Tahoe. This doesn't feel like home anymore."

"I know." I choke back my own pain, not wanting to add it to hers.

"And I miss Rory," she whispers.

I close my eyes and steady my breathing. "Yeah, me too."

We fall asleep, and I don't call Rory. *Because* I miss her, and Willow misses her, and I don't know how to talk to her and *not* miss her. And she doesn't call me either.

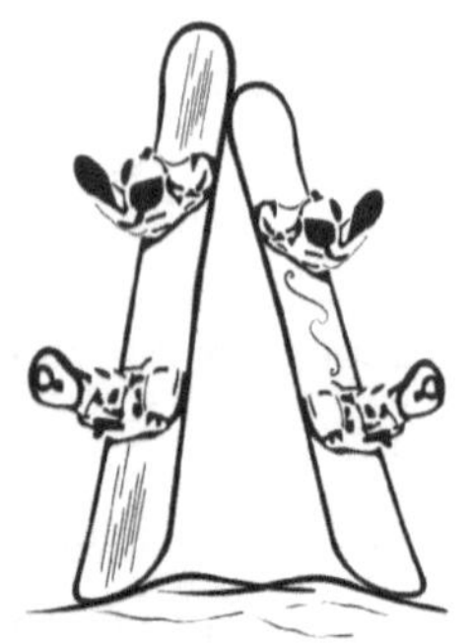

CHAPTER FORTY

RORY

Is this a joke?

It must be a joke.

I'm staring at my computer screen, sitting in the lodge at Empyreal, and I think I might cry.

Friday, March 28, 2025
To: Rory.Anderson@willowtreeelopements.com
From: TylerPlum@sacramentoweddingsmag.com
Subject: Potential Partnership

Ms. Anderson,
I came across some photos you took recently for John and Bree Tanner and was incredibly impressed. They mentioned

you were in the beginning stages of building a new business with a focus on elopements. To be completely honest, this is a market we at *Sacramento Weddings Magazine* would like to cater to and showcase more, which is where this email comes in. I think we could work together in a way that could be mutually beneficial. Would you be available for a virtual meeting on Monday where we could discuss this further? Let me know at your earliest convenience.

I'm a workaholic, so I'll have access to my email all weekend.

Sincerely,

Tyler Plum

Marketing Director, *Sacramento Weddings Magazine*

I pinch my arm. *Yup, I'm awake, and damn that hurt.* I type out the fastest reply in the history of mankind, do a quick read-through for any typos, and hit send before I can think better of it. Then I watch my inbox with bated breath for all of a minute before Tyler's reply pops up.

I have a ten o'clock meeting with the marketing director for a major wedding magazine on Monday. Is this real life?

My chair scrapes against the stone floor when I jump up with a little squeal. The dwindling number of people still sipping hot cocoa or drinks from the bar all turn to look at me. I give an awkward wave and sit back down, doing a little wiggle in my chair instead of a happy dance next to it.

This is huge. This is huge, right?

I grab my phone and the desire to tap on Breck's number almost overpowers me, but I don't give in. I've been avoiding that particular contact for weeks now.

Instead, I hit the name of the very first person in my favorites... Wes. It rings three times before he accepts my FaceTime request. His face is smushed against his pillow and his hair is mussed. Oh crap, it's like six in the morning in Sydney. He groans out my name, so it sounds more like *smores* than *Roars*.

"Sorry!" I say, and he flinches. "Sorry," I say again, quieter this time. "I forgot what time it is there."

"It's fine, but no more shouting. I got in late from work last night, so I've only been asleep for"—he finally opens one eye to look at the phone before closing it again with another groan—"four hours."

"I'm sorry. Oh god, did I wake Joss too?"

"Nah. She's on a trip until tonight, so it's just me losing out on beauty rest today. Hold on a sec." The camera pauses and when it flickers back on, he's propping the phone against something in the kitchen. "So what is it that couldn't wait until a tolerable hour to tell me?"

"I might be partnering with a bridal magazine in Sacramento." The words come out fast and squeaky, but Wes doesn't miss a beat.

"What? Seriously? That's incredible, Rory!" The wide smile that splits his face shows all his pearly teeth and his big dimples.

"It's not a done deal yet, but I got an email from their marketing director today about working together. Wes, this could be huge for me."

"You deserve it, baby sis," he says, and I cringe. "Sorry, old habits. It's hard for me to remember sometimes that you're this super accomplished, super impressive woman and not the kid sister I grew up with. I'm seriously so proud of you, Rory."

I turn red at his compliments. "Thanks, Wessy."

"Real nice," he deadpans, and I laugh. "So, tell me what else is going on? How's the resort? And the business? You holding up okay with both?"

"Yeah. It's a lot, but I have so many bookings from May onward that I won't have time for the resort. Hannah's mostly taken over for me here anyway, and she's so much more into the whole content creation thing than I ever was."

"That's what I love to hear. What about until then?"

"Well, I have whatever comes from this new contract to figure out. The meeting is on Monday, and then I've got a bunch of elopements scheduled for the beginning of April, but I left the last few weeks kind of open." I look away from the screen. "I was going to call you today anyway. I want to come visit you and Joss..." I trail off, worried he'll hear everything I'm holding back.

"Yeah?" he prompts.

"Yeah," I say, giving him nothing.

"And?" He drags out the word, turning it into a question.

"And what?" I snap, but when I bring my eyes back to him, he's smiling.

"And Breck and Willow?" He tilts his head and smirks.

"Yes, okay. And Breck and Willow. Are you happy?"

"You don't have to hide that you want to see them. That you want to see *him*."

My eyes widen at the emphasis and the implication, but I roll my lips.

"Did you really think I couldn't tell there was something going on?"

"Um, yes, I did think that!" I shout, drawing the attention of the last stragglers in the lodge. I lower my voice. "Why didn't you say anything?"

"You're both adults. I knew if there was something I needed to know, you'd tell me. Of course, then it became so damn obvious with how you've been dancing around each other since he left."

"But he's your best friend. You're not mad we—"

"Stop. I don't need to know the details, thank you very much. And no, I'm not mad." He runs a hand through his hair and takes a sip of the coffee I just watched him brew. "I do want to know if you're okay though. He left, and you're still there. I guess I want to be sure I don't need to beat up my best friend or something."

I laugh then put my head down on the table, too overwhelmed by this surprise turn in the conversation to make eye contact with him right now.

"I think I'm okay. He didn't promise me anything. But..."

"You miss him."

"I miss him." I look up, my chin still resting on my hands. "A lot. I just got this huge opportunity that I'm over the moon about, but the person I want to tell more than anyone isn't here." My face falls, eyebrows scrunched together.

"So why'd you call me instead of him?"

"I don't know. We haven't talked in weeks." Admitting it out loud makes my heart hurt, but I guess I'm done ignoring this now. "I know he's trying to figure out his life there. I don't want to overrun it with my stuff. I don't know if I'm making it all up in my head—what I felt when he was here, what I thought he felt too."

Wes sits quietly, and I appreciate that he's such a good listener, just letting me talk.

"I thought if I could come visit and see him—in his element, see that he's good there, that he's where he's supposed to be—I could let go."

"Or you could come visit and see he misses you just as much as you miss him."

"You think so?" I ask with too much eagerness in my voice, too much hope.

"Yeah. I do. Send me those dates and I'll get you a flight."

"I can get—"

"I know you can." His lips tip up in a grin. "Or you could let your big brother do something for you for once."

I nod, love for him filling my chest and butterflies filling my stomach.

I'm going to Sydney.

"Thank you, Wes."

CHAPTER FORTY-ONE

BRECK

I sit astride my surfboard, bobbing in the waves. The heat of the sun warms my face, my chest, my arms. I've sat on this board, with this view of the beach and the city beyond, more times than I can count, but something about today feels different.

Willow and I have been home for almost seven weeks, but with the little progress I've made it feels like no time has passed. I'm still sleeping in the guest room. I'm still just as unsure of what I want to do here—build another business, find a new company to work for... I was fortunate to have the Adventure Chasers money to live off these past five months, but I can't continue on this way. I want to feel the way I did in Tahoe, like I was doing something useful and productive. Like I was wanted and worthy.

A wave lifts me, but I don't paddle to catch it, letting it pass me by. I've been out here nearly every day since we got back. I thought the quiet and the serenity of the ocean would bring me answers, help me find my center again, but I continue to feel off-kilter.

The truth is, I don't need help finding my center. I know where it is, and it's not in Sydney. It's not even in this hemisphere.

It's in Tahoe, with Rory.

Beyond a few business-related emails—that felt too formal, foreign even—and the postcard she sent to Willow a couple weeks back, we haven't talked. That was easier initially. I thought it would help us both move on with our separate lives, but the longer our silence stretches, the harder it is. I don't want to accept that our lives are meant to be separate. It doesn't feel right.

Another wave lifts me, and this time, I let my instincts take over. I dig in, using my arms to paddle and catch up. I'm a little behind it now, but I want it and I'm not going to let this one pass me by. I stretch every muscle of my arms to their limit until I'm right at the crest. I push against the board to jump to my feet, and when the water sprays across my body, it's invigorating.

This is the most awake I've felt in weeks. Pumping my legs, I roller-coaster up and down the face. This is my wave. The one I was meant for today. With my thoughts on Rory and my body in this wave, they feel connected. This wave is the one, and maybe Rory was too. I fall back just enough to allow the tube to engulf me, surround me, until it spits me out and I ride the whitewater as far as it will take me. I'm unwilling to let this ride go...

Just like I keep wishing I hadn't let Rory go.

I paddle into the shore until it's shallow enough I can hop off my board and walk my way up to the beach. The crackling sound of the Velcro on my leash grits against my sensitive nerves. I lay the board down and find my space next to it. I don't care that I'm covered in sand, instead reveling in the gritty texture against my skin. I press my hands in, letting it flow between my fingers.

I turn my head and envision Rory lying beside me, sand in her hair, freckles on sun-kissed cheeks. Would she love to surf? Would she give me a run for my money every day if she was here? The vision changes to the three of us in the snow, making snow angels, and how her hand brushed mine. The mountain is her wave, and she rides it with ease. I know she could take on the ocean, but Tahoe's where she feels at home.

I felt at home there too. I grew up the same as her, on mountains with a board strapped to my feet. I just had to adapt to a different board, to the water, when I moved from the Perisher Valley to Sydney.

My eyes are closed against the sun and I attempt to quiet my brain. I could go back out, but I don't want another wave today. I'm happy to go home with that as my final ride.

I roll over, the sand sticking to my skin as I move to get my board.

On the drive home, I nearly hit Rory's name on my contact list a dozen times.

What am I so afraid of?

Pulling into the driveway, I decide I can at least shoot her a text—try to open that line of communication again.

I take a deep breath, typing out one more because I'm tired of not saying what's on my mind.

I put my phone back into my pocket and head inside for a shower. I don't get a response.

"Hey, Frank," I greet the security guard sitting at the desk of Wes and Joss's building.

"Mornin', Mr. Kylie," he says with a nod of his head and an almost-smile. I've learned you have to really work for a full smile from this man.

"I'll keep asking you to call me Breck, but I know you're going to just keep calling me Mr. Kylie," I quip, and his lips tip up just a hint farther.

"You're right about that. Visiting Mr. Anderson?"

"Yes, sir. Is Joss not here?"

"No, she left a while ago. Have a great day."

"You too, Frank."

I don't bother knocking when I reach their apartment on the sixteenth floor, hollering, "Honey, I'm home," as I enter.

There's a bark of laughter from the balcony and Wes makes his way through the open glass door, wrapping me in a hug. Watching him work through the trauma of his crash, the PTSD associated with it and all that came after, was an inspiration. It's part of what's kept me going these last five months when things felt so hard.

It's not lost on me that we both had Rory to help us get through the hard times in our lives, and that we had each other too. Wes found Joss, and look where they are now. I had Rory, and it makes my heart constrict thinking of where she and I are now. Seven thousand miles separate us, but there's more than oceans spanning between where we were when I left and where we are today.

"Joss left pretty early?" I ask.

"She had a couple errands to run before picking Willow up at school. I'm thinking we order pizzas and just hang out tonight, sound good?" Wes says but there's a twinkle in his eye, mischievousness in his smile.

"Yeah, sure," I say, skepticism dripping from my tone. "What's up with you?"

"Nothing," he says too quickly before pulling open the fridge. "Want a beer?"

"A cold one sounds good. Thanks."

"Balcony?" He nods toward the door and offers one to me.

"Yeah." I grab it and follow him out. "How was your trip? Do you leave again soon?"

He takes a long swig of the beer, resting his head on the back of the white wicker chair. "It was good, long. Joss and I are actually taking the next few weeks off."

I snap my head toward him. "Really? Why?" I wrack my brain for a reason they'd be taking vacation time in April.

He shrugs, trying to hide a smile by taking another drink. Yeah, he's definitely being weird.

"Y'all have anything planned? Another surf trip or something?"

"No, just spending time around here. We've been working nonstop since the honeymoon." He pierces me with his ocean blue eyes. "What about you? Anything planned for the next couple weeks?"

I scoff into my beer. "Ha. No."

"Still haven't had any epiphanies about what you want to do for work, huh?"

"No. Well, I have lots of ideas. Unfortunately, they're all for Rory and Willow Tree Elopements, which doesn't do me much good."

He perks up at this. "Ideas for Rory, huh? Have you shared them with her?"

"Not yet." I let my head tip back now, closing my eyes. "We haven't been talking much. I know she's busy, and I don't want to bug her."

"I know she wouldn't mind."

I nod and sip my beer. "I know but... I... We..." I'm stuttering, rambling.

"You... what?" He raises an eyebrow at me. "Are trying to figure out how to be apart after you let your lives intertwine more than you intended while you were in Tahoe?" he says, answering his own question.

"*What*?" I splutter.

"Breck. I know you. I know my sister. There was something there from the beginning. We could all see it, even at the wedding."

I swallow thickly, prepared for him to get mad or yell. He doesn't do either.

Instead, his face softens. "What do you want, Breck? *Really* want? Not what you think you should do, but what do you *want*?"

The question stuns me, but my answer comes easily. "I want what's best for Willow. She's my priority."

"Okay, of course, and what does that look like? What do you think is best for Willow right now?"

"I don't know anymore. When Talia left, I felt like it was best for us both to take time away. To get some space, find ourselves together—just the two of us. Then we'd come back and rebuild the life we had here. I never planned to uproot her for so long. She's struggling now, and that feels like it's my fault."

"What if the reason she's struggling is because being here isn't what's best for her anymore?" His voice is a little sad, but there are other emotions laced under it that I can't place. When he glances at his phone, a small smile tugs his lips up.

"I guess I'd need to figure out where would be best for her."

"Yeah, and what about you? Where would be best for *you*? Is it here?" He swipes a hand out, indicating the sprawling city around us. "You know I want you here. Always. I love you, man, but does Sydney feel like where you *want* to be, or are you just here because it's where you think you *should* be?"

I shake my head. "Other than you and Joss, nothing about Sydney has felt like home since we've been back."

"That's what I thought. I've never seen you struggle to find your place. You fit in everywhere. You find a home with everyone. You can come up with some harebrained scheme at the drop of a hat. But you're stuck." He puts his beer down and stands up, moving to lean against the railing to face me.

I lean forward, elbows on my knees, and blow out a breath. Then I tell him the truth. "I miss Tahoe. I miss Rory. I want to talk to her all the time. When I wake up in the morning, when I go to bed at night, when Willow says something silly or cute or irritating. I want to talk to her *all the time*, and that scares the shit out of me."

"That's good."

I chuckle darkly. "Really? That's good? It's good that I can't stop thinking about your sister, the one who lives half a world away? The one who didn't even text me back this morning when I finally broke down and told her I miss her?"

"You did?"

I push out of my seat and pace into the living room. "Yeah, I did, and she didn't respond. So what does that tell you?"

"It tells me this is about to be a really good day," Wes says, following me in.

"What?" My brows draw down, more than a little confused.

He doesn't get a chance to respond before the apartment door opens and Joss walks in. She's laughing, the sound mingling with Willow's giggle, but it's the third laugh that stops my heart in my chest.

Time freezes as Willow and Joss part and I see her. A mess of strawberry-blonde waves in a bun on top of her head. The freckles I was imagining just this morning spread across her nose and on her cheeks under turquoise eyes. Eyes that find mine and it's like a defibrillator to my heart, bringing me back to life. Her smile starts small but grows until it overtakes her whole face.

"Daddy! Look who's here!" Willow shouts and bounds toward me. "It's Rory!"

"I see that, baby girl," I say, still unable to pull my eyes away from the vision in front of me.

Rory's face softens and her head tilts to the side, her smile turning from one of excitement to one that holds more. Emotions I'm afraid to put a name to. Emotions that mimic those I feel bubbling in my chest. I don't know what she's doing here, but the time and space between us feels like a rubber band that we stretched too far, and it finally snaps.

I stalk across the space, and when my lips meet hers, I feel like I'm finally home.

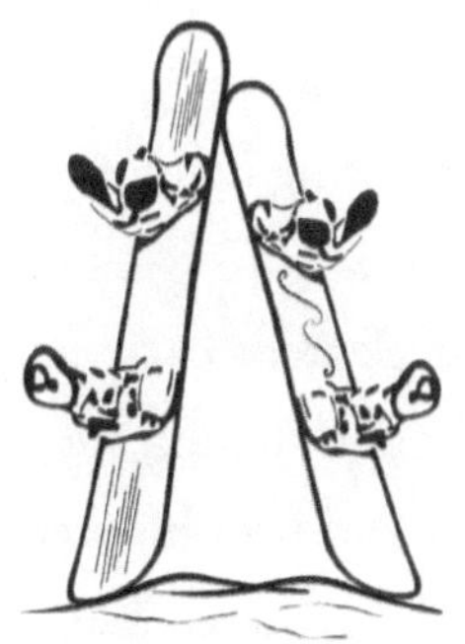

CHAPTER FORTY-TWO

Rory

The moment when Willow saw me standing outside the car at school pickup was perfect. She was so excited, literally running the last thirty feet between us once she caught sight of me. This moment though... I didn't even let myself dream it would be like this. I didn't know what to expect after the radio silence of the past month and a half. Now, with Breck's hands tenderly framing my face and his lips insistent against mine... I know I made the right decision.

I lean into him and inhale his scent. It surrounds me to the point where there's nothing else. No one else.

A throat clears nearby and a giggle follows. Wes and Willow, thick as thieves those two. Breck and I pull apart, still not acknowledging the rest of our little group. His thumbs trace over my cheekbones and his eyes search mine.

"What're you doing here?" he asks, almost reverently, like he can't believe it's me in his arms.

"This," I murmur, pressing up on my toes to kiss him again. It's as good as I remember.

After a moment, Breck steps back, only to pull me into his side like he can't stand not touching me now that I'm here.

He narrows his eyes and uses his free hand to point at my brother. "You—why didn't you tell me?"

Wes shrugs with a wicked smirk on his face. "Can I hug my sister now?"

The apartment isn't huge, but I run the few paces between us and jump into his arms.

"I'm here!" I squeak in his ear.

"You're here. God, I missed you."

"I missed you too."

He holds me a little tighter before finally releasing me so he can look me over. "Your flight was okay?"

"Perfect. A little long. Think you could talk to Qantas about that?" I sigh, grinning. "I could probably use a shower."

"That's probably a good idea," Wes says, pulling back farther and making a face.

I swat his arm. "Rude."

"I only meant because you two," he says, indicating between me and Breck, "are going out."

"Wait, what?" I jerk back.

"Yup." He looks at Willow. "You up for pizza, a movie, and a sleepover with Uncle Wes and Aunt Joss?"

"Hell yes!" Willow bursts out.

"Hey! Language," Breck scolds her, but he looks like he really couldn't care less.

"Well, that's settled. You"—he points at me—"shower, and you two can leave when you're ready."

"But... are you sure?" I ask. I've only gotten to see him for five minutes.

"Would you stop? You're here for two weeks." He waggles his finger. "And you two have a lot to talk about."

Breck steps up next to me, his hand skating along my low back to my hip. "I don't have anything here for Willow. I didn't know about this plan. Rory, you good with this? You must be exhausted." His fingers dance along my cheek to cup my face, searching for the answer in my eyes.

Yes, I'm exhausted, but when he looks at me like that... It's like a shot of adrenaline, and I could ride that high all day.

"Willow's covered," Joss says. She shrugs like they didn't have this whole thing planned well before they had any idea how today would go. Or maybe they had more faith in this happening than even I did.

"You guys," Breck says, the sweetest softness in his voice.

"Oh and," Joss continues over him, "tomorrow, we're all climbing the Harbour Bridge."

Willow bursts in. "Wait, we get to climb the bridge tomorrow, for real?"

"For real," Wes says, then looks at me. "Go. Shower."

Walking out forty-five minutes later, I feel like a whole new woman. The bodice of the jumpsuit I chose for tonight is fitted, from the skinny straps down to my waist, before it flares out into wide-leg pants. I love the way the stone-blue color pulls out the darker facets of my eyes and doesn't wash me out since I'm extra pale from the winter back home.

The room stills when I enter, Breck catching sight of me from where he leans against the kitchen counter. His laughter stills, the smile freezing on his face and the blue of his eyes burning brighter.

"Are you two going to moon over each other like this all the time? Ugh, I don't know if I can take it," Wes jokes and turns to Willow. "Gross, right?" He sticks his tongue out, feigning a gag and making Willow giggle.

"So gross." She nods but then she says, "But that's what you do when you love someone." She shrugs, and with that bomb dropped into the middle of the room, trots over to me and gives me a hug. "You look beautiful."

"Th-thank you." All the adults just look at each other, the L-word hanging between us in that way it only can when it hasn't been said between the people who are expected to say it.

"Well, okay then, y'all should go." Wes clears his throat. "Do you have, um, stuff for later?" He looks at my empty hands.

"For later?" I ask, confused.

Joss walks over and quietly whispers in my ear, "Willow is having a sleepover here, so if you wanted to have a sleepover too..."

"Oh." I look at the guys. Breck's face is a mixture of embarrassment and desire, and Wes looks like he could throw up. I laugh awkwardly and run back into the bedroom to throw an overnight bag together as quickly as possible, feeling my blush all the way down to my toes.

Breck's already at the door and waiting when I emerge.

"Would you rather walk or drive to dinner?" he says, bringing my hand up to his lips. The swoop in my stomach has nothing to do with the quick descent of the elevator. "You must be so tired."

"I'm okay. Walking sounds good."

His eyes trail down my entire body until they land on my wedge sandals.

"You're sure?" he asks.

"Yes. They're comfortable. Now come on, show me your city."

He smiles wide, his dimples stretching across his handsome face. We stop to put my bag in his truck, which he tells me is called a "ute" in Australia. He then informs me I'll have to learn proper Australian-English if I'm going to be hanging out here.

We reach a seawall within minutes, and I pull my hand free and splay both on the concrete, giving myself a second to take in the striking view of the city around me. I've seen it before, but it feels brand new after all these years.

Beyond the landmarks Sydney's known for, it's the sunset—the sky a canvas of purples and blues that bleed down to reds and oranges toward the horizon that falls behind the buildings of the city—that takes my breath away.

"Wow. So beautiful," I say, turning to find Breck lowering his phone.

"I couldn't agree more." He closes the distance between us and threads a hand into my damp hair before kissing me gently.

How did I get through the last seven weeks without him? I lean in just when he pulls back, pressing his forehead to mine, squeezing his eyes shut.

"Rory, I—what're you doing here?"

I duck my head, nerves taking over. Am I misreading all of this? *He* kissed me, right? Now and earlier.

He must read the question in my facial expression because he quickly continues. "I'm thrilled you are, but I don't want to get ahead of myself—or more ahead of myself than I already have. I just... I need to know you're here for the reasons I hope you are," he says, and I relax, relief washing over me.

I cut off his protests, his attempts to backpedal, his worries that I'm not here for him, with a soft kiss. "Hey, don't go overthinking. *We're* a no-overthinking zone, remember." I kiss him again. "How about you buy me dinner and I tell you everything, yeah?"

"Yeah. Yeah, okay." He grabs my hand and pulls me along the harbour to a restaurant with an outdoor seating area.

Once we order, Breck slides his hand across the table and I take it in an instant, hungry for the connection. After almost two months apart, I want to fuse myself to him so I never have to miss it again.

"So," he says, rubbing his thumb across the back of my hand. "Tell me everything."

I blow out a breath and shake my shoulders. I'm about to lay my heart on the line and it's both terrifying and exhilarating.

"First, I couldn't have asked for a better welcome. I didn't want to get my hopes up for how you'd react when I arrived. If I'd dreamt up a perfect hello, it would've been that kiss. I just... I've missed you so much."

His grip tightens and he closes his eyes, breathing out on a sigh. "So you're here for—"

"You. And Willow. Wes and Joss too. But really, I just needed to see you. Needed to know if I was the only one feeling like I was missing a part of myself."

He chuckles lightly. "And here I was hoping you brought the piece of me I left with you."

"Really?" I whisper, scared to let myself believe this is real.

"Yes. I've been walking around this city wondering how it could feel so little like home. I think it's because my heart wasn't here anymore."

"Well, that's pretty much how I've felt too."

His shoulders relax and I swear his smile could light the city. "What's your plan? How long are you here?"

"I have two weeks."

Breck's eyebrows rise. "How'd you make that happen?"

"The ski season ended and I officially left my job at the resort last week. I also left some time open in my elopements schedule so I could come and get the guy. Is it working?"

He stands and rounds the table to kiss me, crowded restaurant and prying eyes be damned. His hands are on my face, lips insistent against mine, and I melt into my chair. There's a whistle and I duck my chin, flushing crimson. "Hell yes it is," he whispers, a sultry heat in his gaze.

He moves back to his seat and takes my hand again, like he didn't just make my toes curl in front of a restaurant full of people.

"You did it then? You're a full-time photographer? God, I'm so proud of you!" He beams with joy.

"I am." I nod my head, feeling embarrassed at the praise, but dammit, he's right. I did do it, and he doesn't even know the best part. "And I signed a contract with a bridal magazine in Sacramento."

"*What?*"

"Yeah. It's a partnership with *Sacramento Weddings Magazine*. I guess you were right that eloping is the growing trend. They want to showcase great locations for smaller, intimate weddings. So they'll send me business and I'll send them features. I have my first shoot for them when I get home."

"Baby." His voice softens on the endearment, full of pride and something else that makes me melt for him. "That's amazing. I'm in awe of you."

"And you know what? That was it." I hold his gaze across the table. This is important. "That was the moment I realized none of this success matters if I don't get to share it with you. I don't know what that looks like exactly—because you're here and I'm there—but I know when good things happen, I want to tell you first. Do..." I stammer. "Do you want that?"

"Yes. God yes. That and more," he says. "We don't have to figure out every detail tonight. I want to share a meal with you. I want you to tell me everything I've missed, and I want to tell you everything.

Then I want to take you home and do all the things I've dreamed of doing for weeks." His eyes grow dark, making everything inside me tighten with want.

"Okay." It's just one word, but it feels like a promise of so much more.

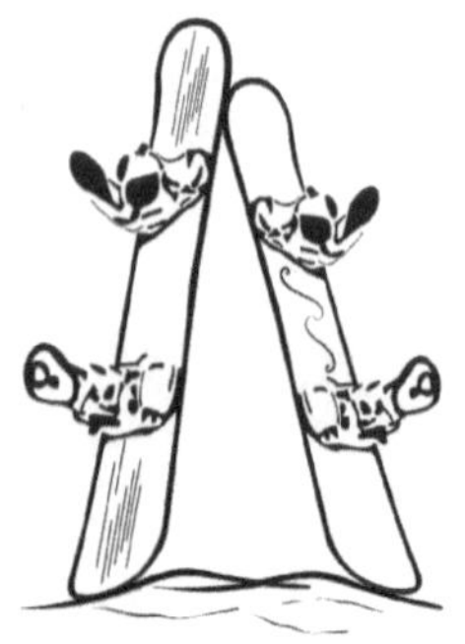

CHAPTER FORTY-THREE

BRECK

I kiss Rory's shoulder, moving across the bare skin of her back until I reach her spine. My lips start a wandering path down each vertebra that's on display for me and she shivers, a small sigh escaping her.

"Good morning, beautiful." I make my way back up with slow precision, landing a kiss just below her ear. "I didn't want to wake you, but I couldn't help myself."

She rolls over, bringing the sheet with her, and covers the expanse of skin I was enjoying.

"Hey! I wasn't done," I pout.

"Well now I'm awake and it's my turn," she says and presses me onto my back. Leaning on one elbow, she trails her hand down my chest and under the sheet. The muscles of my abdomen tighten as her fingers skate across each dip and valley, brushing down the dusting of hair there.

"Rory," I grumble, a warning in my voice, because I won't hold back if she keeps this up.

"Yes?" she says sweetly, like that's what she's hoping for.

"You're playing with fire, baby."

Her fingers move lower, making my breath catch when she whispers, "I'm not afraid of burning, not with you."

I grab her wrist, flipping us with ease so she's pressed beneath me. Every inch of my body lines up against every inch of hers. I don't release her, lifting her arm over her head toward the headboard. Then I follow suit with the other until both her hands are held in one of mine. I smooth my thumb over the delicate underside of one wrist and she melts beneath me.

"I hope that's true." With my kiss, we catch fire and burn until there's nothing left but sweat and panting breaths between us.

I didn't want to leave the warmth of my bed with Rory held safe in my arms. But her excitement, and that of my daughter, to climb the monstrous metal bridge looming before us pulled me from it—reluctantly.

It was always the plan to climb the Harbour Bridge on Willow's eighth birthday, but then we spent it in Tahoe. We haven't prioritized going since being back. I'm glad for that now, because this is perfect. I have both my girls bouncing on their toes beside me, anticipation rolling off them as they look toward the bridge.

Wes and Joss sidle up to us with the guide who'll take us to the top for the most stunning three-hundred-and-sixty-degree view of the city.

"Are you ready?" I ask Willow and she nods, blue eyes alight, dark pigtail braids trailing down her back. I ask Rory the same and she beams her brightest smile, pressing up onto her tennis shoe–clad toes to coast her lips over mine.

"I am."

"Y'all are insufferable," Wes says and laughter overtakes the group, including the guide.

We put on our climb suits and harnesses, and Wes and Joss take the lead, hooking in first with Willow, me, and Rory following after. It's a two-hour journey to the top and back down now that we've completed all of our pre-climb prep.

The sun is shining, there's little to no cloud cover, and there's visibility for miles. There's not much opportunity to talk, but that doesn't stop Willow from trying. She squeaks excitedly and points out different parts of the city to those of us who can hear her.

We stop as a group to take pictures at the top. Rory was disappointed when they told her she couldn't bring her camera up with her. In fact, we all had to empty our belongings into lockers at the base of the bridge because they can't have anything falling from top. We're going to have to trust the professionals stationed up here to capture the moment for us.

"Alright, can you gather the whole family together for this first one?" the photographer asks, and I look at the four people around me. They *are* my family. We squeeze in close and I stretch my arms across the back of the group, letting the feeling of rightness settle over me.

After our group picture, we all take some individual ones. When it's just Rory and me left, I press my lips to hers then pull back a few inches, searching her face.

"I love you." I breathe the words, only loud enough for her. My heart soars at her answering smile before she kisses me again.

"I love you too," she whispers against my mouth, and I want to live forever in this moment. I'm literally on top of the world.

After our climb, Wes all but thrusts Rory's suitcase at me, having packed it into the back of Joss's car.

"No point in her sleeping on the couch at our place when there's a perfectly good bed she can sleep in at yours," he says with the all subtlety of a firework.

Willow's excitement over the prospect of a sleepover with Rory is palpable, especially when she says, "It's going to feel just like being back in Tahoe."

Rory asking if she can tuck Willow in for bed after dinner is different than when we were in Tahoe, though. That was a boundary she never crossed even when we were living together, so her asking for this moment tonight gives me hope that the conversation we still need to have is going to go the way I want it to.

My heart squeezes as I watch them saunter back to Willow's bedroom. I finish up with the dishes we left strewn on the table when we opted to fit in a couple rounds of Attack Uno before Willow's bedtime.

Grabbing the woven blanket off the couch, I head for the back door. The telltale creak as I open it and the mesh of the screen pulling away from the frame feel nostalgic as I step onto the back porch.

I toss the blanket onto the double Adirondack chair I built a few years back and start stacking logs in the firepit. This is my favorite part of this house. It's what I'll miss most if—

I break the thought, not ready to fully go there yet. Rory and I need to talk first.

I look over my shoulder, still bent over the firepit, and find Rory unabashedly checking me out from the stairs.

"Like the view?" I quip.

"Oh, very much. The backyard is nice too."

I laugh, deep and unencumbered.

She's really here.

"Get over here, will you?" I say, bringing the flickering flame of the lighter to the wood and kindling. It catches and I stand only to find Rory right behind me. Her arms slide around my middle and I twist to face her, a smile brighter than the fire spread across her face. "Sit with me."

The flames dance across her expression when she settles next to me.

"Like the view?" she mimics my question with a smirk when she catches me ogling her.

"Very much." I lean into her space and brush my lips across hers, pulling back before we can go too far and I lose this opportunity to talk to her. "I meant what I said on the bridge."

She moves back an inch, taking in the seriousness of my tone, my expression. Her smile doesn't falter when she says, "I meant what I said on the bridge too." Leaning to the side, she slides her legs into my lap so she's facing me, giving me her undivided attention.

I clear my throat, emotion rising in me. "I wouldn't have said it if I didn't. I also wouldn't have said it if I didn't see a future for us. Not just for you and me, but for Willow as well. She's my number one priority. She has to be."

"I understand that. I do." She nods, eyes never leaving mine.

I pull her hand into mine between us, rubbing small circles on her palm. "A future with me means a future as Willow's mom." I swallow, the magnitude of what I'm saying heavy between us. "I want that for her. You know I do, but I have to know *you* want that—that you want *her* as much as you want *me*. You're twenty-seven, and though I've never felt like our age difference was an issue, I'd never want you to feel like you missed out on something or took on too much when you could've been wild and free."

"Breck—" Rory attempts to interrupt.

I can't stop though, needing these words out. "Wait. Please. If you need time to make sure this is what you want, that's okay. I want you take it, because Willow and I are a package deal. I can't see her in pain again. She's already attached to you, and that scares me. She loves you, and I'm terrified to see her lose another person she loves. I won't do that to her, so if a family—us—isn't what you want—"

"Breck," she cuts me off with a hand on my cheek, forcing me to look at her, to stop talking. "Do you think I came here without thinking about this? I've been looking at every angle for weeks now. Every variable. From the moment I realized nothing I had in Tahoe felt like it was worth anything when I didn't get to share it with you, all I have done is think about this. Not just about you and me, but about Willow too."

Her voice is soft but firm. She brings both her hands to squeeze mine on top of the blanket, holding me steady.

"I know you and Willow are a package deal. I know she's your whole world. I know I have to be all in or all out. I'm telling you," she says, releasing my hands and scooting closer, her own coming to frame my face, "I never would've gotten on that plane to come here if I wasn't all in."

My throat tightens and my eyes fill with tears. Dammit, she really has thought about this. I can't speak so she does, wiping away a tear as it falls.

"I didn't know how coming here would go. I wasn't sure if I could trust what I believed to be true in my gut, in my heart. But I knew I'd regret it for the rest of my life if I didn't come and at least *try* to get what I wanted. You taught me that, to go for what I want. With Willow Tree Elopements, and with so much more. I owe you so much."

I press forward to draw my lips across hers. "You don't. That was a team effort. You deserve every ounce of your success. You always had it in you, you just had to find it. And god am I glad you did because it brought you here, to me."

The next kiss is more insistent, everything clicking into place as I absorb everything she's said. "If you've thought of everything, what do we do now?" I ask with a smirk against her lips.

"I think that's a question for you and Willow. She deserves a say. I don't know what it would look like, but I can move here if that's what's best for her, for you both."

"Rory..." I say, overwhelmed by what she's saying.

"No, don't. I know what you're going to say, but that option needs to be on the table. Especially for Willow. Her whole life is here."

"It is, but you've just gotten your business up and running. You have that new contract. You can't walk away from that."

"I can if it's what needs to happen for us to be together. I told you, none of it feels worth it if I don't get to share it with you. We can rebuild Willow Tree Elopements here, find new contracts."

I shake my head. I don't want her to do that. I'm pretty sure I already know what Willow will say, but Rory's right.

"Fine, that option is on the table, but go with me on this. If Willow is on board, we'll move to Tahoe. You have a business there, one we can work at together. There'll be a lot of logistics to figure out whichever way this goes, but I don't expect you to give up your dreams for me and Willow, for us to be a family. I won't let that happen."

I slide my thumb across her cheek and she leans her head into my hand. I pull her forward so she slides farther into my lap.

"I love you, Rory. We're going to find a way to make this work."

"I love you *both* so damn much."

The next kiss doesn't end. It feels like it goes on all night. From the chair beside the fire, to the kitchen counter, to the bedroom. It's a string of kisses that link together into the beginning of a future.

Breakfast in the morning is a family affair. I make the coffee, at Rory's insistence, while she cooks bacon and directs Willow on how to make the pancakes. I was concerned she might be giving my eight-year-old a little too much free rein with the batter and skillet situation, but she only burned one. The first one, and even I can't fault her for that. The first pancake is always a dud.

This kitchen hasn't seen a Sunday morning breakfast filled with this much laughter, light, and love in a long time. Much longer than I care to admit. It feels like the mornings in Tahoe when we'd all move around each other, getting ready for the day, but the raw undercurrent of love is almost overwhelming now.

We're all seated around the table when Willow, in true Willow fashion, breaks the ice with a question. "Are you two going to get married?"

I guess she's not pulling any punches.

I spit my orange juice onto my empty plate and Rory inhales her coffee. She coughs and splutters for a minute, eyes watering. Willow looks between us like we're misbehaving children.

I mop myself up, answering as I dab at my shirt. "Well." I look at Rory and her eyes go wide. Neither of us expected this question, but she looks curious about what I'll say. "We haven't talked specifically about marriage, so I don't have an answer for you on that one, Willow Bear." I shoot Rory a wink. "But Rory and I do love each other. You were right about that."

Rory looks between us, a small line between her brows.

"Willow knew before we did, or at least before I could admit it to myself," I say to her, then turn back to Willow. "We want to be together, as a family. The three of us. How do you feel about that?"

My daughter jumps out of her chair and rushes for Rory, throwing her arms around her.

"Do we get to go back to Tahoe?" Willow asks. There's a brightness in her eyes, exactly like I expected, even if it's covered by tears. They're tears of joy.

"We're still figuring that out. We wanted to talk to you first, because as much as this decision is mine and Rory's to make, it's also yours. And—"

"I want to go back to Tahoe. Please, Daddy!" she begs, pulling on my hands now.

I laugh and so does Rory, then Willow joins in, and this feels like the first day of the rest of my life.

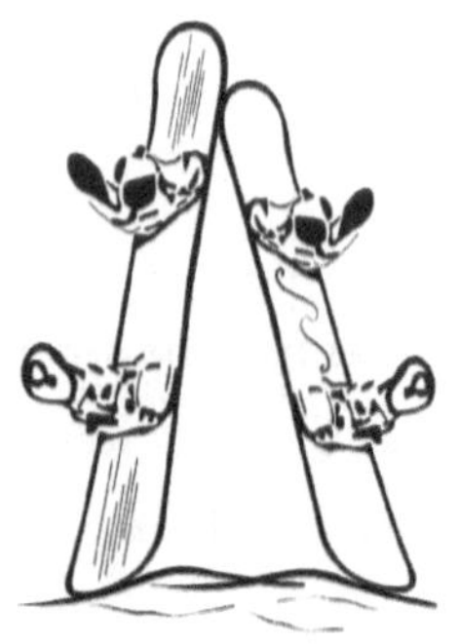

CHAPTER FORTY-FOUR

RORY

Willow decided after breakfast that we needed to spend the day in our pajamas watching movies and eating junk food. I'm not going to even pretend it wasn't perfect. It's only my second full day in Sydney and I feel like we've been going nonstop. It doesn't help that I haven't gotten much sleep the last two nights to help me adjust to the time zone, but you won't catch me complaining.

Wes and Joss only made it about three hours before they turned up, also in pajamas, to crash our plans. I couldn't have asked for a better day with the people I love.

Now, the bonfire burns bright, all of us wrapped in cozy blankets with drinks and discarded paper plates strewn about from the burgers Wes grilled for us.

Willow's asleep in her chair, and I can't blame her as a yawn stretches through me where I sit across Breck's lap. It's reminiscent of last night, but this time, instead of leaning back against the arm of the chair so we can talk, my head is tucked under his chin. His heart is beating a steady rhythm under my cheek.

"So, what happens now?" Wes asks from across the fire, like it's the simplest question in the world.

Breck clicks his tongue, chastising his friend.

"What? I'm just curious. You invited us here—" Wes starts again.

"You invited yourself here," I cut in with a smirk.

"Okay, true, but still. You're all lovey-dovey over there, Willow looks happier than I've seen her in months, so..."

I tilt up my chin and Breck tilts his down. I can't even speak, too caught up in the emotion, the love swirling around us.

"You're leaving us, aren't you?" Wes pouts, jutting out his bottom lip. My eyes meet his and there's real sadness there.

Tears prick my eyes. I can't answer. A small part of me wishes we could stay, but we all know what's best, at least right now, and that's a move to Tahoe.

"I'm sorry, Wes," I say, my voice cracking.

"God, don't apologize." There's a sheen of tears in his eyes now. "Don't apologize for doing what makes you happy, Rory. You deserve all the happiness. All of it. I can't imagine a better man to make you happy."

I hear a sniff behind me—goodness, we're all a mess.

"I tried to convince her we needed to stay here for you," Breck deadpans, and I smack his chest.

"You did not! Look at you throwing me under the bus to try and stay in my brother's good graces."

"Well, he has to or I'll beat him up for going after my baby sister," Wes jokes and I growl at him, garnering laughs from everyone. "Seriously though, Rory. You've given everything of yourself to everyone around you. God, I wish we could all be together, but this isn't about me—I mean, everything is always about me." He chortles at his own joke. "But truly, I'm happy for you guys."

"Thanks, Wessy," I say through my tears and he barks out a laugh, immediately lightening the mood.

Breck squeezes me tighter against him. "It won't be right away. There are details we're going to have to work out here. Willow needs to finish this semester before we take her out of school again. We have to apply for visas and..." Breck blows out a breath. The weight of all that needs to be done is heavy on both of us, but mostly on him.

"There's a lot to figure out," I say, kissing the stubbled underside of his jaw. "But we're figuring it out, together."

"Yeah, we are." Breck leans in to kiss my nose.

"We're here to help. Whatever we can do to make this easier. Do you—" Wes looks around the yard. "Do you have a plan for the house yet?"

"That's one of the bigger obstacles. I don't know if I should sell it or rent it or..."

"What if I have a solution to that particular obstacle?" Wes says and looks at Joss, who places her hand over his.

"Oh yeah?" Breck offers skeptically.

"Would you consider selling it to us?" Wes asks.

"What?" Breck and I say in unison.

"Yeah. We've been thinking about moving out of the city. We love our apartment, but—" Wes stops and looks at Joss again.

"He's trying to knock me up, and if it works, we want something bigger. Somewhere with space," Joss says, not beating around the bush.

"Really!" I yell, running over to my brother and sister-in-law to wrap them both in a hug. It's awkward with them still sitting in their chairs, but I don't care.

"Yeah," Wes says, a cheeky grin pulling his lips.

"It's new, so don't get too excited. Regardless, we love this house. And that way, you'd always have somewhere to come back to when you visit."

Breck joins our hug, making it even more ridiculous. "I think that's the absolute perfect solution. I just—" His eyes tear up. "I can picture you guys here. I can't imagine a better place for you to raise your own brood of children."

"Child... Let's start with *a* child and see how it goes," Joss jokes.

"You're going to be a great dad," I say, hugging my brother tighter. Then I stand and look at Joss. "And you're going to be the best mom. I'm so happy for you guys."

"Speaking of parents," Wes says, bringing the celebratory energy to a grinding halt. "I talked to Mom and Dad last week."

"Both of them—at the same time?" I say, incredulous.

"Yeah. They conference-called me from the office." He rolls his eyes.

"And..." I say, nerves fluttering in my stomach. They've continued to invite me to dinners, and even though I haven't gone, it has opened a small channel of communication between us, making it finally feel like the ball is in my court.

"They—well, *I think* they're finally seeing the writing on the wall for what their relationships with us will look like if something doesn't change. It was the first time I'd talked to them since they kicked you out."

"What did they say?" I ask, chewing at my thumbnail. I never meant for my issues to come between them and Wes.

"Mom said she misses you, misses me. Dad was more emotive than I've heard him in a long time, maybe ever. He said he's been watching the children he raised live their lives completely separate from him and he's starting to see he might be the problem. That *they* might be the problem."

I'm stunned into silence. Breck's hands wind around my middle.

"I'm not telling you what you should do here," Wes continues. "I honestly don't know how I feel about it either. I know my relationship with them was always better than yours, and I'm sorry for that."

"It's not your fault."

"I know, but it doesn't make it okay. I think it might be worth talking to them though, hearing them out. It doesn't mean you have to forgive them or allow them into your life, but I think they're sincerely taking note of how their actions have affected us both."

Joss gives me a sad smile. "You know I don't have any relationship with my mom. That was my choice, and it was the right one. My dad though, he made some terrible decisions, but he's also done everything he can since he's been back in my life to make up for them. Some people deserve a second chance, others don't. I agree with Wes though. It might be worth at least talking to them before making your decision."

I lean into Breck and feel his arms tighten. "You know I'm not a huge fan of your parents," he says, "but I would do anything to be able to have a relationship with mine. Maybe they'll surprise you, or maybe they'll be exactly who you know them to be. Either way, you'll have your answer."

I turn in his arms to face him. "What about you? And Willow? If they're in my life then they're in yours—hers. How do you feel about that?"

His face softens and he ghosts his lips over mine. "I love you."

"Breck," I say with mock exasperation. "That doesn't answer my question."

"If they're really set on changing, then I can give them the chance to do so. I honestly haven't thought about Willow having grandparents in her life before. My parents are gone and Talia's were never in the picture. If I can choose for her to have more people who love her, I will. Always. If they won't accept her, then that'll change things, but we can cross that bridge if we come to it."

"She'll never feel rejected by another person if I can help it," I say, meaning it with every fiber of my being.

"I love you so much, woman." I feel his words all the way to my toes. "How did I get so lucky?"

"You got lucky with me first, mate," Wes says. "If you didn't know me, you wouldn't have her, so you just remember that when you start pawing at her, would you?" He tries to hold a straight face but fails and we all fall into a fit of laughter.

"Fair point," Breck says with one last chuckle against my neck. "You don't have to decide anything about your parents right now, but it's something to think about, yeah?"

"Yeah. I'll think about it."

The next two weeks pass in a blur of school drop-offs and pick-ups, beach trips, coffee runs, touristy fun around the city, cozy dinners, and bedtime stories. Also with Breck and I making love at every opportunity.

He took it as his personal mission to have me on as many surfaces of the house as he could. "Making up for lost time," he said as he bent me over the back of the couch one afternoon while Willow was still at school, or "taking advantage while I can" when he pressed me against the shower wall and lifted me so my legs wrapped around his middle.

In the midst of it all, we talked. And talked. About everything and nothing. About how we would make this move work, what our plans would be when he and Willow got their visas and could officially move to the States.

The rest of the in-between we spent with Wes and Joss. I visited Harbour Grounds nearly every day—the coffee shop Joss's best friend Jaz owns. We spent many mornings on the beach—at least when Breck could haul me out of bed. I'm not a morning person, and he's already said he'll have to figure out a way to fix that.

I took a couple of surf lessons and despite being extremely comfortable on a board on the snow, me and a board in the ocean didn't jive as well as I expected. Looks like we'll have to track down some California waves this summer once he and Willow arrive so I can practice some more.

We went to the zoo, and to see *Guys and Dolls* at the Opera House. Breck and Wes showed me around the University of Sydney and all their old haunts from college. Every day was filled with something new, creating memories. We filled the time to the brim because we knew today was coming.

We're packed into Breck's ute, headed for the airport. Willow's been a sniffling mess all day, clinging to me in one way or another. As the airport looms nearer, I'm right there with her.

Wes insists we park and go in. No goodbyes on the curb today. The minutes tick by too fast. The baggage line empties too quick. Before we can fully process, we're at security. Two weeks, gone in a flash, and I'm missing them already. Even though they're still standing in front of me.

"Why can't we go with you now?" Willow asks, her eyes red-rimmed and voice breaking on the words.

"I wish you could, Bug," I say, leaning down to kiss her head.

"We talked about this, sweetheart. We have to get some things sorted before we can go, but it won't be too long. You'll finish your term here and I'll get our paperwork together. Then we'll go, yeah?" Breck tries for an encouraging tone, but it falls flat, even to my ears.

"Yeah, but I don't want to wait." She pouts and leans against me.

Wes and Joss surround me and Willow, recognizing they won't get a hug if they wait for her to let go.

"I'm going to miss you, Roars." Wes pulls me against him. "We'll start talking about potential trips we can make to see you guys soon. Christmas at the very least." He kisses my temple.

"Travel safely and let us know when you get home, okay?" Joss says and hugs me tight.

"Keep my brother in line, and keep an eye on these two for me," I say back to her.

"I'll do my best," she says with a wry grin.

"I love you both. Gah—I'm going to miss you. Thank you for this trip. Thank you for everything." I'm nearly crying now and I really wanted to hold it together.

"Love you too, sis," Wes says. He and Joss step back to give me a moment with Breck and Willow.

Breck holds my face between his hands, his forehead pressing against mine. "I love you. Thank you for being brave and coming for us."

I choke on the sob that wants to break free at his words. "I-I love you too. Both of you."

"We'll see you in two months. It'll fly by, and you have your shoot for *Sacramento Weddings* next week. You'll barely notice our absence."

"Are you saying that for me and Willow or for yourself?" I chide him with a watery chuckle.

He nudges me playfully, and I absorb his light, his smile, his positivity. "Fly safe, and let me know when you land in Los Angeles and when you get home. You've checked with Jamie about picking you up?"

I nod. "Everything will be fine."

"I know it will." He kisses me then, sliding one hand into my hair while the other wipes away a tear on my cheek. I step back and Breck has to peel Willow's lanky arms from around my waist.

I drop down to my haunches and take a deep breath. "I'll see you soon, okay?" She nods, and the look in her eyes breaks my heart. "Will you take good care of your dad for me?" She nods again. "I knew you would." I lean forward and kiss her forehead.

She leans in to whisper in my ear, the same words from when we said goodbye in Reno. "We love you, Rory."

And I whisper back into hers the same words I said last time: "I love you both too."

An hour later, I'm sitting at the gate waiting for my flight when my phone rings. Jamie's name flashes on the screen. Shoot, I forgot to call him.

"Hey you. I'm sitting at my gate. Still good to pick me up in about a day?" I chuckle, but he doesn't immediately respond. "Jamie?"

"I'm here." His voice sounds strained, distant.

"Okay, good... I thought I lost you. So, are we good for tomorrow?"

"That's actually why I'm calling. I'm at the airport."

"A little early there, Jameson?" I hike my bag up my shoulder and press the phone closer to my ear.

"I'm at the airport because I'm getting on a plane." I can imagine him pinching the bridge of his nose under his glasses, and I pause my movements. *Something's wrong.*

"What? Why? To where?" I ask in quick succession.

"Scotland. My grandfather is sick."

"Oh my gosh, Jamie. I'm so sorry. I—is he going to be okay?"

"It doesn't sound like it. I can't not go. It's been too long since I was there." There's guilt in his voice. He blows out a breath. "I can't pick you up tomorrow."

"I'll figure something out." That's the last thing on my mind.

"I've got you covered. I parked my car in the garage at the airport. I'll text you the location. The keys are in the center console. You know the code to get in so you should be all set to drive it home." He's all business now, and without being able to see him, I can't pick up on his emotions.

"Are you alright?"

"I don't know. I just... I need to be there. I coordinated with Patrick and he can cover all the elopements I was supposed to do for the next month. I don't really know how long I'll be gone yet. I'm sorry I'm going to miss the one for the magazine."

"It's okay, Jamie. We'll figure it out."

"So, did you get the guy?" Jamie asks. There's so much about his history in Scotland he doesn't talk about and I don't want to push, so I let him change the subject.

"I did." I dip my chin and smile. "He and Willow are moving to Tahoe. Breck's hoping they'll be there in time for fireworks on the Fourth."

"I'm happy for you, Rory. I really am. He's a good man. He's good for you. And Willow—she's a great kid. I couldn't have asked for a better family for you."

Family. My own family.

"You're my family too, you know?"

"I know, but this is the one you've always deserved," he says, the words choppy with emotion. I wish I could hug him right now.

"Thanks, Jamie."

"I better go. They're getting ready to board my flight to LA. I wish we were going to be there at the same time so I could hug you. You'll let me know when you get home?"

"I will. You let me know when you get to Scotland, okay? Your grandparents are on Skye, right?"

"Yeah."

"Take a picture on the ferry to Skye and send it to me. I've always wanted to go there," I say, imagining it.

"Maybe you'll have to take a trip there someday."

"Someday," I say dreamily. "Fly safe, Jamie."

"Fly safe, Rory."

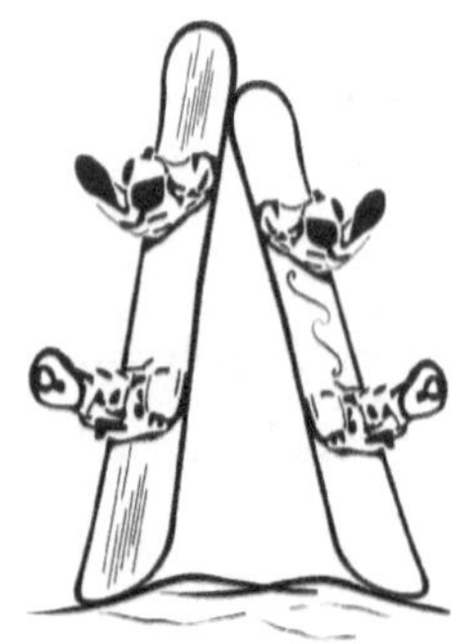

CHAPTER FORTY-FIVE

Breck

2 Months Later

The last two months have been a whirlwind. Willow finished her term at school while I focused on filing for our visas, selling our house to Wes and Joss, and handling the other million things that needed to be done for this move to be a success. All the while, Rory chipped away at things on her end. Finding us a house, doing the legwork for Willow to start school in the fall, and still managing to focus on growing Willow Tree. Today feels like the finish line at the end of a marathon.

This should be the last time we find ourselves in an airport for a while, and there's nothing but joy in the atmosphere.

The escalator out of the secure area is crowded with people, so it's not until we're halfway down that I see her. And the sign in her hands.

It says *WELCOME HOME, BRECK AND WILLOW!* and I think I might cry.

Home.

I squeeze Willow's hand and she starts to jump up and down. This isn't ideal on a crowded escalator with all our carry-ons, especially considering we are not traveling light. The airlines got their pound of flesh on this trip with the cost of the tickets plus the excessive number of bags we checked.

We reach the bottom of the escalator at last, and Willow takes off like a shot. She collides with Rory at full force, knocking her to the ground. When I reach them, they're sprawled on the carpet, laughing and in tears. Instead of attempting to pull them up to avoid a further scene, I climb right on top.

Willow screams, "Daddy!" and the laughter from Rory only increases. It's a laugh I've missed so much since she left Sydney.

I ignore Willow's continued protests, knowing I'm not putting much weight on them, and lean down to kiss my woman. I watch her, detailing everything I've missed. The way her eyes brighten, the freckles across her face, the blush on her cheeks. When I kiss her, I hear as much as feel her inhale.

I pull back just enough to breathe the word "Hi" against her lips.

"Daddy, eww, stop! Get up!" Willow struggles beneath me, little hands pushing and prodding, but I'm not done yet. I haven't kissed these lips in two months and I'm not about to stop because of tiny fists pummeling me.

When she pinches me though, that gets my attention. "Ouch! Hey, little ankle-biter, that wasn't very nice," I say, finally pulling back.

"You're squishing me!" Willow harumphs.

"Am not. If anything, *you're* squishing Rory."

"Am not," she argues back.

Rory's chuckle shakes us as we bicker, and I trail my eyes back to hers. They're perfect. She's perfect, and she's mine.

The 4th of July doesn't hold any real significance for Willow and me, but it's Rory's favorite holiday and she's excited to share it with us. So here we are, gathering chairs, picnic blankets, and a big basket of food to take to the beach.

Beach is a relative term I'm coming to understand means "shore" to those who live around the lake. Is it really a beach if it's not by the ocean? Rory shot me a playful glare when I first asked that question, so I've kept my thoughts on the matter mostly to myself since.

We walk from our campsite in Camp Richardson—camping two days after a trans-continental flight is always a good idea, right?—to find the perfect spot in the sand. Rory told us this is the only way to see the fireworks for the very first time and that next year we'll go to her "secret spot," which doesn't require camping or dealing with the chaos that'll ensue on the roads around the lake as soon as the fireworks are over.

Willow sits on the blanket, while Rory and I take the two chairs, and leans back against my legs as she looks out at the lake.

"It looks so different than it did when we left," she says, eyes scanning the mass of boats on the water and people on the shore.

"Yeah. A Tahoe summer is very different from a Tahoe winter. I'm excited you'll get to experience all of it this year."

"Me too." Willow smiles back at Rory.

The evening sky fades from the bright blue of a summer day into deeper hues as the sun sets. The water on the lake glitters with the changing colors and it's a stunning sight to behold. All around us, groups of people are settling in, wrapping up their frisbee games and donning jackets as the sun sinks lower over the horizon—taking its warmth with it.

I thread my fingers through Rory's in my lap and lean over to whisper in her ear. "Do you remember what happened the last time we were under the fireworks together?"

Her eyes snap to mine, and even in the fading light I can see the blush marking her cheeks. Her hair is pulled up, just a few tendrils escaping to frame her face. The summer sun has added a soft glow to her skin and her freckles are darker, more pronounced.

"I do," she says before she sucks her bottom lip in between her teeth.

"I wonder if I can make tonight just as memorable?" I give her my best smirk.

"It might be difficult with no brick wall and all these people—including your daughter—looking on."

I tilt my head back and forth like I'm thinking it over. "True, but I'm sure going to try."

I tap Willow's shoulder and whisper something only she can hear.

She spins on the spot, big wide dimples on display, and grabs her camera off the blanket. I can hardly get her to go anywhere without it these days, and for tonight, it was a necessity. Rory's watching her with rapt attention, curiosity written all over her face, so she misses the split second where I slide off my chair and come to my knee in front of her.

The shutter clicks behind me and Rory's eyes go wide when they go from focused on Willow to being focused on me. Murmurs filter in around us as others take in the scene.

"Rory," I say, taking her hand from her lap and holding it between both of mine. "I love you. Willow loves you. We agreed this was an all-in kind of thing between us. I can't imagine being all-in without having you by my side as my wife. Will you marry me?"

"Yes!" she shouts without a second of hesitation. She hasn't even seen the ring yet. She grabs my face, pulling my lips to hers, and I can taste the love on them. I vaguely hear the excited whoops and hollers around us, but they're quickly drowned out by the pops and bangs of fireworks exploding overhead. I got the timing just right.

We kiss like that for a few seconds, or it could be minutes or hours. Except, I know it isn't that long because the fireworks are still going when we stop. I pull a velvet ring box out of my pocket and pop it open to show Rory before taking the delicate rose gold band between my thumb and forefinger. I chose this particular metal because it reminds me of how her hair looks when it shines in the sun. Rory's gaze is locked on the two-carat square-cut diamond sitting in the middle and her mouth is open in a little *o*.

Her left hand shakes slightly when she holds it out to me and our eyes clash as I slide it with painstaking tenderness onto her finger. I bought this ring the week after Rory left Sydney, and I've been imagining this moment ever since. I press a light kiss to the ring on her finger then glance at where Willow's sitting cross-legged in front of us, patiently watching the fireworks while we have our moment. She must sense my gaze and glances over her shoulder. An instant later, she's lurching for Rory.

"I love you, Bug," Rory says and hugs her close.

"I love you too…" Willow hesitates, looking at Rory. Then with a smile and tears glittering in her eyes, she adds, "Mom."

Tears flood my eyes as well, my heart so full it could burst. To hear her use that word again, completely unprovoked, a word filled with so much love and no trace of hurt or abandonment, heals a part of my heart I didn't know was still damaged.

The fireworks continue and we end up lying side by side, Willow in the middle, looking up at the sky.

Home. This is my home. This is my family. This is the life I always dreamt of, and I had no idea I'd find it while I was attempting to heal on the slopes of Tahoe.

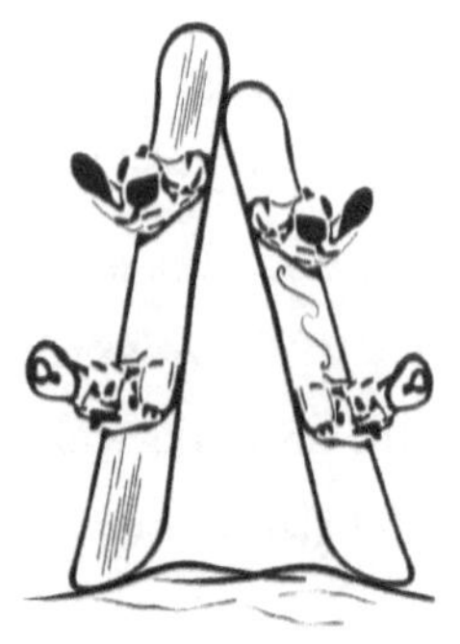

EPILOGUE

ROR4

Eighteen Months Later – Sydney, Australia

T he sound of soft breathing and the occasional beep are the only noises in the hospital room where I sit in a rocking chair in the corner. My eyes drift from the man sleeping on the couch, to the woman asleep in the bed, and then down to the tiny bundle in my arms.

Kai Morgan Anderson is the picture of perfection. Bowed lips that move and pucker in his sleep. An adorable button nose that I've kissed too many times to count. There's a shock of dark hair peeking out from under the little cap they put on him as soon as he was born. They say his eyes could still change color, but when they're open, they fall somewhere between the grey and the blue of his parents' eyes.

His tiny fingers grip the top of the swaddle around him, and I slide my pinky across them until his hand opens reflexively. When he curls it around my finger instead, I melt. I've only known my nephew for a few hours, but I love him *so* much. My heart almost aches with it. It's going to have to grow and stretch to accommodate it, but I know it can. My heart has already grown to accommodate more love than I could've ever imagined in the last couple of years.

The receiver of so much of that love walks through the door, careful not to wake the resting parents when he shuts the door. Breck walks over to me, something tender in his expression as he watches me with Kai. He squats down beside us, kisses my temple, and coasts his forefinger over the place where Kai has my pinkie in his firm grip.

"He's perfect," Breck whispers, and I look into his eyes to see the emotion swirling there.

"He is."

"You look perfect holding him."

"Do I?" I ask coyly.

"You do." He moves his finger up to where my engagement ring sits, nestled against the wedding band he added six months after he proposed. That was a year ago now, almost to the day.

We had to move our annual Christmas celebration to Sydney this year, knowing Joss would be too far along to travel. Thank goodness we did. Kai decided a first of January birthday didn't suit him and arrived the day after Christmas, which was a gift to Joss in and of itself. He was already eight and a half pounds, even a week early.

Our anniversary is tomorrow, and I don't think there's a better way to celebrate than with my entire family and a new tiny addition to love. And I do mean the *entire* family. Mom and Dad made the trip with us, separately of course, but also together. I don't try to understand their dynamic anymore. It took some time, a lot of time really, to figure out how to heal what was broken between us. By the time Breck and I walked down the aisle, my dad stood beside my mom and watched Wes give me away.

I think that stung a little, but he told me he understood. They've grown to love both Breck and Willow. I swear my heart stopped the day Mom told Willow she could call her grandma. Dad thinks Willow is hilarious, and when she asked what she should call him, he said, "Whatever you like, so long as it's grandpa."

There are still some wounds that may never fully heal, but they're trying. We're all trying. They got on a plane and flew halfway around the world to spend Christmas in Sydney and be here for Joss when she had the baby—which meant taking a full three weeks off work, something I've never seen either of them do in my entire life.

"What are you thinking about?" Breck asks, continuing to stare at the tiny figure in my arms.

"Mom and Dad," I whisper.

"They've come a long way."

"We've all come a long way."

"True. Now, back to how good you look with this baby in your arms." He raises his eyebrows at me suggestively. I try to hold in the giggle it elicits but don't quite manage it.

"Stop talking about making babies while you're holding mine," Wes says from the corner. Breck and I spin our gazes to meet his.

"Sorry we woke you," I say.

"You didn't." He yawns. "I was just watching you guys."

"Creep," I joke.

"He's right though, Rory," he says, and my heart squeezes. "Maybe you need to have one."

I duck my chin to look at Kai, a rightness settling over me in this moment.

"Have a what?" Willow asks, startling me. She's just walking into the room with my parents in tow.

Joss stirs and rubs the sleep from her eyes before frantically scanning the room. When they land on me—on Kai—her countenance relaxes.

"Want your little guy?" I ask.

"Not yet." She yawns, stretching her arms overhead. "I need a minute. Let Breck have a turn." She begins to move, and Wes is up in a flash to help her. He walks with her to the bathroom before returning to sit against the side of the bed, watching the door like a hawk.

I do as she said and hand Kai to Breck, who takes him like the natural he is. He looks perfect with that little baby in his arms. All eyes are on him where he bounces lightly, but he doesn't notice. He only has eyes for his nephew.

Joss opens the door, and Wes is instantly by her side, holding her hand and getting her tucked comfortably back into bed. She's watching Breck now too. His head is bent low over Kai, his finger trailing over his hand.

"I think you need one of those," Joss blurts, and we all look at her in surprise. "What, you're all thinking it. I'm just saying it."

"Technically, I already said it, but you were asleep," Wes quips.

We all laugh, but mine catches in my throat. Around the secret we've been keeping. I look at Breck and when our gazes connect, I see the genuine love in his eyes, excitement and trepidation, and in that moment with his tiny nod, I let the secret free.

"I think we need two," I say, letting my hand fall to my stomach, and the room erupts.

Acknowledgements

I dedicated this book to found families, not only because it's a prevalent trope in the book but in my life as well. As a military spouse, I've moved many many times and had to find my tribe—my people—along the way. In every place we've lived I've been blessed with amazing communities who welcomed me with open arms. I'll never be able to explain how grateful I am for the relationships I had the opportunity to build because of the life we've lived in the military.

My found family now encompasses a whole new community. The bookish one. I had no idea when I joined Bookstagram in 2022 that it would change my life. That it would not only put me on the path to become an author, but that it would introduce me to some of the most amazing people I've ever met.

I didn't know I would find a best friend in Stefanie, or that we would bond over a love of Casteel Da'Neer, or that after only a year of friendship I wouldn't be able to go a day without talking to her in one way or another. I am so thankful for you friend. If I look up the definition of found family in the dictionary, your picture would be there.

I have so many others in my bookish community that deserve some serious acknowledgement and hand claps and love. Hannah for always being a light and encouragement to me and all those that call you friend. Thank you to my writing group, Grayson, MJ, Cindy, India, and Stefanie for the weekly chats, daily nonsense, and hourly encouragement, I am so grateful to know you all.

To my betas, Stefanie (oh wait you're my alpha), Hannah, Megan, Dani, Sarah, Ashlyn, Brittany, Christina, Kayla, Grayson, and Sage—I appreciate you all for taking the time to help me make this book the best it could be. To my editing team, Britt and Brooke, for helping me figure out how to properly format dialog punctuation and for making this book as amazing as it is with your feedback and edits. To my cover artist, Sam, who is a miracle worker and takes a vision that exists only in my head and brings it to life in perfect detail.

To my Street Team, thank you for cheering me on day in and day out and for championing my books! To my readers, I wouldn't be here without you. These characters are mine, but they are also yours and I pray that you found them to be relatable and loveable.

As amazing as my found family is, I wouldn't be where I am today without my true family. Traver, thank you for letting me pour my heart and soul (and time) into these books so I could pursue a passion of my own. To my kiddos who put up with me typing away on my computer during practices and at all hours when I was on a deadline, you've given me a lot of grace as a mom and the way you cheer me on never fails to make my heart melt. To my parents and in-laws, brother and sister-in-law, your unwavering support has bolstered my spirit on so many hard days, thank you for always encouraging me and allowing me to talk incessantly about books.

Thank you to the bookstores that took a chance on my debut and that are eagerly awaiting this book to add to your shelves. To the multitude of authors who answered my questions, helped me with my blurb, talked me off the ledge, commiserated over the algorithm or content creation with me... I am so grateful to you all.

I know I've forgotten someone, or many someone's, and in the dark of the night after this book is in your hands I'll remember and sit up straight in bed and cringe. But the fact that I have so many people to thank that it's easy to forget who they all are is a blessing in and of itself. So, if you had a hand in this book, in any way, shape, or form, know that I appreciate you.

Also by J.A. Forde

The Love Along the Way Series

On a Flight to Sydney
On the Slopes of Tahoe

About the Author

 J.A. Forde is a romance writer, Navy wife, and full-time mom to two crazy kids (and a furry pup). She currently resides wherever the Navy has most recently told her to live. You'll likely find her with her nose stuck in a book... or more realistically chasing her two kids with an audiobook in her earbuds.

She loves to travel and go on adventures which is why she decided to set her first book in Sydney, Australia and her second in Lake Tahoe. She hopes to write more books set in fun locales both as an escape for herself in writing, and for you as the reader!

9 798990 576339